THE SORCERESS

A NOVEL

Dear Reader:

Allison Hobbs is on fire, on a roll, on top of her game, and everything else in between. I envision Allison writing more than fifty novels before long because she is that talented. Every book is a page turner; a masterpiece; a journey into the erotic and vivid imagination of one of the most prolific writers to ever grace readers with her words. In *The Sorceress*, she continues on her quest to fan the flames of the freakiness that exists in all people; even if they are not prepared to embrace it.

The Sorceress is Allison's second paranormal novel, a follow-up to the wonderful *The Enchantress*. Allison uses her vivid gift of storytelling to tell the story of two sisters: Tara, who spends her eternity on "The Goddess Realm" and Eris, who has been banished to "The Dark Realm" where evil, sexuality, and life is full of perversion. Eris is hell bent—literally—on seeking revenge on those who betrayed her. Once she teams up with Xavier, who has taken on the life form of a child, Eris' reign of sexual terror and dominion is unstoppable unless someone or something equally powerful comes forward to challenge them.

If you have not read Allison's other books, you have missed out on a lot. Fans of my work will surely appreciate Allison Hobbs. I often state that she is the only woman on the planet freakier than me, and it's the truth.

Her titles include *Pure Paradise, One Taste, Disciplined, Pandora's Box, Insatiable, The Climax, Big Juicy Lips, The Enchantress, One Taste, Disciplined, A Bona Fide Gold Digger, Double Dippin'* and *Dangerously in Love*.

Thank you for supporting Ms. Hobbs' efforts and thank you for supporting one of the dozens of authors published under my imprint, Strebor Books. I try my best to bring you cutting-edge works of literature that will keep your attention and make you think long after you turn the last page.

Now sit back in your favorite chair or, better yet, chill in the bed, and be prepared to be tantalized by yet another great read.

Peace and Many Blessings,

Zane

Zane
Publisher
Strebor Books International
www.simonandschuster.com/streborbooks

ZANE PRESENTS

THE SORCERESS

A NOVEL

ALLISON HOBBS

SBI

STREBOR BOOKS

NEW YORK LONDON TORONTO SYDNEY

Strebor Books
P.O. Box 6505
Largo, MD 20792
http://www.streborbooks.com

ISBN 978-1-59309-175-0
LCCN 2009927609

First Strebor Books trade paperback edition November 2009

Cover design: www.mariondesigns.com
Cover photograph: © Keith Saunders/Marion Designs

10 9 8 7 6 5 4 3 2 1

Manufactured in the United States of America

For information regarding special discounts for bulk purchases, please contact Simon & Schuster Special Sales at 1-866-506-1949 or business@simonandschuster.com

The Simon & Schuster Speakers Bureau can bring authors to your live event. For more information or to book an event, contact the Simon & Schuster Speakers Bureau at 1-866-248-3049 or visit our website at www.simonspeakers.com.

FOR KAMERON HOBBS
I really, really, really love you!

ACKNOWLEDGMENTS

My good friend, Daaimah S. Poole. Our friendship began at the APOOO Book Club Pajama Party back when I was self-published. You were right out of college and already had a book deal. You were so warm and giving and to this day, you have not changed.

To Charlotte Young Foye, my sister of the lip (inside joke). Your husband told me you dug my books a few years before we met. Who knew we'd hit it off and become such good friends? Thank you for giving me "just the right shoe!"

Thanks to the book clubs and the reviewers who have supported me over the years: Yasmin Coleman and Jennifer Coissiere of APOOO Book Club, Tee C. Royal, Paula Henderson, Brenda Lisbon of The RAWSISTAZ Reviewers, Jason Frost of Rubicon-Readers, Radiah Hubbert of Urban-Reviewers, my girl, Chelly/aka PrinceLuva79, Locksie and English Ruler of ARC Book Club, Ladibug and The Strebor Books Book Club, and Nardsbaby, just to name a few.

I want to thank my dear friend, JB Walker, for his numerous critiques and support. He compared my work to Chester Himes. Now that was a first. LOL.

Aletha Dempsey, a poet and I didn't know it!

Zane, words can't express the depths of my gratitude. I want to extend a personal thank you for painstakingly going through this manuscript.

I'm giving Charmaine Parker a special thank-you for always having my back.

As always, my BFF, Karen Dempsey Hammond, who lovingly puts up with me and all my phobias…my neuroses…my endless drama and hysteria! Damn, it can't be easy having me as a best friend. I love you, Karen.

1

Catherine Provost gathered her household staff in the living room of her home located in Chestnut Hill, an affluent cobble stoned neighborhood in the Northwest section of Philadelphia.

Inside the stately home, the atmosphere was tense, and Jen could tell that Ms. Provost was exhilarated by the anxious energy that crackled in the air. She noticed that her employer's eyes had taken on a gleam of sadistic pleasure.

What a bitch, Jen thought, though she maintained a pleasant expression that implied there was nowhere else in the world she'd rather be. She hated being such a wimp. But Catherine Provost was so intimidating, she scared the crap out of Jen.

"George," Catherine said to her driver. "While I'm away campaigning, I won't need you on a regular basis." She paused and nodded her head toward Jen. "The nanny will be taking Ethan to his appointments, so I'll expect you to be on call."

George Hernandez blinked a couple of times. "You're laying me off?"

"With the economy the way it is, the last thing I need is to be criticized for frivolous spending. I'll be traveling most of the time and I really don't need you here on a full-time basis."

Jen cut a sympathetic eye at George. He had a wife and three young children; the poor man couldn't afford part-time wages.

"If you don't want the part-time work I'm offering, please let me know so I can hire another driver," Catherine said, coolly.

Embarrassed, George looked at the floor. A few seconds later, after seeming to get his bearings, he looked up. "Ms. Provost, I...I can't afford—"

"Okay, then," she cut him off. "Thank you for your service, George. My accountant will put your final paycheck in the mail."

"My final paycheck?" George repeated. Offended, he glanced around at the faces of his co-workers, expecting them to be shocked and indignant enough about the injustice to help him plead his case. He didn't get any support. With their own jobs on the line, Lizzy, Carmen, and Jen all kept their eyes focused on the boss, refusing to meet George's gaze.

As much as she hated working as a nanny for Catherine Provost and her horrible little son, Jen needed the pay and the roof over her head until she could sort out her disordered life. Jen mustered a sad smile for George. It was the best she could do.

Catherine caught the quick flicker of a smile and apparently didn't approve of it. "Jen, your presence is not necessary. You can go upstairs and attend to Ethan."

Like a scolded schoolgirl, Jen felt her cheeks flush with shame. She made a discreet nod and slinked away. Catherine, so smartly dressed and sophisticated, made Jen feel like a hick. She'd lived in the big city of Philadelphia for three years, but hailing from rural, Centerville, Pennsylvania, Jen couldn't quite shake her country bumpkin-ness.

Feeling pathetic, she made her way slowly up the staircase. *At least I still have a job*, she thought, trying to make herself feel better. But the reminder did not perk her up. Though she would be broke and homeless for a while, getting fired would have forced her to find a better job with normal hours.

Straining, she tried to eavesdrop, wondering if Lizzy or Carmen was also getting the ax, but Catherine's voice became a distant low drone and Jen couldn't make out her words.

Jen wondered what it must feel like to be able to boss people around. Catherine had run the city of Philadelphia and it was expected that she soon would be the second in command of our nation.

Catherine Provost, former mayor of Philadelphia, had been one of the most popular mayors in the city's history. Unfortunately, the governorship she coveted was not available at the conclusion of her mayoral term. Out of the blue, she'd been selected by her party's presidential candidate to be his running mate.

According to rumors, no one was more surprised than Catherine's husband, Senator Daniel Provost from Pennsylvania. The gossip among the staff was that Catherine had stolen the VP nomination right from under her spouse's nose. The senator had been considered the front runner for the second in command position.

"Hey, buddy," she said to Ethan Provost, her five-year-old charge. Ethan was a weird little kid—nonverbal and uncommunicative. Not only that, the kid was creepy. From the second she'd met him, she'd wanted to ask her agency for a transfer, but she was trying to tough it out. If she bailed on a high power couple like the Provosts, she wasn't likely to get another assignment.

Oddly, when Catherine introduced Jen to her son, she merely stated that he didn't talk, as if that was the extent of his problems. But two days ago, the vice presidential candidate made a public announcement that she and Senator Provost's beloved son, Ethan, had been diagnosed as autistic.

Catherine never gave Jen a personal update on Ethan's condition. Like the rest of America, Jen found out the little guy was disabled from a breaking news report on CNN. That report provoked a wave of sympathy and respect for Catherine Provost, the courageous mother of a disabled child. So far, the press was honoring her plea to leave her son out of politics.

But unlike her fellow citizens, Jen had no pity for Catherine. The woman was cold-blooded and calculating. Catherine didn't have a clue what was wrong with her son but, being on the national stage, she needed an excuse for his lack of social skills. Someone must have owed her a favor because she obtained a speedy diagnosis of the disorder soon after she discovered she was being vetted.

It wasn't that Jen didn't believe Ethan was autistic. He certainly exhibited some of the symptoms she'd heard about, but she wondered why his mom had waited so long to find out what was wrong with him. Denial? A fear of knowing the truth?

Jen was not fond of Ethan. She wanted to like him, but his revulsion toward affection and his silent stubbornness made him unappealing. It didn't help that he had this weird look—a really big, adult-sized head with mean, beady eyes, and a wizened little body that resembled that of an elderly man. Other than his height, there was nothing childlike about Ethan.

Ethan was much smaller than the average five-year-old. He was frail and sickly looking. His light brown skin had an unhealthy pallor and there were dark circles under his beady eyes. Good thing his mom didn't send him to kindergarten; he'd definitely be a target for the other kids. Then again...having that creepy, sinister aura around him might work to his advantage and keep bullies at bay.

Ethan had serious emotional issues. He couldn't tolerate interacting with kids. The cacophony of a schoolyard would make him nuts. He required a quiet and calm setting.

She set out his clothes and personal items and he dressed himself most of the time. She ran his bath water, but she dared not attempt to scrub him down. He didn't like being touched.

Getting him to the toilet was a freakin' nightmare. If Jen didn't grab him and physically carry him to the bathroom, he'd pee in his pants, or so his mother claimed. So far, he hadn't had a toileting accident and Jen prayed he never would. Not on her watch. And if a miracle came her way, her watch would not be much longer.

"Your mom's been selected to run for vice president. How ya feel about that?" Jen asked, knowing he wouldn't respond. "I think it's cool," she answered herself. "If she wins, she'll be the first female vice president." Jen took a deep breath and added enthusiastically, "And she's the first African-American to run for that office." *Shame the first African American female vice presidential candidate is such a snooty bitch!*"

Unsuitable for the campaign trail, Ethan was being hidden from public view and sequestered at home.

Ethan sat behind a tiny desk, staring intently at his computer monitor, little fingers rapidly clicking the mouse, bringing up multiple images of bridges onto the screen: Covered bridges, wooden foot bridges, enormous concrete and steel bridges— every kind of bridge imaginable were the only things that seemed to matter to the child. He was obviously intelligent. She'd heard from other staff members that he'd taught himself how to operate the computer and navigate the internet back when he was only three years old.

Jen checked the time. "Ten more minutes, buddy, and then it's time to go to the potty." She sure hoped the kid didn't stiffen his body in defiance and go rigid on her like he was prone to do when he was pulled away from his computer. The going-rigid routine was appalling enough, but sometimes his eyes rolled into the back of his head, making the experience totally unnerving.

Without uttering one word, the scrawny kid could cause Jen to work up a hell of a sweat. When he wasn't ready to move, he'd swing his head around wildly, using it like a medieval weapon. Jen knew firsthand that when his big head connected, it was as hard and as painful as getting hit with a spiked ball. All the ducking and dodging Jen had to do to get Ethan to the bathroom was exhausting.

Catherine suddenly appeared in the doorway. Jen made a startled sound. Amused by Jen's reaction, Catherine smiled smugly. "Your agency sent a courier over with a ton of paperwork. You'll need to sign an addendum to your confidentiality agreement; a new work agreement now that you'll be pretty much unsupervised. You'll also need to complete some forms that allow you to act on my behalf, in the event of an emergency."

Catherine stared at Jen, holding her in a cold, penetrating gaze.

Uncomfortable, Jen looked away. She hadn't noticed before that Catherine and her son had the same beady eyes.

"Okay," Jen mumbled, fidgeting with her fingers. She bit the inside of her bottom lip to keep it from quivering. The woman emanated power and authority. Being in her presence made Jen nervous as hell.

"I'll be in my office," Catherine said. She looked down at her watch and then glared at Jen, obviously waiting for a response.

"Okay," Jen said for the second time.

"Is your vocabulary as challenged as it seems?" Catherine gave Jen a contemptuous look.

"Uh...no." Jen laughed and began to fidget awkwardly. She felt so belittled. But being as on edge as she was, she couldn't manage a complete sentence.

Catherine ran impatient fingers through her thick, well-behaved hair, and then left Ethan's bedroom. Not once did she even look in her son's direction. He didn't turn around and look at her, either. What a weird relationship between mother and son.

Jen stood next to Ethan and peered at the monitor. "What's with the bridges?" she asked as she slipped her hands beneath his skinny arms and lifted him up.

Refusing to be bothered with walking, Ethan kept his knees bent and his torso erect, as if he were still sitting in the chair. Holding him in that bizarre position, Jen transported Ethan to the bathroom. Luckily, the kid didn't try to beat her up with his head.

Jen tapped on the polished oak door.

"Come in," Catherine said sharply.

Entering Catherine's office, Jen wiped clammy palms over her hips. It reminded her of being called to the principal's office. No; worse. She was experiencing the same trepidation she'd felt when she was summoned to her college counselor's office, knowing she was about to be booted off campus. The lecture she'd been given on the university's low tolerance for cheating was lengthy and humiliating. It concluded that she'd forfeited her scholarship and was expected to hand over her student ID, pack her bags, and get off campus.

Instead of telling her parents she'd been kicked out of school, Jen pretended that she had to hang in Philly for summer classes. But here she was, a live-in nanny, winging it, without any future plans.

Without giving Jen so much as a glance, Catherine kept her head bent, her eyes fixed on the heap of papers on her desk, perusing page after page, and shaking her head in annoyance. She pursed her lips and frowned at the paperwork, making it clear that she felt overburdened by the heap of tedious forms.

Catherine didn't bother to offer Jen a seat. Scowling, she continued rustling through papers, letting Jen stand there shifting from foot to foot, and running jittery fingers through her frizzy red hair.

After what seemed like ten minutes or more, the VP candidate finally acknowledged Jen. "Sign these." She handed Jen a stack of papers.

Jen held the pile and began reading the top page.

Impatient, Catherine exhaled. "Just sign the bottom of each page. It's all standard confidentiality lingo."

"Okay—" Jen caught herself. "All right." She carefully affixed her signature to a ton of papers, hoping her beautiful penmanship made up for her inability to engage in witty banter

Next Catherine handed her a thick binder. "I've detailed your daily assignments. Ethan will flourish in a structured environment. Please don't deviate from his daily routine. I want you to follow my guidelines to the letter. Story time, playtime, music hour…it's all in there. Go to page four." Catherine gestured, impatiently.

Jen quickly found the page.

"Anything that goes on inside this house is absolutely confidential."

Jen shot a look at Catherine and back down at the binder. "Is this the addendum?"

"If you'll allow me to finish—"

"Sorry." Back to one-word responses.

"I have to protect my son's right to privacy. The press has ways of getting their hands on recordings…" She drew in a breath.

"And so, in lieu of a nanny cam, you and I are going to use the honor system."

Great! Jen wanted to shout, but restraining herself, she merely nodded.

"I want you to fill out the comment sections next to each activity. Provide detailed commentary on Ethan's responses to the stimulation you offer throughout the day."

"Sure. I can do that."

"I was going to suggest you fax the reports daily, but I don't want my handlers to have access to such sensitive information. So..." Catherine touched her finger to her forehead, drifting off in thought.

Jen studied the page with her assignments as Catherine pondered to fax or not to fax. The activities were a joke. Catherine knew Ethan would have nothing to do with childish games. When would the woman get it through her head...Ethan was not interested in anything except gazing at bridges.

"Keep everything in a folder. Senator Provost can hand deliver your comments when he campaigns with me."

"Okay," Jen muttered. Smiling sheepishly, she offered an apologetic shrug.

"You'll be happy to know you're getting a pay increase."

"Thank you," Jen said sincerely, but she didn't dare ask how much. She supposed she'd find out when she got her next paycheck.

"The agency will send you copies of the forms you sign."

Okay was on the tip of Jen's tongue, but she nodded instead, giving the distinct impression that hanging around silent Ethan was extremely contagious.

"Is there anything else, Jen?"

"No, not at all," she replied with an uncomfortable smile.

God, she hated it when she behaved like an idiot, but Catherine unnerved her.

"Then, you're excused."

Jen turned.

"Oh, there's something I've been meaning to speak to you about," Catherine added.

Very cautiously, Jen turned back around. Judging by Catherine's somber tone, she was about to impart unpleasant news.

"It's about your appearance."

"What about it?" Jen was no fashionista, but she was neat and clean.

"First of all, I've been gracious enough to allow you to select your own wardrobe. Many women of my stature would insist that the nanny wear a proper uniform…something that identified your status. But, I'm not that rigid. Besides, I think it helps relax Ethan when you're dressed in regular attire. But your hair! Now that's an entirely different matter. Why does your hair always look so frizzy and unkempt? Can't you do anything with it?"

"Uh…" Jen stammered.

"You really need a perm."

A chemical relaxer was out of the question. Jen's mother had warned her against perms and had instilled in her, at a very early age that relaxed hair fell out at the root and never grew back. Jen's wild, wiry red hair had always been a cross to bear for her and her mother. But her mother had taken on the hardship of maintaining Jen's wild red forest of hair without the assistance of chemicals.

Even now, at age twenty-one, Jen's hair was still an issue. She didn't know how to take care of it. She was lousy at blow drying. Or maybe she was too lazy to hang in there, with her arms aching while she raked through her mane, blow-drying until every strand was bone straight.

Hair salons were too expensive for her measly nanny salary. Besides, the luxurious look only lasted a day or two. The best she could do was keep her coarse tresses restrained with jumbo-sized hair clips and scrunchies.

"Uh...next payday, I could make an appointment and go to a salon to get it blow-dried—"

"Blow-dried?" Catherine scoffed. "You need a relaxer." Catherine caressed her own lustrous and chemically relaxed hair and returned her gaze to the paperwork on her desk, silently dismissing Jen.

Jen tried to exit with the shred of dignity she had retained, making purposeful steps toward the door. But her feet somehow got twisted up in the hand-woven, Savonnerie rug, and she stumbled before she made it out of Catherine's office. *Shit!*

2

ROANOKE, VIRGINIA

October 1st, four weeks until Halloween, but the Stovall family was already feeling the holiday spirit. The entire downstairs was ornamented with spooky decorations: flying bats on lamp shades, scarecrows propped in corners, black cats and Jack O' Lantern candy holders, witches, ghosts, and goblin figures were attached to walls and drapery. Skeletons dangled from hooks on the ceiling. The lighting was dim; appropriately mysterious. Creepy organ music played in the background, accompanied by sounds of creaking doors and a witch's laughter.

In the parlor, Kali gazed at herself in the antique mirror. Illuminated by the soft glow of the chandelier, her reflection seemed authentically grown-up. Kali twirled and preened. Standing in high heels, posing with the parasol that complemented her Belle of the Ball costume, she shifted it from one shoulder and then to the other.

Dripping in diamonds and other precious gems, Kali enjoyed having an opportunity to show off her accessories—special trinkets from a collection of vintage jewelry that she and her father had unearthed on the family property.

The sparkling bangles and bracelets that adorned her wrists tinkled together, playing a festive tune. She waved her hand, watching the diamonds encrusted in gold shimmer and dance as they caught the overhead light.

A sudden dark shadow blurred Kali's reflection and she felt the first niggle of fear. Bewildered, she stared at the mirror. A face, hazy at first, slowly came into focus. A woman's face appeared in the mirror next to hers. Kali gasped and dropped the parasol.

Appearing confused, the scary woman whipped her head from left to right and then jerked it up and down. Her eyes, an unusual shade of blue, zoomed in on Kali. Her cobalt eyes grew wide with disdain as they roved furiously over every piece of jewelry that adorned the young child.

The witch in the mirror glared at the strands of pearls that hung from Kali's neck. Kali trembled so badly, her bracelets clashed and clanged as she clutched the pearls; her frightened eyes locked on the ghastly image in the mirror.

The woman was a ghost…a witch, or something equally awful and unnatural, Kali was sure. The evil woman stared at Kali with such malice, the child shrank back in horror. "Mommy!" Her voice came out in an urgent whisper.

"Did you call me, Kali?" her mother called from the kitchen.

"Mommy!" she managed to shout this time.

"Yes, sweetie? Do you need something?"

"Mommy, come quick!" There was panic in Kali's voice.

Ajali Stovall sprinted to the parlor. "Kali, what's wrong?"

"There's a…there's a…"

"A what?" Ajali rushed over to her daughter.

"A mean lady is in the mirror." Kali pointed at her own reflection; her voice quivered in terror.

Ajali squinted at the mirror.

"Do you see her?"

"I only see you and me." Comfortingly, Ajali caressed Kali's terror-stricken face.

Kali noticed that the moment her mother's hand came into focus, the witch bared her teeth and shot a hateful glance at her mother's wedding ring.

The sight of the ring on Ajali's finger prompted the witch to snarl and gnash her teeth. Then she formed her mouth in a way that seemed to hurl harsh and threatening words.

Glowering in full-blown rage, the witch's dark face grew larger and closer, filling the mirror until her gruesome likeness appeared to be superimposed over Kali's and her mother's reflection. Over and over, the witch's mouth opened and closed, as if shouting obscenities.

"Mommy!" Kali's voice pitched high in terror. Stunned, her eyes were riveted to the horrific image in the mirror: a witch spewing a litany of unheard slurs.

"Honey, what's wrong?" Ajali pleaded, stooping down to her daughter's level. Worriedly, she followed her daughter's fearful eyes to the mirror. "There's nothing in the mirror, Kali. Only you and me."

The monstrous woman's lips became still and then stretched into a bitter smile. Standing wobbly in her mother's high heels, Kali's legs quacked. The witch nodded at Kali, a knowing gesture that was so gut-wrenchingly menacing, Kali was certain she was going to lose balance and topple out of the heels.

Remarkably, right before her eyes, the witch's face began to crack into tiny pieces, a sight so appalling that Kali clamped a hand over her mouth, muffling a scream.

Ajali peeled Kali's hand away. "Sweetheart," she whispered, intent on keeping her voice calm and steady. "This isn't like you at all. What's wrong?"

Kali kept her horrified gaze fixed on the mirror as she witnessed the shattered face of the witch whoosh and swirl and then vanish from sight. The child blinked in disbelief. The only trace of the witch was a shade of darkness that hovered, dimming the chandelier's glow.

"Sh-she's gone," Kali whispered, still trembling with fear.

"Who's gone?"

"The...the witch in the mirror. Her face broke apart and then she disappeared."

"Kali, honey. No one was in the mirror. Look!" Ajali pointed at their images. "See, honey. There's no one there except you and me."

"She was in there, Mommy. A wicked witch. I'm not making it up. I couldn't hear her, but I think she was calling me names." Kali began to sob.

"You're scaring me, sweetie. This isn't like you. I've never known you to be afraid of anything."

Protectively, Ajali hoisted her four-year-old daughter on her hip as though she were a baby. Looking cautiously over her shoulder, she treaded toward the sofa.

Ajali sat and positioned Kali on her lap, and then pressed her daughter's head against her heart. "Listen to me, sweetheart," she said, gently rocking Kali. "Wanna know what I think? The dimmed lights cast shadows. I think you saw the reflection of one of the decorations and it really spooked you." Ajali waved her arm, motioning toward the numerous Halloween decorations.

"There is no such thing as ghosts. Whatever you saw was simply an illusion," Ajali insisted, but her words gave her no solace. In fact, she felt a trace of shame at the hypocrisy of telling her daughter such a bold-faced lie when she herself had come face-to-face with pure evil. Had battled for the lives of her future husband and unborn child. Ajali knew firsthand that there were alternate realties—worlds unseen that indeed existed.

She drew in a deep breath as she tried to find words to strengthen her case against the reality of witch's and ghosts. "It's the beginning of the Halloween season. At this time of the year, we're bombarded with frightening images on TV..." She glanced around the room. "And right here in our home." Ajali made a sweeping gesture. "Ghoulish characters are everywhere."

Kali cut off her mother's explanation with a look of sympathy. "You're right, Mommy." She patted her mother's back as if Ajali were the child who needed comforting. "I guess it was my imagination." Bravely, Kali bit down on her bottom lip. "I know there's no such thing as ghosts."

Ajali cradled Kali tighter.

"I'm not a baby," Kali remarked embarrassedly. She wiggled free and eased off her mother's lap. "Witches and goblins are make-believe." She rose to her feet and steadied her balance in the high heels. "It must have been a shadow." She laughed, but the sound that she made was more like a fearful cry than jollity.

A sudden and strong feeling of sorrow grasped Ajali's heart and gave it such a hard tug that, for a few terrible seconds, she had to struggle with the urge to burst into tears. Her precious, overly-mature daughter was pretending to be brave in order to protect her mother from knowing the depth of her fear. Ajali didn't know what to do.

Kali had seen something dreadful in the mirror and though Ajali was as terrified as her daughter, she didn't want to feed into needless fear. Eris was gone forever. She couldn't hurt them. Ajali had watched her burn...she'd witnessed the evil entity's demise.

With the help of the warrior goddess Kali, Ajali had personally cast Eris back to the Dark Realm. Could Eris have once again broken free? Ajali felt an icy gust at the back of her neck. She shuddered.

"Are you okay, Mommy?" Unusually intuitive, Kali was particularly sensitive to her mother's mood.

"Yes, sweetheart. I'm fine," Ajali answered quickly, though her thumping heart disagreed. She smiled reassuringly at her daughter, struggling to keep her face composed.

Should she mention any of this to her husband? *No!* she thought adamantly. The ordeal with Eris had sent both she and Bryce to hell and back. A discussion about Eris would upset the balance of their happy home.

"Kali, if you see that scary lady again, or anything that frightens you, don't be ashamed to tell me."

"Okay," Kali responded, her finger making its way to her mouth. It hurt Ajali to the core to see her daughter chewing nervously on her finger.

3

THE DARK REALM

"Thief!" Eris shouted and shook her fist. "You stole my jewels, you detestable little crook!"

A swarm of depraved souls, who were confined in the bleak environment where the sun, moon, and stars had abandoned the brown-streaked sky, believing Eris' accusation was aimed at them, went scurrying and shrieking into the shadows of the forsaken place.

But Eris was not referring to the any of the wicked spirits confined in the Dark Realm. She was ranting at the thieving Stovall child who had suddenly and miraculously come into her third-eye view.

The pompous brat was masquerading in apparel fit for the mistress of a plantation. But what had really sent Eris into a fit of rage was the audacity of the little rascal to stand, admiring herself, while wearing Eris's precious jewelry.

Centuries ago, when Eris was cast out of the Goddess Realm and down to earth, she was expected to learn humility by assuming the guise of a slave. Eris was not interested in learning lessons or returning to the Goddess Realm contrite and repentant.

Cleverly, she'd seduced the master of the Stovall plantation and then poisoned his wife, weakening the mistress until the nuisance of a woman was bedridden and as thin as a rail. She'd slipped the mistress of the plantation's very own wedding ring off her skeletal finger. But a nosey slave had caught onto Eris's scheme and had brought the mistress back to good health.

Eris was ordered to return the mistress's wedding ring. Before she was flogged and set afire, Eris had managed to bury a crude wooden box filled with stolen trinkets as well as her own goddess ring, which seemed lackluster compared to the shiny earthly treasures.

She had buried the treasure box in a secret place on the Stovall grounds, but it was now apparent that her precious jewels had been unearthed and Ajali, her nemesis, was wearing the mistress's wedding ring.

"Give me my jewels!" Eris shouted. Ajali didn't seem aware of Eris's presence, but her little brat had gawked at Eris, recoiling in fear.

Intending to strangle the girl with the pearls that were draped around her scrawny little neck, Eris reached out to grab her. Instantly, she lost the connection and the revolting little Stovall child vanished, escaping Eris's murderous grasp.

"Come back!" Eris commanded the earth-bound little girl. "You can't have my treasures!"

A fearful hush fell over the creatures. Thinking her eerie cry was shouted at them, a ghoulish throng of known thieves quickly slithered and burrowed deep beneath the soot to hide.

Like Eris, the other depraved souls had been exiled to the Dark Realm, a holding place for wicked spirits. Though shamelessly immoral, none were as evil as Eris. Or as gifted. Not one corrupt spirit dared go up against the powerful, fallen goddess.

Those who'd been cast to this smoky abyss for crimes that did not include thievery assumed they were free to continue snarling, biting, scratching, and screaming obscenities at each other.

"Silence!" Eris shouted and shined her cobalt-colored eyes at the bawdy offenders. Arms flew up to shield eyes sensitive to light. A hush fell over the macabre assemblage of evil. Fear of her superior powers kept the malevolent spirits obedient to her every command. Eris ruled the Dark Realm, but found no joy in her prominent stature.

Satisfied that she'd frightened the ghoulish horde into silent submission, Eris closed her eyes and knit her brows in concentration. Something—someone had been blocking her third-eye vision for quite awhile. *Xavier!*

Xavier was a masterful being. And malicious enough to block Eris's vision just to be spiteful. He was enjoying his life as the offspring of a political couple and was busy planning revenge on his parents, who had betrayed him in a previous life.

The last time Xavier had even bothered to communicate with Eris, he had casually mentioned something about working on building a bridge between their worlds. *Rubbish!* What a prankster. He clearly held a grudge against Eris and did not intend to help liberate her from the deplorable prison she dwelled in.

She'd been sending images of her plight to her sister, the goddess Tara, appealing to the goddess's well-known sense of compassion. Her mealy-mouthed sibling didn't have the guts to confront the goddess council and insist that Eris be given a pardon.

The council was too busy wringing their hands and fretting over the failed health of the goddess Kali to be concerned about Eris's predicament. Eris couldn't rely on anyone except herself.

And now, after catching that little jewel thief wearing her goods, she was more determined than ever to break free.

It seemed like years since she'd last set her sight on the Stovalls. And judging by the offspring's size, several years had indeed transpired. But now that she'd finally managed to once again penetrate the barrier between earth and the Dark Realm, Eris was more determined than ever to maintain a watchful eye on the roguish child and her despicable parents. She'd deal with them more intimately once she was liberated from these accursed environs.

The goddess Kali had cast her here, but her interference had come at a great expense to her. It was easy for Eris to fix her sight on the Goddess Realm. Perhaps that link was easier, being that it was her homeland. Who knew? Who cared? She hardly ever bothered to direct her gaze to the Goddess Realm. They were all so smug and pleased with themselves, she found them utterly boring.

She looked in from time to time to snicker at the so-called mighty warrior, Kali. It looked as though Kali's warring days were over. She lay encased inside a chamber that had the purpose of a coffin. Yet, no one would declare the meddlesome goddess, Kali, dead. The goddess council claimed she was merely resting. *Ha!* Kali had outdone herself by imposing herself in a battle that did not concern her.

Now she lay in endless slumber; depleted of her strength and most of her life force. With Kali quarantined, Eris could wreak all sorts of hellish havoc on earth. If only she could figure a way to break free.

If she couldn't do it on her own and if Xavier continued to ignore her pleas for help, she'd work her mind craft on her sister. Tara's compassion was foolish and ill-spent. Whoever heard of a goddess giving sexual pleasure to a hermaphrodite attendant?

Eris was disgusted when her third-eye bore witness to her sister intimately caressing her attendant's mutant genitalia. Still, Eris would keep in mind that Tara's sisterly love and undying loyalty might come in handy.

Evil thoughts warmed her as she imagined the many ways to wreak havoc, to insert her personal brand of retribution inside the Stovalls' untroubled, pristine lives.

First, she'd retrieve her precious jewels, snatching the box of jewels roughly from the thief's clutching hands. If she had to rip off a limb to accomplish the feat, then all the merrier the deed.

She'd begin her rampage with the child—she'd slowly torture the rotten little spawn, biting off her thieving fingers one at a time. Of course, she'd insist that the loathsome parents witness the carnage and bloodshed as she devoured the fruit of their loins alive.

Next, she'd torment the sniveling father. This time she'd be sure to suck the skin right off his worthless prick and then she'd allow her legions of tiny insects and imps to tear away at the bloody exposed flesh.

Eris cackled gleefully as she imagined Bryce crying out and moaning in agony as he'd done the last time she'd ravaged his manhood.

She'd save the worst form of suffering for that bitch, Ajali. Before nailing the sickeningly pious mother Madonna to a cross, she'd scratch her way into her vile vagina and then tie her tubes together with her own bare hands.

Though they kept their distance, the spirits were becoming restless in the cramped and too-quiet-for-comfort domain. Barely able to contain their lustful yearning for mayhem, the beings emitted quiet, uncontrollable hisses and snarls.

Eris heard the soft, sullen sounds. She shot out an angry beam of blue light at the creatures, making them screech and scatter about. She narrowed her eyes, sharpening her vision so that the light that shone from her eyes was so piercing that, like a laser, it burned a hole through the closest creature within her view. The ghoul shrieked in pain while fanning a smoldering gap in its neck. Eris howled with laughter at her malicious deed.

Then she sighed, resolute.

It was no use. She'd been cut off from the Stovalls's world and she couldn't get back in. Her mind was too restless; it was difficult to concentrate when every time she closed her eyes, she saw a mental picture of her jewels adorning that obnoxious child.

Angry, her rancid pussy emitted a stench so fetid that all who were familiar with the odor skulked out of her reach. She writhed and undulated as she turned her blue lights low and then crept up to her unsuspecting prey.

Ah! Her serpentine tongue flicked at her lips. A new arrival! A man who'd lived his earthly existence as a serial rapist and murderer was promenading around and flaunting a ferocious erection. With her mind craft, Eris willed him to swagger in her direction.

Suddenly she lurched forward and pounced on him.

A horde of cretins gasped and ran, attempting to join the thieves who remained in hiding beneath the soot.

Eris bared her teeth, and then crooked a finger, beckoning them forward. "Hold this varmint down," she implored. Realizing she did not intend to do them harm, the creatures shouted in malicious glee as they roughened up and then wrestled down the foolhardy new arrival, and pinning him to the soot-covered ground.

With legs held wide apart, Eris lowered herself onto the bloated male appendage. Thrashing wildly, scratching at his eyes while she molested him, Eris ground her hips violently against the groin of the new arrival, twisting and gyrating until she felt his penile flesh rip.

Satisfied, she rolled off of the rapist. Eris lay on her back with his detached phallus impaled inside her malodorous cunt.

The sight of Eris with her legs cocked open, pleasuring herself with an amputated shaft, was frightful even to the monstrous brood incarcerated in the Dark Realm. Their eyes bulged in horror as they slowly crept forward, awestruck and enthralled by the disgusting exhibition.

The rapist lay in momentary shock, and then he lifted up and gawked at Eris who was busy filling her cunt with his loins.

His panic-filled eyes roved from Eris and then down to his ragged groin. It had been a swift castration. And now he was left to wander throughout eternity without his most valued weapon. He stared once again at what was left of his manhood. Sobbing, he tenderly touched the shreds of bloodied, hanging flesh.

Eris paused momentarily, stilling her fast moves, and pointing at the cowering crowd of heathens. "Go ahead, you mischief makers. Have at each other," she permitted, and then she lay down upon the obsidian and soot, where she administered to the seeping and heated foul area between her legs.

The unholy bunch growled and shrieked with wanton abandon and began battling each other for no reason other than the thrill of causing injury and impairment.

4

THE GODDESS REALM

Enjoying the beauty of the lotus flowers, the goddess Tara relaxed by the pond. The lotus, a spiritual flower with elegant beauty, symbolized the characteristics Tara represented: peace, contentment, loveliness, and perfection.

Tara, the goddess of compassion, evolved eons ago. Like the lotus, she rose from the mud and grew above the water's surface, looking untouched and magnificent with her long arms outstretched toward the heavens. To this day, Tara was deeply connected to the majestic flower. From the lotus, she derived her enduring strength, beauty, and compassion.

Tara's gentle disposition was a stark contrast from her sister's. Eris, the goddess of discord, had a fiery temperament. Thoughts of Eris made Tara sigh unhappily; disrupting her peace. Succumbing to a strange emptiness, she found her beautiful surroundings suddenly transformed to a dark, despicable place. The brilliant sky became dark and cloudy. She winced as the lovely flowers wilted before her eyes; their scent replaced with a choking stench.

It was Eris. Her sister was making her presence known; sending impressions of her ghastly world to her sympathetic sister. Eris was crying for her help, but Tara was powerless to rescue her.

A sudden howling wind, carrying Eris's scream, whirled and

whipped angrily. Then it stopped as suddenly as it had begun.

Sensing someone approaching, Tara looked up. The sun shone again. The flowers stood as vibrant and as beautiful as before, emitting a fragrance that was wonderfully intoxicating. The spell was broken.

In the distance, she saw Zeta, her favorite attendant, carrying a woven basket and walking swiftly across the meadow. Zeta was a blue-winged, hermaphrodite—a true treasure—who was once a companion to Eris. Eris had treated Zeta with cruelty and routinely abused the beautiful winged maiden.

After Eris's dismissal from the Goddess realm, Zeta was passed on to Tara.

The sun gleamed upon Zeta's blue gossamer wings; it shimmered upon the silver threads in the lace garment that clung to her high breasts and displayed her feminine curves. Of all her numerous attendants, Zeta, a vision of loveliness, was Tara's favorite.

Tara's somber mood instantly lifted. She sent a soft smile in Zeta's direction. In turn, Zeta blew the goddess a kiss and hastened her footsteps. Zeta raised her wings; they fluttered gently, lifting her ever so slightly above ground. Slowly, gracefully, she glided toward the pond, toward her worshipped mistress.

"Good morning, goddess," Zeta greeted as she softly landed. Tara inclined her head, silently nodding a hello.

Holding the basket firmly, waiting for permission to set it down, Zeta lowered her beautiful blue wings, enticing her mistress with the rustling sound of her dark blue feathers enfolding.

Tara's chestnut-colored eyes sparkled consent and Zeta placed the basket beside the pond and then daintily spread the silk blanket on the lush green ground.

The Goddess Realm was a dimension comprised primarily of

female energy. The small population of hermaphrodites such as Zeta, beings who possessed both male and female genitals, produced only meager amounts of testosterone—too insignificant and inconsequential to have any meaningful effect on the predominant female vibration of the Goddess Realm.

Many of the goddesses, including Tara, had ravenous sexual appetites. It was the responsibility of the chosen attendant to anticipate and appease every sexual need and desire of the goddess she served.

Tara extended her hand. Expressing a grateful heart, Zeta grasped and tenderly kissed the top of Tara's hand, her wrist, and her palm, before helping the goddess to a standing position. Once Tara was firmly on her feet, Zeta carefully slipped the straps of her sheer gown off her shoulders, baring beautifully formed breasts. Zeta's knowing fingers eased the flowing gown past Tara's round, womanly hips.

With her outer garment shed, like skin peeled from succulent, ripe fruit, Tara stood proud and gloriously naked. And sexually hungry. For a few, charitable moments, Tara allowed Zeta's adoring eyes to feast upon her magnificence.

"The sun shines upon your beauty, Goddess Tara," Zeta said while hastily pulling her own gown over her wings.

"Thank you. You look quite lovely today as well."

Zeta lowered her lush lashes, obviously warmed by the compliment from her mistress. Smiling, she allowed her feathers to spread and flutter charmingly.

Tara stroked Zeta's wings. Her attendant's blue feathers were soft and soothing, wonderful to touch. "Your timing is perfect, Zeta. It pleases me that you're here."

Naked, Tara and Zeta melted into each other's arms. Their breasts pressed together. Zeta's coarse coils of hair fell into her face as she bent her head to admire Tara's luscious mounds.

Tara, already on the brink of arousal, parted her lips, welcoming Zeta's kiss and seductive, wandering tongue. Zeta's lips lingered for a second at Tara's breasts and then traveled to her ear. "Mistress," she whispered. "I shall pay special attention to your breasts today. My lips yearn to be attached to your dark pearls."

The feeling of Zeta's sweet breath so close to her ear sent thrills down Tara's neck and straight to the nipples of her bosom, hardening them.

Zeta gently nibbled on Tara's earlobe and outlined her ear with her tongue. This erotic gesture caused Tara's swelling nipples to become hugely engorged with yearning.

Gently, Zeta penetrated Tara's ear. Soft sounds of pleasure escaped from the back of Tara's throat. This incited Zeta to insert her tongue more deeply and to murmur softly, "I exist for your eternal pleasure, mistress."

Becoming almost dizzy with sexual desire, Tara ran the fingers of both hands down the center of Zeta's back. Then, her fidgety palms meandered in opposite directions, seeking the solace of Zeta's soft feathered wings to quell her raging need.

"I sense that you are troubled today," Zeta said, her voice tender with concern. "I present my moist lips to kiss and soothe the silken center of your womanhood. I offer a wet tongue to lick between your petal-soft folds. Allow me to wash away your cares."

Tara tightened her strong legs together. Zeta was wise; all her concerns seemed to have gathered and accumulated and the building tension throbbed in her center. Not only was she deeply disturbed over her sister's confinement in the hellish Dark Realm, she was equally concerned about Kali's continuous slumber.

Deep sorrow combined with sexual tension, knotting in her

center and then swirling, and moving to other sensitive parts.

Sadly, Tara reached out and caressed Zeta's wings, yearning to find a bit of comfort in the soft feathers.

"Sweet mistress, I feel your sorrow. With my undying love and well-honed sensual skills, I pledge to relieve your pain and give you unimaginable pleasure."

Instantly, Tara felt her burdens begin to ease. She removed her hands from the downy softness of Zeta's wings and allowed the prized hermaphrodite to lead her to the soft blanket that was spread out for their lovemaking.

Tara lay on her back with her arms stretched upward. Her brown body, glazed by the sun, looked delicious—sweet and edible—like molasses. Zeta sat next to Tara and gazed down, giving her mistress a long, considering look.

"Start with my hair," Tara said, knowing her attendant had been wondering where she should start. Zeta worked her fingers into Tara's hair, massaged her scalp, and then pressed her lips against Tara's neck, tasting her flesh.

Tara, desiring more than kisses, tilted her head, offering Zeta access to the full length of her long, delicate neck. Zeta licked Tara's neck; lapped the heated perspiration that was sweet on her tongue. She bit into Tara's delicate skin. Tara cried out, enjoying the sweet pain. Zeta bit harder, this time leaving behind the indentation of four teeth marks. A soft crooning, a musical sound of yearning, escaped Tara's lips and floated to Zeta's ears, persuading the attendant to lick, suck, and kiss the sensitive flesh on Tara's neck until Tara pleaded for her to stop.

The goddess and the attendant became entwined, lips merging hungrily, their feminine hips undulating together in an erotic, primal dance. Zeta kissed her way down to Tara's swollen nipples. She squeezed Tara's breasts together and used her thumbs to tease the pebbled flesh. She opened her mouth, inviting her mistress to lift up and rest on her elbows as she fed her attendant her plum-colored pearls.

At first, Zeta flicked her tongue against Tara's firm nipples, and then sucked each pearl. Tara, her body flushed with arousal, began to feel a familiar ache as intense heat flooded her body and her thighs became drenched with her juices.

"Use your shaft and take me," Tara uttered breathily and curled on her side, displaying her beautifully rounded buttocks.

"Yes, mistress." Obligingly, Zeta positioned herself behind Tara. Possessing both male and female genitals, Zeta was overly-stimulated. Unbearably so.

Zeta's penis throbbed with yearning, while beneath the pulsing male appendage, her wet vagina clenched with need. But being a superior and disciplined attendant, Zeta suppressed her urges and ignored the hot wanting inside her female organ.

Deftly, Zeta pressed her rapidly growing hardness against her mistress's lovely rump. With an arm draped over Tara's side, Zeta used her longest finger to caress Tara's clitoris. Enjoying the heightened sensation of dual stimulation, Tara rotated her hips and moaned softly as she rocked to and fro', thrusting into Zeta's finger while at the same time bumping against her attendant's rigid maleness.

Now, panting, Tara called out, "Oh, my lovely Zeta!" Tara knew Zeta would recognize her desperate cry and properly prepare her for entry.

As expected, Zeta crouched down, her suckling lips seeking the pleasure of sipping Tara's nectar. Her thirst quenched, Zeta nibbled her way backward, her hands tenderly separating Tara's smooth buttocks.

Gingerly, she licked the ridged rim and then inserted a quick and darting tongue inside Tara's tight and delicate anus, teasing it into opening for her; grazing at the small hole until Tara gasped and whimpered with pleasure.

Zeta withdrew her tongue and spoke with her mouth enclosed in the flagrant valley between Tara's buttocks. "Your taste rivals the sweetest fruit on the Goddess Realm; I could lick your anus for all of eternity if I were allowed to."

Zeta's words stimulated her mistress. Aroused beyond reason, Tara made her needs known before she lost her mind and drifted off into an otherworldly state of ecstasy. "Cover me with your wings. Enter me, now."

Obediently, Zeta kneeled on her haunches and spread her wings. Her feathers caressed Tara's arms gently, reassuringly. She stroked her phallus, moistened it with its pre-ejaculation and aimed the slippery knob lower, toward the silken entry of Tara's pulsing tunnel.

Zeta's thrusts were rhythmic and slow.

"Deeper!" Tara moaned. Zeta obeyed, satisfying her mistress as well as her throbbing hardness. But her feminine part dripped with unfulfilled yearning.

"Harder!" Tara cried, pushing back and demanding more of Zeta's sturdy penis.

Obeying her mistress, Zeta squeezed Tara's buttocks for leverage and then drove her throbbing shaft in and out swiftly. She released one buttock and wound her hand around and down to Tara's puffy labia, tugged on one slippery lip and then the other.

When she sank two fingers into Tara's dewy vagina, her own female opening gripped and clenched with ravenous hunger.

Zeta was not allowed to ejaculate from her penis until Tara was satiated. Needing desperately to quench one of her sexual desires, she plunged her shaft in and out of Tara's tight depths. Tara matched Zeta's rhythm until she exploded.

Now it was Zeta's turn for release. Quickly, she released and, together, she and her mistress shuddered and cried out in one shared vibration.

When Tara's breathing returned to normal, she reached backward; her fingers stretching to locate Zeta's hot pool of yearning. "You can't speak of this. It is our secret," Tara whispered.

"Thank you, mistress. You are so kind and understanding. I promise to never tell a soul," Zeta replied as she changed position. Lying on her back with her wings spread, she waited for Tara's touch.

Tara couldn't resist the urge to caress the length of her attendant's pleasure-providing maleness. Zeta's penis quivered at Tara's touch, but did not grow hard.

Unable to control her desire, Zeta clasped Tara's hand, guiding her mistress's delicate finger to her slippery softness. Spreading her muscular legs, Zeta granted Tara access to the moist place that was hot and aching with unbearable sexual need.

Sadly, the pleasure Tara had shared with Zeta had been only a temporary distraction. Alone now, and feeling tormented by Eris's dire circumstances, Tara sobbed softly. Despite Eris's wicked ways, Tara loved her dearly.

The day was sunny and glorious. Yet, if it weren't for the colorful hues of the lotus and the power they imparted, Tara would have felt as if she were surrounded by dreary clouds.

Gloom hovered closely—too closely. The thorny, dark place where Eris dwelled was alive with evil; the lost inhabitants inflicted unspeakable acts of cruelty upon each other. Their violent howls and piercing screams were being transmitted to Tara.

Eris was sharing her misery and beseeching help from the one compassionate soul who loved her without condition.

Eris had a hand in every quarrel, feud, or disagreement among the inhabitants of the Goddess Realm. It was Eris's nature to cause conflict and to delight in dissension and discord.

Inanna, the goddess of love and war, had passed on each of her dueling characteristics to her two daughters, Tara and Eris. Countless times, Inanna had intervened on Eris's behalf—using her prominent status to veto the council's decision to punish her wayward daughter. However, when Inanna had ascended to a higher realm, the council was no longer restricted from meting out just punishment for Eris's incessant wrong-doing.

Many lifetimes ago, the goddess council ruled that Eris would be dispatched to the Earthly Realm, forced to roam the land in the guise of a slave. It was the hope of the council that having to assume the form a humbled human being would persuade Eris to mend her ways and return to the Goddess Realm grateful and repentant.

Unfortunately, Eris was not humble; she received wicked enjoyment from her earthly displacement. She misused her remaining goddess powers while on earth and was bent on destroying many lives.

The goddess Kali, the protector of children, was summoned to earth to protect the unborn fetus of a female earthling known as Ajali.

Kali assisted Ajali in destroying Eris with fire and returned her to the Dark Realm, a hideous holding place—a loathsome and eternal prison—for depraved, corrupt souls.

Her mighty victory over Eris completely sapped her strength.

Kali returned to the Goddess Realm and collapsed. The attendants of the goddesses carried Kali to a peaceful chamber where renewal and rejuvenation could be hastened with the calming scent of lavender, which permeated the air. Soft music, with its wondrous healing power, played without cessation while Kali slumbered inside a clear, crystal tomb.

Daily, the goddesses formed a circle around Kali's resting place and chanted the sacred prayer of healing. Mental images of brilliant white light surrounded the sleeping form of the warrior goddess. Despite this daily ritual, Kali's recovery was taking much longer than expected.

Unlike their mother, Tara held a much lower position in the hierarchy of goddesses; her opinion held no weight with the council. Seven times, she'd flung herself at the mercy of the council, advocating on her sister's behalf, and seven times her request had been rejected.

Though Tara sent her sister the telepathic messages that the council had stood firmly by their decision and that there was nothing she could do, Eris persisted in sending the atrocious images and impressions; no doubt taking delight in her sister's soul-wrenching, mournful reaction.

5

Ethan wouldn't stop screaming and Jen didn't know what to do. She couldn't distinguish if it was a cry of agony or if he was having some sort of emotional break. When he twisted his face into a grotesque mask that seemed to express pain, Jen yanked the phone out of the base, prepared to call emergency services.

Then she thought about the consequences and hung up. If Ethan wasn't near death, his mother would flip out. Catherine Provost didn't want any unwelcome attention drawn to her son.

Jen covered her ears. He continued screaming. She looked at the clock. He'd been steadily screaming for a half-hour. That wasn't normal. Now, she was scared.

She thought about the whispers between Carmen and Lizzy. Rumor had it that, moments after Ethan's birth, right after he had taken his first breath, he had clearly shouted the word "bitch" and had never spoken another word since.

It was only a rumor but, thinking about it right now, while the kid was carrying on, was really starting to freak her out.

Carmen swore that she'd heard Catherine and the senator arguing over their child. She'd told Jen that Catherine had referred to Ethan as the senator's demon son. And since then, Carmen had kept a silver crucifix around her neck, convinced that Ethan was possessed.

Jen was also informed that the Provost household had a revolving door of nannies; young women who couldn't deal with Ethan's numerous, appalling eccentricities. Murmuring suspicions that Ethan was possessed, many of those former nannies had walked off the job without giving notice.

Jen forcefully shoved those dreadful thoughts from her mind and refocused on the present: Ethan's piercing scream. The shrieking sounded like something straight out of hell. His horrifying wail pierced her ears, threatened to puncture her eardrums.

At this moment, while she was suffering, his mother was living it up, being adored by millions of voters. Jen couldn't take it anymore. It was time to give up this job, go home, and face her parents.

She called Catherine's personal cell.

Catherine picked up. "Yes!"

"Hello?" Jen shouted, trying to be heard above the pandemonium. "Ms. Provost?" Jen said, frantic.

"Is that Ethan in the background?" Catherine asked calmly.

"Yes. He's been screaming for a half-hour. I can't make him stop."

"What's going on, Jen?" Her tone sounded accusatory, as if Jen was torturing her son.

"Th-there's something wrong with Ethan." There was a tremor in Jen's voice.

"What's wrong?" Catherine said, her voice rising.

"I don't know what's wrong with him?" It seemed to Jen that Catherine was trying to mimic the sound of a concerned mother.

"Is he hurt? What's wrong with my son?" she demanded, bringing her voice to what seemed to be a fake, desperate pitch.

"I don't...I don't think he's hurt." Jen looked over at Ethan and he simply closed his mouth and stopped screaming. "Um... Ms. Provost, like...all of a sudden, he seems to be fine."

"Well, what happened? Why was he screaming like that?"

"One minute, he was calm and the next…he…he just started screaming. But he's back to his normal self now." She wanted to add his normal *weirdo* self.

"Did you call the senator's office?"

"No."

"Did you contact any of my staff?"

"No. I didn't call anyone else. Just you. But, Ms. Provost, you should have seen Ethan. He looked really frightening. His face was all twisted and I thought he was in pain. I started to call Emergency Services—"

"Are you kidding me?" Catherine shrieked.

"But I didn't," Jen assured her. "I did exactly like you said to do, in case of an emergency." She took a deep breath and steadied her voice.

"And you didn't call 9-1-1?" Catherine sounded unconvinced.

"No. I only called you. If you hadn't answered, I would have called Senator Provost's personal cell."

"Great," Catherine said. Jen could hear the relief in her tone. Catherine had this obsession about people nosing into her business and she forbade Jen to leave voice messages. Jen was instructed to speak to either the senator or Catherine directly. "What's Ethan doing now?" Catherine sounded distracted.

"He's sitting at the computer. Calm and composed, like nothing happened. He's looking at those bridges he stares at all the time."

"Good…good," Catherine muttered. "He'll be fine."

"But I'm not. I…I'm…" Jen stammered. "I'm scared, Ms. Provost."

"Of what?" Catherine said indignantly.

"Of Ethan. You should have seen him. He was hardly recognizable. His face—" Jen paused and gave a small whimper. "His face was contorted…and…and—Ms. Provost. I know this sounds ridiculous. But there's something about Ethan that isn't right."

"What do you mean, isn't right?" Catherine sounded incredulous. "He's not a serial killer, you know," she added with harsh sarcasm. "He's a disabled child." Then she quickly softened her tone. "For heaven's sake, Jen. What can poor little Ethan do to you? What's there to be afraid of?"

"Ms. Provost. It was really awful. You should have seen him. He—"

"Jen, I need you to get a grip. Ethan was having an episode," Catherine interrupted in a whisper.

"You didn't mention any episodes when you interviewed me."

"It happens so infrequently, I must have forgotten. I have a lot on my mind. I'm a busy woman, you know," she said in a chastising tone. "Ethan is five years old. He's a harmless little child. He can't hurt you."

"I know, but—"

"Honestly, Jen, I don't know why we're having this conversation. It's utterly ridiculous." Cathcrine spoke quickly. She paused, switching to a soft, placating tone. "Hang in there with me until the election. There's a position opening in the senator's office. His assistant is completely incompetent and I've asked him to get rid of her. Working with Senator Provost could lead to un-limited opportunities."

"Really?" Jen asked, excited.

"Yes, but you can't ditch poor Ethan like all those other nannies did. He needs you. To switch his nanny right before the election would not be fair to Ethan, or to me."

"I understand," Jen said, feeling like an idiot. She wanted to quit! But the job offer with the senator was too enticing to pass up. She wouldn't have to tell her parents that she got kicked out of school. She could say the great offer came and she was taking some time off. Her parents would love to brag that their daughter had a prestigious job with a United States senator.

"I'll take care of you. Do you understand?"

"Yes…I'm sorry, Ms. Provost—"

"Apology accepted." Catherine let out an audible sigh of relief.

"Um, right before Ethan went berserk… I mean, right before he had that, uh, episode, your campaign manager called. She wanted to know if you'd checked in with me."

"All right, Jen. I'll get in touch with her. Have a good night. Oh, kiss Ethan for me."

Jen had a hunch why the campaign manager didn't know how to locate Catherine. According to Carmen and Lizzy, Catherine liked to sneak away from her handlers and gaze at the vice president's mansion—her next home. Jen couldn't figure out how the cook and the maid knew so much…it wasn't as if Catherine sat down with them and chatted, bringing them up to date on every aspect of her life.

Jen glanced over at Ethan. He was clicking the mouse on the computer; looking at bridges. *A few more weeks and this hell will be over; I'll be working with the senator.*

Jen gave a blissful sigh. She had a huge crush on Senator Provost; partly because he was handsome, but mainly because being joined at the hip with Ethan was ruining her chances for getting laid.

She couldn't get out the house to meet any guys and the sex drought she was going through was really starting to get to her.

6

Lizzy had finished cleaning and had already left for the day. In another hour, Carmen would be finishing up cooking her specialty: beans, rice, and chicken gizzards—a Spanish meal that wasn't allowed on the menu when Catherine was at home—and then she'd leave, too.

Jen hated this time of the day. She'd be alone with Ethan until his father arrived home and sometimes Senator Provost didn't get in until around ten; sometimes later. It depended.

Sitting in the kitchen, Jen sipped orange juice and thumbed through a few more pages of a gossip magazine, and then closed it. She checked the time and forced herself to her feet.

"Tinkle time?" Carmen asked sympathetically, referring to Ethan's hourly toileting schedule.

"We'll see." Jen gave a resigned smile. She was required to remind Ethan to take bathroom breaks. She dreaded it, but if she didn't insist and physically carry him to the bathroom, he'd sit in urine-soaked undies without a care.

"Seems like the kid might benefit from having a pet. You know, with his disorder and all, I'm surprised Mayor Provost didn't look into pet therapy," Jen said.

"No, he's not good with pets." Carmen took on a worried expression and nervously wiped her hands on her apron.

"How do you know? Has Ethan ever had a cat or a dog?"

"No! God forbid." Carmen made the sign of the cross.

Jen raised both her eyebrows, waiting for the cook to elaborate.

"The senator brought home some gold fish…he put together a small fish tank with the colorful gravel, seashells, and fake plants, and stuff like that…"

Jen nodded.

"Well, the next morning, we heard the nanny scream. Lizzy and I ran up to the bedroom…Madam Mayor didn't budge from her room—"

"Wow," Jen murmured.

"Every single gold fish was lying at the bottom of the tank… torn to pieces."

Jen grimaced. "What do you mean?"

"They were mutilated. Like somebody had cut them up with a pair of scissors."

"Eew. Ethan cut up his goldfish?"

Carmen held up her palms. "Unsolved mystery."

"God, is the kid that warped?"

Carmen's raised her palms higher. "Who else would have done such a vicious thing?"

"You really think Ethan's capable of callously murdering gold-fish?"

This time Carmen didn't respond with words; she crossed her arms over her ample bosom and stared pointedly at Jen.

"If he did that, he's got more than a couple of loose screws. He's evil."

"Evil is the exact word his nanny used to describe him after she discovered the cut-up fish. Then she quit."

"That's understandable." Jen stared down into her glass for a few moments. Jen doubted she could stick it out much longer with this psycho kid. The mutilated fish story was helpful information. Something Jen could add to the excuse she was piecing together for the nanny agency when she asked for a transfer.

Carmen lifted the lid of a big pot, stirred vigorously, her eyes narrowed in unpleasant recollection. "Later that day, Madam Mayor called us together and reminded us that we could be prosecuted if we leaked anything about the goldfish to the press." Carmen shook her head. "She didn't even seem sorry for what her boy had done to the poor fish. I'm telling you, the apple don't fall far from the tree. That woman is as cold as ice."

"You're right. She's not a very nice person."

"She's wicked. That's why she was cursed with that son." Carmen closed her eyes and shook her head. "The poor senator. He loves them both and what does he get in return?"

"Well, in Ethan's defense, his disorder prevents him from showing love or affection. But Catherine…what's her excuse?"

"No excuse. Selfish and mean." Carmen's loyalty was with the senator alone. She detested Catherine and was leery of Ethan.

As though she were taking a swig of hard liquor to boost her courage, Jen took a big gulp of orange juice before leaving the comfort of the kitchen. Instead of moping around and feeling sorry for herself, she really should have appreciated all the free time she had. If Ethan's mother were here, Jen's life would be pure hell.

Catherine was very precise and specific about how her son's care should be given. She made Jen organize the little clothes that hung in his closet by color. No beige pants mixed in with the blues. The same set of rules applied to his pajamas, T-shirts, and briefs that were folded inside his bureau drawers. Everything had to be organized by color. Catherine Provost was so anal.

His bedroom was filled with expensive toys that he never

touched. Jen was assigned to play with specific toys at a precise hour of the day. Entertaining normal little kids with silly games would be bad enough, but having to engage in one-sided play with a disinterested, non-verbal computer geek was so demeaning.

Besides, Jen didn't like his toys. She'd prefer playing with a Barbie doll with a killer wardrobe, a hot car, and a dream house.

She particularly despised having to play with Ethan's toy cars. There were, like, a zillion of little racecars lined up on a complicated ramp. She was expected to operate a remote and give a lively narration of the car race.

With his eyes fixed on the computer screen, transfixed by the images of bridges, Ethan always ignored her and the damned cars, but Jen was expected to start some new dialogue. She had to keep up her miserable performance for exactly a half-hour, or his mom would flip out and accuse her of neglecting her nanny duties. God, her job sucked.

In addition to playing with Ethan's corny toys, she was also instructed to read to him. Jen loved books and since Catherine was totally into exposing Ethan to the Harry Potter series, Jen got a lot of enjoyment out of reading aloud.

But every morning after breakfast, she had to play a CD with interactive kiddie songs that involved sing-along, hand-clapping, counting, word repetition, foot-stomping, and a lot of whooping and hollering.

Jen had to comply with the humiliating sing-song exercise with absolutely no participation from her silent and listless young charge. As long as Catherine could hear Jen's voice belting out the silly lyrics and Jen's hands and feet clapping and thumping, the vice presidential candidate was content that her son was getting the stimulation she felt was necessary to his well-being.

What a crock! Nothing except the sight of bridges interested or stimulated Ethan. Oh, the things Jen had to put up with when Catherine Provost was at home.

But now that Catherine was fully focused on getting elected, Jen was able to float freely, mingling with the cook and the maid, watching TV, chatting on her cell phone with her friends back in Centerville, pretending that dorm life at Temple University was a perpetual party.

She never let on that she was a miserable live-in nanny for an obnoxious, non-verbal little boy.

With Catherine out of the way, Jen only checked in on Ethan at the top of every hour to remind him to take a bathroom break. Sometimes, she felt sorry for him. The kid couldn't help the fact that he was such a creep. It wasn't his fault. Still, no one, not even his own parents, seemed comfortable around him.

Aside from the occasional, God-awful screaming episodes, Ethan was usually silent. The rapid clicking of the computer mouse as Ethan changed images on the computer screen was the only sound in the room.

A stock photo of a bridge popped up on the screen and was quickly replaced by another. This would go on until he became exhausted. When his mother wasn't around, he pretended not to hear Jen when she told him it was time for bed. He'd stiffen his frail body when she tried to pull him out of his little swivel chair. It was a nightmare trying to move rigid limbs into the arms and legs of his pajamas.

"Hey, buddy. How's it going?" she said, entering the bedroom. Naturally, Ethan didn't acknowledge her presence; he kept his back turned to her. "Ready for a bathroom break?" she continued cheerfully. She didn't actually expect a response; she was merely making conversation, the way she'd do with a verbal child.

"You're going the wrong way."

Jen stopped cold, stunned by words that were spoken in a croaked, scratchy whisper and that seemed to come from the little boy. But Ethan couldn't talk. *What the heck is going on?* With a sharp eye, she took in the surroundings, doing a three-sixty as she inspected the bedroom. Nobody around except her and Ethan. Maybe the website had an audio feature, she rationalized.

Now, standing next to him, she chuckled nervously, trying to kid herself into believing that nothing out of the ordinary had occurred. "Did you say something, buddy?" Jen bent down to the child's level and peered at the monitor. There was movement on the bridge.

"Oh my God!" she uttered and then clamped a palm over her mouth. Her eyes bugged out in disbelief as she witnessed a naked black woman with wild raven hair billowing behind her as she ran along the wooden bridge. Jen had seen that exact image of the old-fashioned bridge over a misty waterfall, like…a zillion times or more. Ethan always stared at the same set of bridges. Over and over—the same set of bridges. And the bridge on the monitor was a stock photo. That bridge was not being live-streamed, so what in the freakin' hell was that woman doing on the screen? Jen wanted to scream for help, but was stunned silent.

"Not that way!" Ethan spoke.

Okay, this was getting way too creepy, now. She was ready to bolt, but her knocking knees rendered her disabled. Suspended in time. As hard as it was to accept, there was no denying it. She saw Ethan's lips move; heard the words come straight from his mouth. But the voice he'd used was not that of a child's. He sounded like a cranky old man.

Jen uttered a frightened gasp. She felt the hairs on the back of her neck lift as she watched, shocked and horrified, as the nude black woman, seeming to have heard Ethan, stopped running, turned in the opposite direction, and made a few faltering steps. Changing her mind, the naked apparition on the bridge switched back and continued running until she was no longer within the screen's view.

Like an irritated adult, Ethan clucked his tongue in disgust.

A naked woman on a bridge. Had Ethan logged onto a porn site? Jen blinked rapidly, trying to make sense of what was occurring on the screen. But there was no explanation. It was one of Ethan's favorite bridges. *What the freakin' hell is going on? Is someone live streaming from the bridge?* Unwilling to find out who would appear next on the bridge, Jen's shaky hand turned the computer off. Rigid with fear, her lower limbs refused to move. When they finally cooperated, she fled the child's bedroom.

7

THE DARK REALM

When the portal closed, Eris wanted to scream in frustration, but that sound would have aroused the scallywags around her, sending them into a raucous frenzy, disrupting her concentration.

Trying to reconnect with the little jewel thief, she closed her eyes and waited. Time passed. Minutes…days…perhaps weeks went by, and all she saw was darkness. Then there was a jolt. The connection had been reestablished.

A familiar but unexpected voice spoke to her. "I've constructed a bridge for you."

"Xavier!" she shouted excitedly.

"Hurry! I can't keep this portal open very long!"

"How do I find this bridge?" She needed guidance—explicit directions—and was prepared to ask him a number of very detailed questions.

"You must follow me; do not tarry," he grumbled impatiently before she'd sent him a mental query. "As you know, Wicked One, I have little tolerance for dimwittedness. Do not waste time with your foolish inquiries."

"Very well." Eris had no choice but to go along with Xavier. She forced herself to relax and blindly followed him with her mind until she felt their energy merge. Xavier took hold of her hand and led her out of the darkness.

He let go and, moments later, she was surrounded in brilliant sunshine! Her bare feet were touching smooth, sun-warmed wood. Oh, it was a glorious feeling.

"Run!" Xavier ordered. His voice was no longer close. He sounded as if he were very far away or speaking from under water.

"Where are you, Xavier?"

"Run!" He sounded more garbled and farther away.

So, she ran. Fast. Her feet slapped against wood as fresh air breezed against her bare skin. Earthbound at last, Eris smiled and ran faster. *I'm free!* A gentle wind blew through her hair, lifting her locks as she sped naked along the bridge. Oh, sweet freedom was exhilarating. Such happiness had eluded her for so long, she wanted to express it by engaging in a lewd dance while naked on the bridge, but she had to keep running before the portal closed.

"You're going the wrong way." His distorted voice was filled with disgust.

Confused, she faltered a little before getting her bearing. She whirled around and began running in the opposite direction.

"Too late!" He chuckled scornfully.

"No! Xavier, come back! Help me!" In an instant, Eris felt her body being whooshed into a fast-moving vortex, whirling about for what seemed like an eternity. Xavier's malicious laughter echoed in her ears. Finally, all motion stopped. There was stillness and Xavier's laughter blended in with a distant buzzing sound. The sunshine was gone and the air was dank and vaporous.

Shrouded in darkness and disoriented, Eris's body trembled. She struggled for clarity as she took in her surroundings. Her cobalt eyes swept back and forth. After regaining her focus, her eyes became wide with incredulity. Furious, she inhaled, filling her nostrils with the recognizable noxious odor—the despicable stench that permeated the Dark Realm.

The buzzing in her ears grew louder and became the familiar sound of scratching, clawing, growling, screeching, as Eris's unholy brethren maimed and molested each other.

"Xavier! You bastard!" she cried in her mind. There was no answer; not even the sound of his mocking laughter. Their connection was broken.

Desiring to inflict pain, she randomly selected the first creature that came into view. It was a female creature—a floozy with yellow hair and large brown eyes. The female batted her lashes and enticingly licked her lips. Her undulating hips invited males to get down in the soot with her.

The wanton female was out of compliance with Eris's law. She'd lost sight of the fact that Eris was the Queen Bee of the Dark Realm—all the males' sexual organs belonged to Eris alone. She doled their services out to the females as she saw fit.

Mistakenly, the tramp thought she could secretly solicit sex while Eris was preoccupied in meditation.

Eris cast glowering blue eyes upon the woman.

"Don't!" The female screamed and threw up an arm to shield her eyes from the blinding light of Eris's harsh glare.

A flock of terrified creatures scrambled and leapt out of Eris's sight, blending into the shadows, burrowing into the soot.

Eris narrowed an eye, rotated her head, panning her vision to zoom in on the target. She shot out a penetrating blue light. It burned through the female's arm, scorching her eyeball.

"Aah," the female screamed, covering the injured eye with the palm of her hand. The cry of pain excited Eris, inciting her to keep her burning gaze riveted on the creature's face. She sent another hot beam of blue light to the offensive female's right eye, blazing through the eyeball and socket until smoke streamed out of the back of the creature's head and her yellow hair caught afire before she burst into flames.

Eris's taunting laughter rang out and soon others joined in with a cacophony of hellish squeals, hoots, and cackles. The yellow-haired female burned and the stench of smoldering flesh and hair commingled with the usual foul odor that infused the Dark Realm. Aroused by the fetid air, the vile and demented creatures drooled and hissed; they slithered and gyrated in sexual urgency. Eris nodded her head, permitting them to indulge their perverted desires.

Her eyes gleamed, her body quivered with excitement as she watched the savage ruckus. But the mêlée provided only momentary distraction from her problem. Frustration set in and once again, Eris felt caged and resentful. She had to escape.

Hatching an escape plan required privacy. She needed her own private space—a cavern similar to Xavier's former domicile would give her the silence necessary to concentrate. She called on Xavier for help in constructing her own quarters, but he remained inaccessible.

"Tara!" she cried out. "Tara! Goddess of Compassion and loving sister, I beseech you to have mercy on me! Save me from this dark and unremitting punishment."

8

THE GODDESS REALM

Their fingers laced, Tara and Zeta walked briskly past the garden of bluebells.

"Oh!" Tara winced. Her hastened footsteps faltered as she pressed her hand against her throbbing temple.

Instinctively, Zeta raised a wing, caressing Tara's back her soft feathers. "What is it, mistress? Are you ill?"

"No. I felt a sharp pain. It's gone now."

Unless deliberately inflicted by another, pain and illness was practically nonexistent on the Goddess Realm. Zeta looked confused as she searched Tara's eyes for truth.

Tara looked away. "We must hurry. I'm late."

Zeta didn't question her. They resumed walking, their bare feet moving swiftly. Zeta unlaced her fingers and held Tara's hand in a protective, tightened grip.

"I know that you're troubled, mistress." Zeta's blue feathers rustled nervously. "Were it not for your urgent appointment, I would lift you in my arms and soar heavenward where you could rest upon a cushiony cloud."

Tara set appreciative eyes on Zeta's face. "Thank you." She didn't have it in her to say more. With each hastened step, Tara was haunted by a mosaic of horrid images and maniacal moaning and wailing sent telepathically by Eris. The loud sounds and crude imagery crammed every corner of her mind and made her head throb. Though she wanted to ease her pain, Tara did not possess the power to shut out the images from her mind.

Zeta kept caring eyes trained on Tara's face.

"My sister's confinement is appalling."

Zeta nodded acknowledgment of the statement. Eris was wicked. Zeta, having been on the receiving end of Eris's cruelty, knew that firsthand, but she kept her judgment to herself.

"Eris doesn't deserve to be trapped in that hellish place. My poor sister is surrounded by dreadful beings—" Tara's bottom lip trembled. "Those evil-doers she dwells among are all thieves and murderers. Incorrigible! I'm so afraid they'll influence my sister. Involve her in some ill-doing that will lengthen her sentence."

"She's serving a life sentence, mistress," Zeta reminded Tara. "The goddess of destruction is doomed to the Dark Realm for all of eternity."

"Good behavior and repentance could grant her clemency. As her compassionate and loving sister, it is my obligation to speak to the council on her behalf." Tara turned to Zeta, her blue eyes moist and unhappy. "She's suffering, Zeta. And when my sister suffers, I suffer too." Her sinewy fingers brushed across her forehead.

"Without a doubt, Eris has engaged in a great share of wrongdoing and many unkind acts were committed against you. But, in my heart, I believe my sister's behavior cannot possibly be compared to the depraved misconduct of those deviants she's imprisoned with."

Tara's troubled thoughts propelled her to walk swiftly. Her gown swirled around her as she sped along. Zeta's wings fluttered as she quickened her step to keep up.

"She uses her gift of mind power to get in my head and communicate with me. My sister especially regrets her transgressions against you, Zeta," Tara said softly. "She pleads for your forgiveness."

Zeta walked with her mistress in silence.

"You will forgive her, won't you? I'm certain that Eris can be rehabilitated if she were granted clemency and returned to the Goddess Realm—under close supervision, of course."

"I agree, mistress. No one is beyond redemption," Zeta said, lowering her head to conceal doubtful eyes. Kindhearted, Tara could not bring herself to believe that Eris was so callous she was beyond redemption. She was certain there was a misunderstanding or some reasonable explanation for why or how Eris had managed to escape captivity from the Dark Realm or why she'd revisited the Earthly plane. While on earth for the second time and this time without permission, Eris had not communicated with Tara. Tara did not possess the details of her sister's crimes on earth or why she'd been handed down the harsh life sentence.

She did know that the warrior goddess, Kali, was summoned to earth and was forced to wage battle against Eris. Kali had returned to the Goddess Realm so infirm that not even the magic of the highest healer could restore her health. Her silenced lips could not report the extent of Eris's misdeeds.

But Eris's laments, her cries for mercy, were agonizing; too much for Tara's compassionate soul to bear. If Eris was not released, Tara worried that unbearable sorrow would wither her own radiant smile. The vibrant health she so enjoyed would eventually fail and, unlike her mother, she would not ascend to the heavens. She'd be doomed like Kali, to convalesce inside a crystal tomb, waving between life and death indefinitely.

Zeta accompanied Tara down the glittering gold path that led to the healing chamber. When they reached the door, the winged maiden opened her arms and Tara moved into her embrace. They kissed softly, and then Zeta held open the door and bade Tara farewell.

The goddess circle had already formed around Kali's vault. Instead of praying, their voices resonated in a humming chant. At first, Tara's questioning eyes drifted around the circle and then rested on Kali's still form. Tara took her place inside the circle and reverently bowed her head and, with a heavy heart, she joined in the single-chord mantra, now understanding that Kali's health would not be restored. The goddess chant would help with her transition. It was only a matter of time before Kali ascended to the Heavenly Realm.

9

Eris was a fool. He'd masterminded an ingenious escape plan, created a pathway from her world to his, and she'd bungled all his work. Now he was exhausted; too tired to make another attempt to free her. She was lucky he needed her help; otherwise he would gladly leave her trapped in hell.

Being caged inside the body of a small child restricted him from wreaking havoc or doing physical harm to his parents and the hired help the way he wanted to. Every time he was referred to as "Ethan," the child went into frenzy. His name was Xavier but these imbeciles refused to address him properly.

Since he was perceived as odd and unable to master speech, he went along with the farce, expressing his disdain for the name he'd been given with snarls and wheezing. Xavier could manipulate his facial muscles into numerous unsightly contortions that terrorized anyone unfortunate enough to set eyes on him. But it wasn't enough. He wanted to cause pain.

Daniel and Catherine Provost had betrayed him many lifetimes ago and now that he was inside their home, a member of their family, he intended to make them suffer far worse than they'd done to him.

As parents, they were as detestable as they'd been in their last lifetime together, when they'd conspired to topple him from his throne. Xavier was king and Catherine was his queen. Daniel, the cad, was Catherine's clandestine lover. The two sexual deviants had copulated in practically every room of Xavier's castle.

But committing adultery wasn't the worst of their crimes. Catherine and Daniel had masterminded a scheme, accusing Xavier of treason, leading him to an untimely demise at the guillotine.

The deceitful twosome reigned together for many years and grew old and died peacefully while Xavier's tormented spirit was contained in the Dark Realm.

Happy and successful in this lifetime as well, Catherine and Daniel had yet to pay for their crime. Oh, but they would. Xavier's hatred for his parents knew no bounds. Their demise would not be a gentle smothering or a simple slitting of their throats. They would die brutal deaths. It would be a hellish, bloody massacre splattered on the pages of newspapers for the entire world to see.

The mental pictures of the revenge he would exact upon them filled him with thrills. Pretending to be a child wasn't easy at times like this. Xavier was centuries old in spirit and he had emerged from the womb with the intelligence and the urgent desires of an adult male.

Sexual relief did not come easy. He could look at porn on the computer, but why do that when there was a living and breathing female in the bedroom a few doors down the hall. From past experiences, he knew his current nanny slept nude.

On numerous occasions, he'd used her unclothed body as a backdrop for self-gratification. Controlling his breathing and the accompanying wheezing, he had stealthily eased the sheet off the nanny and gazed at her luscious body.

He didn't even have to touch her perky little breasts or her genitalia. The exquisite form of a living and breathing naked woman was a decadent work of art and the very sight of it was more satisfying than cyber sex could ever be.

As much as it reviled him, he had visited Catherine's room numerous times throughout his short five-year earth life. Though he hated Catherine, to his chagrin, he'd been left no choice but to relieve himself while standing over her wretched body on more occasions than he cared to count. Even during infancy, when he lay close to her breasts. He didn't have a choice.

The cowardly nannies always fled the household as soon as they suspected hanky panky had been going on as they slept. A dollop of telltale moisture on the bed sheets or a sticky splattering upon a thigh or a taut tummy always sent them packing.

Gripping a painful erection, Xavier slid off of the bed and crept out of his bedroom. He struggled to control his wheezing and panting breath, telling himself that relief was only a few feet away as he toddled toward Jen's room. This ineffective child's body that imprisoned him was a nuisance, particularly when adult urgings came down on him.

Stealthily, he twisted the doorknob. In a crouched position, he crossed the threshold. Satisfied that she was fast asleep, Xavier straightened his body when he reached the side of his nanny's bed.

Even in the darkened bedroom, he could see the rhythmic rise and fall of her chest; her peaked nipples taunted him, silently asking to be pinched or bitten. But he restrained himself.

He slithered closer to the bed, caressing his penis as he admired the outline of her perfect feminine form beneath the sheet. Sexual tension radiated from his groin in powerful waves. Spittle dribbled down his chin as he cunningly lifted the sheet. Jen squirmed. He released the sheet.

In the midst of a dream or perhaps a nightmare, Jen fitfully turned away, tucking the sheet beneath her body, offering Xavier only a covered, rear view.

Making the most of the situation, the demon child sneered at her rounded derriere while he lowered his underwear and released his erection. His child-sized palm skillfully encircled the large limb that plagued him. With his face twisted in a grimace, he thrust it in and out with such ferocity, the sound of flesh against flesh, together with his ragged breathing, filled the room. Xavier was too far gone to concern himself with being discovered.

Wheezing and salivating, he stroked his penis. A rush of adrenaline accelerated his heartbeat. Groaning, he ejaculated into his cupped palm, careful not to leave a stain on the bed linen or on the floor. He wanted this nanny to stay awhile. He needed her as his unwitting sex partner until Eris arrived.

As if aware of his presence, Jen twisted in her sleep. The sound of his pounding heart and loud, wheezing breath seemed to disturb her but she didn't wake up. Frowning, she turned over. Lying flat on her stomach, Jen buried her face into the pillow, as if on some unconscious level she was hiding from the pure evil that lurked at her bedside.

Xavier slithered back to his bedroom and powered on the computer. Time to toy with Eris.

10

More than ever, Eris wanted out of the Dark Realm. She knew exactly where her jewelry was hidden—inside that abominable Stovall child's bedroom, encased in a childish music box. Using her third-eye vision, and without any assistance from the prankster, Xaxier, she'd figured out a way to connect with the thieving, young rascal.

Through the moving picture box!

A sharp crackle and flashes of light woke Kali. Sitting up, she rubbed her eyes, and then glanced around. Her bedroom, dimly lit by a nightlight, appeared normal. The room was peaceful and calm—no unusual noises—no sparks of light. Thinking she'd been dreaming, she settled back down, nestling her head deeply into a plump pillow.

A sudden harsh click and the TV powered on. Kali sprang upright and stared at the TV mounted on the wall that faced her bed. The screen was lit, but there was no picture, only a series of sizzling sounds.

She whipped her head around, her eyes frantically searching for the remote. Locating the device on a table near her bed, Kali grabbed it, and quickly hit the power button. Nothing happened.

A hazy image began to appear on the screen. Petrified, Kali stabbed the power button repeatedly with her thumb.

Desperately, she jabbed the button over and over in quick succession, breaking up the forming image, but unable to shut off the TV. She wanted to get out of bed and run to the safety of her parents' bedroom, but she felt paralyzed...unable to scream and unable to move. Murmuring fearful little utterances, she watched as a woman's face began to materialize on the TV screen.

An awful image filled the TV screen—a close-up of the dreadful face of the witch from the mirror. Kali expelled a frightened breath. The witch's mouth, drawn tightly in fury, began to open and close. Her hateful words were at first muted, and then became frighteningly clear.

"They're mine!" the witch hissed, her eyes shifting toward Kali's bureau. Stunned and terrified, Kali looked questioningly at the items arranged on the top of her bureau.

"You stole my jewels...all my beautiful trinkets!" The witch's blue eyes glared at Kali's musical jewelry box and then she pointed a long finger at Kali. The child trembled so violently, her knees knocked together.

"Those treasures inside that box belong to me, you snot-nosed thief!" She shook a fist at Kali, her lips curled with menace. "It's only a matter of time before I break out of here."

The scene changed to a barren, smoke-filled place, a ghastly backdrop for the witch. Muffled shrieks and cries were heard. A wide-shot of the hellish place revealed horrible ghouls and malformed creatures that were battling each other. They all were naked. The witch, Kali now realized, was naked, too.

"When I get out of here, I'm going to pay a visit to the Stovall plantation—"

Kali recoiled, sniffling and whimpering.

"I'm coming after you, you disgusting Stovall spawn. When I get to the plantation, I'm going to put these hands around your neck—" The witch paused and wriggled the fingers of both hands, demonstrating her eagerness to strangle Kali. "I'm going to choke the life out of you, and then I'm going after your parents. The punishment I dispense upon those two will be slow and torturous."

Kali covered her face with both hands. Daring to peek through her fingers, she saw the witch's eyes glowing, aiming twin beams of blue light at the foot of Kali's bed. She gawked in horror as the blue light roved over the soft blanket that covered her feet.

She felt heat. Fearing she was about to feel the sting of the taser-like beams, Kali flew into action, throwing off the blanket, and scrambling out of bed.

"Mommy! Daddy! Help me!" she yelled. A split second later, the TV made a sizzling sound. The screen went dark.

Ajali's heart drummed as she and Bryce raced to their daughter's bedroom. Kali was huddled in a corner, shaking uncontrollably, her face buried in her hands.

She practically pounced on Kali, covering her with her own body, instinctively sheltering her child from whatever harm lurked inside her bedroom.

Meanwhile, Bryce skidded across the room, yanking open closet doors, tossing aside large stuffed toys, searching for an intruder. He raced to the windows and found each one locked.

Ajali tossed a quick look at Bryce, her eyes probing his. Perplexed, he shrugged. She pried Kali's hands away. Her daughter's face was distorted with fear. "What's wrong?" Ajali took Kali's hand, trying to coax her over to her bed.

Kali refused to move. "I don't want to sleep in here, anymore! That mean lady came back. She said she's coming to get me. I'm so scared of her, Mommy." Kali broke down in sobs.

Bryce inserted himself between mother and child. He lifted his daughter in his arms, kissed the top of her head. "What mean lady? There's no one here, sweetheart. Daddy searched the room. I think you had a bad dream."

Kali tried to burrow her head into her father's chest. Ajali stood close by, massaging her daughter's back. "Tell Mommy and Daddy what happened."

Kali lifted her head. "That witch lady said she's coming for my jewelry. She called me a thief," she whimpered.

Ajali and Bryce shared a worried look. "Kali, you know the difference between what's real and a bad dream." Bryce tried to be the voice of reason.

"Bryce, I don't think we should make light of Kali's fear," Ajali said harshly. Her tone didn't go unnoticed. Kali looked at her mother questioningly and then searched her father's confused face.

Softening her voice, Ajali asked, "Kali, what does the lady look like? Can you describe the lady in your dream?"

Ajali kept her eyes on Kali, but she could feel Bryce's stern gaze; trying to dissuade her from feeding into Kali's fears. Ajali ignored him.

"Kali, tell me exactly what happened."

"The witch came back."

Grim-faced, Ajali stared at Kali.

"You had a nightmare about a witch?" Bryce asked.

Kali shook her head. "It wasn't a dream. The witch was here."

"Where?" Bryce asked, his eyes sweeping the bedroom.

Kali pointed to the TV mounted on the wall. Bryce and Ajali both stared at the darkened screen.

"She was on TV," Kali said, her voice quivering. "But she wasn't on a regular channel."

"The TV's turned off, princess. You must have had a nightmare," her father rationalized.

"At first, I was asleep but a noise woke me up. The TV popped on. The picture was blurry and the sound was real scratchy."

Ajali frowned. "Like the sound of static?"

"Uh-huh. I sat up, wondering if I'd accidentally left the remote in bed. But it was on top of the table. I got the remote and tried to turn the TV off, but it wouldn't work." She swallowed hard. "The TV came on by itself, Mommy."

"Do you think you might have programmed it by mistake?" Bryce proposed.

Kali shook her head. "Why don't you believe me, Daddy? I didn't program the TV."

"Bryce! You're upsetting her." Ajali glared at her husband. She reached over and pulled her daughter into her arms; hoisting Kali on her hip, Ajali caressed the back of her hair as she held her child's head to her bosom.

"Tell Mommy what the mean lady looks like." Nervous, Ajali looked over at Bryce. The muscles in his jaw contracted.

Kali raised her head and faced her mother, her tiny mouth opening and closing in panic as she tried to find words to describe what she'd seen. "She looked just like she did that day in the parlor, when I saw her in the mirror."

"What is she talking about?" Bryce demanded.

Ajali glanced away from Bryce. She'd never discussed the incident in the parlor, and had never explained the reason she'd gotten rid of the mirror.

Drawing in a deep breath, Ajali responded wearily, "A few weeks ago, right after we put up the Halloween decorations, Kali said she saw a woman's face in the parlor mirror."

"Is that why you cancelled her Halloween party?"

Ajali nodded. "She's terrified of anything associated with Halloween. That's why I took down the decorations. I donated her costume to charity; she's not going out trick-or-treating this year."

"Why'd you keep this from me, Aj?"

"I didn't want to believe Kali really saw anything in the mirror. I thought the decorations were spooking her, and I didn't want to upset you needlessly." She returned her attention to Kali. "The witch can't come back. The mirror's gone."

"She doesn't need the mirror anymore. She can use the TV. This time I could hear her voice. She called me names—"

"What kind of names?" Bryce tilted his head, the muscles working angrily in his jaw.

Hearing that her child had been called vile names brought a pained expression to Ajali's face. She tried to keep calm, but couldn't. Bitter words escaped through clenched teeth. "What did that venomous creature say to you?" Ajali could feel Bryce's eyes on her, and could imagine his disapproving expression.

But she wouldn't acknowledge his gaze. She wanted to hear what kind of threats that a cursed demon had made against her child.

"Um…she said I was a little snot-nose rascal…" Kali looked up. "Um…and she said I stole her beautiful trinkets and jewelry. And um…." Kali's eyes clouded. "She said I'm disgusting Stovall spawn. What's a Stovall spawn, Mommy?"

Ajali shot Bryce a look of alarm. *Stovall spawn!* That sounded exactly like the type of hateful language Eris would use. But how could she? Eris was dead. Ajali had killed her. With the help of her daughter's namesake, the goddess Kali, Ajali had destroyed Eris with purifying white fire.

She'd witnessed with her own eyes as the blazing flames devoured the evil demon. She watched as Eris screamed in outrage as her wicked spirit was cast back to the hellish place where she should still remain. Was it possible that Eris had escaped the bowels of hell?

"And, Mommy," Kali said urgently, frowning as she remembered more. "At first, I only saw her face on the TV screen—"

"Describe her! I want you to tell me exactly what you saw," Ajali interrupted. Ajali was in a panic, but tried to keep her voice calm.

"Dark skin. Blue eyes with lights that she can turn on." Kali inhaled. "She tried to sting me with those blue lights."

Ajali gasped. Perspiration broke out on her forehead. Eyes filled with horror locked on her husband's face.

Though Bryce had only a few traces of memory of the time he'd been tormented by Eris and her fiends, Ajali could tell from his expression that he vividly recalled Eris's burning blue eyes.

Kali pointed to the foot of her bed. There was a trailing dark spot on her pink blanket. "Did she hurt you?"

"No, she didn't get a chance to sting me. I jumped out of bed."

Enraged, Ajali could feel her face growing hot. She didn't want Kali to witness her fury, but unable to get a grip on her temper, she shouted, "That's it, Bryce. I want every piece of that jewelry out of this house. I don't care how much money those damned jewels are worth. That creature is trying to harm my daughter. I won't let that happen. I swear, I'll give up my life on this earth and claw my way into the burning fire of hell and wage a battle against that depraved demon once again!"

"Calm down, Aj."

"That demon is back; she's threatening our child. I can't calm down!"

"Do demons look like regular people?" Kali asked.

"I guess. Yes, sometimes they do," Ajali answered in a quieter voice.

"The witch lady looks like a regular person, only she's really mean and her eyes have those shiny lights that can hurt. But there were monsters and all kinds of wild creatures in that smoky place where she lives."

Ajali recoiled in dread. "I thought you only saw the woman's face."

"That's all I saw at first. Then I saw her whole body. She was naked." Embarrassed, Kali lowered her eyes. "The creatures—"

"What kind of creatures, sweetie? Were there animals roaming around?" Bryce asked.

Kali shrugged. "Sort of. They were like…part human and part animal. Their hands had claws and they were fighting and scratching each other. Screaming and using curse words. There was broken glass and thick black ashes all over the ground. That place was spooky. Real dark and smoky. That witch lady said if she gets her hands around my neck, she's going to choke the life out of me."

"Oh, my God, Bryce. Eris gave our daughter a glimpse of hell."

"Who's Eris? Do you know her, Mommy?"

Ajali cupped Kali's face. "Yes, I know her. She's my worst enemy and Mommy has to make sure that she stays where she is and doesn't harm you. Now, I know you're a big girl, but I don't want you sleeping in this room alone. From now on, you're sleeping in the bed with Mommy and Daddy. Do you understand?"

"Yes, Mommy," Kali agreed, nodding her head as her father carried her to the safety of his and Ajali's bedroom.

11

E ris was delighted that she had spooked the Stovall child.
That moving picture box, a link to the other world, gave
her unlimited access to the little bandit. Until she broke
out of this hellish penitentiary, she'd have to use that picture
box to terrorize the brat. She'd only singed the bed covers, but
next time her blue light would burn through, searing the child's
feet and legs.

Her plan of revenge was so thrilling, her sexual region visibly
writhed and oozed, sending off an arousing scent that summoned
a horde of lewd and libidinous creatures.

She took them on, two at a time, copulating with a few and
sending some running into the shadows, howling in pain with
their appendage ripped off and munched on by Eris as an extra
treat to appease her ravenous sexual appetite.

Responding to a silent call, she pushed a thrusting ghoul off
her and rose to her feet. Its phallus, pulsing and unsatisfied, the
fiendish creature she'd been copulating with in the soot, snarled
and lunged for her, intending to force Eris to finish the sex act
she'd initiated. Eris shot a burning indigo glare at the beast.
The fiend cowered, shielding its face with a fur-covered arm.

As if being pulled by a magnet, Eris moved forward and out
of his reach. He looked down at his knobby and swollen appendage

and howled in anger. Though his cry was within earshot, to Eris it seemed distant and muted. Creatures squawked and screamed, but the cacophony of hellish sounds had no effect on her.

In a dream-like state that was utterly blissful, she'd taken steps toward Xavier's whispery voice. "Over here," he directed.

She turned her head in the direction of his voice and there it was—a bridge! A different one than before, but once again Xavier had teleported another link between his world and the Dark Realm.

Eris looked around. None of the creatures seemed to notice the wonderful overpass that could lead them all out of hell. Stealthily, she stepped onto the bridge, her bare feet slapping against the wooden planks, hurrying along before the ghouls tried to follow her out of hell.

Her level of joy bordered on euphoria.

"Stop rushing. Walk slowly. You're going to draw unwanted attention." Xavier's voice, filled with disgust, hissed in her ear, ending Eris's euphoria.

"Am I going in the right direction?" she asked worriedly. She didn't want to relive the experience she'd had on the last bridge he'd constructed for her.

"No!" he spat. In his tone, there was strong insinuation that she was an incompetent fool. She loathed his arrogance but was at his mercy.

Obediently, Eris stopped. She turned around.

"Hurry!" he whispered. "Someone's coming."

Below her, she saw a young woman staring at her in horror. Eris glared at the woman. *Busybody!*

All color drained from the gawking woman's rosy cheeks and then she took off; stumbling and running in the opposite direction.

That's right. Scat! Eris hustled along. Midway across the bridge and in what seemed like only a matter of seconds, the wood beneath Eris's feet became creaky and swayed a little as if unable to support her.

Daring to look over her shoulder as she fled, she saw to her horror the expanse of wooden planks and side rails beginning to lose depth. Like a phantom, the bridge was slowly evaporating—disappearing before her very eyes. Eris ran as quickly as she could. She had to make it to the other side.

But the bridge cut off abruptly. Too late to halt her swiftly moving feet, she tumbled off the edge of the bridge. Out into the open air and into the abyss. Outraged that she'd been duped again, she screamed, outraged. Her strident scream that pushed from her throat blended perfectly with the nearby cries and howls.

Disoriented, she tried to collect herself and make out the shadowy environment. As her senses adjusted, she could smell the foul odor, she could see the thick, vaporous swirls that impersonated air, and she heard the demonic wails and the scratching and scraping sound of hooves trampling upon obsidian and soot.

Looking down, she saw all too vividly, the hoofed-like footprints made by her fiendish compatriots.

"Agh!" she cried. Unbelievably, she was back in the dank and putrid confines of her abominable prison of the Dark Realm. Her head turned left and then right, looking for the conduit out of hell. But try as she might, she could not locate the bridge. It was gone. She shook her fists! Xavier, the louse, was having mischievous fun at her expense.

Her abandoned sex partner was still sitting in the soot, murmuring in discontent as he scratched the scabs and barnacles that covered his now flaccid penis. Noticing Eris hovering over him, he looked up and gave her a cold grin; assuming she was gazing at his phallus with renewed interest.

Reaching for her with a clawed hand, he groaned an indication that he was ready to resume their macabre sex play. Spittle gathered in the corner of the beast's mouth as he speedily began to stroke himself to erection.

His cupped hand moved up and down his bumpy shaft, creating a friction that ruptured old wounds and bumps. Sticky yellowish secretions oozed, coating his gnarled hand, but the uncaring creature continued to work on a mighty erection.

But Eris, disappointed and furious, aimed a harsh beam of blue light at his prick, scorching it and adding another well-deserved lesion to his lumpy, scarred shaft.

12

The little boy sat in his booster seat at the dining room table. Scrambled eggs, pancakes, and turkey bacon filled a sectioned scoop-plate. Jen sat across from him, drinking coffee, and feeling agitated by his eerie presence as she turned the pages of the morning newspaper.

"More coffee?" Carmen's eyes held compassion. Her job was easy compared to Jen's.

Jen looked up from the newspaper. "Yes, thank you." She forced a smile, though she felt aggravated and caged being stuck in the house with eerie Ethan while his parents jetted around the country without a care.

Carmen and the day maid, Lizzy, didn't even have a high school education; yet, their jobs were cushy compared to Jen's. Carmen had three days off every week and Lizzy left each day promptly at four.

But Jen was trapped day in and day out with Ethan. No one enjoyed being there. Not even the child's own parents. Ethan's presence was stifling and oppressive. The elegant residence surrounded by mature trees and manicured grounds seemed more like a penitentiary than a stately manor.

Jen was working around the clock. Why? A sense of obligation? No! She wanted to prove her loyalty and gain Senator

Provost's respect. She wanted him to realize she was completely competent. Not to mention, she wanted him to flirt with her a little and then assist her in ending the sex drought. Jen laughed to herself.

The crush she had on the senator involved sexual fantasies, but she'd never act on them. She wasn't the type to get involved with a married man. Her thing for the senator was her personal secret.

"The boy hasn't touched his breakfast," Lizzy said, as she stood on a short ladder, wiping in circular motions as she polished the grandfather clock to a high shine. Ethan was prone to exhibiting violent reactions to the sound of his own name, and the staff, and even his parents, tried to avoid referring to him by his given name.

"Eat your breakfast," Jen said half-heartedly and without bothering to look up.

"Do you think he'd rather have cereal?" Carmen inquired.

Jen shrugged. This time she didn't raise her eyes from the newspaper. She didn't care what Ethan ate. It wasn't in her job description to force-feed the little creep.

"Maybe he's thirsty," Lizzy suggested.

"Drink your juice, kid," Jen said, dryly; her face buried in the newspaper. A rustling sound from overhead drew her attention. Lizzy gave her a wink as she dug inside the deep pocket of her big wool sweater. She pulled out a white plastic bag and tossed it to Jen. "Miniature straws," she explained. "Got 'em at the dollar store."

Jen opened the pack and pulled out a straw. She looked at the bright red stripes and festive balloons and smirked. "Wow, this should put a big smile on the kid's face," Jen said sarcastically.

"You never know," Lizzy said defensively. "Those balloons

and bright colors might make his juice seem more appealing."

"I doubt it." Jen rose reluctantly from her seat. She went over to Ethan and tugged out the clear, ordinary straw that came attached to the side of the package of apple juice and replaced it with the colorful straw.

Ethan didn't move a muscle. He maintained a blank stare. Jen picked up the juice box and shook it in his face, enticingly.

Ethan finally reacted, but he didn't reach for the juice. He recoiled, tightening his lips.

"Okay, kid, you win. You don't have to work yourself into a fit." Jen quickly set the apple juice down and made a face at Lizzy.

Lizzy held a hand up in surrender. "I tried." She turned around and resumed shining the clock.

"That child is possessed," Carmen whispered, running a finger over the silver cross that hung from her neck. Jen chuckled. "I spoke to my priest about the things he does—"

"You didn't!" Lizzy sounded shocked. "You know Ms. Provost doesn't want—"

"There's no rule against a parishioner making a confession to her priest. My relationship with God has precedence over that piece of paper that woman made me sign."

A devout Catholic, Carmen held strong beliefs about a number of things. She'd hinted on several occasions that she thought Ethan was possessed. But she'd never expressed it with such conviction as now. Jen was shocked.

"I asked my priest if he could perform an exorcism on the boy while his parents are out of town, but he said he wasn't trained and, even if he were, he'd need the parents' permission."

"Wow!" Jen exclaimed. It was a noncommittal expression. She wasn't actually agreeing that Ethan was possessed. Something was wrong with him…and it wasn't autism.

Taking care of a child who didn't talk her ear off with a million questions a day should have been easy, but it wasn't. In his own creepy, silent way, Ethan was a real handful.

Jen wished she had the nerve to call her supervisor at the agency and ask for another assignment. *Keep dreaming*, she told herself, knowing she'd have to look for a job with another agency if she left a power couple like the Provosts in the lurch. Who was she kidding? No other agency would hire her. Her name would be mud in the nanny industry.

Maybe she could find work in retail sales. Wal-Mart was always hiring, she'd heard. Oh, God. Why, why, why had she persisted in trying to cheat her way through school? She'd ruined her life.

Something had to give because she seriously doubted if she could stick it out with Ethan much longer. Since that incident with the woman on the bridge, Jen was feeling more freaked out than ever. The kid was so repulsive, his own mother barely acknowledged his presence.

God, she couldn't wait for Catherine to hurry up and become vice president. Jen wasn't going to let her off the hook; she'd promised to use her influence and get a prestigious job working for the senator.

Jen sighed. Catherine was full of it. She was dangling that job to keep Jen shackled to her vile son. Jen would make out better if she went straight to Senator Provost himself and told him about the agreement she'd made with his wife.

He seemed far more honorable than his wife. Jen's heart fluttered. The senator was so distinguished and handsome. Man, she had the hots for him. He'd always been polite and had never approached her in any manner that even mildly suggested that he found her attractive.

He was upstanding and completely professional. Jen would

never actually hit on the senator. His integrity was part of her attraction. She enjoyed having him as her sexual fantasy.

She was going stir crazy and missed being with her own age group. If she didn't get out and have some fun and get some good sex, she was surely going to lose her mind..

According to the Carmen and Lizzy, Jen had outlived all the former nannies. One of the nannies—a blonde with a boob job—was now the senator's personal assistant. That information made Jen green with envy.

Didn't she deserve some sort of compensation for her dedication and perseverance? She figured she deserved a much higher paycheck, as well as a monthly bonus, for putting up with eerie Ethan for as long as she had. A powerful man like Senator Provost could hand her a new career on a silver platter.

There had to be a way to get his attention and make him aware that he should start thinking of her as a…well…a colleague. Jen mused for a while. Then it occurred to her that the senator kept up a brave front and even joked with the press about being the "first guy," but he was only human.

His wife's meteoric rise in politics had to be a blow to his male ego. Jen was more than willing to stroke his ego, if that's what it took to get out of this nanny position. Besides, she admired Senator Provost. She thought he was a nice guy and it wouldn't be like her "stroking" was insincere. Catherine was never at home.

Jen was sure the senator would appreciate having the attention of a woman while he was home. Nothing improper. They'd be pals who laughed together and talked. Of course, she'd have to bone up on politics before she began her campaign to be the senator's new BFF.

With her spirits lifted, Jen imagined becoming chummier with the senator. Being his confidante…oh hell, she'd be his gopher and be proud of it. Any position had to be better than the one she currently held. Jen folded the newspaper and reluctantly turned her attention to Ethan.

As usual, he had a vacant look in his eyes. Then suddenly, he licked his lips and gave her a lingering glance. Jen gasped. Ethan's lecherous facial expression was more reminiscent of a dirty, demented man than a five-year-old child. She scooted back so forcefully, there was a loud screeching sound as her chair scraped against the hardwood floor. "Carmen!" she shouted.

Carmen rushed to the kitchen. She was carrying a colorful plastic bowl decorated with Disney characters and filled with sugar-coated cereal.

"Would you look after him for me? I'm going out for a quick run."

Carmen looked aghast. She cut an eye at Lizzy, hoping for some support when she laid out all the reasons she couldn't keep an eye on the boy.

Lizzy, a short, withering woman with graying hair, did all her chores in what seemed like painfully slow motion, but she now showed a surprising amount of energy as she vigorously rubbed the face of the tall clock.

Usually a busybody, Lizzy averted her attention away from Carmen and Jen, and focused on her task; wisely refraining from adding her two cents worth. She apparently didn't want to get involved in any discussion that might conclude with her being responsible for giving care to the boy.

Seeming to sense that Lizzy was withholding support, Carmen caved in. "Okay, Jen. Uh, you won't be gone too long, will you?" Carmen asked, her voice uneasy as she pushed back eyeglasses that had slid to the tip of her nose. "I have to start making supper for the senator and a few guests. He's entertaining at home tonight. Foreign dignitaries," she added, to strengthen her case that she had lots of work to do and needed Jen to hurry back.

"I won't be long, Carmen," Jen assured, knowing that Carmen, like the rest of the household staff, was as edgy as a cat when it came to being alone with Ethan. "After he finishes his breakfast, park him in front of his computer. He'll be happy there." Giddy with relief, Jen bounded the staircase.

She tightened the laces on her brand new Nikes, and grabbed a fleece-lined, oversized, zip-up hoodie, appliquéd with the Temple University logo.

Jen tromped down the stairs. Instead of running out of the house, she forced herself to check on the boy. Standing near the entrance of the large dining room, Jen observed as Carmen pulled up a chair close to Ethan. She tried to spoon-feed him to speed him along. "Eat!" Carmen prompted. There was no mistaking the irritation in her voice.

Ethan crunched lazily, refusing to cooperate with Carmen, who was practically shoveling the cereal into his mouth.

Impatient, Carmen snatched up a cloth napkin and wiped a ring of milk from Ethan's mouth. She pulled the tray from in front of him and lifted him out of the chair. Grasping only the tips of his fingers as if his hands were covered with slime, Carmen drew her face into a tight knot of aggravation. She rolled her eyes at Jen as she led the tot upstairs and directed him to his bedroom and his computer.

Jen's thick, athletic legs pumped along a familiar path on the side of the road. The temperature was a little chillier than normal for late October, but within a few minutes, her joints warmed up, blood pumping.

The sound of her feet pounding against the earth was sooth-ing. Inhaling fresh air and feeling the cool breeze blowing in her face was so exhilarating, her mind soon cleared of all thoughts of the weird little boy she was employed to care for.

Soon, she had arrived at the end of the path. Time to turn back. But she didn't want to. This freedom felt too sweet and she wasn't ready to deal with Ethan quite yet. She checked her watch and was surprised that only ten minutes had elapsed. She had plenty of time.

Filled with a sense of euphoria. Jen veered off the trail and ran alongside Forbidden Drive, a pebbled dirt road that followed the Wissahickon Creek. Jogging felt so good, she didn't mind that the ground was damp and the grooves on the soles of her new running shoes would be caked with mud.

Running and running, splashing mud like a carefree child, she soon noticed a small foot bridge. Startled, she skittered over the stony terrain; trying to put on the brakes. Her Nikes kicked up soggy dirt and scattered pebbles as she slid to a bumpy stop.

Sheer terror gripped her heart. She clamped her hand over her mouth. Her eyes blinked rapidly and then gawked in disbelief.

Hurrying across the bridge was a naked black woman—the exact apparition that had appeared on Ethan's computer screen. But here she was in the flesh, with her wild hair flapping on her shoulders as she paced uncertainly.

The crazy lady swung her head around and looked over her shoulder and then began turning her head swiftly to the left and then the right. She looked confused, as if she didn't know which way to go.

Taking tiny backward steps, a strangled cry escaped Jen's lips. Desperately, she scanned the motorists who whizzed by; flailed her arms over her head for help. But not one driver stopped or even slowed down. No one seemed to notice Jen or the naked woman on the bridge.

The black woman instantly shot her gaze directly at Jen. An uncanny stream of blue light emanated from the woman's eyes. Now frozen in place, Jen looked down and gaped at the blue dot that had been projected onto the center of her chest, pinpointing her as a human target.

Survival instincts unfroze her feet and Jen turned, tried to run, but lost her balance and went crashing down. Her chin, chest, arms, and thighs pressed into the sludge. She pulled herself up, and then shot a frightened look toward the bridge.

The woman had disappeared. Heaving sobs jerked Jen's shoulders as she careened away from the bridge, running against traffic along the sodden dirt path.

Nerves frazzled, vision blurred, Jen didn't notice the police squad car cruising toward her. The car slowed and then came to a stop, the driver's door opened.

"Something wrong, ma'am?" asked a really nice-looking police officer as he walked around the vehicle.

She shook her head, wiping away tears with the back of her hand.

He leaned against the passenger door. He was medium height, very fit, and had a rugged sex appeal that was even more enhanced by the uniform, Jen noted.

"Are you out jogging or is someone chasing you?" A slight smile tugged at the corners of the police officer's lips, teasing Jen into relaxing and being straight with him.

Then she noticed a frown formed as he inspected her.

There was no hint of a lingering smile in his eyes as they scrutinized her, taking in her mud-covered palms and mud-splattered clothing.

He looked at her face. "Seriously, ma'am...you can talk to me. Did someone assault you?"

"No," Jen protested. "I'm fine." Her trembling lip was a give-away that all was not well. She wanted to tell him about the crazy lady, or entity, or whatever...that had been running around on the bridge. No, he'd think she was nuts. And what could he do to a nonphysical being?

He moved in closer. "Would you like to come to the station with me? Talk to a female officer?"

Jen shook her head adamantly. "I'm okay. Really. I fell."

The handsome cop gave her a doubtful look. Under normal circumstances, if a cop as hot as this one was in such close proximity, her mind would be zooming; trying to come up with a flirty line. But all she could do was emit tiny whimpers.

"Obviously, you're not okay. Can you identify the assailant, ma'am?"

"I'm fine," she protested again, her pitch rising. She lowered her tone. "There wasn't any assailant. Honestly." She wiped her tears with the back of her hand. "Really. Nobody assaulted me. I'm not hurt. I...I just have something on my mind."

The police officer stared at Jen's face, squinting as if trying to get a clearer view of her soul. She squirmed under his intense and penetrating gaze. It seemed as if he was trying to get to the truth of the matter by staring into her eyes. Feeling exposed and self-conscious, Jen dropped her gaze.

"Got your cell on you?" he asked.

"Huh?"

"Your cell phone."

"Oh!" She patted the low-hanging pocket of her hoodie. "Yeah. Why?"

"I want you to take my number in your phone...in case you

decide you want to talk. Unofficially, of course." He pulled out his cell.

She held up her mud-stained palms and shrugged.

"Don't want you to get your phone all muddy, so I'll call you. Make sure you lock my number in."

Lock his number in? Was hot cop hitting on her while she was mud-covered, disheveled, stammering and stuttering, and obviously teetering on the brink of insanity?

What did he find appealing? *Absolutely nothing!* she answered herself. She could tell by his kind expression that he thought she'd been victimized and was disoriented and rambling. He was using some of his police training to smooth talk her into blowing the whistle on the perpetrator.

If she told Hot Cop what she was really running from, he'd probably drop her off at the closest loony bin. "Um, I don't think it's a good—"

He stared at Jen. "You're running, you're crying, and you look like you've been dragged through mud. It's my job to pursue and apprehend suspects. If you give me a description...or tell me what he was wearing..."

Jen shook her head. "There's nothing to tell."

"You don't have to be afraid, ma'am. Just tell me what happened?" His voice was satin. But Jen was no fool. Well, not that big of a fool to fall for his smooth talking.

"Nothing happened. I stumbled on something and fell."

Squinting, he nodded. "I patrol this area every day. Never saw you before. Are you new around here?"

"Sort of."

He looked at her expectantly, waiting for her to provide more details. She merely nodded. He ran his eyes over her hoodie. "You go to Temple?" he asked.

"Uh. Used to."

"Oh, so you sort of live around here and you used to go to Temple?"

Jen sighed. Oh, Lord, why was this man trying to get all up in her business like this? Catherine would have a freakin' fit if she thought Jen was discussing any aspect of her private affairs with an outsider—a law enforcement agent, in particular.

"Yeah, I'm sort of new in this neighborhood. I work for a family here in Chestnut Hill." She skipped over the part about Temple. It was a personal sore spot.

"Doing what?" he asked with a charming smile.

Charming smile or not, his question made her squirm. "You sure are nosey. I mean...I'm starting to feel like this is an inter-rogation or something?"

"No, I'm not interrogating you. Is that how I'm coming across?" His lips spread into a lazy, non-threatening smile.

"That's how it seems. And I shouldn't have to respond to anything because I didn't call for help. You came from out of nowhere and stopped me."

Unperturbed, he laughed. "It's my job to provide aid to a citizen who seems to be in distress. But now that I know you're all right...I was...you know, kickin' it with you."

Jen looked at Hot Cop like he'd lost his mind and backed up a little. *Was he some kind of cute creep who had a thing for muddy joggers?*

"I'm not comfortable having a conversation right now. I really have to get out of these clothes." She frowned down and pointed at the mud that was splattered on the front of her hoodie.

"That's understandable." He looked at her and then down at his phone, used his thumb to rotate a side button, and then looked at her again. "I can't make you tell me what happened to you, but whatever went down shouldn't be taken lightly. I bet you could use a friend."

The nerve—the arrogance of this hot cop—making the assumption that she was lonely, which she was, but still…it wasn't any of his business.

Hot Cop saw the indignation on her face. "That came out wrong. I meant to say, I'm available if you want to talk…unofficially, of course." He disarmed her with another smile. "By the way, my name is Romel Chavis. Friends call me Rome."

"Jennifer Darnell," Jen told him, leaving out the shortened version of her name since she didn't intend to ever talk to him again. He seemed like the type who was used to getting his way. Jen bet he had never, in life, made one booty call. Why would he? He gave out his number and women called him. Shit, if it weren't for Catherine and all her rules, Jen would probably join the long list of female booty callers.

But as it was, she couldn't. She'd lose her job if she started palling around with a police officer. But being polite, and also in an attempt to get rid of the aggressive cop, she recited her number.

Rome hunched over as he punched her number into his phone. Jen stole a look. He was concentrating, like it was serious business; unconsciously holding his lips scrunched together. His mouth looked scrumptious. So kissable. Positively lickable.

When her cell went off, the vibration inside her pocket startled her, sending little tingles down her thigh. Jen felt her cheeks grow warm, as if Hot Cop's hand was touching her thigh, caressing it; his thick fingers migrating toward her most intimate spot.

"That's my number. Put it on lock." He winked.

Oh, God! That wink was devastating, causing her thoughts to take a quick turn, detouring from soft and sensual feelings to inappropriate…mind-in-the-gutter thinking, accompanied by lewd imagery as she imagined her and Hot Cop naked on the ground, their bodies entangled as they wallowed together in a bed of mud.

He replaced his phone in his pocket. "Need a ride?"

"No thanks." Jen rushed toward home. Hot Cop got in the squad car and cruised away.

13

Not only did Kali sleep in bed with her parents, but handicapped by fear, she refused to even go to the bathroom alone at night. She didn't mind being in her own bedroom during daylight hours and right now, with the sun still shining brightly, she felt safe and carefree.

In the midst of a tea party, Kali and her dolls were gathered around a small table, set with cloth napkins and a porcelain tea set. She poured fruit punch from a miniature teapot for each "guest" and then settled back in her seat.

Holding her favorite baby doll in her arms, she said, "Don't worry, Mommy's going to feed you." She picked up a toy bottle. Something caught her eye, startling her.

There was a flutter of movement in the vicinity of her toy chest. Frozen in fear, Kali held the toy bottle in midair. With shuddering dread, she forced herself to put the bottle down. Too frightened to turn around and confront her fear, she rotated her neck only slightly and gasped at what she saw.

Sitting in its place atop a bright pink toy chest, Mr. Bear, Kali's favorite stuffed animal, held its right arm extended upward.

Stunned silent, Kali stared unbelievingly as it slowly lowered its arm. It repeated the up-and-down motion with its left arm.

"Oh, no!" Kali muttered when the stuffed animal began to flutter-kick, excitedly testing the movement of its legs.

Using its rounded plush paws to grip the edge of the toy chest, Mr. Bear hopped off the toy chest, making a wobbly landing on the floor. Arms stretched out at its side, the panda steadied its balance.

Kali drew back in fear.

Mr. Bear, a once cuddly and adorable plaything, now seemed an animated menace. Swinging its arms, the jumbo-sized, black-and-white panda stepped aggressively toward her. It seemed agitated and intent on disrupting the tea party.

Expecting to be assaulted with a barrage of flying cups and saucers, Kali closed her eyes. Ducking her head, she clutched her baby doll closely.

The giant panda approached, but there was no onslaught of colorful porcelain.

Instead of being pummeled with a teapot, she felt the brush of Mr. Bear's fake fur against her arm. Kali was not soothed by the soft touch. Scared out of her wits, goose bumps prickled her flesh.

"You're...in...danger," Mr. Bear said in a mechanical-sounding voice. The faltering words were spoken through lips sewn into a smiling curve.

Kali gasped, and then whipped around, gawking suspiciously at the TV. Surely the witch had a hand in Mr. Bear's unnatural ability to walk and talk.

The TV screen was dark. No spooky images.

Kali listened for strange sounds but there were no shrieks or hair-raising screams from that foggy place where Eris lived.

She let out a breath of relief, but then gazed warily at the black-and-white panda.

Mr. Bear stared at her with unblinking marble eyes. A sound, like the hum of a motor, emerged from its stitched lip. The humming revved as the panda seemed to struggle to produce coherent speech.

This time the panda's curved mouth twitched, breaking stitches, and replacing the happy smile with a lopsided sneer. "The... evil...one—"

The baby doll slipped from Kali's arms. Frozen and scared speechless, she didn't retrieve the doll. She couldn't move or make a sound.

"She...will...harm...you."

It occurred to her to get up and run, but her limbs felt paralyzed. "Who wants to harm me?" Kali asked shakily, surprised that she'd recovered her voice.

The motorized humming went into high gear and Mr. Bear began speaking without hesitation. "You have a ring—a possession that is extremely valuable. It could be dangerous in the wrong hands."

As if overcome with spasms, the bear's broken-stitched mouth zigzagged in various directions. It was a frightening sight.

"I don't have the ring."

"Eris will stop at nothing to get that ring from you. She intends to destroy you. Your parents, too."

"But I don't have her ring," Kali insisted, frowning with fear and distress.

"There will be blood shed inside these walls."

"I'm scared." Kali's squeaked, terror-stricken.

"You must protect yourself with the goddess ring."

Kali picked up her doll and began rocking it frantically, as though the doll was wailing and demanding comfort.

"My daddy gave all my jewelry to charity," Kali uttered helplessly. So many scary things had occurred lately, this bizarre conversation with a stuffed toy was beginning to feel...almost normal. It was Mr. Bear's dire warning about blood being shed that had Kali's heart thumping.

"The goddess ring is here. and it remains inside the box. Keep it with you. It is the ring of eternal life, and it is yours…a gift from the goddess Kali."

"The goddess Kali? That's my name!"

"You were named for her…your godmother, the protector of children. The ring will keep you safe from harm," Mr. Bear explained, voice lowered, the threads that served as its mouth beginning to tangle in a series of disturbing knots.

Keeping her focus away from Mr. Bear's sad mouth, she whispered, "Where does my godmother live? How come I've never met her?"

"She…rests. On…the Goddess…Realm. Watches…over… you." The panda's words were slow. Muffled. And so terribly slurred, Kali felt guilty for asking questions, but she really wanted to know more.

"Is the Goddess Realm near Roanoke?"

Mr. Bear went silent. Looking worn down, the panda's knotted lip hung down in a sad loop.

"Are you, tired, Mr. Bear?" Kali stood up. The stuffed toy flopped down into her chair, its cotton-stuffed body slumped to the side, and then became still.

Kali sighed, realizing that Mr. Bear, once again inanimate, had nothing more to say. She paced to her baby doll's wooden cradle and carefully placed the doll inside. Now irresistibly drawn to the toy chest, Kali crossed the bedroom.

The jewelry and Kali's music box were donated to charity, but the original crudely made wood box that had contained the buried jewels was mixed in with her playthings inside the toy chest.

She found the box, removed the top, and scanned the rough-ened bottom. Wedged in a corner was a glimmer of silver. Kali tugged on the object, splintering the aged wood as she pulled an ancient-looking ring out of the deep groove. The ring bore an unusual design: a cross with an odd, hooplike top.

Balling her fist around the ancient treasure that would protect her, Kali felt a jolt of energy surging through her. Along with the energy came a feeling of immense peace...an inner knowing that her worries were over.

Then she heard these comforting words inside her head: *"There's nothing to fear. The ring will protect you."*

Her mother came into her bedroom. "Having fun, sweetie? I see you let Mr. Bear join the tea party," Ajali said, laughing. Then she scowled at the stuffed animal. "Mr. Bear may need to get spruced up. He sure looks pooped."

As she slipped the ring inside the pocket of her jeans, Kali glanced at Mr. Bear. Slumped like a drunk, the stuffed toy looked out of place at the tea party with the smartly dressed, shiny dolls. "He's sick; his mouth fell down," she explained, without telling the whole story.

"I'll take him to the toy doctor and get his mouth fixed; he'll look good as new," her mother said, smiling. "I bet you're going to have a good time at Marley's house today."

Distracted by the goddess ring, which seemed to pulse inside her pocket, Kali didn't answer.

"Did you forget about your play date with Marley?"

"No, I didn't forget," Kali said absently, her mind on the ring and the mysterious Goddess Realm where her godmother lived.

Regarding her closely, her mother frowned worriedly. "Are you okay, Kali?"

"Uh-huh."

"It's okay to cancel if you're not up to it."

Kali stuck a hand inside her pocket, fondling the wonderful treasure. She really wanted to cancel. She preferred to stay in her room and gaze at her ring all day. Maybe Mr. Bear would come back to life and tell her everything she wanted to know. But when she glanced up, she noticed that mother looked troubled. Her eyes were unbearably sad.

Reluctantly, Kali removed her hand from her pocket. "I don't want to cancel the play date," Kali spoke up, her tone suddenly perky. "Marley has a gerbil, a parrot, and a new kitten. I'm going to help her take care of her pets," she said exuberantly.

She could feel her mother's relief. "You're good with animals, so you should have lots of fun. Today should be lots of fun. By the way, Daddy and I had a conversation and we're thinking about getting you riding lessons—maybe get you your own pony—"

Finally taking her focus off the ring, Kali responded with genuine delight. "My own pony?"

"Maybe. We'll see." Her mother winked at her.

"I'm getting my own pony!" Kali shouted.

"I said maybe."

"But you winked. That means yes! I have to think of a name for my new pony."

"Riding lessons, first," her mother insisted, shaking her head and smiling. "We'll have to find the perfect pony for you and then we'll come up with a name."

"I already have a name for her."

"Her?" Ajali raised a brow.

"Yes, I want a female pony and I'm going to name her, Goddess."

Taken aback, her mother looked shocked. "That's a nice name. But...uh...what do you know about goddesses?"

Kali shrugged. "I heard it somewhere. I like the name. When can I start the riding lessons?"

"Very soon."

"Yea!" Kali cheered.

Ajali closed her eyes as if in thankful prayer. When she opened her eyes, she said, "It's so good to see that cute little grin on your face."

"Guess what, Mommy?"

"What honey?"

"I'm not scared of that mean ole witch anymore."

14

A bundle of nerves, Jen fidgeted with the security keypad at the gate. Too frazzled to punch in the right numbers, she wiped her muddy palms down the front of her pants and took in a deep breath to calm herself.

She finally got the number combination right, jogged up the long driveway, and pounded on the front door.

Lizzy opened the door and grimaced. "What on earth?"

Jen rushed inside. "Lock the door."

"Why?"

"You're gonna think I'm crazy."

Lizzy scowled at Jen. "What happened to you?"

"I fell while I was running," she responded, breathless, and then leaned forward and peeked through the frosted glass pane; straining to see if a cop car or a naked woman had managed to get past the secured gate.

"Must have been some fall. Look at you. You're covered in mud from head to toe."

"Yeah." Jen gave a sigh of relief. The coast looked clear. Hot Cop hadn't followed her home and that crazy naked lady wasn't heading for the front door. Jen was positive that the woman was not a human being.

None of the motorists had noticed her. And how could Jen

account for the same butt-naked woman from Ethan's computer being out in the open—on the bridge. The woman was most definitely an otherworldly entity...with a mean spirit, Jen sensed.

Oh, God. I'm really losing it. Jen felt like crying again. Maybe she should seek help. She wondered if her chintzy health insurance plan covered a psych visit. Probably not, so she made a decision to never run anywhere near the vicinity of Piper's Bridge.

Never, ever again.

Kicked out of school with a meager income, no real-world job skills...her sanity was all she had left.

"Maybe you should take your running shoes off," Lizzy suggested, looking down at the dirty shoe prints that Jen had tracked on the polished marble floor. "Your jacket—" She scowled at Jen. "Take off everything. I'll wash your things for you." Disgust was written all over Lizzy's face.

"No, thanks. I'll wash my own things." Jen took a final peek out the windowpane, making sure she hadn't been followed.

"Instead of looking out the window, you should take a look at yourself! You're covered in mud. It's in your hair, on your face, and all over your clothes."

Jen's fingers began an immediate investigation, traveling over her cheeks and colliding into patches of hardened mud. Jen took a breath and continued the blind examination of her face.

There was a big dollop on her forehead and dried sprinkles on her chin. Hot Cop couldn't have been angling for a booty call. He felt sorry for her; found her really pathetic.

Oh, God! Jen brushed past Lizzy. Mud flakes fell from her jacket.

Lizzy made a grumbling sound. "I'm almost finished for the day. I don't like backtracking. But I'm going to have to go behind you. The last thing I need is for Madam Mayor to make a surprise trip home and find crumbled mud all over the place."

"I'll clean up behind myself," Jen said, raising her voice. "Lizzy," she said, in a hushed tone. "I saw a naked lady on Piper's Bridge." She gazed at Lizzy, waiting for her reaction.

"You saw a what?"

"A naked black woman running back and forth on Piper's Bridge. She looked crazy! I'm sure that I've seen her before?"

"Where?" Lizzy's voice took on a much higher pitch.

Wiping her hands on her apron, Carmen rushed to the foyer. "What's going on?" She took in Jen's appearance and furrowed her brows.

"Jen says she saw an escaped mental patient running around on Piper's Bridge."

"I did. Really."

"She claims she's seen her before," Lizzy piped in, rolling her eyes upward.

"Where?" Carmen put a hand on her meaty hip and waited.

"I saw her on Ethan's computer!"

Carmen and Lizzy both went silent and exchanged doubtful glances.

"I'm serious. I don't think the security system is enough. We may have to ask the senator to hire a private security guard…to watch the house. You know what I mean?"

"Jen," Lizzy said calmly. "The senator is entertaining tonight. Madam Mayor is on the brink of winning the election. We don't need to do anything out of the norm that would draw unnecessary attention." Lizzy had been listening to Catherine so long that she had her reasoning and logic down to a tee.

"But she could be dangerous. An escapee from jail or a mental hospital."

Carmen threw up her hands, exasperated.

"I wouldn't make this up." Jen sounded pitiful.

Carmen changed her tone. Spanish accent and all, she too,

mimicked Catherine's voice of reason. "The last thing we need is for word to get out that a crazy, naked woman was spotted running like crazy near the Provost home. The press will be crawling all over this place."

Lizzy patted Jen on the back. "If she's out there, somebody will report it. You know, we can't get involved."

Carmen nodded. "She's right, Jen. It's not our concern. Besides, we don't have to worry about her getting inside this house. The security system is high tech. We're locked tighter than Fort Knox." Carmen chuckled and headed back to the kitchen.

Lizzy pulled out a plastic trash bag from the pocket of her wool sweater. "Put your muddy clothes and shoes in there." Lizzy's pockets were deep and filled with all kinds of cleaning supplies and other crap. "The boy is in his bedroom, sitting in front of that computer. You'd better check in on him. Probably time for him to use the bathroom," she said with a sympathetic ring to her tone.

"No one took him?"

"That's not our job. Look, I have to get this foyer cleaned up."

"Lizzy, between you and me…do you think I'd make something like that up?"

"Could be your imagination. Being around that boy all the time might be taking a toll on you."

Jen couldn't blame Lizzy and Carmen for thinking her imagination had gone wild. She hardly believed what she'd seen herself. Frustrated and tired, she brushed past Lizzy and rushed toward the stairs.

She didn't check on Ethan. She went straight to her bedroom and peered in the mirror. Her reflection was appalling.

There were splotches of drying mud all over her face. Her bangs were encrusted. Separated and stiffened, Jen's bangs were sticking out as though she'd been electrocuted. A thick layer of mucous created a crusty mustache over her upper lip. She looked like a lunatic.

She washed her hair in the shower, repulsed by the murky water that ran from her body and down into the drain. Then she remembered...*Oh, shit. Ethan!* She hoped he hadn't tinkled in his pants.

She threw on a clean T-shirt and jeans, and a pair of beat-up sneakers. With a towel wrapped around her damp hair, Jen rushed to Ethan's bedroom, hoping to deal with him as quickly as possible so she could blow dry her hair before it became impossibly tangled.

The boy's door was open. She could see the back of his head. A bout of anxiety stalled her outside the door.

Ethan wheezed. The sound made Jen's heartbeat quicken. Every muscle in her body felt tensed. She was a wreck! She should have been used to Ethan's unsettling patterns of breathing, but she was scared. Suppose that nutty woman, or ghost, or whatever, was back on the computer screen?

Feeling uneasy, she stood in his doorway, too afraid of what or who she might see if she got too close to the monitor. From the safety of the doorway, she stood, deliberately keeping her eyes focused on her scruffy sneakers. "Hey! Do you have to tinkle?"

Ethan didn't acknowledge Jen. His beady eyes were riveted to the monitor; his small hand moved the mouse back and forth, busily clicking images on and off of the screen. He looked down briefly at the mouse and Jen noticed his lips moving. She could hear his whispery mutterings.

"Ethan!" she yelled. She needed to snap him out of the zone he was in before he conjured that terrible woman onto the screen.

The tiny swivel chair made a soft creak as the child turned away from the screen. Jen looked up and was informed by the small erection that tented the crotch of his Osh Kosh jeans that Ethan needed to use the bathroom.

Eew! It was sickening, the way his penis stiffened whenever he had to pee. Jen marched across the room. Handling him a bit roughly, she tugged Ethan out of the chair. "Go potty, Ethan," she scolded, forgetting how much he disliked being called by his name.

With a grimace on her face, she patted the child's bottom, prodding him along.

Offended by the gesture and the sound of his name, Ethan spun around. Instead of his usual flat affect, he glared at her, eyes ablaze with menace.

His face began to contort horribly. His top lip jutted upward toward the right and his bottom lip went downward in the opposite direction.

Jen's heart jumped. It was a hideous sight. "Stop making that face, Ethan! Go potty," she said sternly, trying to nip in the bud what looked like the precursor to another screaming episode. *Oops, I called him Ethan!* She remembered too late.

His lips untwisted and a hint of a smile surfaced. For a split second, Ethan looked normal. Then his smile turned sinister; his dark eyes glimmered lewdly, like something vulgar was running through his mind.

Quick as a flash, the child undid his pants and snaked his small hand inside the slit of his briefs. Before Jen could react or jump out of the way, Ethan had gripped his large penis, aimed it at her, and was spraying her with urine from the thigh area of her denim pants down to the sneakers on her feet.

"Ethan, no!" Jen screamed. Calling him by his name again

only encouraged his bad behavior, and made him move in closer; making sure that her jeans were soaked through.

Carmen came running, with Lizzy shuffling behind. "Oh, my Lord!" Carmen spied Ethan's exposed privates through dark-rimmed glasses and took a few steps back; her fingers splayed against her heart.

Lizzy's scowl was drawn to the yellow puddle at Jen's feet and then her gaze roved back and forth from the puddle to her wristwatch. "If I have to scrub one more floor, I'll never get out of here on time." She gave Jen a hard look as if she expected her to volunteer to clean up the mess.

Jen swallowed hard, fighting tears. "Is that all you're worried about? Look what he did to me!" She grimaced at her urine-soaked clothing. "Eew!" She glared at the monstrous child. "That's it. I quit!" She dashed out of Ethan's bedroom, leaving her young charge unattended.

Ethan, now back to normal, had the usual vacant look in his eyes as he stood in the middle of the room seemingly unaware that his pants were down and that he was holding his penis.

Carmen raced behind Jen. "You can't leave me with that child. Lizzy's leaving at four and I have a big meal to prepare."

"I don't care! I'm out of here. No amount of money is worth this."

Lizzy wasn't as fast as Carmen but she was only a few seconds behind. "I can't get involved with that child. I don't have any training with autistic children," Lizzy told the two women.

Carmen was distraught, wringing her hands as she stood in the doorframe of Jen's bedroom. "I'm just a cook; I can't handle him, either."

Standing beside Carmen, Lizzy gave a curt nod of agreement. "We're not qualified to manage that boy's special needs."

Jen grunted with disgust. "Does it look like I can? You need to call the nanny agency." Jen braced her shoulder against a wall. Refusing to touch the urine-stained footwear, she used the toe of her right sneaker to wedge off the left and then began working to pry off the other. "Tell the agency to send someone else. Seriously, guys…I'm out of here."

With both soiled sneakers kicked to the middle of the floor, Jen bent at the waist, looking down at her sodden socks, trying to figure out how to remove them without using her hands.

After a tense silence, Lizzy cleared her throat. With nervous, heavily veined hands, she pulled her wool sweater tightly around her small frame. "Listen, Jen. You have to think about Ms. Provost. She really doesn't deserve this kind of bad publicity right now."

Jen made a scornful sound. "I don't deserve to lose my sanity and that's what's going to happen if I hang around this nuthouse."

"The Provosts aren't nutty," Carmen piped in.

"You're right. They're cool, but their kid isn't. Did you know he can talk?"

Shocked, Lizzy took several gasping breaths.

Carmen reared back and shook her head. "No!"

"Yeah, he says a few words every now and then. Trust me; you don't want hear his voice…he sounds like a crabby old man and it's disturbing as hell."

Carmen shuddered and crossed herself. She didn't have to say a word. That instinctive religious gesture spoke volumes.

"I can understand why you're pleading with me to stay. You don't want to be left alone with eerie Ethan. Though I sympathize…you didn't get peed on by that mean little brat. I did! Now, if you'll excuse me, I have to take a shower."

Jen pulled her T-shirt over her head, signaling them to leave her in peace. When the cook and the maid didn't budge, Jen stared at them pointedly. "Can I have some privacy, please?"

Lizzy unclenched her sweater in defeat. Carmen's shoulders heaved a resigned sigh. Reluctantly, the two women left Jen's bedroom.

Inside the shower stall, Jen didn't reach for her favorite peach-scented bath gel. The fruity fragrance seemed inappropriate for washing away the stench of urine. Using hand soap, she lathered her body, scrubbing her thighs until they were tender to the touch.

Jen's mind wandered to the woman on the bridge. In hindsight, she decided that her mind had been playing tricks on her. The woman was merely a figment of her imagination.

Dealing with Ethan was taking its toll, causing her to hallucinate. Hell, she had so much pent up anxiety, she was slowly losing it. Maybe she'd even imagined that she'd heard Ethan speak the other day. She was definitely becoming unglued and if she didn't get far way from eerie Ethan, she might end up in a psych ward.

The nanny agency would fire her for sure if she walked off this job. *So what?* She would not allow herself to be victimized by that atrocious child for another day. The child was beyond strange. He was so odd-looking; with an adult-sized head and frail little body.

Not to mention his penis! It was huge…vile and unacceptable. No little kid should be hung like a horse.

During her interview, Catherine Provost never once mentioned her son's big dick or any of Ethan's other peculiarities—his finicky food choices; his creepy grimace if he didn't like something he heard you say; his refusal to leave the computer even when he had to urinate; his self-induced catatonia when he didn't want to go to bed. He was weird, weird, weird and impossible to care for.

Catherine Provost had reeled Jen in, dangling an internship in the senate if she stuck around for a while. Well, she'd been on the job for six months. Six months too long.

It was time to find another job. Or just pack up, go back to Centerville, and tell her parents the truth. On second thought, she couldn't do that. It would devastate her parents to know that she'd been kicked out of school.

Solemnly, Jen washed her body. She didn't have a choice. If she expected to save face with her parents, she'd have to continue working for the Provosts until she got the internship.

Working for the senator sounded prestigious—a chance-in-a-lifetime job—well worth missing a semester or two…at least, that's what she'd tell her parents. But would she be able to last long enough to get the darn internship? With eerie Ethan getting worse by the day, Jen truly doubted if she could stick it out much longer as his nanny.

Stepping out of the shower, it occurred to her that aside from going home in disgrace, she had nowhere else to go. A daily hotel fee would cost a fortune; deplete her savings in no time.

A lump formed in her throat. Her future had looked so promising when she had arrived in Philly to attend Temple University on a full academic scholarship. Taking on seventeen credits was more difficult than she could have imagined.

More than half of her classmates had paid two hundred bucks for a copy of the Economics test, but Jen was the one caught with the text messaged quiz answers on her cell phone. The University did not take cheating lightly. Jen was expelled.

Torn between keeping a rent-free roof over her head and losing her mind, Jen decided she wanted to keep her sanity. It was time to go!

In the midst of packing, there were two sharp knocks on her bedroom door. "Yes?" she said and continued to pack.

Carmen opened the door. "The senator would like to speak to you." Carmen's eyes flitted from the open luggage and then over to the phone at Jen's bedside.

Jen took a deep, fortifying breath and picked up the phone.

Before exiting the bedroom, Carmen gave a slight head bow, obviously grateful that Jen was willing to talk to their employer.

"Carmen gave me an update. I don't know what to say, except that I'm sorry. I know Ethan can be a handful at times…after hearing about what he did today…well. I'm completely baffled."

"Senator Provost, I can't work here anymore. There's something peculiar about Ethan. He frightens me."

"I realize he's different than other children his age. He's autistic, but he's still only a little kid," Senator Provost said, his tone, crisp and confident, making Jen feel a little foolish. "He's really harmless, Jen. And he's grown accustomed to you."

The senator was right. How much harm could a scrawny little kid do?

"This is really an inopportune time for Catherine and me to interview nannies. As a special favor to us, couldn't you stay until after the election?"

Senator Provost's words, posed as a question, held such authority…such command; Jen could not stand up to him. And then there was that little crush she had on him.

"Sure, I can do that." Boy, she was such a softy; melting over the sound of the senator's voice.

"Great! I'll see you tonight."

"Okay. Bye." She released a long breath and hung up, blushing as if her employer had whispered lustful promises of a steamy night in bed. Her Senator Provost sexual fantasies were becoming tired and worn.

Jen had been using him to fuel the lust during her self-pleasuring sessions for so long that she was running out of fresh material. She decided to substitute the senator with the hot cop. Tonight, when her hand worked its way between her thighs, she would see Hot Cop's face; she'd feel his lips and his burning touch.

What else could she do except fantasize? She'd never meet any men if she continued to be cooped up in the house with Ethan. Most nannies in the area got to prance around the pricey shops on Germantown Avenue and meet people when they took the kids in their charge to the many activities planned for them on a daily basis.

But not Jen. She was imprisoned inside the house. Among a host of dislikes, Ethan despised the outdoors. So until she got some time off to search for a boyfriend, she'd have to continue to masturbate and mentally hop from the senator's bed to straddling Hot Cop inside his police cruiser.

Ooo, that was such a naughty thought, but with the bad sex drought she'd been experiencing, she'd be a fool to save herself for a bona fide boyfriend. She'd settle for a fuck buddy in a hot second. The weather was changing; she had to hurry up and get a sex partner before she ended up cold and alone in her little nanny bedroom.

She stood still for a moment, pondering her sad fate. The woman on the bridge crossed her mind. The recollection seemed more like something she'd dreamed than actually seen. The woman seemed ghostlike...imaginary...not flesh and blood. Not real.

If there had been a naked black woman on the bridge, cars would have careened. There would have been pile-ups and such a big commotion, Carmen and Lizzy would have heard about it on the news by now. Yes, she'd been under a lot of stress and her imagination was running wild.

Dealing with Ethan was not easy but she'd have to survive the terrible tot if she expected to get that prestigious position with his father.

15

Xavier had pulled another prank. He'd had Eris thinking she was running toward freedom. But once again the joke was on her. That bridge—a wooden link to earth and mankind, cut off. Again. Sending Eris spiraling back to the Dark Realm.

The fall was long and terrifying. And though she was unharmed, she felt traumatized. And helpless. How dare Xavier to continually manipulate her, pull her from the Dark Realm on a whim, and then just as whimsically, send her spiraling back.

Angrily, she kicked the soot; exasperated at being at the mercy of a cruel, demented child.

Eris came up with a plan. Xavier was a prankster, taking his bogus childhood to an extremely annoying level. He had deceived her twice and obviously did not intend to help Eris escape.

But Eris was not to be toyed with. The next time he engaged in child's play and tried to tantalize her with a teleported bridge that could lead her out of the Dark Realm, she was going to use some muscle to get out of this hell.

She'd outsmarted Xavier before, joining him when he escaped the Dark Realm through his mother's birth canal. She'd done it once and she could do it again. Xavier had better beware. Eris intended to exact revenge on him once she broke free from the Dark Realm.

"What's your name?" she asked the ghoul who sat bent over, blowing away the lingering smoke from his phallus, which she'd burned.

He gave her a surly look. "What's it to you?"

"Answer me before I set your balls on fire."

He yelped, scooted back, cupping his scrotum as if it were a sack that contained gold nuggets.

"My name's Boozer," he muttered.

She turned up her lip. "What kind of name is that?

"My last time on earth...I was a thief, a scoundrel, and a helluva a mean drunk." He smiled at the recollection. "I was known as Boozer. My name is the only thing I ever came by honestly." He chortled.

Eris smiled wickedly. She'd found her muscle. Boozer would make a perfect minion on the earth plane. "Shut up, you fool!" she ordered, eyeing his scrotum with her blue eyes narrowed and mean.

He clamped his lips together and grabbed his testicles protectively.

Eris was pleased. Boozer had displayed an appropriate degree of fear and obedience. "How'd you like to take a trip with me?"

He groped his appendage and looked at her with tawdry desire. Though the burning hole was causing him pain and seeped a nasty, bubbling green secretion, Boozer was more than willing to forget his discomfort and roll around in the soot with Eris.

Eris kicked him. "Not that kind of trip, you vermin."

"Sorry." He stopped stroking himself and, instead, began doctoring his wounded appendage, gingerly placing bits on soot on the smoldering hole.

Eris looked around and then lowered her voice conspiratorially. "I'm making an escape soon, and I'm considering taking you with me."

Boozer's eyes widened to twice their size. He slapped his thigh. "Hot damn! How do you plan on doing it?"

Eris gave him a faint smile. "I'd be a fool to tell you."

He nodded in understanding.

"Can you run fast?"

"Oh, yeah."

Boozer was Eris's kind of fiend. But she was curious about the time frame of his last incarnation and where he came from. Was he an earthling or from some other realm like herself?

Once all the fiends were clumped together inside the humid environs, it was hard to distinguish their origin. On the Dark Realm, everyone understood each other, speaking a universal language, via telepathy.

Evil was what they all had in common. But some were more so and possessed powers—like Xavier had. Xavier had honed his skills while on the Dark Realm and managed to retain some of his powers now on the earthly plane.

"Where's your former home?" Eris inquired.

"Mississippi." Boozer puffed up, proud, seeming to forget that his fellow Jacksononians had shot him down like a dog.

Good, an earthling. An American earthling and a Southerner, at that! Eris was extremely relieved that Boozer hadn't come from a foreign country or another, less-intelligent realm. She needed a cohort that could speak English and knew American ways. She hoped he could remember his way around the South.

"You're sober now, so I hope you won't stagger and fall like a drunk when I'm ready to use your services?"

"No, I ain't had a drink in…" He looked upward, his bushy

brow crinkled in confusion as he tried to process time. Unable to come up with exact dates, he went on, "I ain't had a drink since I made my last batch of moonshine," he said.

"What happened after that?" Eris had logged into the Stovall man's computer and done a quick study of American history during her last earth life. Moonshine sounded like an expression that was around during her first visit to earth.

"Some fellas shot me down. Claimed I'd been raping all the women in the town while the men were away at war. They also blamed me for the bringing a bad case of the claps down on the whole town."

"Did you?" Eris giggled.

"Somebody gave it to me. I reckon I passed it on to twenty or so females who I had my way with." He scratched his head. "But I ain't spread the claps to the whole doggone town."

"Where was this town?" she said, hoping it was Roanoke.

"Jackson, Mississippi."

Eris sneered. "How far is that from Roanoke, Virginia?

"By buggy?" Boozer scratched his head. "Hmm. Probably..."

"No! By car!" she snapped.

"By what?" Boozer frowned in confusion

"An automobile, you moron! How long will it take to drive to Roanoke?"

Scowling in bewilderment, Boozer raked a claw back and forth across his scalp. "I don't know nothing about that 'mobile thing, but we could probably hop a freight to Virginny. I reckon it would take a week or so to get to Roanoke."

"You reckon?"

"Can't say for a fact. I never stepped foot out of Jackson." Boozer grinned. "I'm looking forward to getting my hands on some Virginny rump." As though readying his shaft for mayhem, he flicked bits of soot from his injured appendage.

Boozer was a numbskull for sure. She considered giving him another blast of heat for being so stupid, but she restrained herself. She needed him for his brawn, not his brains.

Fuming mad, Eris thought about those damned Stovalls... Bryce, Ajali, and the little jewel-thieving brat, and how they were all living like royalty in the old Stovall plantation. They were nothing more than brazen squatters. It was she who had kept the master's bed warm when his ailing wife couldn't. She was entitled to the deed to that mansion. The Stovall plantation rightly belonged to her!

She looked at Boozer. "As soon as we get out of here, we're heading for Roanoke. I have lots of nasty work for you to do. I'm going to let you loose on a couple of folks who deserve to be ripped, limb by limb."

Boozer giggled maliciously.

Wondering if the creature would be a hindrance as she maneuvered around modern day America, Eris asked, "You never answered my question. Can you drive a car?"

He held up his clawed hands. "I don't know what that thing is, but I can drive the heck out of a buggy."

Disappointed, Eris's shoulders slumped. No telling where that bridge would lead her. She'd have to find herself a chauffeur to drive her to Roanoke to pick up her jewelry Of course, she'd take Boozer along to do what he did best. Maim and murder.

On her behalf, of course.

He could start with Xavier, for taunting her.

The Stovall family, next.

"When the time comes...when I'm ready to leave, I'm going to need you to pick me up and carry me. Follow my explicit instructions and run like the wind. Can you do that?"

Devilment shone in his beady eyes. "That's easy. When are we leaving?"

Exasperated, she scorched his arm with her burning glare. "Stop pestering me with idiotic inquiries. I'm a goddess and you're a mortal moron. I expect you to follow my directions without questioning me."

"Ow!" He rubbed his arm and patted at the puff of smoke. "All right. I'll shut my trap," he mumbled.

"You won't be able to see our transportation, but I will," she confided. "Being a goddess, I possess special powers."

Boozer nodded dumbly.

"When I snap my fingers, scoop me up in your arms and run as fast as you can. I'll point out the direction. Understand?"

"Uh-huh."

"That's not an appropriate response to a goddess." She gave him an evil look.

He shrank back. "O-okay. What should I—?"

"You should say, yes, goddess!" Eris informed.

"Alrighty. Yes, goddess," Boozer obliged without batting an eye. The woman had powers and she was his ticket out of hell. He'd call her whatever name was pleasing to her ears. Boozer was already thinking up ways to stir up trouble with his neighbors in Jackson.

The fact that more than a century had passed didn't enter his mind.

16

C armen tended to stretch the truth. The visiting dignitaries turned out to be the senator's old college pal, Paul
Gooding, and two blondes—one was a strawberry blonde
who did something important on Capitol Hill, and had gotten
her positions in Washington, thanks to her connection with
Senator Provost.

The other was a dirty blonde with a noticeable boob job.

Carmen had pointed out that the boob job blonde was the
former nanny, who was now his personal assistant.

Carmen went home after serving them, and Jen could tell
there was a change in the atmosphere downstairs. The guests,
becoming more animated by the minute, were no doubt, enjoying cocktails.

Hearing the constant tinkling of stemware, along with her
many jumbled thoughts and conflicting emotions, was stretching
every one of her nerves. Had she actually imagined seeing the
naked woman on Ethan's computer? Was she hallucinating when
she saw what looked like a flesh and blood woman running on
Piper's Bridge? How could something that weird happen twice?

Their voices grew louder. Just what were they celebrating?
Jen wondered, closing the novel she couldn't concentrate on.
She flung Ethan an irritated glance. He was parked in front of
his computer as usual.

Bored with Ethan's company, Jen decided to entertain herself by snooping on the senator and his friends. She rose from her appointed chair—a rocker—something the future Ms. Vice President thought was an appropriate seat for a nanny. She then slipped out of Ethan's bedroom and tiptoed downstairs.

Jen crept along a wall toward the dining room and then halted, standing stock still when she was close enough to hear each voice clearly.

"How's it feel to be this close to the White House, Danny Boy?" she heard one of the blondes say in a voice that reeked with flirtation.

"*Danny Boy!*" Jen mimicked, her expression sour. The woman sounded self-assured, and too damn familiar with the senator, to be a casual friend. She wondered if the dirty blonde would call him *Danny Boy* if Catherine Provost was within earshot. She doubted it.

That dirty blonde and her strawberry counterpart would be appropriately respectful if the woman of the house were around. Jen didn't know what was worse—having Catherine at home barking orders or having to endure the knowledge that two hussies were having a wonderful time while Jen was being treated like an outcast.

She couldn't help envying the blondes, and wishing she were an invited guest instead of lowly, hired help. Being a nanny sucked.

"I'll tell you how Danny Boy feels. He feels outmaneuvered and de-balled!" Paul Gooding bellowed. Drunk as a skunk, Paul's voice was loud and cocksure. Paul and the senator were as different as night and day, but were as close as brothers.

"Not true," Senator Provost laughingly protested. "I'm proud of Catherine and looking forward to supporting her all the way through her own run for president in eight years." The senator's voice was crisp and eloquent; his was the only voice that hadn't started to slur.

"What about your political career?" Strawberry blonde asked, her tone petulant.

"I'm trying to talk him into switching parties and running against his wife," Paul retorted. "That would sure spice up politics. Maybe in the bedroom, too. Hey, Danny?"

"You're a sick-o," Senator Provost responded, sounding a little embarrassed that his drunken bud had had let the cat out of the bag; revealing the true nature of his relationship with his wife.

Now the two blondes were privy to the fact that the senator and his wife's love life was a disaster. The political couple had separate bedrooms. It wasn't unusual for a wealthy couple to maintain separate bedrooms.

For all Jen knew, the pair may have been slipping in and out of each other's rooms for comfort or sex. But Jen suspected that her employers did not have a sex life. At least, not together. And apparently, the senator had been complaining to Paul. Now the blondes knew. *Drats!* One of them was going to try to snatch up Jen's dream man.

Jen was sick of listening to all their drunken banter and witticisms. Feeling ostracized and angry now, she quietly moved away from the dining room and hurried up the stairs.

Back in Ethan's bedroom, she marched toward the child and clicked off the computer. "It's bedtime," she said sternly and then exhaled a long-suffering sigh that warned the boy to not give her a hard time.

But, on second thought, maybe an episode from Ethan would bring the dinner festivities to a speedy conclusion. After taking a gander at Ethan in a full-swing episode, those blonde harlots would never set foot in the Provost household again. And after all the guests had fled, the distraught senator would drag himself upstairs to his lonely bed.

Jen closed her eyes dreamily. *I'll comfort you, Dan.* Yes, she called him Dan in her fantasy world. Dan was more fitting and much more dignified than Danny Boy.

Ethan's breathing suddenly changed to rattling and wheezing. Jen let out a small mewl of disgust.

"Do not start!" she warned. "I'm not taking any more crap off of you, Ethan!"

There, she'd called him by his given name right to his miserable little face. Expecting Ethan to throw a fit, Jen calmly waited for the beginning of an episode.

But he didn't tense up or start screaming. What he did was far, far worse.

Ethan looked at her through soulless eyes and displayed a smile that was so chilling, Jen's blood ran cold, and her teeth began to chatter.

"My name is Xavier!" the boy said. His voice sounded like a grumpy old man's.

"Wh-what did you say?" Jen's heart hammered.

"Call me Xavier." His voice emerged in a horrible wheezing, angry whisper.

Jen gasped in shock.

And fear.

Satisfied that his words had a powerful impact, the child's lips stretched into another cold and deadly smile, letting his nanny know that he was fully present—totally alert and not speaking nonsense while in the throes of an alleged episode.

Unwilling to hear the child speak another word, Jen turned and high-tailed it out of his bedroom. Her pulse pounded in her ears as she made fast tracks down the hallway, and then trotted down the stairs.

She barged into the dining room without a second thought to how awkward and unattractive she felt in the presence of the elegant senator and his ultra-sophisticated friends.

"Senator Provost," she said in shaky voice. "Can I speak to you?"

Looking both amused and lecherous, the senator's best friend sized Jen up, undressing her with glittering eyes. The two blondes stared at Jen with disapproval. The senator rose. After excusing himself, he ushered Jen out of the dining room. Once they were able to speak privately, he asked, "What's the problem?"

"Ethan spoke."

He squinted at her. "What?"

"Your son just spoke. Clearly."

A bewildered smile and a head shake. "Are you sure?"

"Yes. He freaked me out. I...I don't know if I can continue—"

"What did he say?"

"He gave himself a new name."

Senator Provost eyed her in disbelief and then let out a small, amused laugh.

"Seriously. Clear as a bell, he told me not to call him Ethan."

He didn't believe her, but Jen didn't care. "He wants to be called Xavier," she said, her voice low and confidential.

"Jen, this isn't funny. Ethan can't talk."

"Come with me. I'll prove it."

Upstairs, they entered Ethan's room together. He'd rebooted the computer and, as usual, the child was in front of the monitor, his back to them as he stared at bridges.

"Xavier," Jen said, feeling powerful like she was responsible for Ethan's ability to speak. Ethan didn't turn around. He remained mute.

"Don't call him that," the senator chastised, quickly approaching his son. "Hey, buddy." He bent down to the child's level. "How's it going? Enjoying looking at those bridges, huh?"

Ethan, his body rocking, his eyes intense and focused on the screen, didn't respond to his father's presence.

"Xavier!" Jen's voice cracked. She placed her hands on the child's shoulder, trying to still his annoying movement, but he thrust forward, forcing her hands to slide off of his small shoulders.

"He doesn't talk. You can't bully him into accepting a name change."

"He told me to call him Xavier. I wouldn't make up something like that. I swear to God…" Jen raised her hand in earnest.

The senator regarded her with a look of weary patience. "You're overwrought…working around the clock is getting to you and I apologize. I'm going to call the agency in the morning and get another nanny."

"Are you firing me?" Jen asked, panicked. "I don't want to lose my job."

"No, no. I'm not firing you. Ethan requires two nannies. It was thoughtless of Catherine and me to put you in this situation with no backup…no support." He smiled at Jen; his eyes were warm and compassionate.

A few minutes ago, she'd been ready to pack it up and go back to Centerville with her tail between her legs. Now, she was prepared to hang in there a little longer—for the sake of the internship. Maybe her imagination *was* getting the best of her, she decided.

Senator Provost patted his son on his shoulders. He looked at Jen for a few moments. There was sympathy in his eyes. "Hang in there, Jen," he said with a sigh, and then left the room to rejoin his guests.

Getting Ethan to bed had been awful. He demonstrated his refusal by stiffening his body and stretching his lips into a tight line. Jen was used to that behavior, but it was the fear that those lips might part and emit sound—words—spoken in an other-worldly rasp.

Sure, she could chalk it up to an overactive imagination later, but while she was in the moment, she was terrified. Jen laid him on his bed with his clothes on. She'd change him into his pajamas after he fell asleep.

In her own bedroom now, Jen massaged her forehead, stressed. Dealing with Ethan had been bad enough, and as if her nerves weren't frazzled enough, the unexpected buzz that caused her cell phone to wobble on the nightstand gave her a terrible jolt.

She picked it up, expecting to see Catherine's name. Jen squinted. She didn't recognize the number of the caller. So many strange things had occurred, it seemed entirely possible that the ghost lady could be calling.

Jen shuddered as she envisioned the female apparition sprinting across the bridge, this time with a cell phone pressed against her ear. Jen gulped down a knot of fear.

"Hello?" she whispered. She was going to freak out and smash the phone against the wall if she heard the slightest bit of distortion or any spooky crackling sounds that were indicative of a phone call from hell.

17

"Jen?" It was a male voice. No distortion, no crackling sounds. His voice was friendly and very familiar. A wave of relief washed over her.

"Yes, this is Jen."

"Hi, this is Rome. Hope I didn't wake you." His voice was silk. Conflicting emotions raced through Jen…relief that ghost lady didn't have her number and agitation at the audacity of this pushy policeman.

Why was he harassing her? Chestnut Hill was pretty peaceful, with a low crime rate, and obviously his job was not fast-paced and stressful or he wouldn't have had time to shoot the breeze when she'd fallen in the mud. But was he that desperate to make an arrest that he telephoned a suspected victim, trying to persuade her to press charges against an imaginary assailant?

"I'm awake," she admitted in a sullen tone. Hot cop or not… she wasn't going to allow him to sweet talk her into telling him what really happened. "I see dead people" might be a powerful line in the movies but if those words came out of her mouth, Hot Cop would think she was a basket case.

"Just checking on you. I waited for you to call, but I got the hint. You're the type of female who likes the man to make the first move. Am I right?"

Jen was annoyed by his self-assurance. "I'm confused. Is this a social call or part of your investigation?" She could have used stronger wording, but Rome was cute enough to get away with it with a mere pat on the wrist.

"Social? Is that a polite way of asking if this is a booty call?" He laughed. Jen didn't. "It's social," he said when he realized she wasn't amused. "But it's also business."

"Oh, really."

"Yeah. See, I like female mud wrestling. I thought you might want to get into the circuit."

"What?"

"The mud wrestling circuit. Need a manager?"

She laughed. A sincere, from-the-tummy guffaw. She hadn't laughed heartily since…since before she had gotten kicked out of school. Feeling perked up, she said, "You're funny. I didn't have you pegged as the comedic type."

"I have my moments. So why did you decide to go out for a run today?"

Disappointment wiped the smile off of her face. She'd almost believed that he was calling because he was interested in her. "What do you mean?"

"You don't normally run along Wissahickon Creek. Why today?"

"I needed fresh air and exercise. I ended up on Forbidden Drive. Look, I thought you said this call wasn't about an investigation."

"Not officially because you claim you weren't attacked."

"I wasn't," Jen snapped.

"I'm not deliberately trying to get on your bad side. Okay? You can trust me. I know something happened to you."

"Yeah, I fell."

"You were running and crying and looking over your shoulder in fear. That's not the normal behavior for someone who simply stumbled and fell." He paused. "If you want to talk about it...you know, without filing a report or anything..." His words came out slowly and in a lower register. As though it were an afterthought, he added, "I'm a good listener."

The offer was so tempting. She paced her bedroom, wondering if she should risk telling him what she'd seen. *No!* she decided adamantly. Carmen and Lizzy didn't believe her and they knew her to be somewhat rational and sane. Hot Cop, Rome, didn't know her from a can of paint, so why should he take her seriously? "Like I said, I fell."

"Okay. I won't press the subject. You don't run every day, do you?"

"No. How do you know?" She glanced at her thighs and hips in the mirror, trying to assess whether her body broadcasted the fact that she rarely exercised.

"Forbidden Drive is in my jurisdiction; it's part of my regular patrol. In the course of a week, I can't count how many times I cruise that part of town. I'm thoroughly familiar with all the popular jogging trails...and the joggers and the pets that run alongside them." He chuckled. "If you were one of the regulars, I'd remember you. A pretty lady like you would be hard to forget."

He was flirting. She wished she had it in her to flirt back, but that would require a level of confidence and a sense of well-being that she simply wasn't feeling. She was too shaken up from all the peculiar events that had taken place to shift into vixen mode.

Knowing that his one and only visual of her was of a running crazed woman who looked like she'd taken a mud bath did not motivate her to respond with a witty remark.

"Thank you," she said sincerely. And that was all she could think of to say. She felt awkward as hell during the following few seconds of silence.

"So...uh...what did you say you do?" Rome asked, his voice penetrating the void.

"Um. I didn't say."

"Is that info classified?"

"No, I guess not. I'm a nanny."

"No shit?"

"Why is that so surprising?"

"You don't strike me as one of those Chestnut Hill nannies that I see shuttling kids to school and transporting them around town in luxury strollers that probably cost more than the truck that I drive."

Jen couldn't stifle a giggle. Rome was right; the people who lived in this affluent section of Philadelphia were loaded. Nannies toting kids around in style was all a part of the Chestnut Hill scenery.

"You just don't seem like the nanny type."

I'm not! Jen didn't have any experience in child care and would have never, in a million years, imagined herself in the nanny role, but a girl's gotta do...

"Is there a stereotypical nanny?" she quipped.

"Well, they're usually a lot older. I see lots of young college kids doing nanny duty, but there's a huge turnover. They don't last long." He paused. "As hard as it is to believe...I had a nanny once...for a couple of days."

"Oh, really?" She didn't believe him. Rome didn't give the impression of being from an affluent family and how many kids whose parents could afford a nanny would aspire to become a cop? He was probably joking.

"I know that being a nanny is like being an extension of the kid you're looking after, so I can understand why the college kids don't last for long. You're not much older than a college kid yourself. How are you managing to stick with the job?"

She wanted to tell Rome that she doubted if she'd last much longer, but that was much more information than she was willing to provide to someone she barely knew.

"How come I've never seen you around town, pushing a stroller or tugging along a screaming toddler?" Rome asked.

"The boy I take care of is...well, he's autistic and uh...let's just say, he's not a people person."

During a couple seconds of silence, it seemed Jen could hear Rome's wheels spinning as he began to put two and two together.

"Are you talking about Catherine Provost's son?"

Jen sighed. "Yes, but I'm not supposed to discuss—"

"I heard her acceptance speech. That thing with her son...his condition. It's really sad."

Jen sighed into the phone, letting him know she was uncomfortable with the direction the conversation was taking.

"Well, it's not a secret. She made the announcement."

"Right. But I have to honor the agreement I signed. I can't discuss the Provost family. At all."

"I know they live in Chestnut Hill—that big house over on Mermaid Lane," he continued. "But it never occurred to me that you worked for the Provosts. Wow," Rome repeated, apparently very impressed.

"Moving along..."

"Got it. Look, I'm not gonna keep you on the phone. I wanted to let you know that I was thinking about you."

Jen softened. "That's sweet. Thank you."

"So look, have a good night. And...uh...don't be a stranger. Give me a call sometime."

"I will."

"Meanwhile, stay off that section of Forbidden Drive. Lately, there's been some strange shit happening on Piper's Bridge."

"Strange? Like what!" She was stunned.

"You wouldn't believe it."

"I might. What happened on the bridge?"

"Oh, man," Rome said with a sigh. "This is confidential, okay. I'm an officer of the law and I can't have the citizens I'm supposed to protect get the idea that I'm off of my rocker. Know what I'm saying?"

"Sure." Jen nodded enthusiastically, as if he could see her.

Rome blew out another heavy sigh. "This is crazy," he said, as if to himself. "So crazy, I haven't told a soul."

"What?" Her voice was a whisper. "Tell me," she prodded.

"The first time I saw it, I had to pull over to get my head straight."

"I can imagine."

"No, baby, I don't think you can. But let me try to describe it the best way that I can."

"Okay…"

"I have this gift. I guess you can call it a gift. Here lately, it seems more like a curse. My grandma said I was born with a veil over my face."

"A veil?"

"Yeah, that's an old-fashioned expression. I was born with a thin layer of skin covering my face."

"Eew."

"I know—sounds nasty, doesn't it?"

"Yeah, really gross."

"You don't talk like a Philly chick. Where are you from?"

"Centerville."

"Where's that?"

"Near Meadville, Pennsylvania."

"I've never heard of either of those places."

"Twelve hours away. It's rural. Farm country. The closest big city is Erie."

"If you consider Erie a big city, you must really be from the sticks."

"Yeah, unfortunately. Living around cornfields and having the Amish as your closest neighbor…well, you can imagine, it wasn't an exciting life."

"Oh, so that's why you're so nice and thick—you're a corn-fed girl," he teased.

Was that a compliment? "Are you deliberately trying to change the subject? You were telling me about that extra flesh you were born with. And by the way, what does your veil have to with Piper's Bridge?"

"Old folks say that if a child is born with a veil covering its face, the child will grow up being able to have visions."

"Visions? As in seeing the future?"

"Yeah, but that wasn't the case. If it were, I'd know what tomorrow brings and I'd make all the right choices in life. I can't complain, though. We learn from our mistakes, right? Can't learn anything or grow as a person if you already have the answers to life's tests."

"That went way over my head," Jen admitted.

"I know; being born with that veil makes me get kinda extra sometimes." He laughed at himself.

"You were about to tell me about the gift you were born with. Bet it helps you fight crime here in tranquil Chestnut Hill."

"Crime is not restricted to the 'hood," he said casually. "Even an affluent neighborhood like Chestnut Hill has its share of law breakers," Rome said.

"True. But I doubt if you've ever had to dodge any bullets around here."

Rome laughed. Jen joined him in hearty laughter.

"So like I said, I don't have the gift of prophecy but I've been seeing ghosts pretty much all my life."

She felt a little chill run over her. "Are you serious?"

"Yeah, they're harmless. They don't bother me. They usually have surprised expressions, like they accidentally stumbled into this world. They don't say "boo" or make things go bump in the night. They disappear as quickly as they appear." He drew in a deep breath. "But that woman on the bridge... Man, she wasn't any ordinary ghost. She's the most menacing spirit I've ever seen."

The hairs stood up on the back of Jen's neck. "You saw a female ghost?"

"Yeah. A black woman. Dark skinned and dig this...she has these spooky blue eyes that she uses like a flashlight, scoping out shit while she's running back and forth on the bridge."

"Was she naked?"

"Butt-ass naked! How do you know?"

"I saw her, too!" Jen pressed her palm against the center of her chest.

"So, that's why you were looking back at the bridge while you were running," he said, enlightened. "This thing has had me thinking I was losing it. Seeing the same ghost is disturbing. It's never happened before. I've been trying to figure out why she keeps appearing on the bridge...acting confused and looking angry as hell."

Jen noticed the noise level downstairs had decreased. Party must have ended. "I don't know. The craziest thing is that I also saw her on—" A sudden crash—the sound of shattering glass. "I have to go."

"Wait. You can't leave a brother hanging like this? Where else did you see her?"

"I'll call you later. I promise." Jen had to check on Ethan; make sure he was all right. She hung up and rushed to the boy's bedroom.

18

Ethan was sleeping like a baby. Well, maybe not like a baby…
more like a tired old man. The house was quiet. The senator's friends must have gone…maybe he'd gone with
them. It wasn't like the senator to leave without telling her.

Rome's admission about the veil thing and his disclosure of
seeing spirits on a regular basis had her spooked. Jen was not
thrilled with the idea of being in the house alone, and she
dreaded having to investigate the breaking glass. Damn, damn,
damn. Maybe she should call Rome back and have him on the
line in case there was an intruder in the house.

Despite her fear, she descended the stairs. Not because she
was feeling heroic, but because she refused to remain upstairs—trapped and at the mercy of a crazed home invader.
Being downstairs gave her a sliver of a chance to escape. *Sorry,
Ethan.* The child would be left to his own defenses, but she was
sure he'd make out okay. If Ethan awoke and felt threatened,
he'd launch into one of his "episodes," scaring the crap out of
a burglar.

To be honest, Ethan didn't even have to perform his dreadful,
high-pitched scream. The sight of his stiffened body and the
added horror of his eyes rolled to the back of his head would
shatter the nerves of the most heinous criminal, sending him
scurrying into the night.

Downstairs, the lights were dim. The guests had gone. Jen's body tensed with apprehension. Having no weapon, she grabbed a silver candle holder and stealthily moved through the dining room.

Scared to death, she couldn't keep her hand steady. Or dry. Her palm was clammy, making it difficult to keep a grip around the silver stem of the candle holder.

Frantically, Jen's head jerked from right to left, searching for the intruder. If someone jumped out at her, she would react like A-Rod up at the plate, swinging the candle holder like a bat, hitting a home run as she knocked the housebreaker's head clean off of his shoulders.

A light shone from inside the senator's study. Senator Provost was home. He must have dropped something. Instantly relieved, her muscles relaxed and she returned to the dining room and replaced the candle holder on the mantle.

Then the house phone rang. Her heart leapt. Any sudden sound made her jumpy. Jen whisked through the dining room to the kitchen wall and picked up the phone.

"Hello," she heard the senator say. He'd answered from inside his study.

Instead of hanging up, Jen kept the phone pressed against her ear, unable to resist an opportunity to eavesdrop on the senator and his wife.

"You left three urgent messages. What's the emergency? You know this is the most important time of my life," Catherine Provost said, fuming.

"Sorry, but I thought it was important. Our nanny is at her wit's end. She needs some help. We're going to have to employ a second nanny."

"This is the worst possible time for you to bring this up,"

Catherine Provost complained. "I already spoke with Jen and she told me that she understood the historical importance of hanging in there with Ethan. With less than two weeks until the election, why would she put us in this terrible position? Is babysitting a little kid too much to do for your country?"

Jen was offended. Catherine was duping the public. The vice presidential nominee was no sweetheart. She was a tyrant and a merciless bitch.

"She's overworked, Catherine. I don't know if it's in Ethan's best interest to have one nanny working around the clock."

"We're ratcheting up the campaign stops. I don't even have a minute for myself, so how can I possibly squeeze in the time to fly home and interview a new nanny?"

"I think your popularity would skyrocket if you took a day or two off to…"

"At this critical time?" Catherine practically shrieked. "I don't think so. And by the way, pal, your absence on the stump has been duly noted. The press is having a field day, hinting that your absence is a silent, jealous tantrum."

"That's not true and you know it. I sent out a press release explaining that our son has an aversion to unfamiliar people and that he's most comfortable at home. During this critical time, with one parent constantly away, it's in Ethan's best interest that I be here with him."

"Yeah, I heard about your press release. No one is buying it, Daniel."

"Who cares? I'm being completely honest. We didn't know what was wrong with Ethan until a few months ago. If you weren't being vetted and didn't need a reasonable explanation for his odd behavior, who knows how long it would have taken us to discover that he's autistic. For the life of me…after all those evaluations, why didn't one of those doctors diagnose him years ago?"

"Autism is often hard to diagnose," Catherine explained. "I'm grateful that we finally have an answer."

"You're right. Well, one of us has to show some support for the little guy. I've been approached about being a spokesperson for autism—"

"Oh, really?" Catherine sounded delighted. "Hey, that's a great idea—politically speaking. Having my husband standing up for something charitable…you know…doing the type of work that's expected of a first lady is really foreword thinking. Kudos, Daniel. I'll talk to you later."

"Catherine!"

"I have to go."

"Since I'm assuming the concerned parent's role, I figure I might as well go all the way. First thing tomorrow, I'm calling the agency. I'll be interviewing nannies, tomorrow. Wish me luck."

"The media will be out en mass if they get wind of that."

"Don't worry. I'll be very discreet."

Wow! The senator had stood up to his wife on Jen's behalf. Feeling flattered, Jen couldn't suppress a smile. She waited until the Provosts disconnected and then quietly replaced the phone back into its base. Still, the walls were starting to close in on her. Jen was on edge and needed to get out of the house.

With Ethan finally asleep and the senator at home, maybe he wouldn't mind if she went out for a few hours. Rome was waiting for her to call him back. And she intended to.

She'd been in a sex drought for months and Hot Cop was the de-stressor her tense body was craving. But as tempted as she was to make a booty call, now was not the time for sex play.

She and Rome were experiencing the same paranormal occurrences—both witnessing a ghost lady running around on Piper's Bridge. Jen needed to get to the bottom of the phenomena.

Perhaps, putting their heads together, she and Rome could make some sense of what was going on and, hopefully, with his history of ghostly encounters, maybe he could figure out a way to make the sightings stop.

Standing outside the senator's study, Jen raised her fist, prepared to tap on the door. She heard a woman's low murmur.

"Why so glum, Danny Boy?"

Jen bristled. It was the voice of the dirty blonde. Hanky panky! Annoyed but nevertheless intrigued, Jen pressed her ear against the door.

"We shouldn't be doing this. It's not right," the senator said.

"I'm sorry about that broken vase. I lost my temper when you started texting your wife. I'll replace it if you promise to stop sulking."

"I don't care about the vase."

"Then, what's wrong?"

"Us. We're wrong. I'm a faithful husband and I really think you should leave."

"Come on, Danny. The cat's away and you should play. Let's have some fun. Want me to go find a broom and a dustpan? I'll pretend to be your French maid while I clean up the broken glass."

"That's not necessary."

"Why do you let her get you so uptight? I can help you unwind." Dirty blonde was speaking in a sultry, extra-breathy voice. What a slut. Jen really hated the woman for having the prestigious position as the senator's assistant—a job that Catherine had promised she'd get for Jen. Jen could forget about that opportunity now that the dirty blonde was securing her position by adding blowjobs to her job description.

The next sound from the study was the senator's breath, which came out in ragged gasps of arousal. Dirty blonde was no doubt on her knees, having her way with him. Jen sucked her teeth. With the senator preoccupied, Jen would have to remain cooped up with Ethan. Shit!

Maybe not. The boy was sound asleep and the senator would be too busy to notice if she slipped out for a couple hours. Well, she hoped he wouldn't notice. Leaving Ethan unattended were grounds for dismissal. But she'd simply have to take that risk.

Outside of the gate and a few feet away, Rome waited for her in his truck.

"Hi." Jen climbed inside, and then strapped the seatbelt in place. Dressed in jeans with a washed-out denim jacket covering a T-shirt, Rome was hot—maybe hotter out of his policeman's uniform. But Jen didn't allow herself to think about the high-voltage sex appeal he radiated.

"Glad you could get out. Do you have a curfew?"

"Yeah, I snuck out, so I have to be back in an hour or two."

Rome looked incredulous. "You left the little boy home alone?"

"No. His dad is there, but he was occupied and I didn't tell him I was leaving." She made a face and gave a helpless shrug. "I'm a wreck. This thing with the ghost lady is taking a toll. Right now, talking to you is more important than peeking in on a sleeping child. He usually sleeps through the night. He'll be all right."

"This is wild."

"What? Ghost lady?"

"Yeah, that and the fact that you're the nanny to the first African-American female VP candidate."

"Yeah, well…things aren't always as they appear."

He scowled. Jen waved her hand. "Forget I said that. I'm not myself. I'm sure you understand."

"I haven't been thinking straight either. So, where would you like to go?"

Jen shrugged her shoulders. "Doesn't matter. Anywhere outside of Chestnut Hill."

"I know a spot you might like. Quiet. Good food, nice atmosphere. It's in Mount Airy—not too far from here."

Jen thought about it for a few seconds. "I'm not hungry and I don't think I'd enjoy being around people tonight."

Rome nodded in understanding. "We can go back to my place, if you're comfortable with that. I live in Germantown."

"Sure. Sounds good."

Lost in their thoughts, Jen and Rome were both quiet for the first five minutes of the ride. Curiosity got the best of Jen. "You said you've been seeing spirits since childhood?"

"Yeah, my whole life…for as long as I can remember."

"When you were little…uh…how could you tell the difference between a spirit and a living person?"

"Spirits don't seem to have the same substance as humans. I can't see through them or anything, but they're sort of translucent. And they move differently than we do."

"What do you mean?"

"At a different frequency. It's hard to explain, but I always knew the difference between the living and the dead."

"Were they friendly?" Jen asked, hopeful.

"Not exactly. No, I wouldn't say they were friendly. But definitely non-threatening. I would have sensed malevolence. Like I said, the spirits I've seen always appear to be startled by my presence. "

"But the lady on the bridge is different, right? More human in substance."

"Right. She's a whole different species of ghost. And the nudist aspect..." Rome shook his head. "That really has me thrown off. Normal spooks dress in the clothes from their era."

Jen nodded. "And those freaky blue eyes. Have you ever encountered spirits that shoot off beams of light from their eyes?"

"Nah, never." He looked mystified.

"That naked lady is one ornery ghost. I freaked out after she aimed blue light at the center of my chest—targeting me like I was prey."

"Now that I know the entire story, you rolling around in the mud makes a lot of sense."

She punched him in the arm. "Hey, I fell in the mud. I didn't roll around in it."

"Just playing with you, trying to lighten up the mood." He turned up the volume of the music that was playing from the radio. "You like rap?"

"Yeah!" she answered. "Who doesn't?"

"I thought you might be into country or some cornfield music that doesn't get airtime in Philly." Rome laughed. Jen joined in. Their laughter rang out as he drove along Wissahickon Drive. He made a sudden left and drove up a gravelly road called Hermit's Lane. Rome parked in front of a quaint cottage home that was off the main road and hidden from view.

"Charming." Jen gazed questioningly at Rome and then at the white stucco front cottage.

"It's not a very masculine-looking home. My grandma lived here. She passed away recently—"

"Sorry for your loss." Jen didn't know what else to say.

"Thanks. She left me her house and though it doesn't reflect my taste, I can't bring myself to sell it. Not yet." He unlocked the door. It had a very homey feeling inside. A plump, comfy sofa decorated with lace-trimmed pillows, frilly curtains, and floral paintings on the walls. It reminded Jen of home in Centerville. There were dozens of framed pictures of family members…most of the photos chronicled the stages of a cute little boy, starting with infancy and all the way to adulthood, smiling broadly, sitting inside a police cruiser.

"That you?" Jen pointed to a picture of a crying child sitting on Santa's lap.

"Yeah, they're all me." He smiled sheepishly.

"Grandma's favorite, huh?" Jen teased.

"You could say that. I'm the only child of an only child. My mom…" He blinked, his eyes turned sad, and shot downward. "We'll discuss my mom some other time." Taking a deep breath, he regrouped and looked up. "Haven't had time to redecorate. I've only been here a couple of months," he explained.

She wanted to ask if his grandma's spirit wandered about, and if so, did his grandma act surprised to see him occupying her house? But Jen didn't ask; she figured that type of questioning would be insensitive and in poor taste. The pain of his loss was apparent in his brown eyes. And there was something about his mom that added to the sorrow.

"Can I offer you a drink?" Rome asked.

Jen nodded. "Yeah, I could use one."

"I don't have any wine, no Alize, or anything sweet." He chuckled. "Sorry, all I have is a bottle of Jack Daniels."

Jen smiled. "Sounds good to me."

19

Inside Rome's grandma's small kitchen, Jen and Rome did shots to take the edge off. Drinking hard liquor, straight with no chaser, seemed a bit irreverent considering the folksiness of the kitchen with its ruffled gingham curtains, a "Home Sweet Home" plaque on the wall, old-fashioned appliances. There was even a ceramic cookie jar with the word, "cookies" spelled out invitingly. In a kitchen like this, one would expect the aroma of homemade bread, banana muffins, or an apple pie baking in the oven instead of the harsh smell of Jack Daniels that permeated the air.

"It's so hard to believe that we both witnessed the same blue-eyed, naked ghost." Rome threw down another shot.

"Want to hear something even weirder that that?"

Rome raised his brows.

"I saw her on the computer before I saw her outside."

Frowning and coughing from the bitter taste of the liquor, Rome said, "Come again."

"This is between you and me." She stared at him intently.

"Got it. Confidentiality and all that shit." He gestured for her to continue.

Jen started laughing. "It just struck me as funny that I'm bothering to worry about the Provosts' privacy when there's a furious ghost on the loose who might have it in for me."

"Why are you taking it personally? I saw her, too."

"I take it very personally," Jen snapped. She pointed a finger. "You were born with that extra skin over your face. You're accustomed to seeing ghosts. I'm not."

"That's true."

"But what I can't understand is why I'd see that particular apparition, twice? I think it's very strange that I saw that awful woman on the internet and then again on Piper's Bridge."

"Don't worry, baby. I know how to deal with spirits."

"Oh, yeah? How are you going to deal with her the next time she makes an appearance? What are you going to do? Arrest her for indecent exposure? Are you going to take her to the station for questioning?" Jen started laughing.

Feeling the liquor, Rome joined in with loud laughter, smacking the top of the table as his shoulders shook. The table smacking made Jen laugh so hard, tears formed and her stomach muscles clenched.

When their liquor-induced hilarity subsided, Rome's face turned serious. "You saw that same female ghost on the computer?"

Jen sighed. "Long story."

"I have time."

"The little boy I look after…Ethan Provost…he doesn't play with toys like regular kids. His only interest in life is looking at stock photo images of bridges. Ethan doesn't talk…but one day, I heard him talk. I looked over his shoulder at the monitor and there was a black woman on one of the bridges Ethan admires. She was naked and running back and forth. I heard him tell her that she was going the wrong way."

"Wow!" Incredulous, Rome shook his head.

"He also told me that his name is Xavier. And the voice that comes out his mouth sounds ancient. It's scratchy and terrible, like how you'd envision the Grim Reaper would sound."

"Wow!" Rome repeated.

Jen shot him an irritated look and then went on. "I told his father that Ethan started talking, but the senator doesn't believe me. He thinks I'm overworked and overwrought." She narrowed an eye at Rome. "Please don't say wow!"

"I don't know what else to say. This is not a typical, every day conversation."

"I realize that. That's why I'm here. We have to try to figure out what's going on and how it might affect us."

"Maybe it doesn't."

Jen gave him a long look.

"Ms. Provost is going to be the vice president. There's no doubt about it. Her running mate is getting up in his years. Old boy might not make it through his term and that would make her the president."

"Yeah, and…"

"And maybe this is a hoax or some kind of a plot. You say you saw the same woman on her son's computer—"

"I did!"

"So it sounds to me like someone hacked into that computer. This whole thing could be a terrorist plot aimed at Ms. Provost. That's why the ghost lady didn't have the translucent quality of a spirit. And that blue light… That could be some high-tech terrorist weapon."

In her inebriated state, Jen thought Rome's deductions made a lot of sense. "I think you're onto something." Jen was pleased that Rome had solved the mystery.

"But you should look for another job," he warned. "Might be best for you to put some distance between yourself and the Provosts."

"I know. And it's not like they'll listen to me about this terrorist plot."

"No. If you tell them you think they're being targeted by terrorists, they'll think you're some nutjob, conspiracy theorist."

"You're absolutely right. Hell, they might even blame me; try to pin the commuter hacking on me!"

Rome held up the near empty bottle, offering Jen the last shot. Shaking her head, Jen declined. "The senator is going to be interviewing nannies for the next couple of days. After he finds someone suitable, I'm going to resign."

"Wise choice." Rome stood. "I'm twisted. I gotta lie down. Come on upstairs. I won't bother you."

"I'm not going upstairs with you." She ran her eyes over his muscular frame and was tempted to give it up right there in the kitchen. On the floor. But she wasn't intoxicated enough to give it up before their first official date. "Hey, you can't go to bed. You have to take me home."

"I need a half-hour to sleep this liquor off. I promise to keep my hands to myself." He held up his right hand as if making a solemn oath.

Getting caught shirking her nanny duties was not the end of the world. Jen could deal with having to face an angry senator, but that ghost lady...whew! The prospects of having to deal with an evil spirit were more than she was equipped to handle.

So, relieved that the naked woman was part of a terrorist plot and not an evil spirit, Jen was practically giddy as she trotted behind Rome up the stairs.

Rome's bedroom was very different from the other rooms in the house. His personal space was stunning but the word "sensual" described it best. The room was ultramodern and manly with natural tones.

The leather headboard and chocolate suede bedding on the king-sized bed had a strong masculine appeal. Spellbinding tapestries accented the walls. These wall hangings depicted ferocious wild animals engaged in the chase and Jen wondered if this art was a reflection of Rome—agile, muscular, bold, and ferocious…in bed?

Jen was very curious. And totally horny. An onslaught of decadent fantasies rushed through her mind. Rome's bedroom had all the trappings to persuade the most levelheaded and prudent woman to strip out of her clothes and offer up a session of no-strings attached sex.

Yawning, Rome obviously had other things in mind—like sleep. He held up an oversized white T-shirt. "You want to put this on?"

Jen gave him a look, all the while thinking how badly she wanted to touch and be touched by him.

"I'm not trying to get you naked or anything…though that would be nice." He gave her a lopsided smile that was so cute… rugged and boyish at the same time. He rubbed his tired eyes and even that innocent gesture was a turn-on. She wanted to do really naughty things with this man.

"I thought you might want to put this on so you don't wrinkle your clothes."

"Okay. You only need a half-hour, right?" Jen said, raising a concerned brow and feigning reluctance as she accepted the shirt.

"I need to chill for about thirty minutes. After a quick power nap, I'll be straight and we can roll out."

Jen smiled to herself. She liked the off-duty Rome a lot more than the inquisitive cop she'd met on Forbidden Drive. Hot Cop was sexy, but he was even sexier out of uniform and in the relaxed environment of his home. She hadn't realized until now that Rome's speech pattern had changed from formal police lingo to casual, Philly talk.

He was easygoing and had a great sense of humor. And the

mere sound of his voice aroused her. She caught herself staring at the bulge inside his jeans, wishing he'd unzip and give her a peek. Everything about Rome was so perfect, she was certain that his dick was wonderful, too.

She wanted to taste him, feel his dick, hard and urgent, entering her mouth. She wanted to feel him stretching her inner walls... She covered her mouth, muffling a moan. If he could read her mind, he'd think she was a terrible slut.

Rome was nothing like those college boys she'd wasted her time with. He was a grown man and Jen wanted him. And not for one night, which would be the case if she gave up the goods without allowing him the opportunity to engage in the chase like the animals on his walls.

"Bathroom's down the hall. You can change in there."

Aw, Rome was a gentlemanly womanizer. Jen accepted the shirt and trekked down the hall to change. She located a bottle of mouthwash. She swished the liquid inside her mouth, getting rid of the smell of whiskey and giving her breath a fresh minty scent, in case she decided to give Rome a kiss. Nothing more. Just a kiss.

She was no sexpot. Her frizzy hair refused to cooperate with the brush she quickly pulled through it. Rome's T-shirt was long, but not long enough to completely cover her thunder thighs. She tugged on the bottom of the shirt one more time, trying to force it to stretch down a little further. The fabric stayed in place, revealing her extra-thick thighs, big hips, and big booty. As far as Jen was concerned, her boobs and flat tummy were her only saving grace.

When she returned to the bedroom, Rome had thoughtfully dimmed the lights and she was grateful for that. But he couldn't dim the heat of his gaze as it traveled from her face, her boobs, her thick thighs, and the swell of her ample hips. Forgetting her dissatisfaction with her body type, she met his gaze, revealing the desire that burned in her eyes as well.

His jeans were tossed on a chair. Bare-chested, he relaxed on the bed, wearing only boxers. She pulled her eyes away from his broad shoulders and amazing chest but mistakenly settled her gaze on his thighs, which were roped with steely musculature. Her mouth watered. She swallowed a lump of desire and averted her gaze.

"Hey, you look cute in that shirt," he complimented, his voice cutting through the sexual tension that was thick inside the bedroom.

Jen wanted to yank off the T-shirt and let it pool on the floor beside the bed, but she controlled her urges. Ignoring her overactive hormones, she sat on the edge of the bed, hands folded on her lap.

Rome got under the covers and tugged at the fabric beneath her butt. "Lie down. Get under the covers. I'll be a gentleman. I promise," he said softly.

Jen pretended to be reluctant, easing cautiously beneath the suede duvet and the sheets.

"Half-hour," he reassured her, tugging her arm gently until she was curled beneath the covers, her buttocks merging into the contour of his body. He draped an arm loosely over her. She could feel his manhood pulsing against her derriere, each beat tightening the knot of desire within her core.

A slight brush of cotton fabric against her nipples made them flush and harden into small beads that pleaded for attention. Overly sensitive, her pearls yearned to be touched…pinched… suckled.

But his fingers did not wander toward those dangerous, peaked regions. Instead of fondling her luscious breasts or soothing the hot spot between her legs, he stroked her wiry tendrils, his fingers concentrating on taming her wayward strands of red hair.

"Your hair smells good," he murmured and inhaled a full breath of her scent and continued smoothing down her wild mane.

The air from his nostrils tickled the back of her neck, arousing and tormenting her to the point of wanting to scream. She forced her body to become stiff and rigid, not to ward off any potential advances, but to keep herself from twisting around, ripping off Rome's boxers and molesting him.

Jen bit the inside of her lip as she fought the building desire. Rome didn't appear to be struggling the way she was; he seemed content with his gently pulsing dick and with the nearness of her. Then she felt the pounding of his heart as it thumped against her back, beckoning her to join him...to connect her body with his.

She didn't notice it happening. Didn't feel her defenses breaking down. It seemed like the most natural thing when she finally relaxed and allowed her body to move, uncensored... unrestricted by rules of morality or even common decency.

It was the most natural thing for her to turn toward him and press her feminine mound against his groin, moving rhythmically against his concrete manhood.

Rome squeezed her hip, caressed her thigh. "Baby...You feel so good."

She couldn't bear it. His low groan was so sensual...too sensual. Made her want to do things she knew she'd later regret.

"I wanted you the first time—"

She couldn't listen to sexy murmuring and be held accountable for her lustful actions. Desperately, her mouth covered his, silencing him with her minty kiss.

He groaned and began groping at the shirt, urging her to take it off.

Obliging, she pulled it over her head and tossed it to the floor.

Rome watched with anticipation as her luscious breasts gently bounced and then settled. He reached out and touched one rosy nipple and then the other, feeling them grow hard under his heated touch.

She hooked a finger beneath the elastic band around the V of his waist. "Your turn," she purred.

He quickly shed his boxers. Now all barriers between their burning fleshes were removed.

She devoured his naked body with her eyes. His dick looked good at half-mast but when it became engorged and stood at full attention, it was a husky, good-looking dick and Jen wanted to cover it with her lips and bathe it with her tongue. But she restrained herself.

She gave good head, she'd been told. But wasn't sure if she should display all of her talents on the first night with Rome. Maybe she'd give him a sneak preview of her oral skills.

Rome captured her lips; she opened her mouth for him, permitting his tongue to wander freely. At first he entangled his fingers in her wild hair, pulling handfuls until she cried out in pain and writhed in pleasure. He abandoned her hair, his hot hands scorching her skin as they traveled to her shoulders… squeezing, caressing and then sliding down and tenderly cradling her breasts.

A primal sound rumbled in the back of his throat as he lowered his head and drew in a ripened nipple. His tongue lashing against her hardened flesh gave her surges of delicious sensation.

"Rome," she whispered, her voice filled with unmistakable pleasure.

"What, baby?"

"I want you."

"You got me, baby. It's you and me, now," he responded, his voice hoarse, his words emerging in broken chords.

It was only sex talk. He didn't mean what he was saying. A man like Rome could have any woman he wanted and he was what—about twenty-four or twenty-five? Too young to settle down in a committed relationship. Still, his words made her flush with joy. "I want to feel you inside me," she clarified.

She wished she could make their short time together memorable. She'd love to lick some honey, whipped cream, or chocolate syrup off of his beautiful body, but there was no time to raid his kitchen for naughty treats. She kissed his neck. He moaned.

She sucked his small male nipples and licked her way down to his stomach. His dick thumped her cheek, impatiently. She broke her rule and feasted on his shaft, slurping, sucking…loving it.

Then he maneuvered her around, palming Jen's ass cheeks as he pressed her moist kitty against his ready lips. One hot tongue flick and Jen tensed; couldn't concentrate on sucking. She relaxed her mouth briefly while she enjoyed the sensation of his warm tongue sliding between her labia, lapping up generous amounts of her sweetness.

"Mmm," she murmured. "Ah," she moaned as his tongue moved up and toggled her clit.

"You like that, baby?" His muffled voice brought Jen back to reality. They were in the "69" position and she was supposed to be giving as well as getting.

Working her jaws again, she concluded that his dick was exceedingly delicious and didn't require the sugary topping she'd wanted to drizzle up and down his thick shaft. Adding honey or chocolate syrup to something so sweet would give her a sugar high.

She was still tipsy from the shots of Jack Daniels…adding a sugar rush could be a dangerous combination.

"I like it a lot," she finally answered after she'd had her fill of oral sex. "But I want something else."

"Is that right?"

She didn't answer. She mounted him.

"Oh, it's like that?" He smiled. "You're taking charge?"

"That's exactly how it is," she said breathily as she wrapped her hand around his length, which was bulged with thick veins.

"Oh, so you're just gon' take what you want?" He faked a frown, but couldn't maintain the expression as his shaft, eager for her warmth, began to vibrate in Jen's hand.

The frenetic energy of desire mounting made Jen shudder. "Uh-huh, I want it and I'm taking it," she said, her voice husky with lust. She used the head of his manhood to separate her petals and guide him inside her moist and receptive place.

Rome griped her shoulders and thrust upward, lodging himself deeply. Jen's pussy was so hot and wet, it made sloshing sounds as he plunged in his immense thickness. He became still. Motionless.

"What's wrong?"

"Nothing." He flipped her over. Lay on top of her. The full frontal contact was electrifying. He kissed her as their hips rocked together, swiveled, gyrated in smooth rhythmic motions. He stopped again, looked down at her, staring at her face as if she might disappear if he blinked. "You're so beautiful, baby."

There was such intensity in his gaze, such tenderness in his tone, that she had to close her eyes and press her lips together to keep from blurting out, "I love you, Rome. Let's get married. I want to have your babies."

Had she said what was in her heart, words she had no business speaking, she would have been perceived as talking crazy, speaking the type of gibberish of a woman coming out of a long, hard sex-drought. But this feeling they were sharing was the closest she'd ever come to feeling love.

Love, marriage, and babies. Universal female urges that could not be denied. Or admitted. She'd have to keep those desires secret or risk chasing Rome away.

So she let her body do the talking. Lying beneath him, she arched her back, meeting his impassioned plunges with her own ardent thrusts. Their body's enflamed, the pace quickened. No longer careful and gentle, their bodies crashed together in a frenzy to satisfy their overwhelming and voracious hunger.

Like the animals on his walls, Rome was wild and passionate. His male groan was primal in its sound. Jen clutched handfuls of the sheet as she felt the beginning of a gigantic climax... building and coursing through her. She gritted her teeth, trying to hold back the high-pitched cries of passion. But couldn't.

After reaching a screaming crescendo, Jen trembled uncontrollably. Rome drove deeper, speeding up his strokes, and working his way to salvation. Joining her, he liberated a growl as pleasure exploded.

20

The goddess Tara appealed to the council, pleading on her sister's behalf. "Eris is reformed," she testified.

Goddess Diana looked at Tara skeptically. "How do you know?" she inquired.

Tara lowered her gaze, ashamed. "She's been communicating with me."

"And you allowed her to penetrate your mind?"

"She's my sister. I couldn't shut her out."

The council gave a collective sigh.

"Tara, we are aware of your compassion. It is in your nature to feel the pain of others deeply. Too deeply, sometimes. And it is in your sister's nature to be destructive. We put up with her wicked ways because your mother vetoed all our votes to dispatch Eris to the Dark Realm. Your mother, the goddess Inanna, has ascended now; she no longer sits at council and it is our decision to keep Eris contained with others of her ilk—the wretched and wicked with souls beyond redemption."

Diana drew in a breath; her eyelids fluttered in frustration. "We did not dispatch your sister to the Dark Realm. We sent her to earth to begin a new life and possibly redeem herself. But she continued her wicked ways. And even after her escape from the Dark Realm, she returned to earth over a hundred years later and still made mischief.

"Because of Eris, our dear goddess Kali must slumber throughout eternity, unable to ascend to the highest place for honorable souls such as she." Diana shuddered.

"After all her crimes against mankind on earth and the sexual abuse she inflicted upon your dear winged attendant, I would expect you to join this goddess council in our decision to keep Eris trapped inside the Dark Realm, forever!"

Diana stood. "This meeting is adjourned," she asserted.

The members of the goddess council stood.

Distraught, Tara returned to the pond, accompanied by Zeta, whose wings were folded down in sorrow. She draped an arm around Tara and wiped her tears.

Finally, Tara stopped weeping. "Zeta, my lovely winged one. I need solitude. Please leave me."

Zeta raised her wings, enticingly, a signal that her phallus was readied. She pulled up her gossamer gown. Tara cast a glance at her attendant's beautiful sex organ. It glimmered in the sunlight, while beneath the rigid shaft; Zeta's female opening revealed a dewy desire.

"My dear servant, I can see that you are in need of release."

Zeta lowered her head, ashamed.

"I want you to leave me now. Go join the other winged attendants and choose the one with largest and finest phallus and tell the hermaphrodite that the goddess Tara has granted permission for her to penetrate your lovely flower."

Zeta squeezed her thighs together, aroused by Tara's generosity, but pained by her mistress's obvious suffering. "I cannot leave you in anguish. It is my duty to serve you, goddess. I am committed to care for you. Using the gift that I am endowed with, I can take your mind off of your trouble. I beg you, goddess, pay no attention to the lack of discretion of my undisciplined vagina."

"You have dual urges and I am just one woman. I can only offer you penetration with my slender finger. If the goddess council ever found out—" Tara shook her head, unable to continue.

"Don't worry, mistress. We are very discreet."

Tara nodded. "To be totally happy, you need to be with your own kind—a hermaphrodite who can satisfy you fully."

"No, mistress. I only need you. I can ignore my feminine urges."

"You shouldn't have to. Zeta, I know that my sister punished you when your feminine desires occurred."

Zeta made a little whimper, recalling how the goddess of destruction had spanked her feminine area whenever it moistened with desire. And Eris, enjoying causing pain, had thought of crueler and more inventive ways to punish Zeta's genitalia.

Tears sprang to Tara's eyes. "You are so beautiful. I love you, Zeta. It saddens me that the goddess rules are so rigid."

"Your compassion is as beautiful as your face, as sensual as your bosom. I am your devoted companion; I will never indulge my own sexual cravings. I exist to cater to your every sexual need."

"My only pleasure in life is parting your legs and sliding this into your plush depths." Zeta's sturdy penis quivered in her palm.

Tara moaned. Zeta pulled her closer, and then caressed Tara's shoulders with her wings.

Tara's eyes began to well again. Zeta's love and devotion were so unyielding and pure; she wanted to weep with gratitude but didn't allow herself to. One day, after the matter with her sister was resolved, she would seek permission of the council to return the love that Zeta gave to her.

There shouldn't be rules that prevented her from satisfying her winged lover's feminine core with her fingers and her mouth. "These rules are outdated. The love between a goddess and her attendant should be respected and honored. If a goddess wants to grant her attendant an equal status, she should be able to,"

Tara would argue with the council, one day...when she was feeling a lot stronger.

Tara dismissed Zeta with a soft kiss. She watched until she could no longer discern Zeta's departing figure from the distant and towering trees and the foliage.

Tara's lashes lowered. Concentrating on the image of her sister, she closed her eyes, opening her mind, allowing Eris to penetrate. But instead of the pitch black force field that usually engulfed her and the piecing wails that hurt her head when Eris came through, she saw nothing.

She heard nothing except the sound of her own worrisome contemplations running through her head. "My poor sister. The council has denied my request. You must remain in that wretched place."

She sent out a thought form. "Eris, can you hear me? Where are you?"

No response.

"Eris!" She called in her mind. Eris didn't answer.

Tara shed a tear for her sister. "Despite the devastation you've brought upon so many, I still love you, my sister. I pray that the day will come when you will mend your wicked ways. In the meantime, I can only pray that you haven't been harmed by those wretched souls in the Dark Realm."

Eris heard her sister. Loud and clear. And she was fuming mad that she was being forced to listen to the bad news that Tara delivered. "You've made your announcement. Now go away, you nuisance," Eris spat. Her spineless younger sister had most likely presented such a weak and unconvincing proposal on Eris's behalf, the council had easily denied the request.

Eris hated Tara for her sniveling, useless compassion. All the other goddesses were known as warriors, protectors...famous for strength, power, intelligence, fertility, courage, and wisdom. Her silly sister, on the other hand, was burdened with the worthless trait of compassion.

If she ever made it back to her true home...the Goddess Realm...the first thing on her agenda would be to rid the realm of the likes of Tara. She'd gladly obliterate her useless sister right now if only she could reach her hands through the gates of hell and strangle the life out of the insufferable goddess.

"Be safe, my sister," Tara's annoyingly sweet voice went on. "Forgive me for letting you down. I will not forsake you. I won't give up. I'll keep petitioning for your pardon and safe return to the Goddess Realm. "

Eris covered her ears, trying to shut out Tara's annoying lament. Eris wanted Tara to go away. "Leave me alone, Tara. Go play with Zeta...the winged one you acquired...the whining hermaphrodite who is responsible for my unfair banishment."

"I will plead your case until the day I ascend to the heavens—"

"Blah, blah, blah," Eris shouted, trying to drown out her sister's voice. Where was that little brat, Xavier? He was the only soul who could liberate her from this crude holding place. But being stuck in the tiny child's body had soured his disposition and turned him into an awful prankster.

"Remember, dear sister, my love for you is unending."

Eris sucked her teeth. Her wimpy sister was relentless, going on and on...yakking inside her head, distracting her with her whiny apologies and empty promises. "Be quiet, Tara!" Eris yelled in her mind, but of course, Tara didn't hear her.

"Keep in mind the power of your goddess ring," Tara reminded. "It will always keep you safe. It is the one thing that can protect you from those ghouls who surround you."

Eris became still and listened with interest. The goddess ring had powers? Eris didn't know that. "Tara!" she hissed. "Why didn't you tell me about the powers of the ring? That information would have been useful when I was banished from the Goddess Realm."

But it was one-sided conversation. Unable to hear Eris, Tara made no response.

Livid, Eris continued to rant. "These stupid demons can't hurt me. I rule this hellish domain. It's those earthlings who keep finding ways to dispatch me to this revolting habitat. Humans are shrewd beings. They're full of trickery. I am so insulted that my own sister kept such valuable information from me." Eris shouted. "Listen to me, Tara!" She trembled with anger.

Tara couldn't hear her, but that didn't stop Eris from venting. "When I was captured and taken in as a runaway slave, my ring was turned over to the master. Slaves were not allowed to promenade around wearing trinkets. I didn't care about that ring. I didn't know it had any value. But I know where it is. It was mixed in with the mistress's fine jewels, which I stole and hid inside a crude wooden box. I wasted years, coveting the mistress's sparkling jewels, when my very own goddess ring would have imbibed the power to rule nations!"

Infuriated as she envisioned the snotty-nose Stovall child with access to her fine jewelry and her powerful goddess ring, Eris kicked up a swirl of bristly obsidian. "I hate you, Tara. I lost my earth life twice. I could've ruled the entire earth, had I known about the powers of my goddess ring. Now, some little scallywag of a child is prancing about and wearing my jewelry. A snot-nose little twit has my life-preserving, all powerful, goddess ring!"

Overwhelmed by the desire to cause pain, Eris shot sparks from her blue eyes, sending stinging pops to any creature lurking nearby. She derived a small measure of excitement from hearing their yelps of pain. But the thrill was short-lived. She wanted revenge on Tara.

"You're going to pay dearly for the error of omission, you stupid, compassionate fool. I'm going to make sure that you and your winged playmate die slow and torturous deaths. If I have to escort you to the Dark Realm with my own bare hands, I'll do it. You deserve a taste of this kind of unrelenting suffering!" Eris snarled and shook her fists. The nearby ghouls, fearing they'd be burned or lose an appendage, scurried deeper into the shadows.

In the midst of her tirade, she noticed wooden planks. Could she be actually seeing what she thought? She turned up her blue gaze, illuminating the mysterious sight. And there it was…a beautiful, well-constructed, sturdy bridge! But it was located in a different place, much further in distance than the previous one.

Ever the prankster, Xavier was having great fun taunting her by constructing her passage from hell far away. Afraid she might miss another opportunity to escape incarceration from this stifling and forsaken place, Eris shouted, "Boozer!"

Boozer came running.

"Hurry!" she implored him.

Like a running back, Boozer knocked down ghouls that stood in his path as he heeded Eris's call. He scooped Eris up in his arms and ran like hell, speeding in the direction she pointed.

"Are we gonna hightail it out of this hell?"

"Shut up and run."

Boozer galloped along blindly. "I don't see nothing, goddess."

She jabbed her finger toward a sight that only she could see. "Do as I say! Speed it up!"

Boozer brought his fur-covered knees up higher to add power to his fierce gallop.

"Faster!" she demanded. "Stop lollygagging, you clumsy oaf."

Boozer increased his speed, looking down at Eris in astonishment when his bare hooves touched on something smooth and cool. "Hot damn!" he exclaimed, excited as he looked down at his hoofed feet, expecting to see something reminiscent from his earthly existence.

But his hooves were still embedded in soot and obsidian. Confused, he arched a scraggly eyebrow. "Are we still in hell?"

"No time for questions, numbskull. Run! Hurry, we're almost there. Make haste before that damned portal closes up on us."

Suddenly, Eris and Boozer inhaled air…fresh night air.

"We made it."

Boozer looked around. "It don't look we're in Jackson. But we're damn sure outta hell." He lowered Eris's bare feet to cool planks of wood.

Bathed in moonlight, Eris and Boozer joined hands and launched into a macabre jig, both butt-naked, howling with malicious pleasure as they danced on Piper's Bridge.

21

Kissed all over and sexed in numerous positions, Jen was finally satisfied. After three badly needed and deeply appreciated orgasms, she fell asleep wearing a contented smile. A few hours later, she opened her eyes. Momentarily startled, she blinked at the darkness inside the unfamiliar room.

Though still asleep, Rome cuddled closer, comforting her as if he sensed her confusion. The musky aroma she inhaled was Rome's own natural scent and it was intoxicatingly arousing, but Jen kept her hands from roaming along his strong, athletic body. She smiled and caressed the top of his hand.

Her eyes searched and set on the red digits of the clock. Four a.m. She sprang upright. She glanced at prince charming sleeping next to her, hoping she didn't jolt him out of what looked like a peaceful sleep.

Hopefully, she could rejoin him under the covers. It all depended. Stretching her hand down to the floor, she picked up her handbag and routed around until she located her cell.

She pressed a button, lighting up the small screen. No messages. *Fantastic!* The senator was distracted by his clandestine affair and his wife was totally preoccupied with her campaign. Apparently neither of Ethan's parents knew or cared that Jen was not inside the Provost home.

Rome woke up and gawked at the clock. "Damn!" He looked at Jen, his eyes soft with concern. "I'm sorry, baby. I didn't mean to keep you out this late."

"What time do you get up for work?"

"Usually at six. But I don't have to work in the morning. My day off."

"Oh. Then, lie down," she whispered. "Let's sleep for a few more hours."

Rome didn't argue with Jen. He pulled her close and drifted back to sleep. Wrapped in his arms, warmed by his body heat, and lulled by the beat of his heart, Jen was quickly pulled back to dreamland.

When the alarm went off at six, they were both jolted awake, but Rome kept her locked in his embrace.

Jen hated having to extricate herself from his arms.

"I don't want to let you go," Rome muttered, reaching for her.

"The maid starts work at six and the cook gets there at seven. I could call Lizzy and ask her to cover for me…" Jen paused, trying to come up with a lie. "She could tell the senator that I went out for an early morning run."

Rome sat up, yawned, and then stretched. "No, we have to get dressed. It was selfish of me to keep you out so long. Get up, baby. I don't want you getting in trouble because of me."

"But I'm not ready to leave," Jen's said, her voice lilting in frustration.

"Can you get some time off tonight?" A devilish smile crept on his lips.

She shrugged. "I don't know. Depends. The senator is supposed to be conducting interviews today. Adding another nanny to the staff, so I can get a break."

"So, up until this point, you haven't been getting any time off?"

"No. But it didn't matter. I have some personal problems…"

She looked down, ashamed of the way she'd been kicked out of school. "To be honest, trying to work through my issues were more important than having an active social life."

"I can dig it." Rome patted her back. "It's okay. You don't have to talk about it."

God, how she adored this man. She wanted to stay in this bed with him forever. He was gorgeous; even with sleep in his eyes. She felt herself warming inside, becoming moist with need, and it was all she could do not to jump his bones right there on the spot. She took a deep breath and restrained herself. Maybe this wasn't a one-night stand.

"I'm not comfortable keeping you from that little boy you take care. So, get dressed and I'll give you a call later to find out if you can come out and play tonight. Okay?"

If she didn't think it would make her appear reckless and desperate, she would have picked up her cell phone, called the senator, and quit on the spot. But Rome was a keeper and she didn't want to scare him away.

Rome wound his fingers in her tangled hair. "I miss you already." Tilting her head, he kissed her.

Oh, my God, I'm in love!

With windblown hair, frizzled out and covering her head like a red helmet, Jen used her key and let herself inside the house. She tried to creep toward the stairs, unnoticed by Lizzy. But Carmen entered the house a few moments later.

Carmen cleared her throat. Jen paused and turned around. "Am I seeing things or did you get dropped off outside the gate by a man driving a blue truck?"

"Shh." Jen held a finger to her lips. "It's personal."

Carrying a dustpan filled with shattered glass, Lizzy came out of the senator's study, brows furrowed in curiosity. "You've been out all night?" Lizzy asked Jen.

"I'm grown. God, you two act like I committed a crime."

Jen went into the dining room and sat down, prepared for an interrogation.

"Who's been watching the little terror?" Carmen inquired.

"No one. He dressed himself and he's sitting in front of that contraption, staring at bridges. I know this sounds strange, but the grumpy little boy seems...sort of cheerful," Lizzy said, scratching her head.

Carmen gave a big hearty laugh. "Maybe he's happy that he didn't have to put up with his scheduled tinkle time. He might be sitting in a puddle of urine...happy as a lark."

Jen sighed at the thought of having to deal with Ethan's incontinence. She instantly switched her thoughts to her new romance.

"Aren't you anxious to find out if he peed his pants while you were out gallivanting with your mystery man?"

"For your information, the senator is going to interview nannies today. Someone else is going to have to deal with Ethan's tinkle time," Jen informed with a giggle.

"They're replacing you?" Lizzy frowned at the thought of a new personality in the household.

"No. The new nanny will be part-time. A fill-in so I can have some time off."

Lizzy chuckled. "Ah! So, you need some time off to be with your new boyfriend, huh?" She nudged Jen with her elbow.

"Ow!" Jen grabbed her arm playfully.

"Stop fooling around. My elbow didn't hurt you."

"Thank goodness your bony little elbow is cushioned by that heavy wool sweater. Otherwise you could have stabbed her," Carmen chimed in, laughing. Lizzy and Jen laughed. For the first time since Jen had started working for the Provosts, there was genuine fun and laughter inside the solemn home. Of course, her rendezvous with Rome had a great deal to do with her cheerful mood.

"So…what's the story? You got a secret lover?" Carmen pried.

Jen rolled her eyes upward. "I'm not telling."

"Look at you. You're blushing. And you have a glow." Carmen looked at Lizzy. "She's glowing, isn't she?"

Lizzy smiled and nodded. "You can trust us," Lizzy prompted. "By the way," she said in a lowered voice, "Jen's not the only one in this house with a secret lover." Lizzy pointed to the ceiling. "A woman is in bed with the senator," she whispered.

Carmen's brows knit together in disapproval. Aghast, she shook her head. "Sinful," she said quietly and then made the sign of the cross.

"She stayed overnight?" Jen queried.

"Apparently. She's in there with him. And they've been pretty noisy." Lizzy grimaced.

"Disgraceful. He has a child in this home."

Lizzy and Jen gawked at Carmen, surprised that she was defending Ethan's honor when she usually complained that he was possessed.

"It's not the boy's fault that he's possessed," Carmen said, responding to the looks she was getting. "Instead of burying their heads in the sand, his parents should have converted to Catholicism, had the child christened, and then, if that didn't work, they could have asked the priest to call in an exorcist."

Lizzy defended the senator. "His wife neglects him something terrible and a man has his needs."

"Mrs. Provost is a piece of work. Very ambitious, but I don't think she's out on the campaign trail sleeping with other men. That woman may be a lot of terrible things, but she's not an adulterer. She respects the sanctity of marriage. I'm shocked at the senator. He seemed like such a noble man."

"You know, guys…it's really not our business," Jen piped in. "I'm going to bring Ethan down for breakfast. Don't worry, Carmen. I'll fix him something to eat."

"You can't cook." Tying on her apron, Carmen placed a hand on her hip. "I don't want you fooling around in my kitchen."

"You're stressed and I don't want to add to it." Actually, Jen was floating on air over Rome and she didn't mind taking on the extra chore of preparing Ethan's breakfast. In fact, she'd be daydreaming about the passionate love they'd made last night while Ethan fiddled with his food.

"I'm not stressed. I'm disappointed in Senator Provost. Committing adultery in his own home," Carmen muttered.

Lizzy had been holding the dustpan throughout the entire conversation. She finally went into the kitchen and emptied it. "Oh, get off your high horse, Carmen. The senator is entitled to a fling or two. Ms. Provost might not be cheating with another man, but that woman is having a love affair with the entire country."

"She's not violating the sanctity of her marriage," Carmen insisted.

Jen rose to her feet. "You two go right ahead and debate the issue. I'm going to check on Ethan. What time should I bring him down for breakfast, Carmen?"

"I'm not sure." Carmen threw up her hands, disgustedly.

Jen gave her a perplexed look.

"If I'm ordered to whip up a fancy breakfast for the senator and his trollop, I won't have time to place a variety of selections in front of that finicky boy."

No longer in a playful mood, Carmen grumbled as she peered inside the fridge.

22

"Hi, buddy," Jen said to the back of Ethan's head. Only yesterday, the eerie little guy had peed on her and here she was calling him "buddy." She shrugged. *Love makes you do and say crazy things.* "Hungry?"

She was about to lift him out of his swivel chair, and then pat his bottom to check if he'd had an accident, but her cell phone began to vibrate. Forgetting all about Ethan's appetite and tinkle time, she breezed out of his bedroom and headed for her own, groping inside her pocketbook to grab her phone.

"Hi," she said breathily, without checking the caller ID.

"Jennifer, I understand that Daniel is going to be interviewing nannies…"

Ew! It was Catherine. She'd been expecting to hear Rome's sexy voice; not Catherine's testy tone. "Good morning, Ms. Provost. I think the agency is sending someone over today."

"You think?"

"I didn't schedule the appointment, I believe the senator did. You'll have to speak to him," Jen said with a little edge to her voice. She was sick of being bullied by her employer. *If you can tear him away from the blonde bombshell,* Jen thought with a smirk.

She felt feisty. That good loving she'd gotten was the perfect antidote for dealing with Catherine's attitude problem. Jen wasn't in the mood to tolerate the woman's bitchiness and she was no longer willing to be her personal punching bag. She didn't want that job in the senator's office.

Not anymore. In due time, she was going to face her parents and tell them what had happened at school. This household was a nightmare and was driving her crazy. Being with Rome made her realize that there was a lot of happiness out in the world, but she wouldn't find it if she continued to hide out in this nuthouse.

"Are you there, Jennifer?" Catherine snapped.

"Yes, I'm here."

"Then, say something."

Jen pointedly remained silent. Catherine couldn't intimidate her anymore. It was a small victory when she heard Catherine sigh in frustration. "Look, I can't get the senator on the phone. Lizzy said he's sleeping in. Would you please knock on his bedroom door and tell him that I insist that he pick up his phone?"

"Uh…"

"This is so exceedingly frustrating. Listen, Jennifer, I want you to bang on his bedroom door, barge in, and hand him your cell. My schedule is insane; I don't have time to wait for his return call. I need to speak to him right now."

"Not a problem," Jen said, deliberately sounding as cavalier as she felt. *Good sex is the remedy for all of life's problems*, she thought to herself. Without a care, she trekked down the long corridor and knocked sharply on door. "Senator Provost," she called.

"Barge in!" Catherine hissed into the phone. Jen ignored her. She didn't want to witness him and the dirty blonde in a compromising position.

"Senator Provost." She knocked again. "There's no answer," she told Catherine.

"Young lady…open that door right now and place your phone against my husband's ear." Catherine was seething.

With a shrug, Jen finally opened the door. The bedroom was empty. No senator and no dirty blonde paramour. But from the looks of things, they'd been pretty busy. The exquisite bedding was tangled and hanging off of the bed. Wine was spilled on the carpet and smudges of chocolate were everywhere! On the pillows cases, the headboard, the walls, the telephone, and the lampshade. My, my! Blondie was seriously trying to wreck the Provosts' home.

"He's not here, Ms. Provost."

"Then he must be downstairs. Go see if he's having breakfast."

Nothing could ruffle Jen's feathers. She really didn't care where the senator was hiding but, humoring his wife, she trotted down the stairs and was greeted by the sight of Lizzy and Carmen pointing to the front door, miming the words, "He's gone!" The senator and his floozy had executed a great escape.

"Ms. Provost, the senator has already left the house. I had no idea. Sorry you missed him. Maybe you can try his cell—" Click! Catherine hung up on Jen. Jen pulled the phone from her ear, and then looked at it in astonishment. "She hung up on me!"

Lizzy and Jen broke out into hysterical laughter. And even sanctimonious Carmen couldn't help from joining in. The senator had pulled a fast one on his wife and he was going to have hell to pay.

The phone she clutched beeped. She glanced at the screen and smiled at Rome's text: *Call when you get a minute.*

Running up the stairs, she stopped and looked over her shoulder. "By the way, Lizzy. I hate to break the news to you, but you have a heck of a surprise waiting for you in the senator's room."

Lizzy's shoulders slumped like it was the end of the world. "Take lots of cleaning spray in there with you," Jen said with a devilish giggle.

"She sure is a comedienne today," Carmen observed with a wry smile. "I think I liked her better before she fell in love."

Lizzy mumbled discontentedly, with spray cleaner in hand as she climbed the stairs.

Jen didn't have the heart to tell the poor woman she was going to need a bucket of soapy water as well. She'd soon find out and Jen had a pressing personal matter to attend to. Standing outside Ethan's bedroom, she sent Rome a text:

Can't talk right now. Have 2 give the kid his breakfast and that can be a really long, torturous ordeal.

Rome and Jen texted back and forth:

I'm going to try to make you forget the ordeal. Can you come out 2nite?

Not sure if I can get away. I'm going to try.

I hope so. I miss u.

Oh, yeah? What do u miss?

I miss the feeling of your soft skin laying next 2 me. I miss holding you in my arms and I miss the tickly sensation when your hair brushes against my chest. I even miss listening to you snore. LOL

I don't snore.

I wouldn't lie. You snore real cute. Do you miss me?

Of course. I miss your kisses. Being held in your arms. You make me feel protected and warm. Wow! I don't' think I can get thru this nite w/out seeing u. BRB! I'm going to ask the maid if she'll fill in for me 2nite.

Jen stepped inside Ethan's bedroom and walked over to his desk, but carefully avoided looking at the screen. She didn't want any ghostly images to ruin her good mood.

"Come on, buddy, it's time for breakfast. Feel like having

some waffles? How about a bowl of cereal? Or maybe you could munch on a breakfast bar," she rattled on. "Yeah, a strawberry breakfast bar is really yummy. Easy to handle and nutritious," she said and then headed for the doorway.

"You just stay put and I'll bring up your breakfast snack," Jen said, hoping Ethan didn't make her jump out of her skin by giving her a verbal response. She rushed out of his bedroom and hurried downstairs.

Jen was surprised to find Lizzy in the kitchen, seated at the banquette, and thumbing leisurely through a gossip magazine. "Did you see that big chocolate mess the senator and the boob-job blonde left behind?"

"Sure did," Lizzy answered lazily and then turned another glossy page.

Carmen, in the midst of a hot flash, held her personal battery-operated fan up to her face with one hand and held a fork in the other hand, turning over a few strips of bacon that was sizzling in a frying pan.

"I hope that boy has an appetite. The food that gets wasted in this house could feed all the starving children in the world," Carmen complained. She covered the frying pan, pressed some buttons to reduce the heat and went and plopped down on the banquette next to Lizzy. Perspiring badly, Carmen threw her head back and cooled her neck with the breeze from the little fan.

Lizzy cut an eye at Carmen. "Why don't you take medication?"

"And give myself cancer. No, thank you."

"Go ahead and suffer then. Suit yourself." Lizzy buried her face in the shiny pages.

Lizzy was such a hard worker and neat freak, Jen couldn't understand why she wasn't upstairs tackling the senator's chocolate-smeared bedroom. "If you saw the messy bedroom, how come you're down here, chillin'?" Jen teased, mimicking the casual way Rome spoke.

"I'll get to it in due time." Lizzy sucked her teeth. "That hussy should be ashamed of herself. She used to be Ethan's nanny. She has a lot of gall coming in here, sleeping with the senator, and leaving a trail of nastiness for me to clean up."

"Anyway, Ms. Hot Flashing is the one who needs to be chilling." Lizzy nodded her head toward Carmen. "Why does she work herself so hard when nobody's around?"

"Because I'm a good employee." Carmen's eyes roved to Jen. "More than I can say about some."

"What's that supposed to mean?" Jen asked.

"Didn't your mother teach you to carry yourself with dignity and respect?" Carmen fussed.

Jen didn't know what Carmen was talking about.

"Since when did you start staying out all night? I don't know who that fella is who dropped you off, but I do know that he kept you out all night. You should know better than to sleep with a man before you're married. Why buy the cow when you can get the milk free?" Carmen shook her head at Jen's reckless behavior. "At the rate you're going, you'll never get a wedding band—"

"Did the senator mention what time he's coming back," Jen broke in. She was not offended in the least by Carmen's old-fashioned notions. She was eager to set up her next date with Rome and didn't have time to listen to a long-winded sermon about her immorality.

"No, he didn't say one word," Lizzy answered. "He brushed past me and nodded like it was an ordinary thing for him to come down the stairs with a dirty blonde, fake-breasted, former nanny trailing behind him."

"She's his assistant, now," Jen said.

"She's a glorified hooker. She's getting something out of sleeping with him. Special favors…maybe she wants to move up the ladder to an even better-paying job. Shoot, she might be using sex to blackmail him. Don't be surprised if she turns up with a dress with a glob of his DNA. The senator is a lonely man, but he needs to be a little more discreet and careful."

"I guess he's not well-versed in the art of cheating," Jen offered.

"He'd better learn before he costs his wife this election," Carmen added after clicking a switch and turning off her hot flash fan. "Don't get old, Jen," she cautioned as if aging was something Jen could opt out of. "All this perspiring is a pain in the you know what."

"I told you what to do." Lizzy pointed at Carmen as the woman ambled back over to the stove. "That one is such a martyr. Women don't have to suffer through menopause."

Carmen dismissed Lizzy with a brusque hand wave. "I'm not risking my health. I'm going to have to ride this thing out."

"I don't recall Jen and I agreeing to take that ride with you. We're sick of feeling the breeze of that little fan, and don't think we don't feel the chill every time you throw open a window."

"Oh, that little bit of air doesn't hurt you."

"I'm anemic." Lizzy tightened her wool sweater around her frail body. "That chill goes straight to my bones."

Jen smile warmly at the two women. "You two are comical. I'm realizing how much I love both of you; even with all your back-and-forth bickering. You're both real cool peeps."

"We're what?" Carmen asked, frowning. "That new fella you slept with is a real bad influence on you. I can tell by the way you're talking.

"He's really nice. You're gonna love him. He's a police officer and I can't wait to introduce you both to him," Jen gushed.

Carmen brightened. "A police officer? Then there might be some hope. It'll only take me a few minutes of conversation to know whether or not he's on the up and up." She winked at Jen. "By the way, breakfast will be ready in a few minutes. You can bring down the little holy terror. I'll set up his booster seat."

"Actually, Ethan's not having a hot meal this morning. He's having a few cereal bars in his room."

Carmen rolled her eyes to the ceiling. "Thanks for getting around to telling me. I could have saved myself this trouble. It's a crime, the way food gets wasted around here. With all the poor starving children—"

"Pile it on a plate. I'll eat it," Lizzy placated to shut Carmen up. Carmen had a thing about wasting food and would go on and on endlessly.

Jen got the cereal bars out of the cabinet and took them up to Ethan. She didn't say a word and didn't look at the computer screen. She set the bars on the desk and whisked out of his bedroom.

Back in her bedroom, she texted Rome: *What time is our early dinner?*

Seconds later, he responded. *Six-thirty.*

Okay. Pick me up outside the gate.

He responded with a smiley face, which of course made Jen smile. She didn't have a plan, but was determined to enjoy Rome's company for the second night in a row. If she weren't encumbered with Ethan, she'd be able to run wild with her new man.

Wow, did she just call Rome, her man? Yeah, she did. That's how he made her feel. Like they were an official couple, involved in a committed relationship. She appreciated that he wasn't playing any head games. The idea of seeing him tonight was so exciting, she called the senator's cell without even bothering to rehearse what she'd say.

"Hi, Senator Provost. It's Jen. Sorry to disturb you. Listen, I know you were planning on interviewing nannies—"

"Gee! I'm so sorry. It completely slipped my mind."

"Well, I was wondering if you could pitch in tonight. I really need to get out for a few hours."

"Uh, sure, it's the least I can do. I guess." Senator Provost didn't sound very enthusiastic with the idea of being saddled with his son for a few hours.

"I'm leaving at six-thirty and I'll be back by nine. Is that okay?"

"Yeah, that's fine. You deserve a break. Ask Lizzy or Carmen to stay over until I get in tonight. I'll pay double time."

Yes! Another hot date! Jen wanted to leap up and pump her fist in the air, but she maintained a calm demeanor and professional tone. "Thank you, Senator Provost." Now she had to go downstairs and deliver the dreadful news to Lizzy and Carmen that one of them would have to look after Ethan until the senator came home.

Senator Provost had no idea that neither woman would be excited about the extra pay. If it weren't for the fact that they couldn't afford to up and quit, both women would flat out refuse to babysit Ethan; despite the generous overtime the senator was offering.

23

It was Jen's first time at The Continental Restaurant and Martini Bar, one of the popular hot spots in the trendy Old City section of Philadelphia. The interior was chic and eye-catching. Jen couldn't take her eyes off of the hanging olive-shaped halogen lamps pierced with huge toothpicks.

"Those olive-shaped lights. Cool idea," Jen remarked, as her eyes flitted around, delightedly taking in the neo-diner atmosphere.

"If you think this is interesting, you should see the upstairs. Hanging basket chairs and pony chairs situated around the bar. And you're expected to saddle up." He winked.

"Sounds fun, but I'll pass on the pony chairs. Wouldn't want to fall off my horse, if I drink too much."

Jen and Rome chose to sit inside one of the retro-décor booths. Their waitress handed them rainbow-decorated menus.

"Even the menu is gorgeous. It looks like a work of art," Jen whispered. "If I had my own place, I'd frame this menu and proudly display it in my kitchen."

"Do you want me to ask if you can have a menu?"

"No! I'd be mortified. Just because I'm from the sticks doesn't mean I have to advertise it by asking for a menu like a googly-eyed tourist."

"I'm just saying…if you want a menu, I'll get you one."

"And do what with it? I don't have a kitchen," she said, laughing. "Everything here is so high-end, yet it's not pretentious or stuffy. I love it. Thank you for bringing me here, Rome."

"My pleasure, Pretty Red. Hey, that's what I'm going to start calling you…Pretty Red."

Jen blushed; she couldn't help it.

"They have fifteen different kinds of martinis. After all that irrational reasoning I came up with last night…talking about terrorist plots and all those conspiracy theories, I figured we'd leave the hard liquor alone and have some frilly, fun drinks tonight."

"I thought you were serious."

"Hell, no! That was the liquor talking."

Jen's eyes widened in grave concern. "Oh, shit. So, we're back to square one? That naked woman is a real ghost?"

"More than likely. But I told you the dead can't hurt anyone. She's probably lost and confused. If I see her running on Piper's Bridge again, I'm going to park the squad car, get out, and have a talk with her…see if I can help her get to where she's trying to go."

"I thought you said the spirits never talk to you."

"Not with words. It's more like a mental thing. I get a feeling of what's going on with them. Sometimes they keep going and sometimes they look scared and lost. When they look scared, I tell them to find the light."

"How'd you learn how to deal with them?"

"My grandma. She read up on life after death and she told me they're all trying to get to the light."

"Is the light God? Are they trying to find their way to heaven?"

"I hope that's where they're headed. I don't know all the answers, but they usually look relieved when I mention the light and they go on their way."

"But you said they look scared. Our ghost lady does not look scared. She looks furious."

Rome laughed. "Yeah, she's pretty fired up about something. She's probably mad because she's lost...that's why she does that confused running thing. A few steps forward, then whips around and starts heading in the other direction."

"I honestly can't handle seeing her again. So if you bump into her while you're out patrolling the area, please make sure you give her good directions. That lady is in desperate need of some white light."

"I think she's gone already. She's the first spirit I've seen more than once."

"But I saw her twice, also," Jen reminded, looking worried. "I saw her on the bridge and before that, I saw her on Ethan's computer. You've got to admit, there's something weird about all this."

"Hey, it's not the dead we have to worry about. They can't hurt us," Rome reassured. "She's gone back to wherever she came from or she finally found her way to wherever she was going."

"How do you know?"

"I can feel it."

After their meal, Jen and Rome sipped their second round of fruity martinis and listened to the soft music in the background. Jen stole a glance at her watch. Her face completely stoic, no one could tell that she was horrified that so much time had flown by.

She was already fifteen minutes past her expected return time. She hated to have to end such a wonderful evening, but her nanny duties beckoned and she was going to have to call it a night real soon.

"So, you grew up around cornfields...what was that like?" Rome asked, seeming to have forgotten that she had to be back on her nanny job by nine.

"Boring. And like I said, the nearest neighbors were the Amish kids and they weren't allowed to play with me. They kept to themselves and worked all day."

"Sounds rough."

"I wouldn't call it rough, but I had a lonely childhood. Just my folks and me. Oh, and Pogo, the family dog. Pogo wasn't much fun, though. He was old and cranky, ever since I can remember. Blind in one eye, crippled, and could barely run."

Rome started laughing. "Aw, damn. Excuse me, but the way you're saying it is really funny."

"I'm serious. Pogo would growl and even bite me whenever I tried to play with him."

Rome leaned over and gave her doubting look. "Your own dog bit you and your parents didn't have it put to sleep?"

"No. They loved Pogo and blamed me for being too rough. He belonged to my dad. He had Pogo for years before he had me."

"That's fucked up, that they let that dog bite you. I woulda shot that mutt if he bit my baby girl." Rome scowled, his voice filled with fury.

"Do you have a daughter?"

"No, but I'm just saying. If I did, I'd shoot a muthafuckin dog for sinking its teeth into a child of mine."

Jen started laughing. "You're taking it the wrong way and getting all worked up and mad. I wasn't abused by Pogo. I was raised to be gentle with him because he was sickly and cranky. He never bit me hard enough to break my skin and he certainly never attacked me like a pit bull gone wild. He mainly snarled and snapped."

"Oh. All right. So, what about school? Didn't you have friends at school?"

"I had a few white friends but they didn't live nearby. Our community is rural...people live miles and miles apart. There weren't too many black kids in our neck of the woods and certainly none with fire-red hair." She touched her hair, which she'd painstakingly blow-dried for her hot date. "I got teased a lot."

"Why?"

"For being different."

"I love your hair."

"You do?"

"Yeah." He looked at her bone straight hair and frowned. "I even like it slicked down the way you're wearing it tonight."

"I went through a lot of trouble working on my hair. Just for you!"

"Don't do me any more favors. I like it natural—wild and untamed."

Jen scrunched up her nose. "Are you serious? You like my hair when it's looking like barbed wire."

"Barbed wire?"

"That's how my mother always referred to it."

"I think your hair is beautiful."

"Yeah, I guess," she agreed, squirming at the compliment. "But it's too much work to keep it looking this way."

"It's beautiful either natural or straight, all right? But I like it when it's all fuzzy and windblown like it was yesterday."

Jen looked down; her cheeks flushing.

"Your red hair is beautiful and unique and so are you."

She couldn't keep her head down forever, but his compliments were putting such a gigantic smile on her face and she was too ashamed to look up. "Thank you," she muttered.

"Look at you, all blushing. That's cute. There's nothing fake about you, Jen. I dig you. Now, will you please look up?"

"Okay, but you have to promise me…no more compliments. I'm not used to getting too much praise for my looks. That's enough for one night," she said, laughing.

"No, you can't stop me from speaking my mind. You're beautiful and you need to know it. Mothers can seriously mess up a kid's self-esteem."

"My mom didn't mean any harm," Jen said, finally looking up as she came to her mother's defense. "I have a ton of hair and it gets impossibly tangled and it's a lot to handle when it gets wet."

Rome looked at her. "No offense to your mom, but she has you thinking you need to waste valuable time straightening out that crazy curly hair that I happen to enjoy the challenge of running my fingers through."

Smiling, Jen shook her mane of temporarily soft tresses. "Sorry." She laughed.

"Seriously, though. Your hair looks good in whichever style you wear it." He gave her a big, approving smile.

"Thank you. Now, tell me about *your* childhood. Which part of Philly did you grow up?"

His sunny expression darkened. "I spent a lot of time at my grandma's house."

"How come?"

"My grandma is really the only mother figure I ever had in my life."

"What happened to your real mom?" Jen asked, recalling that he'd mentioned his mother the night before, but hadn't gone into any details.

Rome shifted in his chair. His facial muscles tensed and Jen braced herself to hear about a tragic death—from cancer—or a brutal and unsolved murder. Maybe that's why he'd selected law enforcement as a career, Jen thought…to avenge his mother's death.

Rome smiled sadly. "I have two mothers, but neither one of them really wanted me."

Jen had to use great restraint to keep her jaw from dropping open. "What do you mean?"

His mouth tightened into that sad smile again. Jen wanted to reach across the table and smother him with her inexperienced version of a motherly hug. "Well, there's my father's wife, Sylvia. Her name is on my birth certificate. And then there's my birth mother, Twyla, who paid a large sum of money to get her name expunged from all records associated with me."

With this shocking newsflash, Jen lost control. Her jaw dropped wide open and remained in that unhinged state. With her eyes wide and mouth agape, she held her breath and became very still as she waited for Rome to offer an explanation that would bring clarity to his sorrowful and bizarre beginnings.

24

Rome waved his hand in front of Jen's face, snapping her out of her stunned stupor.

She finally blinked, closed her mouth, and gulped. "*The* Twyla Tanning! The big star known as the Big Tee? She's your mother?"

Rome nodded.

"Wow! I heard the rumors that Tee had a child, but from what I read, I thought she had a girl...who'd be around—"

"Around my age—twenty-five," he said solemnly. "She wanted her career more than she wanted me. And unfortunately, my pops took the money without giving a shit about what that lie would do to his son." Breathing hard, he clenched his fist in anger.

"You don't have to talk about it—"

Rome gave a rueful laugh. "I want to talk about it. I've been keeping this bottled in for most of my life. Just like you, a confidentiality clause or some bullshit like that has kept me from opening my mouth. And the one time I slipped up...believe me, I learned it was wiser to keep my mouth shut."

"You signed an agreement?"

"Hell no. My father and his wife did all the signing for me; a few months before I was even born. They got paid big bucks to do it. Up until I was six years old, I thought Sylvia was my mother. But one day, after a big fight with my pops, I heard her talking to one of her friends over the phone. She said my pops *and* his son could both kiss her ass. She was sick of playing mommy to some other bitch's child."

Jen reached across the table and patted the top of his hand.

"I asked my grandma if I was some other bitch's child. My poor grandma didn't have anything to do with those decisions that were made and she told the truth about my parents. According to my grandma, Twyla and my pops were two teenaged recording artists trying to get a hit. Twyla got hers first. My pops never did. Twyla's big break happened when she was seventeen years old and six months' pregnant. It was too late for an abortion, so the bigwigs from her record label, along with her family, paid my pops to keep his mouth shut. My pops was eighteen. Too young and dumb and too damn greedy to refuse. In my opinion, he sold his soul…and offered up mine along with the deal." Rome's voice cracked with emotion.

"Where is your dad—still in Philly?"

"State pen."

"You're kidding! What for?"

"Bad checks."

"I thought he had a lot of money."

"Used to. He lived the life of a big baller, but the money stopped coming in when I turned eighteen."

"Do you visit him in prison?"

Rome grimaced. "Hell no. I don't owe him anything. Ain't no love lost between me and my old man."

"But he was only eighteen when you were born. He was a kid who made a big mistake."

"People are supposed to apologize after they realize they've made a mistake. My pops never even came close to saying he was sorry."

"Did he put any of that money aside for your future?"

Rome shook his head. "He didn't have to. Twyla took care of me." He paused. "Financially, I'm set for life. But everything isn't always about money. On the emotional side of things, I'm as broke as a joke." He laughed wryly. "Especially with my grandma gone."

"No other relatives?"

"No, my pops was an only child. No cousins or aunts or uncles on his side. It's just me now."

Now Jen felt guilty about the way she'd taken her parents' love for granted. Resented them for raising her in a boring, rural community. Trying to live at a faster pace in Philly was her way of rebelling.

Now Rome was pointing out that family love was really one of the most important things in life. She was definitely going to call her parents. After the Provosts hired a new nanny, she'd take a trip home. Invite Rome to meet her folks. Show him the cornfields. Hmm. Make love in the cornfields. She wondered if he'd be willing to try that.

"If you could see the situation from your mother's teenaged perspective, maybe you'd understand the decision she felt forced to make. Things were different twenty-five years ago. She had that squeaky clean image to live up to back then. After she turned twenty-one, she threw away that good girl image and became a sex symbol. When you think about it, the Big Tee persona, with all the surgery and the humongous boobs, seemed like an angry young person, mad at the world. She was probably furious because she'd listened to the people who forced her to give you away."

"She wasn't forced. She willingly went along with the decision. What kind of heartless person could give up their child and never look back because she doesn't want to tarnish her public image?"

"Probably more stars than we realize have made similar choices."

"None that I ever heard about. Everybody has heard about Twyla's abandoned daughter. Fucked-up part is that she doesn't have a daughter...she has me...a son."

"Have you ever met your mother?"

A shadow fell over Rome's face. "I met her once. A long time ago." His Adam's apple became visible, bobbing up and down as if something were caught in his throat—something really hard to swallow.

She'd unwittingly conjured a memory that Rome was having difficulty reliving. Jen didn't know what to do or say. She caressed his hand; her eyes filled with an apology for bringing up an unpleasant topic.

While staring at him, she started to see some of Twyla's features in his face. The features Big Tee possessed when she was a cherub-faced young woman. Before the outrageous breast implants, ribs removed, liposuction, and before she started allowing plastic surgeons to restructure her face. Today at forty-two years old, Twyla Tanning barely resembled her former self.

"What was she like?" Jen asked, filling the uncomfortable silence.

"Distant."

"Oh." Jen lowered her head, sorry she'd asked.

"The fucked-up thing is that if I had kept my mouth shut, I could have spared myself some additional pain, but when I was in the elementary school, my classmates were really feeling Twyla. The girls danced like her and tried to imitate her hairstyles. The boys...well suffice it to say, my mother was the fantasy of every little boy. One day, trying to get some props, I blurted out that Twyla Tanning was my real mother. And like I said, there aren't any birth records to prove it and I became a laughingstock."

"That's awful."

"Yeah, I know all about being the butt of jokes."

Jen touched her hair self-consciously. Her hair issues seemed so minor compared to what Rome had gone through and obviously, from his pained expression, he still hadn't made peace with his mother's abandonment.

"My grandma was furious about what I was going through. She tried to get her son...my pops...to get in touch with Twyla, but he refused to make waves. He wasn't trying to stop that gravy train he had coming in. Finally, my grandma took it upon herself to contact Twyla's people. After about six months or more, she finally got a call from my mother. It took a year of negotiating before she sent for me."

Jen smiled. "What did you two do together?"

He shrugged. "Nothing. She met with me in a hotel room. She came in looking beautiful, surrounded by bodyguards. She smiled at me and shook my hand like I was an underprivileged child who'd won a contest to spend five minutes with her. She didn't introduce me to her security team and I really wasn't sure if she actually knew I was her son. I mean...for real...she treated me like a fan. As she was breezing out the door, I told myself to yell, 'Mom,' just to make sure she hadn't mistaken me for one of her kiddy fans."

"Did you?"

His eyes hooded over. "No. I punked out. She left me with a hired nanny who was instructed to show me a good time."

Hit with a flash of memory, Jen recalled Rome telling her that he'd had a nanny for a couple of days, but she hadn't taken him seriously. "That was it? Your mother left you like with a stranger?"

"Yeah. She called my grandma and told her that she'd held up her end of the bargain—she met me. She told my grandma that if she continued to pester her, she would have her lawyers contact her—with a lawsuit that would cost her everything she owned."

"So, your grandma gave up?"

"What could she do? She couldn't force my mother to love me? She held up her end of the bargain."

"Did you meet your relatives on your mom's side of the family?"

"No, she didn't introduce me to anybody." His voice broke again, revealing his immense pain.

"She sent me a birthday card for my eighteenth birthday. It was generic and didn't mention the word *son*. But she signed it, *Love, Tee*, and that card gave me the hope that one day when the fame and the beauty faded, maybe she'd come around and be a loving grandmother since she missed out on being a mom. It's a fantasy of mine," he said with a very sad smile.

His story was so sad; so unfair. Jen wished she could give that selfish Twyla Tanning a piece of her mind. Feeling helpless, she hung her head and joined Rome in silent sorrow.

"Now you know more about me than I've ever told a soul. And you know what, I feel much better. I feel purged."

Jen looked at her watch and made a face. "I have to get back. I promised the senator I'd be home by nine." Jen didn't miss the disappointment that shot across Rome's face.

"Aw, damn. You have to go?"

She nodded. "But after he hires the new nanny, I'll have a lot of extra time."

"It's cool. I understand. Just a little disappointed. I had a big surprise for you."

"What?"

"It's a surprise. I get off work at six tomorrow. Think you can get away?"

"I'm going to make it my business to get away. I want my surprise."

Leaving the restaurant, Rome put an arm around Jen. His hand slipped down and publicly caressed her butt. He caught himself and smiled that boyish smile of his. "When I'm around you, it's hard to keep my hands to myself."

25

Jen didn't have to use the key pad. The senator, impatiently waiting for her, pulled open the door.

"Sorry I'm late."

"It's okay, really. You deserve a lot more free time than a few hours. I hope you had an enjoyable evening." The senator seemed antsy, raking his fingers through his hair as he spoke.

"I had a very nice time," Jen said, noticing how ill-at-ease the senator seemed.

"Ethan's asleep. If you don't mind, I'd like to talk to you about something." He dragged his fingers down his face so severely, Jen was surprised there weren't welts left behind. God, she'd come home feeling good, but now she was starting to feel squirmy and anxious. He paced quickly toward his study. She had no idea what was on the senator's mind as she tagged along.

Inside the impressive, mahogany-walled room, lined with beautiful artwork, bookcases and leather-bound books, Senator Provost sat in the high-backed chair behind his desk. Jen took a seat in a plush upholstered chair opposite his desk.

Her hands folded in her lap, she politely waited for the senator to get down to business. Senator Provost was a handsome man, but being weak and totally henpecked detracted from his good looks.

As if he'd forgotten why he'd asked her into his study, he looked at her blankly for a few moments, then sprang suddenly to his feet. His expression was troubled. "Excuse me for a second." Jen nodded as he took rushed strides toward a locked mahogany cabinet.

While the senator searched his key ring, Jen allowed her mind to wander to the pleasant thought of Rome, wistfully recalling the sexy pat on her ass. Then she wondered what he had in mind as a surprise. She decided that she would have a surprise for him as well. She'd make it a really hot night.

Tomorrow was Halloween, the perfect occasion to dress like a slut. She'd awaken Rome's dirtiest fantasies when she took off her coat, revealing erotic lingerie. In keeping with the holiday, she'd experiment with makeup, going for a dramatic look: smoky eye shadow, a vibrant shade of blush to make her cheekbones pop, shimmering pink lip gloss, false lashes—the works.

But first, she'd have to plead with Lizzy and Carmen to keep an eye on Ethan while she dashed out to purchase some sexy undies. She imagined Rome's reaction when she entered his bedroom wearing a revealing negligee and a pair of four-inch, slutty stilettos.

To Jen's utter shock, the senator returned to his desk carrying a bottle of vodka. Once known as an excessive drinker, the senator had been sober for years. From what she could tell, he seemed sober the night of his dinner party.

What was the catalyst for this break in sobriety? Judging by the generous amount of alcohol he poured and chugged down in a matter of minutes, the senator had every intention of getting tanked tonight.

"I have to join my wife on the stump," he informed and guzzled more liquor.

Ah, so that's why he was drinking again.

"Unfortunately, I'm not going to be available to interview the nanny, so I've asked the agency to send their best candidate over."

Jen gave a half-hearted head nod. "Does Ms. Provost know about this?"

"No, and she's too busy to care."

"Okaaay…" Jen wasn't too sure about that. Catherine Provost would definitely want a dossier on a person taking up residence in her home.

"I asked for a live-in. The agency will handle the background check, the confidentiality agreement, and all that jazz." He waved his hand, as if dismissing the paperwork as a bunch of nonsense. "The new nanny can have the spare room next to yours."

Jen nodded again, picturing Carmen and Lizzy's reaction to the newest member of the household. If they treated her the way they'd treated Jen when she first started, the new nanny was in for a rough time.

"I have an early morning flight and won't be around to meet the woman, but I'm sure she'll be competent. I requested someone who's had experience with autistic children." He looked at Jen; took another swig. "I'll be with Catherine for the next few weeks. I'll try to make it home whenever possible. But it doesn't appear that I'll be here too often. Not until after that damned election," he grumbled.

So, it was true. The senator was jealous of his wife's meteoric rise. "Catherine and I will be in constant contact." He gave Jen a smile that was meant to be reassuring but failed miserably. He stood. "Have a good night, Jen. As you can see, I'm getting slosh-faced tonight." He held up the bottle of vodka and smiled at it like it was a dear friend.

Jen splashed water on her face and then dabbed it dry. She never wore makeup, but occasionally wore a little lip gloss. Looking in the mirror over the sink, she applied a neutral-tone lip gloss as a makeup trial for her hot date tomorrow night. She winked at her reflection.

When Rome saw the creamy shine on her lips, she wanted him to recognize it as a promise of extended oral sex. The blow-job she'd given him the night before was a sample. Now that she was feeling more confident, she planned to put a lip-suctioning on him that he'd never forget.

She gazed at her reflection. In her opinion, she wasn't pretty… her facial features didn't even add up to cute. But according to Rome, she was beautiful. Little goose bumps ran up her arms and she blushed in response to the memory of his compliment.

Being with Rome was dizzyingly blissful. In less than twenty-four hours, she'd join him in his bedroom and lathe his goodies with her tongue. He didn't seem real comfortable with her taking on a sexually aggressive role, but he was flattered. She could tell. Maybe tomorrow, she'd switch it up and role play as a submissive.

She wondered how he'd handle that. Would he be embarrassed if she asked him to arrest her because she was sexually dangerous? Jen giggled at the thought. But she seriously wanted to bathe his entire body with her tongue. The man was delicious… scrumptious. She wanted to lick him all over from head to toe.

She gave herself one last look and blinked in surprise. There was a shadow cast over her reflection. She took in a loud, startled breath and spun around in a panic; her heartbeat accelerating at a frenzied pace.

Her wide-stretched eyes swept back and forth in apprehension. She was alone. So what had cast the shadow? She jerked her head toward the mirror again. The dark blurry thing was still there. Only larger and more menacing.

Jen cringed.

Then it moved.

"Oh, God!" The words came out in a two pitiful squeaks. Instinctively she looked upward, yanking her head back so hard it was a wonder she hadn't snapped her neck.

A dark figure was crouched on the skylight. It was the worst thing she could have ever imagined seeing.

She gasped and then covered her mouth on impulse, so stunned her breath felt trapped in her lungs, choking off a scream. Something ghoulish and inhuman was grinning down at her. Salivating hungrily, its eyes burning with unrestrained yearning, as it yanked on the latch—noisily and impatiently trying to get in.

Her hand fell away and her mouth opened in a silent scream. Every nerve in her body tightened in apprehension. Her limbs felt locked—paralyzed with fear.

Frozen, her gaze was riveted to the skylight.

Until the shadowy creature growled.

Surely this wasn't happening. *I'm having a bad dream. This couldn't possibly be real*, she told herself as she blinked her eyes in disbelief. Under the circumstances, being paralyzed with fear and all, her lashes were the only thing operating, and rapid blinking was the best she could do to try and wake herself up from the nightmare.

The creature snarled, its claws scraping metal, scratching and tugging hard on the handle, and finally lifting the glass dome, admitting a stream of chilled night air.

Jen's eyes became enlarged with fear. Fueled by increasing spasms of terror, she opened her mouth wide, gulped in a burst of air and, at last, she forced out a scream.

The skylight slammed closed.

"Jen!" Senator Provost yelled from downstairs. His staggering footsteps seemed to be taking forever to make it up the stairs.

Standing in the doorway of Jen's private bathroom, Senator Provost squinted at her, and then tilted his head to one side and then the other, as if he could determine what had happened to her by looking at her from a variety of angles.

Too smashed to stand up straight, he leaned against the door-frame for support. "What's wrong? Sounded like you were being murdered." He stared at her. "Your face is completely drained of color. Why are you looking so grim? Did you see a spider? A mouse?" He grimaced, eyes darting around the bathroom.

"Somebody. I mean…some *thing* was—"

Too distraught to go on, she buried her face in her hands and gave into racking sobbing. Clumsily, the senator put his arms around her. He reeked of alcohol.

"Now, now. Is it a bad relationship? Forget about him; you're too good for the slime ball bastard. Don't worry; you'll find someone new. It's going to be all right." He tried to comfort Jen in a voice that was slurred.

The senator was drunk and didn't have a clue what he was talking about. Jen pulled out of his flimsy embrace and stared at him. Trembling, teeth chattering, and eyes tearing, she pointed a finger upward. "Something was up there."

His eyes followed but he saw nothing except the dark sky. "What was up there?"

She dared to take a peek. The atrocious thing was gone. "Th-there was some kind of creature lying across the skylight," she stammered. "It was staring down at me. Smiling this vicious smile and it had thick slobber spilling down its hairy cheeks. Ew! It was hideous."

"Jesus, are you sure?" He shot a wary glance upward.

"Yes, absolutely. I saw something grotesque and monstrous. It yanked the skylight open… That's when I screamed. I guess it ran off."

The senator frowned up at the skylight, his unsteady body leaning perilously as he strained to see if the thing that had frightened her was still up there. Jen followed the senator's gaze, nervously biting a fingernail.

"I don't see anything up there except the sky. It's dark, but there's nothing else. Just pitch-black darkness. Maybe if we add some fireworks, we can light up the night…" he raised both brows suggestively, attempting to calm her with levity and a bit of drunken flirtatiousness.

"This is serious, Senator Provost." She took a step back. "I really saw something up there." She shuddered. "Its face was waxen and covered with tufts of fur and it had hairy, clawed hands. It was gruesome. I wish that I could believe that some nutcase is on the loose, but that thing in the skylight was not completely human."

"Not *completely* human?" Senator Provost erupted into a burst of drunken laughter. "Then we have nothing to worry about."

"No. I meant…the way it was snarling like an animal, it seemed barely human."

Suddenly amorous in his intoxicated state, the senator pulled Jen into his arms and smoothed her hair. His lustful affection was creepy. Struck with an idea, she looked at the senator and desperately clutched his shirt. "We should call the police."

Consolingly, he patted her back, but only briefly. Meeting her gaze, he gave her a patient smile and amazingly, he appeared suddenly sober at the mention of the police being called.

"Honestly, Jen…you'd have to have a two-part extension ladder to get up on that roof and no one could climb up there without making a great deal of noise."

"I know what I saw," Jen insisted, gnawing on her fingernail. "I think I should talk to this police officer I recently met. Tell him what I saw."

"You can't go public with this!" The senator looked horrified.

"He's a friend. He'll come and investigate, but he'll keep it confidential."

Senator Provost's brows knit together. "That police officer will think you're off your rocker," he said pointedly. "Come on, Jen, it's merely your imagination. You're overworked and that's why, starting tomorrow, you're going to have some time off." The senator pasted a consoling smile on his lips.

Jen sighed helplessly.

"If it will make you feel better, I'll go outside and take a look around, but believe me, no one can get past the gate or get on the roof of this house unless we're talking about Spiderman."

His carriage erect, facial features serious, and actually looking somewhat noble, the senator said, "Go in Ethan's room and lock the door. I'll go inspect the grounds. I guarantee you, I'm not going to find a ladder hanging down from the roof," he teased, his jovial tone intended to calm her nerves.

"That thing I saw wouldn't need a ladder to get on top of the roof," she moaned. "It probably flew up there…like a vampire."

He chuckled as if she were a simple-minded child.

Jen had always considered the senator to be a pretty decent guy. And despite his untoward advances, which she totally blamed on the alcohol, she still thought pretty highly of him. It seemed a cruel and selfish act to allow him to go outside without a weapon. He needed a gun…or maybe a cross and some garlic… he needed some type of defense because he definitely was no match for what was out there lurking in the shadows. She wanted to grab the senator; beg him to let the proper authorities handle the dangerous matter. But he whirled around and dashed out of the bathroom. There was no way to keep him from running into harm's way when he refused to take her seriously.

Biting her nail down to the quick, her eyes traveled back to the skylight. There was no moon in sight. Utter and complete darkness. The hairs on the back of her neck stood up. Afraid to be alone, Jen rushed from the bathroom, crossed into her bedroom, and followed the senator out into the hall—far from the skylight and the disturbing, moonless night.

"Senator Provost."

"Be right back," he responded. Showing a lack of fear, he whistled as he made his way down the stairs. Seconds later, beeping sounds indicated he was disarming the security system and an electronic voice announced that the front door had opened.

Hardly able to breathe, Jen didn't go and lock herself inside Ethan's room. She was too scared to move. Murmuring a prayer, she waited.

26

His chest rose and fell as he lay in bed appearing asleep. Entranced, the child communicated with Eris. "Did you really believe I'd set you free without conditions?"

"What are they?" Eris's voice was desperate. "We're roaming around, lost. And my physical form is starting to fade," she complained.

"Had you not disobeyed me, you'd be welcome inside the home where I stay, but you're so devious, Wicked One, I can't let you inside. You can't be trusted."

"Not true," she protested.

"Why'd you bring that oafish ghoul?"

"For protection…against your…your trickery and deception."

"Ah! So his blunder on the roof was beneficial?"

"No." She cut an angry eye at Boozer. "He's not comfortable in his skin. He needs more practice. Soon, he'll learn to maneuver in human form."

"Speaking of human form… Yours is not holding up very well."

She cast a worried glance downward. Her legs had practically disappeared. They were transparent. She let out a frightened yelp. "It's happening so fast, you have to help me, Xavier!"

A wheezing sound filled the boy's bedroom. But the telepathic sound that reached Eris's ears was a harsh chortle, a clear indication that her dire predicament provided the demon child with extreme and wicked pleasure.

She held out her arms and witnessed the fading process that was beginning at her fingertips and swiftly moving down the length of fingers and to her wrists. "Do something, Xavier!"

"I'm at a loss," Xavier replied.

She glared at Boozer; her eyes roving up and down his dark frame. "His body is still intact. Why isn't he fading, too?"

Boozer stepped backward as if her words might curse his human form and cause him to start fading as well.

"Your oaf was once human. You, my dear, are a goddess. Isn't that what you proudly proclaim?"

"I am a goddess."

"What a pity. Your goddess status doesn't seem to serve you well on the Earth Realm. If you recall, you always had trouble keeping your human form."

"You're right and I need human essence to survive. Help me, Xavier. There's a girl in there with you. I need her. Get me that girl!"

"Get her yourself," Xavier taunted.

"Boozer tried! He couldn't get in."

"And you believed him? Isn't he a known thief? A murderous rapist and liar?"

Eris narrowed an eye. "What happened up on the roof?" she asked Boozer. "You told me you couldn't get in?"

"The girl screamed."

"So what?"

"When womenfolk scream, men come running to save 'em. If I woulda had a chance, I woulda choked her scrawny neck to shut her face up!"

"You are despicable. I brought you here to help me, not to change my predicament from bad to worse."

"I coulda got in. But that there girl wouldn't keep her trap shut." Boozer lowered his head in contrition.

Eris tried to punch him, but her hands had vanished. "You deceitful, lying piece of crud. Wait until I get my hands on you. I'm going to…" She tried to think of human punishment and recalled what the slave master's wife had done to her during her slave incarnation. "I'm going to string you up and whip you good. Nine and thirty lashes aren't enough for the likes of you."

"That's enough bickering," Xavier groused. "You're wasting time. You brought that miserable oaf without permission. Dispense punishment later; right now you need to concentrate on getting inside the house."

"How?"

"The front door has been left ajar. Slip inside. Make haste! Do it now, while that idiot who thinks he's my father is outside exploring the grounds in search of a prowler." Heavy wheezing filled the child's bedroom as Xavier snickered.

Eris and Boozer began slithering across the lawn, rustling the autumn foliage, but were quiet enough not to alert the man. Moments later, they slid through the partially opened door.

Inside the foyer, going in confused circles, Eris and Boozer bumped into walls and crashed into each other.

"Hurry!" Xavier shouted. "Walk straight ahead. Swiftly!"

They obeyed. Naked and crouched, the pair of unsightly ghouls skittered along, following Xavier's directions.

"Through the pantry. Turn right."

Boozer turned left and banged into a steel rack. It clanged violently.

"Be quiet!" Xavier hissed. "Tell that oaf of yours to tread lightly."

Without the assistance of feet, Eris crept along slowly and unsteadily. Boozer, on the other hand, possessing both sets of limbs, should have handled the task with ease. But he didn't. He slipped and slid and skidded around the high-polished floors like a car spinning out of control on a road covered with ice.

Xavier sucked his teeth at the spectacle. "Open that door on the left. Take the stairs. And hide out in the wine cellar. Quickly. Scurry, you beasts. The man is returning. Get out of sight."

Tiptoeing down the stairs, Boozer sniffed the air, taking in the smell of wine. He licked his lips and smiled in delight at the thought of being confined with libations.

Disgusted at Boozer's outward show of lust, Eris tried to kick him in the shin, but her transparent foot went straight through bone and flesh. *Drats!* "No drinking, Boozer! You have lots of work to do."

"Aw, why you wanna be like that? It's been so long. I only want a little taste."

"No! You have to stay sober until we get my body repaired." With great disgust, she perused her vanishing body parts.

Brooding, Boozer poked out his lips. He gripped his chin, his claw-like fingernails furiously digging into his flesh.

Jen listened intently, thinking she heard movement down-stairs. When she heard an unmistakable clang, her heart leapt. She ran inside her bedroom quickly clicking the lock on the door. She was too frightened to come out of her room and trek down the hall to check on Ethan. His father would have to handle that task.

Shaking in terror, she looked around for some type of pro-tection. The only thing that could possibly serve as a weapon was a rather weighty alarm clock, which she snatched up, planning to wing it like a baseball at the misshapen head of that waxen-faced monster. She kept her eyes fixed on her doorknob, her heart knocking inside her chest as she imagined the beast turning the knob and then banging against the door, trying to force its way inside her bedroom.

Oh, God. I need to talk to Rome. She raced across the room to grab her cell phone. She had to let Rome know what had happened. He'd believe her.

Just before she picked up the phone, there was soft rap on her door. "All clear," the senator said and knocked again—this time slightly harder. "Open the door, Jen. It's okay."

She cracked the door open. "Are you sure?" Jen wrung her hands. "I thought I heard noises downstairs. A loud clang." She wrinkled her brow in thought. "Maybe it was the sound of the ladder. You know…the metal scraping against stone."

"There was no ladder. I'm positive." He draped an arm around her shoulder. "And there's no one inside except you, me and Ethan." Senator Provost drew in a deep breath. "Jen, you're seriously overworked and I know you don't want to hear this, but in my opinion…well, I honestly believe you're experiencing sensory overload. You know, like someone who is sleep deprived."

"But I'm not sleep deprived."

"I know. I know. I'm simply using that as a comparison. You need a break. That's all I'm saying. I can't leave you here in charge of my son while you're in such a distressed state. Catherine's not going to like it, but I'm going to speak to her and let her know that I have to stick around at home for an additional day. I'll tell the agency to send over several applicants. I'm going to personally interview and hire the first nanny that arrives. There's no time to be picky…at this point, any qualified nanny will do."

Jen nodded. The senator was right…any nanny would do. The woman would not have to be a rocket scientist to sit and watch

Ethan navigate the internet and to remind him to use the potty, point him toward his bath water, and then put him to bed.

However, she'd have to possess the patience of Job to watch him revisit the same websites. Bridges. And more bridges. Hour after hour. And nerves of steel to endure his wheezing and his horrific episodes. Dealing with Ethan was enough to drive anyone batty.

"After the new nanny is situated and comfortable, I want you to take a few days off. Get out of the house for a while. That's an order. I'll pay for you to stay in a five-star hotel. I want you to take advantage of room service and any pampering services the hotel offers. Deal?"

Jen had been lost in thought. She came out of her reverie and nodded. The senator seemed completely sober now and was back to his normal, kind self. His generous offer was probably exactly what she needed. Acceptance washed over her. Once again, she'd hallucinated.

She'd gone from imagining seeing a naked woman to a vicious and snarling, fur-covered ghoul crouched in the skylight. She shook her head. Caring for eerie Ethan was pushing her to the brink of insanity.

"I'll check on Ethan. Why don't you get some sleep?" Senator Provost spoke softly, using the cautious tone one would reserve for the mentally unstable.

Jen felt guilty for shirking off her responsibility to her charge. "I'll go with you to check on Ethan. I heard him wheezing like crazy while you were outside, but I was too afraid to come out of my room," she admitted.

Together, they peered in on Ethan, who seemed to be sleeping soundly.

"No wheezing," the senator said.

"Good. I feel so sorry for him when he's breathing like that," she lied. What she actually felt when Ethan started wheezing was agitation and, most often, fear.

"There's no explanation for the occasional labored breathing. He doesn't have asthma or any upper respiratory problems." Perplexed, he shook his head.

"It's a mystery," Jen agreed, shaking her head as well. She laced her fingers fretfully. Though the child appeared to sleep peacefully, the atmosphere in his bedroom seemed charged with something malevolent.

"Senator Provost, uh, this is going to sound silly..."

He gave her a patient smile and waited for her to continue

"Well, I was thinking...since you're going to hire a new nanny, why not let her have my room? She'll be closer to Ethan. I'll move into that vacant room further down the hall."

"Shouldn't you two nannies be in adjacent rooms?"

Jen gave him a pitiful expression. "Just for awhile until I get over this irrational fear."

"Okay. Sure, but after the election...Catherine will be home from time to time and I can assure you, she won't appreciate rooms being changed without her permission."

"I know, sir. The change will be temporary."

"I understand. But don't start moving your things tonight. Let's wait until we have a new nanny assigned and her belongings moved in."

She tried to give him a smile of gratitude, but feeling miserable, her lips turned down.

In her own bedroom, she finally got around to calling Rome. No answer. She thought about texting him, but she had too much to say to fit into a text message. Weary from a busy day and terror-filled evening, Jen undressed and eased her tired body into bed. Jen lay on her back, staring at the ceiling.

She refused to look around the room at the furniture and other objects that had taken on a scary look in the dark bedroom. Jen sat up and considered turning on the light. No! With the light on, she'd be forced to look at her bathroom and, even with the door closed, her eyes would stay focused in that direction, revisiting the hallucination of the skylight and the ghoul she imagined had tried to force its way inside.

Jen shuddered. That thing had seemed so real and so brutal and murderous. The thought of ghosts and even terrorist attacks seemed almost laughable when compared to her delirious vision of a brutal monster trying to get at her and seeming to have the single-focused, killing instincts of a vicious, wild animal.

She lay back down, but sleep wouldn't come. Fear knocked her knees together beneath the blanket. She yearned to feel Rome's protective arms wrapped securely around her, comforting her throughout the long and scary, dark night.

From Ethan's bedroom, she thought she heard a voice murmuring. *Oh, God.* Jen dove under the covers, too petrified to go and investigate. She hoped she could make it through the night without having to pee. No way she was going inside her bathroom with the menacing skylight and she'd be damned if she'd wander out of her room to use any of the numerous bathrooms in the Provost household.

For Jen, sunshine and morning light couldn't come soon enough.

27

Too weak to intercede, Eris watched helplessly as Boozer, too sorry a creature to have the wherewithal to uncork the wine, broke off the bottle by the neck, spitting out shards of glass as he downed the pungent spirits. He belched boisterously and then wiped off his mouth with the back of his furry hand.

A dim glow of blue emanated from her eyes and roamed the darkened cellar, looking for an escape route other than the stairs. She spotted a false floorboard and directed her weak beams of light beneath it. *Drats!* There was only a small dark room without an exit.

She'd have to depend on Xavier for further direction. Xavier was such a trickster with a twisted and deviant mind, he didn't know the meaning of the word "loyalty" and Eris doubted if she could completely trust him.

But she was fading fast and could only hope the little menace had hatched a plan to get his female caregiver down the steps and into her clutches. Eris would take it from there.

Really? she asked herself and then gazed at the ends of her wrists where there should have been hands. How would she subdue the red-haired trollop? No hands…no feet or legs. And she was swiftly losing her upper limbs. She slid a glance at Boozer.

He was as drunk as a skunk. No help at all. The ghoul was absolutely useless. She narrowed her eyes and strained as she tried to burn him with her gaze, but the light that emanated from her eyes had no power or glow. She couldn't ignite even a tiny flash of light. That special ability that served as superior night vision, as well as for inflicting scorching pain, had been compromised.

Eris snarled. She'd use Boozer for target practice after she regained the full use of vision. She'd burn so many holes in him, he'd think twice before he disobeyed her orders again. He'd be lucky if she didn't decide to cut her losses and light him up until he burst into flames.

No sunlight filtered into the wine cellar, but the annoying melody of chirping birds told Eris that morning had finally arrived. There was no more time to waste. Her lower arms and legs were gone, with ragged pieces of skin drooping from her elbows and her kneecaps as if her limbs had been hacked off by a maniac surgeon.

The urge to self-preserve kicked her senses into high gear. She sniffed the air; her eyes flickered about the darkened place, searching for a source of life force. She'd be damned if she was going to sit back like a bump on a log and allow her body to fade into complete nothingness.

She heard a noise overhead. Beeping sounds. Someone had entered the home. Ah! So her hearing was still intact and quite keen. Delighted, Eris smiled and then stabbed her companion from hell with her elbow. "Boozer, wake up!"

Boozer, slouched, legs splayed. His penis, large and pulsing, awakened and extended from inside its fur-covered foreskin.

"There's a female mortal overhead. Climb up those stairs and bring her down here to me."

Boozer looked down at his swollen appendage. The urge to copulate made him drool.

"You'll get your satisfaction from her. Now go get her. Drag her down here if you have to, but make sure she's alive when I get my hands on her." Eris licked her lips in anticipation.

Boozer, hung over from the wine, could hardly maneuver his oversized wobbly body. Head pounding, phallus throbbing, he groaned as he crawled up the stairs.

"Silence!" Eris hissed.

Boozer clamped his mouth closed and crawled to the top of the stairs.

Deceitful behavior was second nature to him. Stealthily, he twisted open the door and then crawled toward the scent of a human female. Taking an arm out of a gray jacket, she stood near a hook on the back of the pantry door, her knit hat pulled snug around her head.

Boozer looked around in wonderment at all the shiny machinery positioned around the kitchen. He'd never seen any of the appliances and would have loved the opportunity to tinker with them and see how they worked.

As his eyes roved swiftly, he was awestruck by the craftsmanship of the wood cabinetry. He wished he could sit a spell and take in the marvels of modern man, but he had a pressing need and Eris wouldn't appreciate the time wasted with him browsing around.

Quietly, he slithered across the shiny tile floor and when he reached the back of the female's ankles, he lurched to his feet. She let out a breath of surprise. Boozer quickly clamped his clawed hand over her mouth, muffling her scream.

Boozer hauled the squirming, resistant female to the cellar stairs and softly closed the door behind him. She kicked mightily, forcing him to tighten the grip he had around her waist. He heard a snap and looked around suspiciously. The sound had a familiar ring to it. The woman stopped struggling and went limp.

Old memories flooded his mind. Then it came to him...he'd cracked one of the female's ribs. That used to happen quite often, back in the old days when he had to simmer down a feisty female in order to have his way.

Smiling at the fond recollections of molestation and mayhem, he delivered the injured prey to Eris. Proudly, he laid the unconscious female in front of Eris. Slobbering and grinning, Boozer waited to hear Eris murmur words of approval.

"Pick her up and hold her close to my mouth," Eris barked. There was a time when she would have siphoned the life force out of a human, leisurely taking in the essence of both males and females. But she was too bad off; she needed to go straight to the bloodstream.

Boozer lifted the woman, whom he would have considered hefty during his human life. But in his current form and with his enhanced strength, she was as light as a feather. Her jacket hung off of her shoulders; her hat was now twisted and sat lopsided on her head. The female's leg dangled from beneath her skirt; her thigh flush with Eris's face.

Eris could hear the rush of the life force she desperately needed coursing through the woman's veins. She bared her teeth and ferociously ripped away nylon pantyhose, tearing into the soft, spongy flesh of the ample woman's thigh.

The female awakened, her enormous eyes filled with bewilderment and pain, and pleaded for mercy. Eris bit her again, expecting to hear her howl in agony, but the female, too shocked to scream, produced only a sharp gasp.

Eris watched the female closely while she chewed her flesh. The woman gaped at Eris's blood-covered lips and then down at her own ravaged thigh. Now, her mouth was stretched open, preparing to liberate an explosive scream.

"Shut her up!" Eris ordered, still chewing on a large chunk of meat.

Boozer covered the woman's mouth.

With the female silenced and held still, Eris swallowed and then attacked the woman again, this time sucking the open wound, greedily slurping out blood and tendons, exploring the ravaged region with her tongue.

The female writhed in agony as Eris feasted. Savagely, she bit through marbled flesh and soft tissue until her teeth scraped against bone. The woman's anguished groan was heard; despite the tight seal Boozer's wide palm had made upon her lips.

The victimized woman succumbed to unconsciousness as Eris lapped blood and munched on olive-colored skin and red meat, filling herself with pulsating life force. She could feel the mortal's essence rushing through her. She felt vibrant and very much alive.

"Look!" Boozer gawked down to Eris's feet, which amazingly were beginning to materialize.

Excited by the progress she'd made, Eris chomped deeply into the other thigh and moaned at the succulent flavor of fresh human flesh and blood. Awed and inspired by the rush of life she was infused with, Eris crunched into the flank of flesh, devouring juicy muscle and stringy tendons. She quivered with glee when she saw the appearance of her extremities and finally her hands.

The female bled profusely from her open wounds. Her blood, dark and thick, pooled and streamed across the floor. The mortal was no longer useful. Eris frowned at the half-dead female. With her newly formed hands, she shoved the bloody mortal away.

Fast as lightning, Boozer stuck out a hairy hand and grabbed the bleeding female by the ankle. He snatched her from Eris's grasp, yanking her into the shadowy bowels of the cellar.

Though he didn't crave blood or yearn for the taste of flesh, he had a ravenous sexual appetite—a need so primal it was debilitating, causing his head to throb. The room seemed to spin, and his vision blurred.

Again the mortal female awoke and opened trembling lips. Shutting off her scream before it started, Boozer covered her mouth with his roughened palm and then angrily slammed her head against the floor, sending her back to oblivion.

Voraciously hungry for sex, he hoisted the limp female's skirt around her waist. Boozer used a claw to slash through the nylon and cotton panty barriers. Inhaling the tangy aroma of female loins, he became drunk with lust.

He pulled her limbs apart so viciously, the harsh crack of thick bones echoed through the cellar. Undeterred by her drooping torso and lolling head, Boozer worked to make her groin more accessible. He stretched the older woman's thighs. The broken bones made it easy to pull the bloodied flanks of flesh widely apart until her legs were stretched absurdly taut like a young gymnast performing a straddle split on a balance beam.

He positioned her lower body atop his mammoth fur-thatched loins.

The cook's lids fluttered open as she felt the monster brutally thrust inside her, impaling her. And puncturing vital internal organs.

As her life seeped out, Carmen's lips moved rapidly in prayer. With a quivering finger, she made the sign of the cross.

28

A loud clatter pulled Jen from a sweet dream. She sat up and looked around. Sleepily, she glanced at the bedside clock. Six-thirty. *Carmen must be banging around in the kitchen, getting breakfast ready*, she told herself as she lay back down, tugging the down-filled comforter over her shoulders.

As she'd hoped, the morning sunshine had driven away all fear. It was a new day and last night seemed like a remnant of a bad dream. Smiling, she remembered that she had a hot night planned for her and Rome. She wondered if the new nanny would arrive in time for her to go pick out her sultry lingerie.

Lizzy had the day off, and Jen wondered if she could persuade Carmen to look after the boy. Come hell or high water, she was getting out of the house to pick up her sexy wardrobe.

Rome! Rome! Rome! She couldn't wait to see his face. The man was incredibly gorgeous. And after all he'd been through in life, he was so kind, considerate and level-headed. As badly as Big Tee had treated him, Jen was sure that Rome would forgive her and welcome his mother with open arms. He didn't seem like the type of person who would hold on to a grudge.

Jen wished she could give him the gift of his mother's love, but she couldn't. But she wasn't going to hold back her feelings or try to keep them hidden. Lizzy and Carmen would probably accuse her of rushing things, but as far as Jen was concerned, there were no rules or no set time frame that determined when it was permissible to fall in love.

She was falling in love with Rome and tonight she was going to tell him. In the meantime, she wished she had something of his…a shirt, a hat…something that held his scent; that would make him seem close to her while they were apart.

A warm filling poured over her. Her hand wandered inside her panties. Her finger located her clit as she imagined snuggling close to Rome, his tongue replacing the finger that pressed against her nub.

No sooner had Jen began stroking herself, striving to provide self-induced satisfaction, when the phone blared, jolting her like an alarm. It only rang once. Senator Provost or Carmen must have picked up.

The senator had clout. Jen figured he must have left an urgent message on the agency's voicemail last night. On the ball and striving to please, someone from the agency was handling the situation before normal business hours, calling to inform them that the new nanny was on her way.

Jen threw on a robe and padded down the corridor to the senator's bedroom. Maybe they should have a morning chat, make sure they were on the same page before the nanny arrived.

Outside his door, she heard him speaking. "I didn't realize it was that important. Why didn't you tell me about the photo op with the troops? Of course, I'll be ready." There was a weary sluggishness in the senator's tone. "I promise you, I'll see you soon."

Soon! How soon? Jen wondered. She and the senator had nanny business to conduct together.

She knocked on his door. "Senator Provost, may I speak with you?"

"Yes. Come in, Jen."

She'd expected to see him sitting up in bed with a breakfast tray in front of him, eyes roving between open copies of both the *Washington Post* and the *Philadelphia Inquirer*. But instead he was slumped down in bed, having a liquid breakfast, drinking straight from a bottle of Grey Goose. He looked a haggard mess, with bloodshot eyes and a blotchy face.

"That was Catherine." He spat his wife's name as if it were a dirty word. "My de-balling wife has summoned me and she's not taking no for an answer." He guzzled more vodka, some spilled down the side of his mouth, and wiped it with the back of his hand. Not a good look for a photo op with the troops.

Jen couldn't help but wonder how this obvious lush was going to make himself presentable. But more importantly, she wanted to know what he'd meant by... *"I'll see you soon."*

"Are you canceling the nanny interview?"

"Catherine insists that I join her," he bellowed. Jen had never heard the senator raise his voice. Being the Second Man, or however the nation intended to refer to the senator after his wife won the election, was really getting under his skin and causing him to try to drink away his bruised ego.

"You aren't going to leave me alone, are you?" she blurted, her calm composure gone; desperation raising her pitch.

Senator Provost gave her an odd look, like he was seeing her for the first time. "Uh, yeah. Looks like I'm going to have to join her for this spur-of-the moment photo op with the presidential candidate, his wife, and some damned troops...uh, somewhere. I can't remember where we're going. I certainly hope we're not going as far as the Middle East."

Jen hoped he wasn't going too far, also. She needed him to hire the damn nanny. "Well, what about the new nanny? Remember, you told me you were going to hire one today?"

He held up his hands, frustrated. "Someone on Catherine's staff is going to take care of it. They put in an emergency request. The agency will be sending applicants over this afternoon." He brushed back oily strands of hair that had fallen in his face and then scratched his scalp as if he had fleas. Jen grimaced when he started picking his nose.

The senator's aristocratic manners had transformed overnight to crude and unrefined. Not that she really cared because her main concern was getting out of the house for her lingerie shopping and then, later, for her hot sex-filled night with Rome, but she couldn't help but wonder if the senator would be able to pull himself together before he joined his wife and the future president.

"I'm in a tight spot, Jen. Think you can handle the interviews for me? You'd know better than I would who'd be the best nanny for the little guy."

"Sure. No problem. When will you be back?"

"Tonight. Possibly tomorrow."

Tomorrow! She wanted to scream. "I'm not sure...like...what do you want me to say to the new nanny. What's her salary and when should she start?"

"The agency handles the salary. You know that. Tell her we need her to start right away. I'm sure the agency will handle all the fine details. I need you to check her out for me and make sure she and Ethan will be a good fit. Go with your gut instincts." Daniel threw off the comforter, got out of bed, stood in his boxers and stretched, and then scratched his groin. And farted. He did this double-brow lift thing, like passing gas was absolutely adorable.

What a pig! How had he pulled off the well-bred persona for so long? She wanted to call Rome, but refused to make contact until this nanny thing was worked out. She did not want to give her man any bad news.

He shot an eye toward the clock and frowned. "I wish I had time to walk you through the questions you should ask the applicant. But Catherine's people are sending the presidential plane. I have to be on time. Like I said, go with your gut." He winked and staggered toward his dressing room.

"Wait."

He stopped mid-stagger and turned around. Annoyance glinted in his bloodshot eyes.

"Do you know what time she's going to arrive?"

"Who?"

"The nanny applicant!"

"No clue," he responded nonchalantly.

Jen's face crumpled. She couldn't hide her disappointment.

"Hey! Cheer up. We'll pick up where we left off as soon as I get home tonight."

"What are you talking about?" When she'd had a crush on the senator, she might have thought this alcohol-laced forgetfulness was funny…even cute. But he was disgusting. Oh, she was so over him!

The senator frowned—wrinkled his nose as if he smelled something bad. "Oh, that wasn't you…got you confused for a moment with my assistant, Gwyneth. You know, the hot little blonde who stayed over the other night."

The man was totally intoxicated and without shame. The censor guy inside his brain was apparently asleep at the wheel and allowing the senator to say whatever came to mind. It was going to be a doozy of a photo op today.

"Well, back to you." He glowered at Jen.

What had she done? Nothing that she could think of. Quick

as a flash, his blotchy face had lost any semblance of warmth. His bloodshot eyes burned with anger.

Jen shrank back, confused.

"This isn't an appropriate time to be bombarding me with questions. Do I have to point out that my wife is running for the second most important office in the nation? When I'm called on to give my support, the last thing I need is to have to deal with your insecurities."

He walked back toward the bed. Jen backed up, thinking he might strike her, but he picked up the bottle of vodka, then tucked it under his arm, intending to take it with him into his dressing room. "I'm thinking you should go check on Ethan," he said, his tone frosty. "I'm sure he's pretty hungry by now."

"Sure, I'll get him ready—"

He didn't allow Jen to finish her sentence. "Carmen has probably been at the stove heating and reheating my son's breakfast while his nanny has the audacity to come into my bedroom and grill me. The question and answers session is officially over," he announced firmly as if speaking to persistent members of the press.

Coming to his bedroom as if they were pals was a big mistake; Jen realized that now. The senator had made it abundantly clear that she had a heck of a lot of audacity to consider herself his equal. Drunk mind...sober tongue? Jen couldn't quite recall the saying but it certainly applied to this moment. The senator paid her wages and expected her to do the duties she was paid to perform.

"Sure, I'll go check on him," she said, eyes downcast in embarrassment. Abruptly dismissed and feeling sullied, Jen tightened the sash of her robe and turned to leave. She was sure her cheeks were flaming red. The senator's harsh treatment of her was degrading and a bit uncalled for.

The way he was acting, you would have thought that she'd barged into his room, thrown back the duvet, plumped up a pillow, and lay next to him, expecting to share the lavish breakfast Carmen had prepared especially for him.

She really should quit on the spot. But where would she go? Would Rome still find her appealing if she turned up at his door, jobless and without a roof over her head? She doubted it.

"One more thing."

Jen stopped.

"I'm trusting you to take care of my son and to hire a competent nanny. When Catherine calls to find out how things are going, I expect you to paint a glorious picture."

"Yes, sir. I'll do that," Jen said with all the deference she could muster. She could not afford to be without a paycheck.

The senator turned his back to her and picked up the phone. Jen didn't know whether she should remain standing or give him some privacy by leaving. She chose to remain in his room. No point in getting the drunkard more worked up than he already was.

"This is Senator Provost. I need a car service. Uh, I need pick up at..." He looked up in thought and then noticed Jen still standing in the doorway. Irritated, he waved her away.

Humiliated, Jen closed his bedroom door. What had she said to set the senator off? Nothing she could think of. Blaming his discourtesy on his large consumption of alcohol, she took unhurried steps down the hall toward Ethan's room.

Her thoughts were jumbled as she tried to figure out how to get out of the house and enjoy a sleepover with Rome. With a new nanny underfoot and the senator's obvious withdrawal of support, the possibility of a hot date was looking slim.

29

Ethan was curled in a tight fetal knot...the way he always slept. The poor thing had never had any motherly affection. *No wonder the kid is so screwed up*, Jen thought bitterly. Catherine Provost had the country duped. She was a terrible wife and a rotten mother. The child was weird, but he still deserved his own mother's love, Jen reasoned.

She eased the covers off of Ethan. Jolting him awake could prompt a screaming episode and quite frankly, after the way the senator had treated her, she was already on the brink of tears. Her feelings were too close to the surface to put up with Ethan going off the deep end.

"Good morning," she said softly and very gently shook his shoulder. She watched him guardedly, waiting for the first sign of heavy wheezing or any indication that he was going to launch into that terrible siren's scream. Ethan's eyes popped open but were hollow and unfocused—like normal. *Good!*

"Let's get you washed up. I bet Carmen made your favorite breakfast," she said, knowing she wouldn't get a response. Or at least hoping she wouldn't. She still hadn't fully recovered from that time she heard Ethan speak. *Imagination...hallucination. Yeah, whatever,* she thought with a smirk. *Just don't let it happen again, kid,* she thought to herself and then rustled the child's hair.

Ethan shot her a dirty look. His eyes, dark and unforgiving, bored into her.

"Oops, sorry, kid. Forgot how much you hate anything remotely friendly. I guess you're a chip off the old block, after all, huh?" she quipped and gave a wry laugh; thinking about how mean his father had treated her.

"Let's get you washed and dressed." She lifted him out of the bed, keeping her eyes focused away from the tented groin area of his pajamas. The kid always woke up with an erection and it annoyed her. "Go tinkle." She pointed to his private bathroom. "I'll come in and help you wash up and brush your teeth in a few minutes."

As she waited for Ethan to urinate, she felt her tummy rumble. Today she wouldn't turn down the fattening meal Carmen would try to tempt her with. She was down in the dumps and could use some high-caloric, comfort food.

Then her brows crinkled together. Carmen was awfully quiet this morning. In fact, now that she thought about it, there was no smell of breakfast wafting upstairs. By this hour of the morning, she should have caught a whiff of bacon or the yummy aroma of Carmen's homemade muffins. "I'll be right back, kid," she told Ethan and went to investigate the status of breakfast.

She rounded the corridor and felt her heart sink at the sight of the senator's closed bedroom door. She hated being a pest but she really needed to try and repair their rift. She needed him on her side. He'd promised days off, a posh hotel... Jen took a deep breath and tapped on the door.

"Yes?"

"I'm going downstairs to check on breakfast. Would you like some room service?" Jen groaned to herself; she sounded so meek and subservient. "I meant...I know you're in a rush and won't have time for breakfast but I can bring up your coffee if you'd like."

"No, thank you," he snapped. He actually was irritated by her considerate offer! "I'll have coffee in the limo."

"Okay. Um…did you…uh…" she stammered, but determinedly pressed on. "Do you want to say good-bye to Ethan before you leave?" God, she was practically begging, but having some free time to spend with Rome was worth a little kissing up. She had to get back on the senator's good side so she could continue her new romance without fear of losing her job.

The senator sighed. The sound was loud and weary. "No, Jen. I really don't have time. I'm running late. I'll see Ethan when I get back home."

God, he sounds really pissed. This couldn't be about me. He's mad because he has to join his wife and pretend to be a supportive spouse, when he really would like to switch places with her. "Sure. Okay," Jen mumbled and backed away, gnawing on her lip and trying to figure out how to ask him for the night off. She thought she and the senator had bonded. He'd said that her hallucination last night was the result of being overworked. Now he was acting like it had never happened; like he'd never promised to set her up in a five-star hotel…he was treating her like the scum under his shoe and she'd done nothing to deserve this. *Damn you, Catherine Provost.* Everything was going so terribly wrong. Moping, Jen turned around and sadly headed for Ethan's room.

The doorbell chimed. Senator Provost hurried down the stairs. Jen turned around and rushed to the top of the staircase, hoping he'd turn around and say something like… "Enjoy your night off." At this point, she didn't care about the hotel or the pamper session; she just needed to get out of the Provost home and spend some quality time with her new man.

She heard the senator tell Carmen good morning in a cheery voice. Jen could picture Senator Provost hurrying past the kitchen, walking purposefully toward the front door.

Surprisingly, Carmen didn't say a word. She didn't pitch a fit when Jen heard the senator add, "The limo's here. No breakfast for me. I have to run."

There were no disgruntled sounds from Carmen, and that was odd. Carmen fawned over Senator Provost. She took it personally when he rushed out of the house without eating the big breakfast she had prepared for him—the most important meal of the day, she often reminded him. Then she'd argue to herself in Spanish, complaining about how the Provost family wasted so much food.

But not today. Today, the cook was uncharacteristically quiet, keeping her irritation and opinions to herself, Jen supposed.

Jen shrugged. If Carmen was holed up in the kitchen, silently brooding over wasted food, that was her problem. Jen had bigger troubles. Should she call Rome's cell and postpone their plans? No! Not a good idea. The new nanny might be totally capable of dealing with Ethan alone on her first night. Jen refused to cancel her date unless absolutely necessary.

And exactly what time was the woman planning to arrive? Jen sighed. Her trip to Victoria's Secret would have to be cancelled. She doubted if Carmen would be in the mood to look after Ethan. Maybe Lizzy would watch him. But Lizzy was off today, Jen remembered. Feeling somewhat forlorn, Jen headed back to Ethan's room. She peered in the child's bathroom.

He was standing in front of the toilet, holding his big boner. *Eew!* Jen grimaced and glanced away and kept a safe distance. After that last incident, she didn't want to place herself in the line of fire. "Did you tinkle?" she muttered, her lips pinched together in disgust.

"Hey, kid, did you tinkle?" she repeated in a raised voice. Though she definitely didn't expect or welcome an answer, Ethan had a way of responding. One way would be to start urinating if he hadn't or, if he'd finished, then he would tuck his pecker back inside his underwear.

She crept up behind him with her eyes squinted, trying to determine if the water in the bowl was tinted yellow. His breathing pattern suddenly changed and his small shoulders rose and fell rapidly in time with the tempo of his appalling wheezing. This was not a good sign.

Ethan spun around and stared at her sullenly. His gaze narrowed; a menacing glint surfaced, replacing the vacant look that was usually in his eyes.

Jen shot an alarmed glance downward and went cold with dread. She wanted to run but she couldn't move. She felt frozen in place.

"Did...you...uh...tinkle?" she stammered.

"Not yet!" he responded in a terrible voice that sounded gravelly and ancient.

Her limbs loosened in response to her brain's desire to take flight. "Carmen!" Jen cried, keeping an eye on the menacing child while she quickly backed away. The boy, his expression deadly, his temples pulsing in rage, paced toward her, his steps hastening as he aimed his penis as threateningly as if he were pointing a gun.

"No! Don't!" Jen tried to run but tripped over the sash of her robe, which had come undone.

Expecting at any moment to feel the hot splash of urine, Jen grimaced and curled into a ball on the floor.

But she felt something else. The vibration of footsteps bounding up the stairs. *Carmen?* No, the footsteps were much too heavy—so heavy the house seemed to shake. Felt like more than one person was running up the stairs. *Lizzy and Carmen?* she thought hopefully. *No, not Lizzy either.* The maid was a tiny thing; she couldn't make the house quake—and she had the day off. Besides Carmen, there was no one else inside the house.

Ethan's wheezing escalated to his piercing scream. A shock of fear made Jen's heart double its rhythm. *Oh, shit. An episode.* She needed help. "Carmen?" she called aloud, her voice squeaky with panic. She came out of the fetal position, propped herself up on an elbow, her neck stretched in the direction of the pounding sound that was growing closer.

Unbelievably, from her vantage point on the floor, she saw slender ebony-colored female feet. Rushing past the ebony feet and with a furious pounding were a pair of something thick, furry, and clawed. Something that could only be described as…a pair of hooves.

30

E than stopped screaming. The room became ominously
silent. Then there was a strange and unfamiliar rumbling…
like the hoofed animal was growling deep in its throat, ready
to attack.

Jen scooted back and slithered under Ethan's bed, hoping she
hadn't been detected. Trembling, she prayed the boy would start
wailing again. His ear-piercing shriek might scare off the bare-
foot woman and the wild beast she'd brought with her.

"Hello, Xavier. Well, look at you." The woman's voice was
tinged with amusement.

Holy shit! Xavier! That was the name Ethan had called himself.
The urge to get up and run like hell was overpowering, but she
shook so badly, she didn't risk trying to make a half-cocked escape.

"Childhood does not become you, my friend."

"I agree. Unfortunately, I'm stuck in this tiny human frame and
I need your help. That's why I brought you here. You wanted to
get out of your ghastly dwelling and I assisted you.

"Is that your governess, huddling beneath the bed?" the woman
asked with a bored sigh.

Shit! She'd been spotted. Jen had hoped for a miracle.

"Not anymore," Ethan replied ominously.

"Poor thing's trembling so bad, the bed is quaking. I think
she's afraid."

"As she should be," Ethan answered in his raspy voice. "I'm furious that you brought that growling fiend. He wasn't in the plan." Ethan changed the subject as if Jen's terrified presence was of little consequence.

"As I said, he's my protection," the woman answered. The growling sound intensified as if the hooved beast was ready to maim on the woman's behalf.

"Protection?" the boy echoed, outraged. "From what?"

"From you. And anyone else who would seek to harm me."

"Oh, yea of little faith. Wicked One, you have to learn to trust me. I'm insulted." *Wicked One? What in the name of God is going on?* Jen wondered.

"I know you, Xavier. You are the most deceitful spirit I've ever encountered. You are the last soul I'd trust," the woman said. Oddly, her scathing accusation came out sounding like a compliment.

"I'm no more deceitful than you. So, there. It's out in the open. You and I will put the past behind us and become partners again. We have lots to accomplish. Lots of planning to do. First things first. You can't go around naked. You need clothing. My mother has an extensive wardrobe. Help yourself."

"What about Boozer? He'll need attire as well," the woman said.

Ethan snorted. "Boozer's a beast. There's nothing in this house that will fit him."

"We'll hire a tailor."

There was that awful growl again, scratching through the air like it had emerged from a throat filled with razor blades.

"That ogre is disgusting. Take a good look at what you dragged from the Dark Realm." Ethan scolded. "It's barely human. It won't fit in around here; it needs to return to hell. I'm sending it back."

"You'll do no such thing," the woman said firmly. "I need him."

"You don't need that creature. You have me!"

"You're a child," she scoffed.

"He's a beast; the sight of that thing will cause humans to shriek in horror. How can I exact revenge against my parents with that fiend lumbering about? It's not likely that he'll go undetected. Did it occur to you that you can't drag a mortal who has been cast to the Dark Realm back to earth and expect it to retain its human appearance?"

"You were once mortal."

"I came back through the birth canal and have the appearance of a normal human."

Eris gave him a sidelong look. "Normal? I wouldn't go that far. Besides, you didn't arrive through a typical birth. You slipped inside an unsuspecting fetus and stole its life."

The boy smirked. "Merely semantics. Unlike that monster you yanked from hell, my natural birth cannot be disputed. Being a goddess and all, I thought you were of superior intelligence. I'm starting to doubt your wisdom and cunning. Didn't it occur to you that Boozer wouldn't fit in?"

"I'll keep him hidden from sight."

The boy snorted. "Hidden? Where do you propose to hide that thing? Boozer is gigantic—pretty hard to miss."

Jen could hear the padding of Ethan's small feet as he paced. "Wicked One, Wicked One," he said with strained patience. "For someone who claims to be a wise goddess, you repeatedly make foolish choices. Aren't you weary of getting torched and burned to a crisp every time you return to earth?" He gave a malicious chuckle.

"Don't remind me. Boozer stays. And I won't be burned again… not with Boozer protecting me."

"And where do you suggest we conceal your... uh, security guard?"

"I discovered a false floorboard in the cellar that leads down to a secret dungeon. I doubt if the owners of this home know it's there."

Jen groaned inwardly. The conversation between the boy and the scary woman was going from bad to worse. The air was thick with evil. She would have never imagined that evil had an odor. But it did. The stench was so God-awful, Jen fought to hold her breath. She lost the battle when she drew in a strangled burst of air, bringing undesired attention her way.

"Governess!" the woman said sharply. She stalked over to the bed and kicked beneath bed ruffle, jabbing Jen in the side. It wasn't painful but Jen understood the implied threat. It was time to crawl out and come face-to-face with a trio of monsters—Ethan included.

Cold fingers of terror clutched at Jen. It occurred to her to start banging her head against the hardwood floor and succumb to merciful darkness until help arrived. But the woman kicked her again before she could put her plan in motion. Feeling sick to her stomach, Jen prepared herself for the worst.

Not wanting to rush the inevitable horror that hovered above her, Jen moved in slow motion, raising her head as slowly as possible. What she wouldn't give to click her heels and be back in her dreary hometown.

She'd give anything to have a lengthy conversation with her boring parents; she'd hang on to their every uninteresting word. If only she could escape this horror, she'd rejoin her family and make peace with the humdrum rural life she'd fled.

With that promise to herself, Jen uncovered her head, sat up, and reluctantly opened her eyes. She drew in several startled, deep breaths.

Ethan, with his privates tucked back inside his blue pajamas, stood over her. The coal-black woman from Piper's Bridge was with him and she was still naked. Jen couldn't help but notice that she appeared very comfortable in her nudity. The female apparition had the form and substance of a living person. Her cobalt blue eyes flickered in anger.

"What an ill-mannered governess you are. Get up and make yourself useful. Search every closet and storage place until you find something suitable for Boozer to wear!" The woman was accustomed to giving orders. Her tone held more than a hint that a tragic consequence would befall anyone who didn't adhere to her demands swiftly.

"Yes, ma'am. I'll look everywhere." The tremor in Jen's voice made her words indecipherable. Compensating, she nodded her head, conveying her willingness to cooperate. She did not want any trouble and would do whatever she was asked to do.

Actually, she planned to flee the moment she was out of that scary woman's eyesight. She'd run screaming all the way down the driveway. Once she got outside the gate, she'd flag down a vehicle; bogart her way inside some unsuspecting motorist's car. She'd plead with her rescuer to call the police or, better yet, drop her off at the nearest bus depot.

The police would most likely drag her back to the household to identify the perpetrators. And that wasn't going to happen. Once free, there was no way she was going back inside to rejoin these goons from hell—not even with police protection. She wanted to be safe and sound in her parents' warm and welcoming home.

She imagined herself living quietly and peacefully with her parents…like, forever. The vision wasn't that bad. Compared to her current situation, living in a calm, rural community was a very appealing lifestyle.

Jen accidentally cut an eye at Boozer and wished she hadn't. Boozer was the most grotesque creature she'd ever seen. It turned out that she hadn't been hallucinating last night. Boozer was the same hideous fiend that had grinned at her from the skylight. It hadn't been a figment of her imagination.

It was real and was here in the house.

And it was atrociously huge.

Up close, it was even more gross-looking than seeing it in the skylight. The beast named Boozer had a grayish complexion and grizzly tufts of fur jutting out of different parts of its mal-formed body. It was naked and was like…partially human…and partially beast.

She tried not to look at the thing's groin, but involuntarily, her eyes wandered in that direction and she gasped. Boozer's dick was gigantic. And covered with fur…like an animal's genitals.

Boozer's tongue slipped in and out of his mouth, vigorously licking at feral lips, while a trail of spittle ran down his chin. *Eew!* Each tongue flick delivered promises of unspeakable sexual acts.

What had she been thinking? She'd known from the start that Ethan was a weirdo. She should have run for her life the first time she'd witnessed him having one of his ghastly episodes. She could see it all so clearly now. Both Ms. Provost and the senator had used her. They never intended to get her a position on Capitol Hill.

Did the Provosts have a clue that their son was not autistic… that he wasn't even a child? And very possibly, Ethan or Xavier, or whoever he was, wasn't really even completely human? No, of course they didn't know their progeny was a demon out for revenge. Had they known, surely they would have done the right thing and drowned him at birth.

And while the Provosts were out on the stump, smiling and waving to adoring crowds, Jen was trapped in their lunatic son's bedroom with a couple of his friends—ghouls he'd personally summoned straight from hell.

Jen suddenly inhaled a breath of hope. Ethan's grudge was against his parents...not her. She was innocent and had nothing to do with any of this. Maybe he'd let her go.

As if reading her mind, Boozer, behaving like an agitated dog, let out a long, low growl. Then he flopped down on the floor, like an ornery child. Sitting on his big, hairy butt, he kicked his hoofed feet out in a tantrum. The soles were thick and grooved with deep, crisscrossing lines. Jen grimaced and looked away from Boozer.

"Be patient, Boozer. After I've finished with her, you can keep her as your plaything—she'll keep you company down in that dungeon beneath the cellar."

Boozer's plaything! Kept in a dungeon? Oh, dear God, please help me! The warm splash finally came, but not from Ethan. Petrified of what the beast had in store for her, Jen peed her panties.

THE GODDESS REALM

The time moved differently between the Dark Realm and the Goddess Realm. It seemed to Tara that all communication with her sister had stopped for several weeks. Poor Eris, she believed, was probably so afraid, being held in captivity with those vicious creatures and without the comfort of hearing her sister's voice.

Several times a day, Tara peered into the pond, trying to make a connection with Eris. To no avail. It was as if Eris's life force no longer existed on that realm. Had she plummeted to the very lowest realm? Tara gasped. *No!* Imagining Eris being tormented by Satan himself was a ghastly thought.

Eris didn't deserve to be in such a depraved place. She was high-spirited, a little mischievous at times, but she couldn't help herself due to her nature. She wasn't as wicked to the core as those who dwelled in the fiery, lowest realm.

Tara cried up to the heavens, beseeching her ascended mother to help her find Eris. "Oh, Mother Inanna. Hear my cries. Guide me; tell me what I should do. My sister was sent to earth as a temporary home to teach her a lesson, but she misbehaved and was sent to that dreaded place. Now she's lost. The goddesses should have never sent her so far away from her home. She was lonely and probably kept company with the bad types.

"Now through no fault of her own, she is made to dwell with those evil beings that slither and screech in the realms deprived of sunlight. Give me a sign, dear mother. Please! My sister... your daughter is lost!"

And every day that Tara sobbed, her winged attendant wiped her eyes, covered her with her wings, and comforted her in the only way she knew how.

31

Ordered by the woman to wipe up the puddle on the floor, to change her clothing, and to clean herself, all done with the hulking monster overseeing her, Jen, freshly scrubbed and changed, was marched back to Ethan's bedroom. Red-faced, she stood before her minor charge and the woman named Eris, who was referred to as "Goddess." To Jen, she seemed more like a witch than a goddess.

The woman sat atop Ethan's desk. "What should we do about her?"

The boy sat in his swivel chair, stroking his chin in thought. "Punish her," he remarked casually.

Eris looked at her slender hands. "I can't. I just acquired these." She held them out to be admired. "Too lovely to risk damaging."

"Nanny, we do not tinkle on the floor," Ethan chastised, throwing Jen's own words at back at her.

"Talk, talk, talk. Stop all that jabbering and give her thirty and nine and be done with it," Eris suggested.

"What, pray tell…is thirty and nine?" the boy asked, eyes gleaming with amusement.

"Lashes," Eris explained, frowning at the boy's ignorance. "It's a pity we don't have the whipping post I was hoisted to during my life on the plantation," Eris said and gave a grievous sigh.

Red-faced, Jen dropped her head. She felt utterly hopeless. Then she thought about Carmen and her heart lifted. She'd heard the senator speaking with her on his way out, so where was the cook? She probably slipped out undetected and was running down the road to get help, Jen told herself. Carmen would be back with the entire police force and then this nightmare would end.

"You want to reprimand her in the way you were dealt with when you were a rebellious slave?"

Lashes? Whipping posts...and slavery! What the hell are these lunatics talking about? Please hurry...save me, Carmen! Jen's legs began to wobble. If only she could reach her cell phone. These demons were out for blood. Her blood! Something had to be done. Rome said that the dead can't hurt you, but these ghouls that Ethan had released from hell were of solid form. The phantom world had merged into the real world and these supernatural beings, mutant as they were, were visible, lifelike, and they could hurt her. Really badly, Jen feared. She gave an involuntary whimper.

"This sniveling governess deserves far worse than what I was given. But I'll settle for thirty and nine lashes."

"And who should dispense the lashes? I'm a child. I haven't the strength," Ethan rasped in complaint. Jen almost smiled in relief, but caught herself and maintained her terror-stricken look.

"Boozer can do it," Eris offered.

"No!" Jen yelled. "He'll kill me."

Eris and the child exchanged a significant look. "She's right," Eris said. "Boozer doesn't know his own strength. Furthermore, I need her alive. I have no idea how long this physical body is going to last. It seems unwise to risk losing her when I may need to feed on her for my own well-being."

Feed! On me? A shiver of extreme fear worked its way up her spine. Perhaps she'd stumbled into some sort of alternate universe. Yes, that had to be what was going on here because nothing made sense or seemed real.

Ethan began wheezing. "Are you suggesting the naughty nanny should go unpunished?" The sound of his raspy adult voice was unpleasant and very hard to get used to.

"Of course she should be punished," Eris said. "But not by Boozer. You should give her the lashes."

"I can't." His voice was low; he sounded depressed. "I'm too small. I've been anxiously awaiting your assistance, Wicked One."

"I'll assist you," Eris said brightly. "I'll coach and guide you." Then her voice changed to a disapproving low tone. "Really, Xavier…you're not like your old self. Who would have thought you'd be resisting an opportunity to inflict pain."

"Okay, I'll do it." The boy stood and stepped around the small desk.

Eris turned a searing gaze at Jen. "Go fetch a whip."

The boy rolled his eyes. "These are modern times. I've learned much about this time period from my computer. Only sexual fetishists use whips and such gadgets. On the other hand, my father has a vast collection of belts in an array of leather and exotic skins." He cut a knowing eye at Jen. "I'm sure you would have preferred to be taken over my father's knee," the boy said with a trace of amusement. "But I'm afraid the discipline you require won't be of an erotic nature. Now, go get a belt…something sturdy that will leave marks when I strike your buttocks. Be quick, nanny!"

Eris gave the boy a nod of approval. "That's the spirit! Now, you sound more like the Xavier I once knew."

"Stay close to her, Boozer," Ethan instructed. "We don't want Eris's lifeline to get away."

Her lifeline? Jen thought, bewildered.

Boozer trudged across the room and shoved Jen so hard, she stumbled forward and crashed into a wall. Unwilling to even imagine the beast's next move, Jen composed herself and got moving.

Inside the senator's bedroom, she yanked open a closet and swiftly ran her eyes over the rack that held the collection of belts, while warily looking over her shoulder to make sure the monster who loomed over her, panting and salivating, didn't suddenly lunge.

Though she was repelled by the sight of Boozer, she didn't like having her back turned to him. She didn't linger over the selection process and grabbed a thin belt. Seconds later, she rushed back to the boy's room with Boozer close on her heels, and was comforted in a weird way by the sight of Ethan.

With his acquired mastery of language and menacing facial expressions, Ethan no longer seemed even remotely childlike. But at least he was small. Being so puny, she doubted Ethan could inflict any serious harm.

With a stiff upper lip, Jen handed Ethan the thin leather belt.

Eris sneered at the flimsy belt that dangled from Jen's hand. "Your governess chose something suitable for your miniature grasp," she mocked.

The boy padded toward Jen. So small, his head barely reached her thigh. He stood for a moment glowering at her, his tiny hands fisted at his sides. Then he stood on his tiptoes and wrenched the belt from her grasp.

Giving in to a fit of cackling laughter, Eris eased off the desk. "This should be very interesting."

"Strip down. Bare your buttocks."

Jen looked aghast. Hearing Ethan speak was unsettling enough, but his request was way over the top and terrifying.

"Do as I say!" he shouted, his face twisted with pure evil.

Timidly, Jen tugged on the waistband of her jeans.

"Wait!" He pointed toward his bed. "Go over there and bend over."

"Wouldn't it be better if she stood?" Eris interjected. "Boozer can hold her and make sure she keeps still."

Both ideas were bad—absolutely nauseating, but all she could do was wait until a decision was reached.

"Yeah, lemme at her!" The words rumbled out of Boozer; his voice deep and coarse with yearning. His mouth watered; saliva spilled; his facial muscles twitched with anticipation.

"No!" She shrank back from his beastly gaze. It was inconceivable that her fate lay in the hands of a witch, a hulking monster, and a demon-possessed child. Jen trembled uncontrollably.

After brief consideration, the boy said, "Go ahead, and grab her. Get her ready for me, Boozer."

In a matter of milliseconds, the beast locked his hairy hand around Jen's wrist, jerking her so ferociously that her body slammed against his. As she tried to wriggle away, he roughly worked her jeans over her hips.

Jen looked stricken. "No! Please, don't hurt me. I'll find clothes for Boozer to wear. I'm sure there's something here that can fit him," she pleaded, her eyes focused on Eris, who seemed to be calling the shots. "With clothes he won't have to hide out in the cellar. He can come and go...and you know...mingle, with people." Jen swallowed hard.

Eris considered Jen's words. "Do you know how to get to Roanoke?"

"Uh, Roanoke, Virginia?" Her head bobbed up and down. "Yeah, sure. It's about six or seven hours from here." Jen forced her trembling lips into a smile.

"Good. I'll need you to drive me to the Stovall plantation."

Drive you where? She shouted in her mind, but nodded dumbly. She'd promise anything to buy time to save herself.

"Eris! You're getting time periods confused. The place that you're so fixated on existed hundreds of years ago. As you well know, from your last visit here, slavery ended. We're in a new millennium. No slaves, no plantations—Stovall or otherwise."

Eris gave the boy a thoughtful look. "Times may have progressed since I was in Roanoke, but I know for certain that the modern-day Stovalls are living on that same plantation where my jewels were buried. I used my third-eye vision to track them. My wonderful trinkets have been unearthed and handed over to a snotty-nosed child." Eris spoke through clenched teeth. "I want my property back."

The boy snorted. "I didn't work hard constructing that bridge so that you could go traipsing off looking for trinkets. We will stick to the plan."

"I don't take orders from you, you little brat," Eris hissed.

"And you don't want me to start screaming my head off like one. My parents are a very powerful political couple…a call from this house to emergency services will bring the police and the news media in a scant few seconds." The boy smiled wickedly. "You'll be suspected as kidnappers. It'll be a real mess when the authorities realize that the suspects aren't quite human. No pulse, no heartbeat, and flesh that's subject to emulsify without proper nourishment." He glared at Eris. "Is that what you want? Hmm? Do you want to literally rot in jail?"

Eris looked away, considering the boy's threat. Ethan folded his scrawny arms and waited for her to see things his way. The disharmony between the ghoulish trio gave Jen some time to think. She needed to get to a phone. Her mind searched frantically for a way to reach the closest cell or landline.

Her cell was in her bedroom; too far away. There was a land-line telephone in practically every room of the house. All she had to do was slip away from these creatures and sneakily dial 9-1-1. She wouldn't even have to utter a sound. Like Ethan said, a call from the Provost household would instantly bring in the calvary.

"Your threats don't frighten me," Eris retorted, cobalt eyes glittering. "But…" She paused and nodded toward Boozer and rolled her eyes upward. "I can't depend on Boozer to help with the planning. I'd better think this through before I rush off to Roanoke. So let's make a deal right now. If I help you destroy your parents, will you assist me in retrieving my jewels?"

"Yes. It's a deal," the boy readily agreed. "Now, let's make arrangements for their demise. First, we need to dress you, Eris, so you can give the appearance of being a human mortal. As for Boozer…well, not even the finest clothes will help his image. He'll have to be kept hidden." He stared at Eris challengingly.

"Fine. But Boozer has his needs and the governess may not be enough for him. Where is the rest of your household staff? Boozer needs a generous supply of women."

The boy arched a brow. "The cook should be here by now."

"Boozer already had the cook. Aren't there others?"

Oh, no! What did she mean by, had *the cook? What happened to Carmen? Something really bad*, Jen surmised. Suddenly forlorn, her shoulders slumped. She wanted to bury her face in her hands and weep. All hope was gone. Carmen would not be huffing up the stairs accompanied by a SWAT team dressed in battle gear and equipped with lethal weapons.

"No, my parents keep a small staff. The maid is scheduled to work tomorrow. He'll have to suppress his appetite until then." Ethan lifted a brow. "That is…unless you're willing to share her." He nodded his oversized head in Jen's direction.

"No, I need her. She's mine."

Jen felt lightheaded, close to swooning. The discussion between Ethan and the naked woman was sheer lunacy—something from the *Twilight Zone*, but until she escaped Jen would have to co-exist with them in this twisted, altered reality. There was nothing she could do except stay alert and attempt to stay alive.

Eris turned her scary eyes on Jen. "Let's go select my new wardrobe, shall we? I hope the mistress of this house has refined taste."

Away from Ethan's earshot, Jen started rambling. "I know there's something here that can fit him. He shouldn't have to stay caged in the basement. We don't get many women here at the house, but there are hordes of them who roam the streets at night. If he goes out after dark, no one will suspect that he's not quite human."

Eris's eyes lit with hostility. Irritated, she motioned for Jen to lead the way.

32

With the naked ghost lady at her side, Jen exited Ethan's bedroom, giving a swift backward glance at Boozer. To Jen's relief, he was not tagging along. He glowered and snarled at Jen, but at least he was staying put. Jen figured the woman must have given the brute a warning signal to keep an eye on Ethan. *Good!* Without the assistance of the cloven-foot beast, the ghost lady might not be a strong opponent. Perhaps Jen could subdue her, outrun her, or outsmart her and get her hands on a phone.

Heart in her throat, Jen moved from one room to the next, frantically plotting an escape. Buying time, she slowly…mechanically searched closets, trunks, bureau drawers, and as expected, continually came up empty handed.

She knew there was nothing in the house that the big ogre could even fit an arm or a leg inside. He was monstrously large. Without meaning to, Jen conjured up an image of Boozer.

She grimaced at the thought of those claws, the tarnished sharp teeth, the hooves…and that big furry dick. *Eew!*

On second thought, she preferred Boozer to be dressed and out of the house as quickly as possible.

Yes, it was terrible to unleash such a hellish terror upon society. And it was an act of cowardice to try to spare herself while Boozer rampaged through the populace of Philadelphia and the entire tri-state area, she admitted, somewhat ashamed.

But...she'd never claimed to be a humanitarian; she simply wasn't brave enough or kind enough to deliberately martyr herself to save many. Wanting him, or *it*, or whatever Boozer was...far, far away from her, Jen began an enthusiastic search for jumbo-sized male attire.

Eris sighed impatiently. "Forget about Boozer. I want to be fitted in the mistress's finest garments."

The title Madame Vice President was going to be difficult enough for Jen to stomach, but referring to Catherine as *mistress* was really taking her bossy employer's status a bit too far.

Misery loves company and Jen truly wished Catherine was home right now, experiencing this horror-show right alongside of her. But she wasn't. That hussy was somewhere visiting the troops, and enjoying the fawning press and the thunderous applause that erupted whenever she made an appearance.

With her lips turned down in defeat, Jen muttered miserably, "Sure, follow me, I'll show you the mistress's wardrobe."

Eris swept into Catherine's grand bedroom as if it were her very own. Her eyes sparkled in delight, dancing over the sights of the luxurious and well-made bed, the Moroccan rug, the sleek furnishings, and the silk drapes that hung at the windows.

"This is lovely. Almost as lovely as my personal quarters on the Goddess Realm."

"Excuse me?"

"The Goddess Realm—my true home."

"Okay..."

"I'm a goddess," Eris spat, insulted that Jen hadn't recognized her goddess-like qualities. Jen stared dumbly. Eris gawked at her if she were a blithering idiot who needed to be told a fact that should have been apparent.

"Oh, you're a goddess?"

"I'm Eris, the goddess of destruction."

"I see."

"You don't see. Your effort at humoring me is contemptuous." Tiny sparks of fury flickered from Eris's eyes.

More frightened than ever, Jen calmed the quick-to-anger goddess. "I knew there was something special about you," she placated Eris as she led her to an adjacent room that closely resembled a posh boutique. Catherine's luxurious walk-in closet— featured suspended shelving, and a dressing area with excessive mirrors.

"These are her power suits!" Jen exclaimed and pointed to a multitude of tailored separates in an array of colors and textures. Owning only a meager wardrobe, Jen was no fashionista, but even she, with her predilection for comfort rather than frill, knew that Catherine Provost's wardrobe was stuffy and conservative. She hoped witchy woman wouldn't mind.

Frowning, Eris cradled her chin as she took inventory of Catherine's business suits.

Near the open door was shelving and drawers that contained accessories, sweaters, and other clothing items. Jen meandered over to a stack of pastel-colored cardigans. Needing something to do with her nervous hands, she lifted a random stack of sweaters and anxiously squeezed, crumpling the perfectly folded pile.

Her eyes bounced around and lingered longingly at the threshold she yearned to sprint across. Maybe she should disable Eris and then escape. She surveyed the room in search of an object to bash the wicked woman upside the head.

She needed something heavy enough to cause severe head trauma or, better yet, a death so swift and permanent, the creature would be cast back inside the computer or back to that "realm" she called home. But Jen saw nothing except satin clothes hangers, wimpy power suits, and plushy soft sweaters.

Her eyes shot over to the many rows of shoes arranged in cubbies. Jen scanned them, hopeful. But the shoes were totally useless. All sensible pumps and flats. Not one pair of pointy, killer stilettos among the many pairs of conservative footwear.

She struggled with the impulse to dash out of there. She was a strong runner; she could get downstairs and out the front door in record time.

But she didn't know what powers Eris possessed. Her claim of being a goddess could be true for all Jen knew. Being a goddess, maybe she didn't need to run fast. Maybe she would take flight, whipping through the air in pursuit of Jen.

Anything was possible in this household that had suddenly become a three-ring circus…a loony bin. No, the Provost home had become far worse; it was a haunted house with evildoers from other realms.

If she thought hard enough about her grave circumstances, or gave in to her fears, she would pee her pants again, faint, or succumb to a fatal heart attack. But survival instincts would not allow her to give up without a fight.

So, instead of running, Jen thought it a better idea to try to slip past Eris while she browsed through Catherine's clothes. She stared at the door and then at Eris, who was sweeping through the sea of suits.

Calculating her stealthy movements, Jen's eyes shifted around, making sure Eris was preoccupied. She was, but not with the wardrobe. For some inexplicable reason, she'd shifted her attention to her hands and was holding them up to her face, flipping them back and forth, smiling a wicked smile as she marveled at her palms and then at the backs of her hands as if they were precious stolen goods that she'd cunningly confiscated.

They were nice enough hands with long, slender fingers, but really...what was the big deal? Jen shrugged. Seizing the opportunity, she promptly returned the rainbow hues of cashmere inside the lavender-scented drawer. With the toes of her left foot pointed, she prepared to make her sneaky move.

"These garments are deplorable!" Eris's voice suddenly filled the quiet room. "Where's the mistress's finery?"

Caught in the act, Jen took in a harsh gasp of breath. Her heart fluttered erratically. "Her finery?'" she asked, her face scrunched in confusion.

Ghost lady had her furious bright blue eyes fixated on her, and Jen, too intimidated and too guilty to meet her gaze, hung her head low. Her escape attempt was thwarted but, too absorbed in her repulsion, Eris didn't seem to notice Jen's outstretched leg.

Resignedly, Jen lowered her foot. She was stuck. There'd be no making a run for it or any stealthy tip-toeing out of there.

Strutting around the well-organized room with an air of confidence not typically associated with someone in dire need of clothing, Eris made a flourishing gesture with her long arm. "There nothing suitable here. When I take my trip to Roanoke, I want to be swathed in the finest lady-like apparel. I refuse to be seen in any of these unsightly garments. There's not even a decent frock in sight."

Pants and skirt suits lay in a colorful heap on the floor. Wearing an expression of loathing, Eris dropped a black skirt and fitted jacket combo on top of the discarded pile of business wear with such force, a gust of air fluttered and lifted Jen's bangs from her forehead.

What the hell is a frock? Jen scratched her head. *Oh!* Suddenly illuminated, she realized that Eris was stuck in slavery times and wanted to wear a dress, but not just any dress...she wanted something fancy like a Scarlett O'Hara, belle-of-the-ball type gown. A gaudy little number with a brocade fitted top, cinched waist and layers and layers of voluminous satiny skirts. Why would a black woman, even a partially dead one, yearn for such a crude reminder of high times in the Antebellum South? Jen almost shook her head in disgust, but caught herself. She dared not risk making a gesture that would possibly raise the hackles of the ill-tempered goddess.

"I thought you wanted…you know, something casual. Catherine keeps her gowns separate."

As if expecting the ball gowns to be as humdrum of the rest of the gear, Eris gave a contemptuous snort. "Well…where are the frocks?"

"This way." Jen led Eris to the opposite side of the vast room. "Her evening gowns are stored in air-tight bags," Jen explained, forcing a smile that strove to please.

Jen swung open the double doors of a heavy closet. Eris was right behind Jen. So close, her naked breasts pressed into Jen's back. Her nipples felt like daggers, giving Jen the willies. Eris was completely comfortable in her nudity, desiring clothing only so she could make her journey to Roanoke.

Feeling an urgent need to get the goddess dressed and her pointy boobies properly covered, Jen unzipped a clothing bag.

"Oh shit," she muttered softly. It was the gown Catherine was planning to wear to the Inaugural Ball. The lady of the house would shit bricks if something happened to the gown.

Reminding herself that this was a matter of life or death, Jen yanked the gown out of the bag, handling the delicate fabric roughly in her haste to accommodate Eris's finicky taste. "What do you think?" She held the plain mauve chiffon gown up for inspection.

Eris sneered at the chiffon dress.

Sweating bullets, Jen unzipped six or seven airtight bags containing smooth, sleek, and flowing chenille, satin, silk, and chiffon ballroom finery. Eris turned up her nose at each offering and unceremoniously flung the dresses to the floor.

Jen's face lit when she remembered a costume that Catherine had planned to wear to a Halloween party tonight. That was before she been offered the nomination. Now off somewhere with the troops, Catherine had no need for the costume that was the perfect frock for this pesky witch.

It wasn't an Antebellum era gown; it was from the Victorian period. But what the heck. She displayed the gaudy costume.

A flicker of a smile crossed Eris's face.

Great! While the goddess caressed the fabric, Jen investigated the path to her escape. There were no cumbersome items to jump over or negotiate around. The door was wide open and she had a clear path. It was time to make her move.

"Stop daydreaming. Help me with this!" Eris broke into her thoughts.

"Sure." She shot a longing glance at the open door.

On her knees, Jen held the skirt of the gown open, allowing Eris to step easily into the circle of soft fabric. Jen rose and pulled up the bodice, carefully zipping the back. "Beautiful," she murmured, trying to infuse delight into her tone.

Eris glared at Jen, her cold blue eyes seeming to inform Jen that she didn't need her pathetic approval. Eris waltzed over to the floor length mirror and stared at her image.

Then something freaky happened. Behind Eris's reflection, there was an image of a child's bedroom. A very elaborately decorated little girl's room. Incongruous to the frilly décor was an old brown wooden box.

Eris gasped. "My jewels!" she screamed.

Quick as a flash, the scenery in the mirror disappeared. And something else started disappearing. Jen covered her mouth and gawked at Eris in shock.

Eris's fingers blurred and looked distorted. Jen rubbed her eyes, trying to sharpen her vision, which she was certain had begun to fail her. Then unbelievably, one by one, Eris's fingers started evaporating right before Jen's very eyes.

Eris held up her fingerless hands and howled; the sound long and discordant like an annoying alarm.

Heavy hooves could be heard stampeding down the hallway. *Boozer!* Jen wanted to cry. There'd be no escaping with that big oaf around.

Boozer galloped into the wardrobe room, his ugly face contorted in confoundedness. "What's wrong, goddess?"

In silent response, Eris held up her arms. Her hands were gone, they'd completely disappeared. Jen had never seen such a frightful sight. She wanted to yell her head off, but she kept her wits about her.

"Don't worry, goddess, you'll grow back another pair," Boozer told Eris and then put an arm around her. While the monster was comforting Eris, Jen took creeping steps toward the door, acknowledging the sad fact that even if she made it out of the house unharmed, she doubted if her mental status would remain intact. She'd seen too many bizarre things in a short period of time to remain sane. But her survival instincts pushed her forward.

Until Eris said, "Bite her for me, Boozer! Your teeth are stronger than mine."

Jen froze. "Wh-what? Bite who?"

Eris looked at Jen with venomous eyes. "Stop sniveling. I have to feed." She turned her gaze on Boozer. "Don't be greedy. Just break the skin."

"No!" Jen shouted. She bolted from the room, arms propelling as she powered down the long hall. But she didn't get far. Boozer grabbed her by the back of her collar; his claws deliberately digging into the flesh of her neck as he jerked her into his hairy grasp.

"This should be done in private. Xavier has been an amused spectator, spying on me when he's in a trance state, but I refuse to grant him an audience to my weakness while he's fully awake. Take the governess to the cellar."

"No!" Jen kicked out her legs and swung her arms, fighting for release. But Boozer contained her easily, covered her mouth with his hand, and tightened his grip around her waist, cutting off her circulation and making it difficult for her to breathe.

33

In the dreary cellar, the air was saturated with an awful odor that Jen couldn't identify. Boozer uncovered her mouth.

"Please! Please, don't hurt me," she choked out.

Ignoring her plea, his features hardened and knotted, mutating further his hideous face. He made a roaring sound as he drew back his enormous hand and slammed it hard against her face.

The sound of the slap echoed. Jen could feel the heat of pain emanating from her cheek into her tormentor's calloused palm. The blast of heat must have compounded his desire to do more harm.

Using clawed fingers, the beast mauled her, etching four red lines into her cheek.

"Help me! Somebody, please help me!" she cried out, a shaky hand protectively covering the injured side of her face.

Boozer growled a low and deadly warning. Fearful of what he'd do next, she trembled violently, teeth chattering as she struggled to quiet herself down. As she shuddered and whimpered helplessly, the creature peeled her hand away from her face.

Her eyes went wild as he straightened out her arm and then pressed his hairy nostrils against her skin, inhaling her scent the way an animal sniffs its food.

Eris made an impatient sound. Jen glanced at her, using saddened eyes to beg for compassion. With her mouth tight, Eris glared down at Jen with cold-hearted contempt. Jen dropped her gaze in dismay.

"Hurry." Eris spat. "Bite her before I begin losing my feet as well as my hands."

Before Jen could emit another plea, Boozer attacked. He bit into her arm with such ferocity, Jen swooned. Her legs gave out and her body sagged to the floor as unbearable pain exploded through her.

Boozer didn't try to hold her upright. Crouching, he joined her on the floor, his teeth still attached to her flesh as he pulled her limp body closer.

The agonizing sensation of teeth embedded in her flesh left her woozy, but unfortunately, she remained conscious. Adding to her suffering, the monster sank his teeth even deeper and began sucking out blood.

Jen couldn't comprehend if the vicious assault had rendered her crippled or if the shock of it all had overwhelmed her, but as much as she'd chosen to fight for her life, she was powerless to keep her torso upright. She slumped over, her head drooping feebly on Boozer's shoulder as the cad slurped blood from the gash he'd made into her arm.

"Enough!" Eris shouted. "She's mine!"

With the snarling resentment of a wild animal being forced to relinquish the prey, Boozer begrudgingly raised Jen's wounded arm up to Eris's waiting lips.

Wanting to know what was going on, Jen hazarded an upward glance and instantly regretted her curiosity.

Wearing the ball gown, Eris looked a frightful, macabre mess as she licked her lips and then hungrily latched onto Jen's arm. Her mouth sealed around the open wound as she suctioned out streams of blood.

Shouting strident pleas for mercy, Jen jerked and twisted to no avail. Her weakened body was held inside Boozer's vise-like grip.

Eris stopped sucking momentarily and observed the area at her wrists where hands should have been. Lips pursed in dissatisfaction, she resumed feeding. Slowly now and despite Jen's shrieks for her to please stop, Eris sucked unhurriedly—daintily as if she were taking sweet sips from a glass of wine.

Finally, Jen became quiet, her screams replaced by quiet murmurs as a peaceful darkness fell upon her with the gentleness of soft blanket, escorting her to merciful oblivion.

Oblivion was replaced with dreams. Very pleasant dreams. In one happy scenario, she played with the old family dog. In the dream state, Pogo was alive and vibrant. He didn't seem cranky or sickly.

Running and leaping, Pogo chased a Frisbee and actually caught it, exhibiting the clear sightedness and vigor of a frisky puppy. In another dream, she sat in a classroom paying rapt attention to the professor's lecture. Then she raised her hand, waving enthusiastically. With a twinkle of delight in his eyes, the professor nodded, encouraging Jen to enlighten the class with her vast knowledge. In her dream world, she didn't need to cheat her way through the semester.

The distant ringing of a telephone dragged her from sweet peace. She opened her eyes to pitch-black darkness. And pain. Everything hurt—especially her arm. *Why?*

Gingerly, she stroked the area that throbbed. With a squeaky yelp, she retracted her hand. *What in the name of God?* Against her will and her better judgment, her fingers returned to the injury. At the touch of the bloody open wound, horrific memories flooded her mind.

At the same time, there was a creak. Her heart skipped several beats. Then footsteps were heard overhead. She tried to orient herself to the surroundings, but the distinctive sound of Ethan's wheezing sent her scooting backward, blindly trying to find a place to hide. On her knees, she scampered beneath a wooden structure and prayed that she wouldn't be detected.

A door opened, followed by the click of a switch. Bathed in light, Jen squinted and shielded her eyes. She trembled with dread as footsteps descended.

"Come from under that table, nanny," Ethan said, announcing his agitation with increased wheezing.

Holding on to the leg of the table, Jen shook her head; refusing to leave her place of refuge.

"My father is on the telephone. He wants to speak with you. On your feet now—get up, nanny!"

"Please don't make me face those monsters again. Look what they did to me." She held out her arm.

Ethan snorted. "That's nothing." He made a dismissive, *tsking* sound.

"Please."

He shrugged. "Can't help you. Eris needs your blood."

"Why?"

"Female trouble," he said sarcastically. "I don't know. She's extremely vain. Has something to do with the appearance of her hands and her feet."

Jen recalled the horror of witnessing Eris's vanishing hands and resisted the urge to sprint up the stairs, burst through the front door like a cartoon character, leaving behind a cut-out impression of her body as a testament of her absolute fear.

"That Boozer is a wacko, a real basket case." The boy shook his head. "Did you know he was a serial killer in his previous life...and a rapist?"

Jen shook her head mournfully while frantically considering escape options.

"In case you haven't noticed, he's hung like a horse. If that fiend has his way, he'll skewer you."

Jen uttered a sound of sharp anxiety.

"I told him you were saving yourself for marriage..." Ethan gave a wheezing chuckle. Jen groaned. Ethan's sense of humor was cruel and obnoxious. "You're safe from the fiend for now," he went on. "But if you don't get yourself up those stairs right this minute, I'm turning you over to Boozer so he can satisfy his hunger."

"No!" She held up her hand; the motion sent pulses of pain up and down her arm. Wincing, she lowered her arm, and then circled a comforting finger around the open wound.

"Come upstairs and speak to my father," he said impatiently. "I can't stay down in this smelly cellar much longer. The odor is stifling; it's making me wheeze." He immediately began the heavy wheezing that usually preceded an episode. "If I become incapacitated," he rasped. "I can't promise that I'll have the strength to protect you."

Using her good arm, Jen pushed herself up and rose to her feet. Sadly, she trailed the young agent of the devil and slowly ascended the cellar stairs.

"Tell my father that Eris has come with high recommendations from the agency. Tell him she has lots of experience with autistic children."

At the top of the stairs, Eris stood. Miraculously, her feet and hands were attached. Crusted blood—Jen's blood—trimmed the square neckline of Catherine's Halloween costume. Eris looked Bride of Frankenstein frightful; except for her hair. It wasn't sticking out like she'd been electrocuted.

Amazingly, Eris's hair looked fantastic with the heavy coils fashioned into a perfect upsweep. Her body was perfection—toned, slender, and strong. Her mean expression couldn't hide the beauty that she possessed. But the wicked woman's physical attributes were overshadowed by the pure evil that she emanated.

"I've spoken to your employer—introduced myself. He seems satisfied but requested to speak with you." She glided over to nearby phone in the dining area. "Tell him that I'm making remarkable progress with Xavier...I mean, Ethan." Eris's expression soured when she spoke the demon child's given name. "Don't add any unnecessary details. Keep the chitchat to a minimum."

"Hi, Senator Provost." Jen sounded distressed and hoped to God he could hear her silent plea for help.

"How's it going, Jen?" he said brightly, a stark contrast to his dark mood earlier. "Everything going okay?" He sounded bubbly and had paid no attention to Jen's anguished tone. "The new nanny sounds like a real gem. Lucky for us, huh?"

"Uh...yeah," she said, a bit more upbeat after Eris shot her a hateful glare. Then she added, "I guess..." attempting to infuse some doubt in the senator's mind.

"Good...good. Glad things are working out. She told me about her success with autistic children."

"Oh, she told you about the work she does?" Jen said, speaking slowly... softly... her tone filled with warning, hoping that the senator would read between the lines... hear her inner scream.

"She's a very impressive woman."

Ohmigod! Don't you hear the terror in my voice? She wanted to shake her fist and shout, but with two pairs of evil eyes on her, Jen could not express her frustration. All she could do was breathe out a heavy sigh of disappointment.

Proving to not have a shred of clairvoyance or even paternal instincts, the senator continued. "Listen, they've amped up Catherine's schedule. She's going to be making additional campaign stops. Her agenda is really brutal..."

"Yeah, all that campaigning sounds brutal." She darted an eye at her arm and flinched. It took every ounce of restraint not to shout, *You wanna see brutal? I'll show you brutal, pal!* But she said instead, "When will you be back?"

"That's the thing... I'm not sure. The press has noted my absence. With the election so close..."

"Ethan needs—"

Eris waved her hand and Boozer materialized, tramping into the room with his menacing eyes focused on Jen.

"Okay, well, I'll handle things here," Jen blurted, her voice suddenly pleasant.

"Oh, make sure the nanny agency faxes over the privacy forms that Eris signed. Catherine doesn't want her staff involved in any aspect of Ethan's care. It's a private matter."

"Maybe you or Ms. Provost should call them; I doubt if the agency I work for would be willing to trust me with any private documents." The new nanny from hell certainly hadn't come through the agency and perhaps a call from the senator or Ms. Provost, requesting paperwork, would alert them that something was amiss.

"You're right. I'll call the agency and I'll check in with you later tonight."

"Good. Okay." She hung up with confidence that the calvary would be arriving soon.

Ethan clapped his little hands, sarcastically applauding her performance. "Very convincing, but my opinion doesn't matter. Did you persuade my father to stay where he is?"

"Yes."

Ethan nodded. "When is he returning?"

"I'm not sure. He didn't say."

"She can't be trusted," Eris interrupted. She pointed a well-formed accusing finger at Jen. "The next time your employer makes contact, be sure that I speak with him before you disconnect."

"Okay." She cradled her injured arm. Her eyes roved worriedly over the mangled flesh.

Ethan wrinkled his nose. "That wound looks pretty nasty. It should be treated before it becomes infected."

Unconcerned, Eris shrugged.

"Didn't you purport to have healing skills in that slave life of yours?"

"That's what I told those fools on the plantation. But I know nothing about healing humans nor do I care about their injuries. My one concern is keeping this mortal body intact." She stared at her hands, checking to make sure they were undamaged.

"She's no good to you if her blood is tainted."

"What should I do?"

"You're going to have to close that wound."

"How?"

"I don't know. We can look up the instructions for administering sutures on the internet. If I'm correct, we may need to acquire the intestines of a cat, which we don't have. Can Boozer be trusted to make a quick run outdoors to find us a stray?"

"He's naked. And he looks too peculiar to run around chasing stray cats in the light of day."

"Good point," Ethan agreed and began stroking his chin in thought.

No, no, no! Jen was horrified. Instinct told her to get herself to the closest hospital before she ended up with gangrene, but these cads were without mercy and completely unreasonable. She couldn't rely on them to get her proper medical care. Thinking it best to treat the bite wound herself and before Ethan started working on her poor arm with a needle and a string of cat guts, she blurted, "Uh…it's only a surface wound. It doesn't need stitches." She shook her head emphatically. "Some peroxide and a sturdy bandage and I'll be fine."

The three demented beings eyed her warily. Jen worked her mouth into a reassuring smile and nodded her head for extra emphasis.

34

All three ghouls accompanied her to her bedroom where she retrieved a first aid kit from a closet inside her personal bathroom. Wincing in pain, she administered to the bloody gash right above her wrist. Boozer kept watch. Hulking over her, the beast breathed down her neck, while Eris and Ethan conspired in whispery voices outside the open bathroom door.

With no clue what was in store for her next, she lingered inside the bathroom, trying to maintain self-control as a fur-covered dick pulsed against her spine. Hot beastly breath raised the fine hairs on the back of her neck, and a fountain of saliva spilled onto her shoulder.

Biting down on her lip, it was all she could do not to break down and wail. Her eyes swept the bathroom and landed on the skylight. Frantically, she calculated a getaway. *How can I get up there without a ladder?*

"What's taking so long?" Ethan asked, interrupting her thoughts.

"I'm almost done," she said gaily…too gaily for someone being held captive by a phallus that was as deadly as a dagger.

Boozer was unaware of the incongruity of her tone and her dire circumstances. His mental capacities were limited at best, but the little brain power he possessed was momentarily disabled due to his primal hunger for sex.

But Ethan's mind was sharp. His suspensions were triggered by Jen's unreasonably cheery tone. The boy took hasty steps to the doorway of the bathroom. Checking on her, his face darkened with mistrust. He eyed her arm, which was properly decorated with white gauze and adhesive tape.

But needing a reason to linger a while, she leaned close to the mirror above the sink. Scowling, she ran her fingers over her cheek and grimaced at the fiery lacerations Boozer had slashed across her cheek.

The boy studied her face. "You'll survive. Your cheek doesn't require emergency attention. Let's go."

"Where? Can't I stay here—in my room?" she asked in a withering tone.

"Eris is having problems again. She needs you."

"NO!" With her arms outstretched behind her, she clung to the sides of the sink.

"Get her, Boozer," Ethan said calmly, and then left the bathroom.

Hoisted over Boozer's hairy shoulder, Jen was carried, kicking and screaming, to one of the guest rooms that Eris had claimed as her own.

Gawking at her hands, which were now fingerless, Eris did not present a pretty picture.

"Bite her." She sighed and wearily cupped her face with her fingerless palms.

"Not again. I can't take anymore," Jen shrieked, terror-stricken by the prospect of enriching Eris's life with her blood.

Boozer flung her onto the bed and flopped down beside her. "Same spot as before?" His roughened voice was jarring. Boozer sounded as if sandpaper was trapped in his throat, making each word come out croaked and scratchy.

"Ethan, help me. Please," she beseeched the child. Boozer

locked a hand around he neck to silence her. Jen kicked and twisted, her eyes bulging.

"What are you trying to do, kill her?" he sternly addressed Boozer. With a grunt of dissatisfaction, Boozer released Jen's neck.

Eris inhaled noisily; her features tight with indignation. "You don't call the shots, little man! Boozer belongs to me. He is such an obedient servant, he burst through the portal of hell, carrying me protectively in his arms—"

"How very touching," Ethan interrupted, rolling his eyes.

"Boozer will not listen to you or anyone else."

Taking a wide stance, Ethan folded his arms. "He needs to listen to someone who has sound judgment."

"And that would be you?"

"Absolutely. As usual, Wicked One, you're not using your head. Your last visit to earth lasted how long?" He looked toward the ceiling. "It took only a few weeks for your recklessness to send you back to the Dark Realm. Eris, I know you need your limbs but your thoughtless behavior could result in terrible consequences."

"Such as…"

"Such as bringing the authorities to our door." Ethan's brow creased with concern. "You let that brute murder the cook… perhaps we can cover that up, but if he starts a killing spree right here in this house…well, my plan to destroy my parents goes right down the tubes because law enforcement will most definitely get involved."

"I am a goddess! I don't answer to your law enforcement. And I don't care about your plan. I'm only concerned about myself…I'm losing my hands!" Her eyes aflame with fury, she shouted at Boozer. "Rip off that bandage. Reopen her wound."

Murmuring incoherently, Jen wept bitterly as Boozer stabbed a sharp claw beneath the gauze that covered the nasty gash in her lower arm.

"No…never mind, don't bother with the old wound," Eris groused. "That stream of blood is deficient… I need blood from a stream with a longer-lasting time span. Bite her somewhere else. Do it now!"

Boozer grabbed Jen's good arm and began sniffing up and down, his signature ritual before brutally ripping into her flesh.

Ethan clucked his tongue and shook his head. "Such idiocy! I'm shocked by your ignorance. It doesn't matter where he bites her; it's all the same blood."

"I'm not an idiot," Eris protested. "I'm frantic and I can't think straight. You've always claimed to be such a wise old soul, so what do you think I should do?"

Boozer paused. Instead of biting, he ran his roughened lips over Jen's arm, warming her flesh with his hot breath while he impatiently waited for Eris and the boy to reach an agreement.

"Obviously, a few ounces of her blood are not beneficial for very long."

"Tell me something I don't know."

Arms folded, he took a few moments to mull over her words. "I could do some research on the computer if you'd like. There's a wealth of information on the internet. I spend endless hours doing online exploring."

Eris fixed a fiery gaze on the boy. "I don't have time for you to spend endless hours looking for a solution on that stupid machine."

"Stupid! I'll have you know that it was through computer technology that I was able to bring you and that barbarian here."

She held up her wrists, which hung limp from the complete loss of her hands. "My fingers…my palms. Gone! Are you satisfied, Xavier?" Her voice was shrill with accusation and rage.

"Calm down. Your lifeline is right here." He pointed to Jen and gave her a wink, which under the circumstances was a cruel thing to do.

Petrified, Jen shook her head repeatedly. "I'm not her lifeline! I gave blood already. Leave me alone. Please!" She appealed to Eris. "Goddess...ma'am, I'd help you if I could. But I don't think my blood's gonna work for you. Could be because I'm B-positive. Maybe you need another blood type," Jen rationalized. Her mind raced to find a drawn-out explanation to support her claim. She was willing to go to great lengths to prevent another dreadful encounter with Boozer's choppers and Eris's blood-sucking lips.

"She has a point," Ethan agreed.

Jen exhaled. There was hope. It was a pity that she was such a gutless girl, willing to allow an innocent victim to be lured inside the lion's den to save her own hide. She felt so sorry for the unsuspecting stranger that she made a fervent vow to escape and get help while the three demons were distracted with violating the unfortunate captive.

"The only other mortal in this house is you, little man," Eris threatened. "Are you offering a taste of your blood?"

Her safety was on the line. Holding her breath in anticipation, Jen waited for Ethan to respond—to do the right thing and contribute his own blood. When the boy issued a wicked chuckle, any hope she'd held was instantly dashed.

"Wicked One, Wicked One..." He paused and regarded Eris with devilish amusement. "I'd gladly offer my blood, but I'm not a healthy mortal. As you can see, I'm quite frail. The loss of blood could be my ruination. You need me healthy and alive to execute your diabolical plan."

"You served your purpose. I don't need you."

"You'll need my family's resources to venture out into a world that requires hard cash to make it from one day to the next."

"I have valuables in Roanoke."

"You'll never get to Roanoke without money. You've lost your ability to flit about, traveling as a stream of mist."

"I realize that," she said, frowning down at her feet that had started losing toes. "Shut up, Xavier!"

Eris was losing extremities at an astonishing rate and her predicament did not bode well for Jen.

"All this jabbering is a waste of time. No more talk; I need blood!"

Three pairs of eyes settled on Jen.

Arching a brow, the boy looked at Jen. "Until we can figure out why Eris keeps losing her limbs, you're going to have to tough it out."

"What do you mean?" Jen squeaked, but she knew exactly what he meant.

35

It seemed like she was in the midst of an out-of-body experience. Numb and still as a statue, she felt nothing. Instead of flailing or going into spasms when Boozer sank his incisors into her limb, Jen hadn't flinched. Through an amazing but unintentional act of disassociation, she sat with Zen-like calmness as the ogre ripped a chunk of flesh from her arm, creating a bloody crater. Jen didn't blink an eye.

Inside the deep crimson hole, Eris inserted a straw. Ironically, it came from the cheerful pack of kiddy straws Lizzy had given Ethan. The joke was on Jen. Ethan wasn't and never had been a kid. As bizarre a sight as it was to see a plastic straw jutting out of her arm, even stranger was the fact that Eris's lips were puckered around the end of the brightly colored straw, drawing out Jen's blood as casually as if she were sipping a refreshing beverage.

Jen showed no emotion and felt no pain. Ghost lady had been using her and feeding on her so frequently, Jen had detached from her own body. Her will to survive was diminishing. She was peaceful. Probably close to death from blood loss, she surmised. Evil had won the battle. She could no longer keep up the good fight. Not physically or emotionally. Somewhere in her hazy mind, she surrendered, admitting to herself that death had to be far better than living like this.

"Take her away," Eris commanded. Boozer did as he was told, yanking Jen by the collar. He dragged her out of the room and down the stairs. She didn't feel the bump of each step that the beast descended. She felt nothing except the peaceful release of life slowly leaving her body.

In the lightless cellar, the air was heavy with a revolting smell... a stench so thick that it brought Jen back to awareness, making her retch and dry heave. The beast grabbed her by the collar and dug a claw into her elbow, ensuring that she was awake.

She witnessed him lifting a floorboard and a blast of foul odor assaulted her nostrils. Jen resisted the beast's pull on her arm. He was trying to drag her into a hidden underbelly of the cellar; a place where mice and rats and God knew what else were swarming.

Boozer yanked her down two or three stairs and then let her fall the rest of the way down. Her body hitting concrete wasn't as bad as the feeling of suffocation from the toxic-smelling stink.

Boozer replaced the floorboard, leaving Jen in utter darkness. No rodents approached and it didn't matter. She could feel the curtain of this life coming down and felt herself sinking. Soon, sweet eternal sleep would claim her. Jen welcomed death.

But it was a cruel joke. Jen had only slept. She awoke to total darkness and a sickening stench, that was unlike anything she'd ever smelled. Momentarily disoriented, she wondered why she was lying in darkness, why did she hurt all over, and what was that putrid smell?

Oh, God! Horrific memories flooded her mind. Ethan, apparently in cahoots with the devil himself, had somehow unleashed two demons and invited them into the Provost home.

No longer willing to just lie down and die, Jen flattened her hand against the cold concrete floor and tried to push herself up. Agh! Excruciating pain shot through her arm; she collapsed, her head banging against concrete. She'd landed sort of sideways and the horrific odor seemed closer. With every breath, she inhaled the awful smell.

Oh, Jesus! I have to get out of this house. Desperate to escape, she lifted her head slightly, but the pressure on her neck was too painful. Lying prone, Jen turned her head from one side to the other, trying to make out her surroundings...maybe locate a window or a secret escape hatch. But there was nothing except total darkness. And that atrociously foul odor.

Jen wrinkled her nose. *What the hell is that fetid smell? Spoiled wine? Rotted food? A dead mouse? Or a dead rat? Ew!* Jen shuddered. Repelled, she drew up her legs.

Even after suffering the appalling assaults at the hands of Satan's evil deed-doers, she still didn't think she could handle feeling her feet brushing up against a nasty, dead rat.

She uttered a helpless cry. Not too loud. She whimpered low and pitifully, careful not to draw the monsters down to the basement. Honestly, if she heard that thing named Boozer clomping down the stairs, she'd kill herself by running full speed, headfirst, into a wall. If that didn't do the trick, she'd have no choice but to bash her brains out against the concrete floor.

God, she wished she had her cell phone on hand. She'd speed dial everyone in her contact list...Rome, her parents, her geek friends back in Centerville, the senator, Ms. Provost. She'd call information and ask to be put through to the FBI...the CIA... *The National Enquirer*...TMZ... Hell, she'd even send a text message to Mediatakeout.com and that blogging queen, Perez Hilton.

Jen would reach out to anyone who could get the word out and draw some attention to this demon-infested house. Somebody had to save her before those maniacs started biting on her and siphoning out her blood again…with a straw.

She rolled her eyes, infuriated as she recalled Lizzy proudly pulling those weapons out of the pocket of her big sweater. How had something that appeared so innocent ended up being used as an instrument of destruction?

Rome! Oh, her heart hurt. There'd be no hot date tonight. Or ever. These monsters, fitting in perfectly with Halloween, were not going to let her go.

There was no way she was going to lie down in this basement waiting for that hairy, wax-faced maniac to come and fetch her so Eris could have herself another drink of blood. This madness could on indefinitely, with Eris expecting a hemoglobin cocktail every time she broke a freakin' fingernail.

Jen would rather die right now than endure another brutal biting and more blood sucking. Determined to at least attempt to escape, she propped herself up with her other arm.

It hurt badly but she pushed past the burning pain, panting desperately as she struggled to lift her torso from the floor. Finally, she made it to an upright position. Feeling winded like she'd just finished a 10K race, she gasped, and then had to rest for a moment as she tried to catch her breath.

When her heart rate calmed down a little, she squinted in the dark. Time to move into the next phase of her great escape, but she needed something to grab onto so she could pull herself off the floor. With feeble motions, she waved her aching, mangled arm through the air, hoping to hit upon something solid, but all that hand waving was creating a really funky breeze.

She waved high. Then low. Her hand smacked into something

soft. And gooey. Gooey stuff was all over her hand. And it stank to high heavens. Smelled worse than a truck filled with five weeks worth of garbage. *Eew! Eew! Eew!*

"Oh, Jesus," she moaned, tears beginning to pool as she frantically wiped the mush from her hand, trying to get it off by smearing it across the floor. What had she touched? A person? Jen wanted to scream. She'd been dumped inside the wine cellar, confined with a dead body lying next to her. And she'd been victimized further by ending up with a really stinky hand.

She needed some soap and water. No, that wouldn't help. She'd need something a lot stronger for the residual mess that was clung to the spaces between her fingers and under her nails.

It felt as yucky as it smelled. Now, her problem had escalated. In addition to trying to stay alive, she needed to find a container of Lysol…a bottle of bleach…or some freakin' Mr. Clean!

"Get it together, Jen. Focus. Deal with the smell," she murmured to herself, attempting to talk herself into a state of calmness. As her eyes finally began to adjust to the darkness, she realized that she was not in the main part of the wine cellar, but had been placed in some hidden space where it would be hard for someone to find her.

She cut an eye at the dead body next to her. At first she blinked in disbelief. Then she had to cover her mouth to stifle a scream. Carmen's favorite plaid skirt was hitched up over her abundant behind, where big hunks of flesh had been ripped out. *Oh, my God. No! Carmen!*

"I'm sorry, Carmen. I'm so sorry," she sobbed softly. Grimacing, she pulled back both feet and pushed them into the cook's mutilated backside, shoving the decaying carcass as far away from her as possible.

36

Even though Kali no longer seemed afraid and was back to sleeping in her own room, the family did not plan to celebrate Halloween. To Ajali, donating Kali's Halloween costume to the Children's Hospital was a good idea.

An even better idea had been contacting volunteer services at the hospital and committing to spending several hours a week reading to the sick children. Tonight, she had asked if she could bring Kali along.

The Children's Hospital was bustling with Halloween activities. The staff as well as many of the children wore costumes. On a trick-or-treating excursion, some of the children walked, others propelled wheelchairs as they paraded through the hospital, making stops at various nurses' stations, and yelling: "Trick or treat!"

In spite of the colorful display of holiday decorations, the mood on the fifth floor was less than festive. A dozen or so children were assembled inside a large playroom. These pediatric patients, with conditions too fragile to participate in the costume parade, were quiet. A somber bunch. Some sat in wheelchairs, but most lay prone on recliners, their eyes closed—presumably asleep.

"This is Ms. Ajali Stovall and her daughter, Kali," a nurse dressed in a ballerina costume spoke cheerfully to the sedate group of kids. "Ms. Stovall is going to read you Halloween stories.

Isn't that nice?" Those who were awake responded with slight head nods and weak smiles, but one little girl gave a big, snaggle-tooth smile and yelled an exuberant, "Yes!"

Feeling an instant connection, Kali took a seat next to the bubbly little girl. "Hi," Kali said shyly. "My name is Kali."

"My name is Shanice," the child said, her expressive brown eyes bright with excitement.

"Hello, everyone and happy Halloween," Ajali began. All of a sudden, Shanice groaned, her face, etched in pain.

"Excuse me, Ms. Stovall," the nurse interrupted. "I'm going to take Shanice back to her room."

"Is she coming back?" Kali asked.

"I don't think so," the nurse said. "Shanice gets really sleepy after she takes her medication."

"Can I keep her company until she goes to sleep?" Kali asked the nurse, cutting an eye at her mother, silently asking permission. Ajali nodded.

The nurse straightened the orange blanket around the little girl's legs. "Is that okay with you, Shanice? Do you mind if Kali visits with you in your room?"

Nodding, Shanice sent a faint smile in Kali's direction. "You can play with my Game Boy if you want to." The little girl tried to sound cheerful, but her pained voice was a fractured whisper.

Inside Shanice's room, the nurse transferred the little girl from the recliner to her bed. She raised the bedrails and then pushed a button, cranking up the top of the small hospital bed. "I'll be right back with your pain pill." Trying to cheer Shanice, the tutu-wearing nurse made a series of awkward twirls toward the door. Kali giggled. Surprisingly, Shanice managed a smile.

"The game is in—" Shanice flinched as though struck by a stab of pain. Moaning, she pointed shakily to her bedside table. "It's in the drawer."

"Do you have a tummy ache?" Kali asked.

"I have sickle cell anemia." A stream of tears began rolling down her brown cheeks.

Kali had never heard of the disease, but sensing Shanice's evident distress, she figured it was something serious. She glanced toward the open door, looking for the nurse, hoping she'd hurry back with the medicine.

"Oh!" Shanice whimpered, her facial features contorting badly.

Kali patted Shanice's shoulder. "Your nurse will be right back." Shanice was obviously in a great deal of pain and Kali had no idea how long it would take for the nurse to return. Needing to do something to help her new friend, Kali stuck her hand inside her pocket and took out the goddess ring.

Too large to fit her ring finger, she slipped the silver ring over her thumb. Swept by what felt like tidal waves of adrenaline, Kali stood held onto Shanice's bedrail, steadying herself as she waited to adjust to the overwhelming power of the ring. She leaned in closely, her face fixed in concentration, as she wiped away Shanice's teardrops with the pad of her thumb.

When the nurse returned holding a plastic med cup, Shanice had shown Kali how to lower her bedrails and was out of bed. "Shanice!" Mystified by what looked like a miraculous recovery, the nurse looked at Kali. Smiling, Kali shrugged. She slipped the ring off her thumb, and snuck it back inside her pocket.

"Can I put on my Halloween costume? I want to go trick-or-treating with the other kids," Shanice said, bouncing energetically.

"Are you sure you feel up to it, honey?"

"I really feel much better. I don't need a pill anymore."

"I don't know, Shanice." Frowning, the nurse looked torn. "You were in severe pain only a few minutes ago."

"I know, but Dr. Hutchins said my pain meds are to be taken as needed," Shanice reminded, sounding extremely mature. "The pain is gone and I don't need it. I want to wear my costume." Emphasizing her improved condition, Shanice jumped up and down, grinning and yelling, "Please, Nurse Rachel! Please!"

Giving in, the nurse helped dress Shanice in her costume, an elaborate, belle-of–the-ball gown, with a matching parasol.

"Look at you. You're beautiful...a true belle of the ball," the nurse cooed.

Beaming, Shanice looked at her reflection in a full-length mirror that was affixed to the closet door. Happy, she spun around and around.

"Be careful, honey. You don't want to wear yourself out," the nurse cautioned.

"You look fantastic," Kali exclaimed

"Thank you, Nurse Rachel." Shanice was beaming, and then her smile faded. "Do you have an extra costume for Kali?" Shanice's luminous eyes were wide with hope.

"I'm sorry, most of the costumes were donated and we gave them all out."

"That's okay," Kali said, never letting on that Shanice was wearing the costume her mother had donated—the gown that had been custom-made for her.

"I do have an extra bag if your mom says it's okay for you to have candy. Let's go ask Kali's mom if she can come along."

Holding hands, Kali and Shanice skipped into the playroom. Pausing from reading the story, Ajali stared at Shanice, surprised at her miraculous recovery.

"Can I go trick-or-treating with Shanice?" Kali asked her mother.

"Sure," Ajali agreed, gazing at Shanice unbelievingly.

"Shanice is a feisty one, but I don't ever think I've seen her quite this lively, Ms. Stovall. Your daughter seems to have really lifted her spirits. I don't know what she did, but whatever it was, it needs to be bottled." Nurse Rachel chuckled. "Okay, girls, let's go join all those ghosts and goblins."

As Ajali returned to the story she was reading, she noticed the dull sheen had left the eyes of the children who were awake and had been replaced with something else. *Hope?*

She knew for sure that the bleakness that had permeated the playroom was suddenly gone. It seemed entirely possible that these sombrous children might too, find a reason to smile.

37

In the kitchen, Boozer writhed on the floor, moaning and digging his claws into the hardwood floor as if in agony.

Disgusted, the boy grabbed the chrome handle of the refrigerator, pulling the door wide open, and displaying the contents; a large selection of colorful and eye-appealing groceries. "Do you see anything in there he can eat?" he asked, irritably.

"How would I know?" Eris snapped. "You brought us here; don't you know what he needs to survive?"

"I didn't bring that cretin here." The boy looked down at Boozer with scorn. "That was one of your tricks and now it's backfired. Just look at him," the boy said, repulsed as he observed Boozer.

Lying on his belly with his claws fully extended, Boozer wriggled, snake-like, across the slippery, high-shine, hardwood floor. Howling in sexual agony, the beast undulated, and gyrated, marring the beautiful hardwood, etching a trail as he slithered along, dry-humping the floor.

The boy grimaced. "I doubt that it's actually food that he desires. He's entirely animalistic and so very primitive; his problems are well beyond my scope." The boy shook his head. "Knowing how impulsive you are, I shouldn't be surprised, but I must admit, I'm disappointed in you, Eris. It was a very risky undertaking.

You took advantage of my generosity when you brought that nasty creature along."

Eris pushed the boy aside and slammed the refrigerator door shut. Emboldened by her restored limbs and no longer in need of his advice, she grabbed the child by the collar and lifted him off his feet, bringing him close to her face. She stared at him with incredible intensity. "Watch your tone, little man. I'm in command, now. You can't control me, like you did when we were in the Dark Realm."

"Put me down," the boy hissed through clenched teeth, his small chest heaving in rage. The ragged breathing that often preceded an episode commenced.

"Shut up!" Eris shouted in his face. "That rattling sound you're making is terribly and completely annoying. Stop it at once!"

Ethan ceased wheezing. He'd mastered the symptoms of an asthma attack and had often faked labored breathing as a warning to the household staff, as well as his parents, that he was dissatisfied. Unfailingly, his wheezing would have everyone scurrying about, quickly trying to pacify him before he worked himself up to a strident wail. But Eris was not so easily deceived. And there was fire in her indigo eyes that threatened to harm his fragile human body. "Bitch!" he snarled.

Eris released him from her grasp. He toppled down to the floor.

He scrambled to his feet. "I should have left you—"

"But you didn't. You brought me here and this time, I intend to stay. You're not as clever as you think. I'm superior to you, Xavier. I'm a goddess, and don't you forget it."

"You're a fallen goddess! You don't possess enough power to keep your hands attached to your wrists." He snickered maliciously.

"Your nanny will keep me well-nourished and in vibrant health."

"The poor nanny, dumped in the dungeon with a rotting corpse, is going to end up with a nasty infection in those wounds. Her blood will be tainted and what will you do then?" He arched a taunting brow.

"Oh, there will be others to feed on. Like you, for example," she said in a threatening tone.

He backed away. "I'm frail and anemic. My blood won't last very long nor do you much good. Besides, you need female blood," he said, making that claim off the top of his head. He actually had no idea what Eris needed to stay in human form. He looked up in thought. "Another thing…you'll never get to Virginia without my help."

Eris sneered. "When I was cast from the Goddess Realm, the goddesses crafted me a human form that was sturdy and beautiful and, most importantly, it remained intact." She gazed at her reflection in the chrome front of the fridge. "But during my last earth life, in which you provided the transportation—"

"I did nothing of the kind. I didn't invite you to join me at that time. I had plans for you to come later, but you were so impatient, you made yourself a stowaway inside my mother's womb. It wasn't my fault that your impatience and deception deprived you of a substantial human form."

"That was then. What about now? You brought me here on your own accord. So tell me, genius, why does this body keep falling apart?"

He shrugged. "Maybe it has something to do with that fiend you slipped through the portal without my knowledge."

"Talk, talk, talk. That's all you've ever been, Xavier…nothing but talk. Why can't you admit it? You don't know how to fix this problem. You're no mastermind. You used that contraption in your bedroom. I found the directions printed out and hidden in the bottom desk drawer."

Exposed, the boy flinched.

"Ah, you didn't think I'd discover your little trick?"

He was a pitiable sight with his hands behind his back, his large head held low.

"What happened to you, Xavier? You were once so wise and all-knowing. Or so I thought. I had so much respect for you while we dwelled together on the Dark Realm. You taught me to use my third eye vision, so what has happened to your skills?"

"It's this human form. It's terrible being trapped in this body."

"Why couldn't you retain your power?"

"I was born of woman…as a human child," he lamented.

"It's good to see you for what you really are…" Eris paused and smiled a wicked smile. "You're nothing but a very tiny, egotistical, and ineffective little man. A sideshow magician, duping spectators with card tricks, has more skills than you possess." Bending down to his height and narrowing her eyes at him, Eris jeered, "Smoke and mirrors, Xavier…that's all you are… that's all you ever were."

"I hate you, Eris and I hope you lose your head along with your limbs."

"Silence! Your voice is as annoying as a buzzing insect. You're useless to me now. Be gone!" She threw up a hand. "Go back to your bedroom and play with your computer toy." She glimpsed her hands, and then her gaze shifted to her feet. Satisfied that she had all ten fingers and toes, Eris drifted off in thought.

Chastised, the child turned to leave, then he whirled around wearing a devilish smile. "Where's Boozer?" he asked. There was a malicious glint in his eyes.

Eris jerked her toward the area where Boozer was last seen.

There was a long, crooked trail of etched scratches, leading toward the hall. But Boozer was gone.

"Boozer!" Eris shrieked.

The boy held up his hands. "Too late. He's probably in the cellar, gobbling up your evening meal. Instead of standing here puffed up with your goddess status and taking pleasure in belittling me, you should have kept your eye on that lowlife you thought had your best interests at heart."

Eris gasped and fled the kitchen, slip sliding along the way.

The boy toddled behind her, shaking his large head. "I guarantee you, he's devoured her completely. I can't imagine how you're going to get hold of another female the next time your limbs begin to disappear."

Eris froze, horrified by the boy's prediction. "Shut up, Xavier, before I turn you over my knee, you annoying little brat. I hate that you returned to earth as a child. It's just so unbecoming."

Out in the hallway, Eris breathed a sigh of relief. The lock on the cellar door was in place. "Boozer!" she called him again, this time using an alluring lilt in her voice.

Boozer didn't respond. He didn't have to. Eris and the boy heard him groaning. They rushed toward the sound of the senator's study and were both appalled to find the beast trying to get out of a window. His waxen buttocks were booted in the air. His hairy legs and malformed hooves were dangling inside, while his head, torso, and upper limbs hung outside the window.

Ethan shook his head in disgust. "I presume disarming the alarm system at the front door was too complicated for your idiot beast."

Boozer was too large for Eris or the boy to struggle with. Using the heat of her gaze, Eris burned a hole in the creature's backside.

Boozer howled and shimmied back inside, dropping to the floor, rubbing his smoking behind.

"Did you think I'd allow you to escape, you moron? You are here to protect me, not to roam and rampage these streets." She stood over him, the light in her eyes turned to a low beam that warned of continued burning if Boozer made one false move.

"Say you're sorry, you imbecile."

"I'm sorry."

"Now get up."

Boozer rose to his feet. He rubbed his buttock again and then began pacing and scratching his arms, like an addict in dire need of a fix.

"I don't know what I'm going to do about him," Eris confided to the boy.

"Let him have the nanny. The maid will be here in the morning. You can drink her blood."

"I've acquired a taste for the nanny." She held up her hands. "See how pretty. And look at my skin. It's absolutely glowing. I don't want to risk switching blood unless it's absolutely necessary."

Boozer's groaning grew louder. He began stomping back and forth, fists balled. Eris burned his other buttock. He smacked the smoking area, but despite the threat of more fiery pain, he continued to growl, enraged. "I gotta get outta here," Boozer bellowed.

"You can't go out; someone will see you," Eris argued.

"But I'm hun-ga-ry," Boozer roared, adding a syllable to the word "hungry." "Staaaarving!" He stretched out that word, bending at the waist, rubbing his thick, fleeced phallus. He pulled back the fur-covered foreskin, and frowned down at his engorged waxen-colored penis. It throbbed and oozed a grayish, semen-like substance.

The boy sucked his teeth and averted his gaze. "Your body-guard is despicable. The next time you make a selection, I beg of you to exercise better judgment—for the good of mankind."

"I don't care about mankind! I only care about me!" Eris screeched.

"Without mankind, who will sit and worship at your...uh..." He lowered his eyes, smirking down at her feet. "So far, so good," he taunted.

Eris ignored the boy's sarcasm. "Maybe we should force him to eat something. He was once human; he should still enjoy the taste of food. With something in his stomach, maybe he'll be less sexually aroused."

"He's an animal, Eris. He's in heat. Food is not the answer to his dilemma. Now, either offer up yourself as a treat or..."

Eris bristled. "Or nothing! I'm a goddess! Copulating with a beast is out of the question."

"You didn't seem to mind groveling in the soot with the ghouls on the Dark Realm," the boy reminded her.

"Different times; different circumstances."

Boozer's groans escalated to a howl, much like the sound of a wolf. "I need a female," he bellowed, stroking his dripping appendage. His grayish discharge had begun to puddle on the floor.

The boy threw up his hands. "This can't go on. That half-wit is going to bring the authorities to this door. He's going to ruin my plot against my parents. All that planning I did..." The boy sighed and then shook his head wearily.

Boozer howled again, this time he beat upon his chest with hairy, balled fists. At the same time, there was a buzzing coming from upstairs.

"I keep hearing that sound. What is it?" she asked the boy.

Though he knew perfectly well that the buzzing was the nanny's cell phone, he'd be damned if he'd willingly provide the ungracious goddess with any more information. He'd noticed that the nanny's phone had been intermittently making a succession of sounds for the past few hours...going from ringing to buzzing when a text was left, and finally, beeping whenever the frustrated caller left a voice message. Most likely one of his parents was trying to get through. It was odd that they didn't use the landline phone. Oh, well, eventually, they'd get worried. Perhaps his negligent, power-hungry mother would decide to come home. To leave the campaign trail to check on her disabled son would be good for her public image, he was sure. *Hurry home, Mother!* The boy shivered with delight.

"What are you daydreaming about? I asked about that strange noise."

The boy shrugged, his facial expression the perfect imitation of an innocent child's. "I have no idea what that sound is."

"I've spent too much time here. I've got to get to Roanoke as soon as possible."

Boozer opened his mouth wide and roared and then began pounding his chest again. The sound of his voice was coarse and discordant and his chest, taking a beating, vibrated like a tom-tom drum.

Infuriated, Eris sent a burning beam in Boozer's direction. "Listen, you fool, I can't let you run amok out there with the humans. You're dim-witted with a brain the size of a pea and if I let you out, you'll do something stupid and have the authorities swarming all over this place. I have business in Roanoke and I refuse to allow your primal urges to stand in my way."

"Roanoke, Roanoke...I'm sick of hearing about that place," the boy cut in. "I've risked everything to get you out of the Dark

Realm and you reward me by bringing this Neanderthal with you. My plans have precedence over yours and I can't think clearly with him stomping about and pounding on this chest."

"Your childish revenge will be dealt with when I return from Roanoke with my jewels," Eris said as she patted her coiled hair, taking the loosened coils and twisting them back into the glamorous upsweep secured with Catherine Provost's hairpins.

"Why do you care about that old-fashioned jewelry? If it's diamonds you're after, my mother has plenty of those locked in a safe. And I know the combination," he said smugly.

"I don't want your mother's inferior jewels. I'm going to Roanoke to retrieve my very own powerful and precious goddess ring."

Before the boy could comment, Boozer bellowed again. Leaning against a tall bookcase, he worked on his erection, using frantic hand strokes, irritatingly audible as his calloused hand scraped angrily against his thick phallus that pulsed with raw desire. The release he desperately sought did not come and Boozer dropped his head in frustration and wept. His tear drops, thick and oily, were a wretched sight. "Lemme outta here," Boozer sobbed.

38

"I'm going to let you out, but you have to promise me that you'll be careful and do your deed with discretion."

"I promise," Boozer croaked, holding up a malformed hand.

"You're making a grave mistake," the boy cautioned.

"Listen to me, Boozer, you must use stealth. Leap up to rooftops and then crawl across very quietly. Use your sense of smell to sniff out a female. If you detect a male scent, move on to another house. Do you understand?"

"Yes, goddess." Boozer smacked his hands together with glee. Eris led him to another room with a side door. He dropped to his hands and knees. Poking his head outside, he cautiously looked left and right. Determining that the coast was clear, he raced outside, running low along the wall of the house, and then scampering up the gnarled trunk of a tree. Leaping from treetops, Boozer avoided the long driveway that led to the main road.

"Nothing good is going to come of this," the boy said ominously. "But then again, being that tonight is Halloween, Boozer might fit in quite nicely." Tauntingly, the boy arched a brow.

"Who cares if he fits in or not? I'm going to Roanoke with or without Boozer. The nanny is going to take me."

"How is she going to manage that? You left her down in the

cellar depleted of blood; she's probably half dead by now." The boy snickered. "Oh, Wicked One. You never listen to reason and you never learn from past mistakes."

"Be quiet. What do you know? You're a boy?"

"I'm a man," the child insisted. "And I have manly urges. Now that Boozer is out on the prowl, I'd hoped you and I could spend some time together—pick up where we left off."

He closed his eyes in blissful remembrance of the wanton times they'd spent together on the Dark Realm. "Wicked One, I've been waiting for this day for so long." He held out his small hand. "Come join me in my bedroom. Lie down with me."

Eris's cackling laughter echoed in the quiet house. "You amuse me, little boy. I refuse. That miniature body you chose is appalling. Now, be a good boy and go upstairs and operate your contraption. Go to that source of vast information—"

"The internet," he informed sullenly.

"It doesn't matter what it's called; just find out if there's anything else I can use to help keep my lovely body glorious throughout all of eternity."

"All of eternity?"

"Of course. Do you think I plan on returning to the Dark Realm?"

"No, but I assumed that eventually you'd want to go home—to the Goddess Realm."

"Never! I refuse to allow those self-righteous goddesses to have power over my fate. I do, however, plan to lure my sister, Tara, to this Earthly Realm."

"Whatever for?"

"Let's just say…she deserves her comeuppance."

"Is she pretty?" He looked hopeful.

Eris shrugged. "I suppose, but not as pretty as me. We're complete opposites in our appearance and temperament."

"What does she look like?" The boy stroked his hairless chin.

"She's compassionate and weepy."

"Her appearance..." he prodded.

"The fair maiden type. Long bronze hair, chestnut eyes, with honey-colored skin."

"And her body? Is she well-endowed?"

"Her breasts are very large but her hips are narrow, her legs slender and, did I mention that she's not physically strong?"

The boy was wheezing. "She sounds scrumptious. I must meet her."

"Why?"

"You've rejected me based on my appearance. I'm sure your sister will see the real me...besides, there's something about goddesses that I find extremely arousing. Once you've been with one, an average woman simply doesn't measure up. Do you mind if I work my charms on Tara before you exact revenge?"

"Sorry, little boy. You're not her type."

The boy flinched and then pouted. "She's a compassionate goddess. She'll understand that although I'm trapped in this deficient little body, I'm of superior intelligence, clever... and I've always been quite the ladies man."

"Tara doesn't like boys or men. She's in love with a half-bird."

He peered at Eris questioningly. "Half-breed?"

"No! I call her a half-bird. Her lover's name is Zeta; she has wings like a bird. Zeta is very unique. She pleasures Tara with her two sets of genitals. Zeta has a male appendage as well as a female opening. Tara adores her. Think you can compete with Zeta for my sister's affection? I think not!"

"You're probably right. I can't compete, but I'm thoroughly aroused." The demon boy began to pant with lust. "I want to fornicate with both of them."

"If you figure out how to keep my limbs intact, I'll try to

work something out. I'll lure Tara and her lover here. Then I'm going to break Tara's heart. I know how to cause her deep pain...pain so severe, she'll keel over and die!"

"Make sure you keep her safe and sound until after I've had my way with her and the bird woman."

"I'll keep that in mind. Once you've been satiated by Tara and Zeta, I'm going to castrate her half-bird lover, right in front of Tara's eyes. If that doesn't do the trick, then I'll force Tara to watch as I rip off the wings that my sister absolutely adores!" Eris grinned. The smile twisted into a sneer when the buzzing upstairs commenced again.

"That's the nanny's cell phone," the boy explained.

"Oh, one of those tiny talking mechanisms? Yes, I remember tinkering with one during my last visit here. Why does it keep buzzing?"

"It's probably my father. Trying to get in touch with her to find out how you're making out in the new nanny position."

Anxiety twitched the muscles in the boy's face. "If he doesn't speak to her, he's going to become concerned. Who knows what might happen. He or my mother might become alarmed enough to slip away from the campaign trail and come home."

"Good!"

"Not good," he disagreed. "I'm not ready yet. My plan is not in motion."

"Then hurry up! I have to get to Roanoke. The sooner your mother gets here, the sooner I can be on my way. I don't know why you're holding a grudge against her for something she did hundreds of years ago."

"You're a fine one to talk. You're still obsessed with those Stovalls."

"Not really. I simply want my jewels. The gall of that obnoxious child to frolic about adorned with my precious jewels. When I arrive in Roanoke, she'll prance no more. I'm going to maim that little jewel thief of a child—break her arms and legs and disable the pompous rascal for life. After that, I'll leave the Stovall family alone. They are really out of fashion with me and totally irrelevant now. My latest grudge is so much more exciting; it makes me tingle with wicked desire. As I told you, my mealy mouthed sister and her winged lover are the focus of all my wrath and rage."

"Don't harm her until after I've sampled the goods," the boy reminded Eris.

Eris checked her hands and smiled, satisfied that they were remained undamaged. "Bring me that buzzing contraption that belongs to the nanny. I want to have a word with your mother."

"No! You'll ruin my diabolical plans."

"I can't wait around here forever, you know. You're going to have to trust that I know what I'm doing. Don't you want your mother to come home without guards or even her husband for protection?"

"Yes, most definitely. It would be ideal to get her here alone."

"Then leave it to me. I know exactly what to say that will bring her here, quickly and without a horde of security guards."

The boy's smile spread wide. His beady eyes twinkled with malice. "Good idea."

"When she arrives, we'll end your mother's miserable life and then I'll summon Tara. Now bring me the nanny's talking device."

"That's not a good idea. The nanny's not in any shape to talk. We don't want to arouse my parents' suspicions."

"Don't question my judgment, Xavier. I know what I'm doing."

"If you say so." He shrugged and left the room. If his mother came home unexpectedly, then so be it. Eris would be caught with her guard down, but he'd have a devious plan already in motion.

Death was too good for his mother and his former unfaithful wife. She deserved far worse. He intended to involve Catherine Provost in a scandal that would end her political career and send her to prison. Child molestation was a terrible crime. Pedophiles were reviled—even in prison.

He began to formulate a sinister plan and could hardly control the urge to howl with malicious laughter. He'd set up a hidden camera. When his mother arrived, he'd pretend to be violently ill and trick her into his bedroom.

Eris didn't need to know the details of how he planned to finally settle a centuries-old score. The press would salivate when they got their hands on the footage of Catherine Provost molesting her own child. The presidential candidate would be wise to have another vice presidential nominee on hand as a back-up.

Excited with his idea, he raced into Jen's room, and grabbed her phone off the night stand. Downstairs, he handed the cell to Eris.

As if on cue, the cell phone vibrated against Eris's palm.

"Catherine," Eris said, reading the name that appeared on the screen of the small phone.

"I tried to warn you," the boy said grimly. "Should I fetch my ailing nanny?" he asked with a smirk.

Eris ignored his sarcasm. She flipped the phone open. "Hello, how are you Ms. Provost?" she said, using a voice that was identical to Jen's. "Oh, Ethan is fine."

She flung the boy a triumphant smile and continued talking to his mother. "The new nanny is great. Ethan seems to really like her. She's with him right now. Reading to him while he's sitting in front of his computer…you know…looking at those bridges." Eris's words were followed with a nervous giggle, giving an uncanny impersonation of Jen.

"Wicked One," he whispered, impressed.

Eris shot a smug look in his direction.

Gesturing, he gave her performance an enthusiastic thumbs-up.

39

"Baby, you got me stalking you. What's up? Why you avoiding me? Pick up the phone." Rome put laughter in his tone, trying to use humor to hide the hurt that he was feeling in his heart. "I got my Obama look tonight...a black cashmere coat...a fly suit—I'm looking all GQ for you, baby," he continued, sounding playful and lighthearted, though inside he was anxious and confused.

He gave another burst of nervous laughter. The sound rang so false, Rome couldn't go on pretending. "Look, I have to keep it real. I'm sitting in my truck, not too far from your house. I've been waiting for a couple of hours. I guess I should take a hint and recognize that I've been stood up. I can't understand it. Why didn't you call and tell me something?"

He sighed. "I don't know what I could have said or done that pissed you off like this. I mean, damn...you won't even take my calls. Listen, whatever I did, I apologize. Okay, Pretty Red? Another thing, I don't care whether you're mad at me or not, I'm not giving up on us." He paused again, his mind racing for something else to say.

"So...um...I'm about to turn around and head on home. I'll be in the crib if you decide you want to talk. Bye, baby."

Rome backed up and made a U-turn. Instead of zipping onto

Germantown Avenue, which would be a speedy route home, he drove slowly, taking a scenic tree-lined winding road with bubbling brooks and a picturesque autumn landscape.

Normally, the beauty of nature both soothed and mesmerized him. Sometimes he marveled at the majesty of a red maple tree or gazed in awe at a sturdy oak that stood at least fifty feet tall and could well be one hundred years old or more. But tonight the beautiful scenery was meaningless.

Rome's cell was set up in the cup holder next to his seat. He kept picking up the phone and checking to make sure he hadn't mistakenly turned the volume too low. Jen's call was important; he didn't want to miss it.

Acting like this wasn't cool at all. For so long, he'd guarded his heart. He was probably a classic example of a male all messed up in the head with an Oedipus complex. Yeah, he'd had a childhood crush on his mom, he admitted to himself. The way she danced in her old videos, that look in her big doe eyes made her every young boy's dream.

He couldn't honestly exclude himself. But after she'd rejected him, acting like she forgot she was his mother, he grew into manhood keeping a close watch on his heart, never opening up or allowing himself to be vulnerable. Never letting another woman get close enough to break his heart.

Jen was different. So wholesome and sweet. Nothing city slick about Jen. *So what went wrong?* he wondered, anguished. Damn, he missed his baby. He wanted to see her pretty face; hear her laugh; hold her again. He swallowed. He wanted to feel her skin against his, even if she told him it would be the last time.

The night that held so much promise. Rome patted his coat pocket and felt the square box that contained a ring. He shook his head. Wrong move. Jumped the gun; moving too fast. Only a love-struck sucker would think it was a good idea to buy an engagement ring in this early stage of the game.

Good guys always lose, he told himself. Still, too stubborn to admit defeat, Rome continued cruising down the long, winding road. Wasting time, lingering around Chestnut Hill, hoping Jen would return his call.

"What the fuck!" Something big leapt from a tree and shot across the sky. He screeched to a stop, lowered the window, stuck his head out, and craned his neck upward.

"Oh, shit!" He flinched as he gawked at the huge, shadowy figure that was leaping from one treetop to the next, in pursuit of something. It was happening so fast, the creature was a blur, but from what Rome could make out, the thing looked like a flying ape or a soaring Sasquatch.

He threw the truck into park and grabbed the gun he kept under his seat. Standing outside his truck, he walked a few paces, his head upturned as he scanned the tall trees. There was no movement and he didn't see a thing except the dark sky, the stars, and the eerie light of the half-moon.

Was it some sort of high-tech Halloween prank? There were a group of Goth teens in the area. Known troublemakers. Rome had to haul a few of their asses into the station on more than one occasion for disorderly conduct, disturbing the peace, and other misdemeanors. He doubted if those zombie-looking kids were capable of pulling such an elaborate stunt.

That flying Sasquatch was some serious, supernatural shit. *I'm trippin.' I'm starting to see bizarre, horror-movie scenes. It's time to get off this dark, lonely road and take my ass home.* Rome tugged the handle of his truck, but rustling sounds made him whirl around, gun drawn.

He looked up. The top of a maple tree swayed in the moonlight.

Something had definitely jumped off of that tree. What? A wild animal? And where had it gone? Hell if he knew. He'd better call the station and let the officers know that there was some mysterious activity—

A woman's distant scream interrupted his thought. Rome knew the area well and the only home in this remote area was the Abramson home, a gorgeous colonial about fifty yards past the bend in the road. Ms. Abramson, a recent widow, lived alone.

A sudden sweat dampened his brow. Acting on instinct, he quickly climbed back inside the truck, and got behind the wheel. Without mulling it over or devising any kind of plan, he tore off in the direction of the Abramson home.

The front of the house was dark. He parked the truck, got out, looking up, scanning the treetops. Nothing going on up there. Maybe he'd imagined it all. Breathing more easily, he started to walk up the steps to the house and ring the doorbell and ask Ms. Abramson if everything was all right; perhaps warn her to keep the house locked up tight. Just in case.

But an odd sound coming from the back of the house disturbed the quiet. On high alert, he crept toward the back of the house, weapon in hand.

Concerned that the moonlight might illuminate his approach, Rome dropped to a crouch, hoping to blend in with the dark shrubbery and trees surrounding the house as he advanced toward the sound that was a groaning roar, a beastly echo of the past. Like listening to a soundtrack of *Jurassic Park*.

He would have fired his weapon immediately if he didn't think his eyes were deceiving him and, for a few terrible moments, he stood frozen watching an inconceivable sight. He looked away from the atrocious scene for a few seconds. He surveyed an overturned trash can, and its lid that had been flung a few feet away. In an attempt to comprehend the sight that his brain refused to grasp, he continued focusing on inanimate objects, like the stuffed green trash bag with red handles, that slowly rolled back and forth near the toppled trash can.

Steeling himself, Rome forced his eyes to zoom in on what appeared to be the wide V-shape of a woman's outspread legs. There was something on top of her. Something vicious, inhuman, and unafraid. The thing didn't jump up in shock; it didn't dart off into the night after being caught in the act of rape.

Unapologetically, it humped, growled and clawed the ground as it ferociously thrust itself in and out of Ms. Abramson. The widow didn't move. Her body was still. Lifeless. The poor woman was better off dead, Rome decided as he finally steadied his hand, aimed, and fired.

The gunshot was loud. The creature's pained howl was louder. The big hairy thing rose up, revealing an angry face with fur-tufted ears, cheeks, and forehead. Rome froze, unsure of what he was looking at. The thing was hideously ugly, with its mouth agape, roaring mad and dripping thick saliva.

While Rome stood, momentarily transfixed, the creature bounded up the trunk of a tree, swung from its branches, raced to the top, and then launched itself across the abyss between trees, hurtling through treetops like nothing Rome had ever seen.

Rome fired off wild, badly aimed blasts in rapid succession, splintering bark, shooting off limbs and branches, while the beast ran free. Determined, Rome dashed between trees, tripping and stumbling, arms stretched skyward as he continued to fire shots.

There was a sudden thump of something hitting the ground. Thinking he'd most likely toppled one of the smaller trees, he moved forward to investigate. Rome stopped cold. The creature, big and animalistic, lay on its back, groaning in pain. Rome stepped closer, forcing himself to look at the monstrous thing. It twisted and panted and foam bubbled at the corner of its mouth. Its growl was weak, yet laden with menace.

Standing at close range, Rome fired over and over into the beast's snarling face until he'd emptied the clip.

Unbelievably, the maniac's bullet-ridden face ignited and became enflamed. Nanoseconds later, the fire raged down its hairy body. A sudden whoosh and the creature became a dark swirl of thick smoke that swiftly tunneled deep into the earth, as if hell bound.

There wasn't much left to identify the killer; just a few smoldering clumps that quickly turned into a pile of ashes.

The crime scene indicated that the widow was taking out the trash when the beast attacked her. Rome knelt down to look for a pulse, but didn't expect to find one on the poor ravaged woman. His eyes involuntarily swept downward, settling on the gaping, bloody hole in the crotch of her pants. He cringed.

As an officer of the law, Rome should have secured the crime scene at the Abramson home and reported the murder. But what could he say about the assailant? That it looked like Sasquatch and had burst into flames after being riddled with bullets?

Would anyone believe that the perpetrator had gone poof? It was a preposterous story, and Rome knew that he'd be considered a suspect, taken into custody, and labeled a maniac cop.

At the top of their long list of questions, the investigators would want to know why Rome had been prowling around Chestnut Hill while off duty. Mentioning his planned date with Jen would inevitably bring up the names of her high-profile employers. Jen wouldn't appreciate him dragging the Provosts into this mess.

It was too late to save Ms. Abramson, and there was no point in voluntarily surrendering himself to an interrogation that could last for hours. At least not now. He'd deal with the interrogation and possible arrest after he knew for certain that Jen was all right.

Of course, DNA found on Ms. Abramson would eventually exonerate him, but in the meantime, wild horses couldn't stop him from getting to Jen.

Leaving the dead woman lying on the ground, he raced to his truck. A beastly murderer had been on the loose in Chestnut Hill. Jen and the little boy she took care of were most likely at home all alone, and Rome's single-minded thought was to make sure Jen was unharmed.

40

Confident that her looks mesmerized, Eris admitted the dashing young man inside, sizing him up with an unmistakable glimmer of approval in her eyes. She'd seen him before, sitting in an automobile gawking up at her during her precarious attempts to cross a bridge that would evaporate in the blink of an eye if she dared to dawdle.

During those distressful times, she didn't have a moment to spare and had never appraised the gentleman. Now she realized that he was a fine looking male specimen, elegant, and garbed in high-quality finery. His physical qualities appealed to her. This human male looked worthy enough to be her mate. It was a pity his life would have to end tonight.

Eris had heard the desperate messages the man had left on the nanny's talking device. "I love you, I miss you, I need you," he'd declared over and over. His words had burned Eris's ears. She despised it when male attention was focused on another female. After hearing his love pledges, Eris had flown into a jealous rage, prompting her to bite and inflict pain on the red-headed governess even though her she had no immediate need of nourishment.

Her limbs were holding out quite well and showing no signs of fading. Still, the governess had no right getting compliments.

In a jealous rage, Eris had stomped down the cellar stairs to bite the little trollop with her own razor-sharp teeth.

Surprisingly, the feeling of her teeth cutting into human flesh and the girl's responding scream gave Eris a bout of dizzying pleasure. Now that she'd developed a liking for biting, Boozer would no longer be necessary for that task.

She batted her lashes and fixed her indigo eyes on the chivalrous young man, who was there to save his damsel in distress. Well, it wasn't going to happen.

"Greetings," she said, ushering him in. "I'm Eris, the new governess." A magnificent smile blossomed on her face.

"Romel Chavis," he replied. Though he was shocked to find himself face-to-face with the ghost lady from the bridge, he forced himself to appear as calm and as normal as possible. This particular spirit usually wore a mask of anger; her smile was unexpected and disarming.

Her satiny, dark skin looked life-like, as if it would be soft to the touch. She had strong features and her blue eyes enhanced her unusual beauty. No longer naked, she was wearing an old-fashioned ball gown.

There were blood stains on the bodice, making Rome wonder if her last breath had been stolen by a violent and jealous lover a couple of centuries ago.

The presence of this apparition probably had Jen freaked out. No wonder she hadn't returned his calls. Most likely, she and the kid, terrified that a spirit was roaming openly throughout the house, were huddled together, hiding somewhere in the enormous home.

Rome knew that the average lost soul believed that he or she was still alive. This ghost was badly confused and would have to be guided to the light with gentle kindness. She struck him as having the potential to be become stubborn and malevolent if she was told she was dead. He sighed, his eyes bouncing around the foyer, straining to spot Jen.

It wasn't customary or usually necessary for Rome to have to speak to ghosts. And he hadn't met one yet that had spoken to him; until now. He felt foolish, talking to something that was apt to vanish into thin air, but he went through with the ritual anyway. He even went so far as to extended his hand, hoping the spirit who called herself Eris would go poof the moment her ethereal hand passed through his solid, human limb. Her palm pressed against his. It was warm and soft to the touch, shocking his senses.

"Would you like to join me in the living room? It gets rather lonely at night after I put the little one to bed."

Rome eyed the outdated ball gown. "I don't mean to be rude, Eris, but you're not the governess. I'm not calling you a liar; I'm sure you were on top of your nanny game back in the day." He chuckled at his humor. Eris stared at him blankly.

Rome cleared his throat. "What I'm saying is that I think you're lost."

Eris winced. Offended, she placed her palm against her chest.

"Seriously. I'm not trying to upset you or anything, but the child you took care of is no longer with us and you would be better off if you joined him."

Eris smiled a patient smile. "He's upstairs and he's tucked safe and sound in his bed."

This wasn't going well. And after that weird-ass encounter with that crazed creature, he needed to check on Jen and make sure she was all right. This talkative ghost was holding up progress.

It was time to speed things along and point her in the right direction. *Which is?* he asked himself. Hell, if he knew where the white light was located. He'd never had to take his finger and physically point it out.

Merely making the suggestion to go toward the light usually helped the spirits on their final journey. But after watching Eris running around on Piper's Bridge, something told Rome that she was going to require a GPS or a printout of Mapquest directions. She seemed too complicated a personality to simply take his word and keep it moving.

Rome regarded Eris closely, his eyes dead serious. "Listen, you're a spirit now and you don't belong here. There's a new governess...well, we call her a nanny. Her name is Jen. She has flaming red hair; she's pretty unforgettable," Rome said, unable to suppress a sudden smile as he pictured Jen's face.

The spirit maintained an amiable expression, but there was a change in the atmosphere, subtle, but unpleasant, making him more anxious than ever to talk to Jen.

"Will you let me help you find your way to the light?" he pressed.

"Pardon?" Eris asked, her mouth upturned pleasantly, while sparks flickered in hrt eyes, informing Rome that her smile was fake. This was a discontented spirit.

Rome's palms felt suddenly clammy. *"The dead can't hurt you,"* his grandma had always said. Remembering her words, he tried to ignore the angry flashes in Eris's eyes.

Okay, granted the dead can't hurt you, but what about that creature that raped and killed Ms. Abramson. There was no doubt in Rome's mind that the Sasquatch-looking monster was something from another dimension.

What if the beast had gotten its claws into Jen? Suppose there was more than one Sasquatch on the loose? For all he knew, there could be a pack of hellish rapists terrorizing Chestnut Hill.

With the grotesque image of that maniac fresh in his mind, he pushed Eris aside, and sped through the living room. Overcome by a growing sense of dread, he moved swiftly from room to room, yelling, "JEN!"

Darting through the kitchen and out the exit at the opposite end, a padlock dangling outside the cellar door sent a chill through Rome and paralyzed him with fear. Jen was down there. He could feel it. "JEN!" he bellowed as he tried to shoulder the door open. The lock rattled against the wood but the door didn't budge.

His gun was reloaded and tucked in his waistband. He considered blasting his way into the cellar, but he couldn't bring himself to fire through the closed door. If Jen and the little boy were down there, it would be inexcusable and completely reckless to put their lives at risk. Yelling profanities, Rome raised his foot and tried his best to kick the door off its hinges.

Huddling in a corner, trying to leave lots of space between her and poor Carmen's rotting corpse, Jen shook, her body still in shock from the vicious mauling Eris had inflicted. Eris was merciless. Wicked. Biting Jen over and over and in different places for no reason other than unadulterated evil. During the sadistic attack, Jen hoped to disassociate…to transcend from her body and escape the pain like she'd done before. But it didn't happen. Jen was very much present. She was totally aware of the agonizing pain as Eris brutalized her with razor-sharp bites, pulling back flesh, and peeling off thin layers of skin.

It seemed to go on for hours…maybe days. The teeth sank in savagely, causing Jen to scream and convulse.

A banging overhead made Jen's teeth chatter in fear. *Oh, my God!* It was too soon to go through the biting ordeal again. But then again, maybe it was time. Jen had lost all concept of time. She inched further into the corner of her dreary holding place.

Another loud bang and it seemed like she heard someone shout her name. She had to be hallucinating; the monster didn't call her by any name. It just growled and bit her. Ghost lady called her "the governess" and the demon child referred to her simply as "nanny."

Jen dropped her head in defeat. Very soon, one of those horrible creatures would lift the floorboards. The soul-shuddering fear, the useless screaming, the pleading for mercy, and the blinding pain...It would begin all over again.

41

There was a strange odor seeping up from under the cellar door. He'd smelled it before. A cold chill ran up his spine. *Jen!*

"Rome."

With his leg raised and ready to give the door another hard kick, he was startled by the sound of Jen's voice calling his name. The sound of bare feet smacking against the marble, hastily approaching, couldn't be ignored. Rome dropped his foot and spun so swiftly, his black coat swirled around his legs. The spirit was persistent, rushing toward him, and the beam of light shining from her eyes was turned up so high, the brightness was blinding, forcing Rome to shield his eyes.

"There you are. I thought you'd never get here."

Jen? It really sounded like her voice. Baffled, he pulled his arm away from his face. The high beams were turned down several notches; a soft, mesmerizing glow emanated, taking his attention away from the cellar door.

The spirit was smiling again; proud of her ability to perfectly imitate the sound of Jen's voice, and pleased with her powers of seduction that had him baffled and spellbound.

"Let me take your coat," she said, still mimicking Jen.

Confused, Rome removed his coat and hesitantly gave it to the apparition.

"You won't need that," the apparition remarked, pointing to the gun sticking out of Rome's waistband. "Give it to me." She stuck out her hand.

He knew he should refuse, but for some inexplicable reason, he was unable to resist the command. Rome handed over his weapon.

"You'll be more comfortable without it. Besides," she added with scoffing laughter, "there are no criminals in this house." The apparition strolled off in the direction of the kitchen. She returned a few moments later, empty handed.

His gun now forgotten, Rome gazed at the spirit. She smiled at him. Something wasn't right. Why didn't Jen look the same? Her smile seemed so insincere—and so eerie. And what was that bad smell coming from the cellar? The stench had his heart pumping with fear. Apprehensive, he turned back to the pad-locked door. There was a reason he was standing there, but for the life of him, he couldn't remember.

"I'm so happy you're here. I've been so lonely." The spirit was messing with his mind and he knew it. "Let's sit in the living room. It's so comfortable in there." She took his hand. "I missed you, Rome," she said, borrowing Jen's tone and inflection, soft-ening his resolve. He could hardly tell the difference between real and illusionary occurrences.

His vision blurred as he moved in slow motion, taking extreme caution with each footstep. His depth perception was off and each step he made toward the living room seemed precarious and life-threatening.

Holding hands with an apparition with a voice that sounded exactly like the tone of the woman he loved had a similar effect as the time back in school when he'd accepted a joint that was laced with PCP. Though he hadn't smoked weed since high school, he'd heard the effects could resurface at any time for years to come.

Was he hallucinating from that bad shit he'd smoked way back then?

He looked over his shoulder at the locked cellar door, brows furrowed, trying to remember why he found that locked door so disturbing. He couldn't recall.

Rome inhaled deeply and scowled. His sense of smell was off the charts. "What's that smell coming from the cellar?" he asked as he was led into the stylish living room.

"Sewage backup. I've called the plumber. He'll be here first thing in the morning."

Made sense.

"I heard your message. I didn't stand you up. The new nanny was a no-show."

Rome frowned. "I met the new nanny." He shook his head vigorously. "Hold up. I feel like I'm high as hell."

She giggled. Like Jen. The musical sound relaxed him. Things started making sense. "I don't want to freak you out, but that ghost we saw on the bridge was in this house," he confided, his tone hushed.

"The dead can't hurt you."

"That's what my grandma used to say." Rome was definitely starting to relax. "This house is nice," he said, looking around. "We could get one like this one day."

"Really?"

"Yeah, I have the money; just never had anyone to share it with."

"Now you have me." Eris turned and began unbuttoning his shirt. Her hands didn't look like Jen's hands, but that was okay.

The PCP was messing with his vision. He wondered if the

doctor could prescribe something to keep the hallucinations from returning.

She opened his shirt and ran her fingertips across his nipples. He closed his eyes and issued a low groan, his nipples hardened under her heated caress. He cupped her face. His fingers traveled upward, eager to get tangled in her halo of red hair.

He jerked back his hand. Her hair felt different. His eyes popped open. Her hair was dark and coiled like the confused spirit.

She kissed his chest. He closed his eyes, savoring the feeling of her lips pressed against his skin. "Did you miss me?" she asked in a sweet voice that sounded like music, making him forget that her hair was a different color and texture than Jen's.

"Yeah, baby. I missed you," his voice broke with emotion. "I thought I'd lost you."

She didn't speak. She kissed a hot trail down his chest. He inhaled sharply as her lips nibbled at his navel. His erection was massive. Painful. He wanted to release inside her warm mouth and the sensation was overwhelming.

She wriggled down between his thighs and began licking the fabric of his pants, saturating the fabric with the moisture from her tongue as she warmed the growing bulge inside his pants. Chills spread through him. She unzipped his pants.

Gathering willpower, he pulled her up. It was too soon. He had to give his baby some pleasure first. Make love to her the way she deserved. He placed his lips over hers and kissed her.

The taste of her was addictive. Tenderly lapping the sweetness from her mouth, his tongue stroked hers until she uttered soft murmurs deep inside her throat. Her hands were spastic; clenching and unclenching his shoulders.

He felt her fingernail moving downward, scratching softly, then digging deeper. He moaned from the pain and from the pleasure.

Rome squeezed his eyes shut, giving her permission to unleash her passion. She scratched bloody trails down his chest. Rome writhed as she rubbed his shaft with a blood-smeared hand, and licked the wounds on his chest, lapping the drizzling blood.

She wound her hand inside his fly. Desire pulsed through his shaft. She took possession of his dick, liberating it. With her other hand, she reached up and embedded her nails into his chest. Her fingernails penetrated as deeply as four deadly daggers.

Rome cried out. Eris soothed him, enveloping his thickness with her lips, licking the smooth head of his dick with a tongue so hot, it seemed to vibrate. Blood trickled down and pooled at her lips. She slurped and sucked until he exploded. Long after his eruption, Eris continually pierced his skin, sipping generous amounts of blood.

And now, hours later, she had him turned onto his stomach as she raked her nails down his back, licking the fresh wounds she had created. Rome shuddered and groaned, feeling himself weakening from blood loss.

With his face buried into the seat of the sofa, his agonized groans were muffled by the cushiony fabric. His hands gripped the spongy soft texture as he endured the incisions of long fingernails and tolerated a roughening tongue that seemed to grow in length as it traveled over the length of his back.

Rome bore the pain, convincing himself that Jen was expressing her wild side. It was okay to let her drink his blood. Just this once.

THE GODDESS REALM

Bright sunshine lit the pond. Tara stared at the water, her only way of making a connection with Eris. Suddenly, Eris's face shimmered on the surface. Tara gasped in delight. "Eris, I've been searching for you. Where have you been?" she whispered, afraid that raising the volume of her voice would cause ripples in the water that might make her sister's image fade.

Eris didn't respond. Her attention was focused on a something else. Clearly, she was no longer in that abominable place. She was wearing grand attire and seemed completely at ease. Tara determined that Eris had managed to escape the dreadful, dark prison and was once again on the Earthly Realm. Eris was speaking to someone. Tara placed her face close to the water, straining to see—to hear. She listened to the conversation between Eris and a very small being—an evil-doer who had deceived many by pretending to be an innocent child.

After a few moments of eavesdropping, Tara cringed when she learned that her sister despised her and was plotting to disfigure Tara's precious, blue-winged lover. And there was someone else Eris planned to harm—a child who would be granted goddess status though she lived on the Earthly Realm.

She'd heard enough. Angry, Tara immersed her hand into the pond, swishing the water until Eris's evil face became indistinct and sank beneath the surface.

Rising to her feet, Tara took strode purposefully toward the chamber where the warrior goddess Kali slumbered with her two mighty swords at her sides.

42

Jubilant, the boy bounded down the stairs clutching a sheaf of papers. Eris stood preening in front of a mirrored wall.

"My eyes are much more vibrant, don't you agree?" She batted her lashes and then patted her hair. "It's thicker and has more luster." She proudly cupped her breasts, which had grown fuller and more plump, and bulged out of the top of the blood-splattered bodice.

The boy scrutinized at the moaning man on the sofa. There were blood stains and gashes on the man's back. "Who is that?"

"Oh, him?" She cast a look at the tortured man. "He's your nanny's former beau." She smiled. "He belongs to me now."

The boy giggled. "You are clever, Wicked One. I have the information. It's right here." He shook the pages excitedly. "I don't know how you figured it out, but it's right here in black and white. You need the blood of both a human male and a female to stay intact and alive."

Eris patted her parted lips, mimicking a yawn. "That's yesterday's news, Xavier. Tell me something I don't know."

He rustled through the papers, speed reading, his face flushed pink with embarrassment. "I couldn't find anything else on the subject."

"Since being born of woman, you have lost your cunning ways and your wisdom. You are completely deficient. I am the superior one. Don't you agree?"

He rolled his eyes and then released a bitter sigh.

"I am a goddess who deserves to be worshipped by all—especially by you, Xavier. It's hard to believe that I once allowed you to treat me as an inferior."

"You were inferior. I counseled and advised you. I taught you many lessons when we dwelled on the Dark Realm—"

"That was then. What can you teach me now?"

He searched the ceiling for an answer.

Eris grinned and crooked a finger. "Come here, you little insignificant male."

The boy bristled at the insult. Stubbornly, he balled his fists at his side.

"Xavier!" she said sharply. He jerked his head up, his beady eyes burning with irritation. Eris stared at him, sparks of blue flashing from her eyes as she attempted to mesmerize him.

Wisely, he closed his eyes, resisting her hypnotic powers.

"X-aaa-vi-er." This time Eris sang his name, making each syllable sound like a note of a seductive melody.

He squeezed his eyes even tighter. "Leave me alone, you sorceress!" he hissed through gritted teeth. "I was a fool to release you."

"And you're being an even bigger fool to refuse this opportunity to sample my ripened fruit." Eris was quiet for a few beats, waiting for the boy to cave in. He didn't. Wearing a hideous grimace, his eyeballs moved rapidly beneath his lids as he struggled to keep them closed.

"Look at me, Xavier," Eris goaded.

"I refuse." Adamant, he shook his head.

"The governess's blood has enlivened me. I'm more beautiful

than ever." She released a dramatic moan. "My loins have become unbearably inflamed."

Xavier groaned as if agonized. Hunched over and wheezing, the gaunt boy humped against his hand.

"I suppose I could wait for Boozer to return," she said grimly. "But I prefer to copulate with you. Oh, the times we had together on the Dark Realm. Your sexual prowess is extraordinary. Unmatched! Nothing and no one compares to you."

Pride placed a hint of a smile on the boy's pinched lips. Eris tried an additional ploy. "If it makes you happy, keep your eyes closed. But please don't deny me the pleasure of viewing your extraordinary phallus."

The wheezing and groaning intensified. Using both hands now, he appeared to wrestle with the enormous protrusion that tented his pants. Eris smiled knowingly. It was obvious the little sex fiend couldn't control his urges.

Maintaining his "see no evil" expression, Xavier unzipped his pants and liberated his massive erection.

"Ah! You're extremely well endowed," she flattered. "Come to me. Let me caress your gigantic rod with my tongue."

The bedazzled boy toddled toward the sound of Eris's spoken promise. With his eyes still closed, he looked like he was sleep-walking. Now standing in front of Eris, he uttered in a voice hoarsened by lust, "Lick me, Wicked One." He shivered. Pointing his dick upward, he offered Eris a taste of his hardened flesh.

Eris got down on her knees. Eagerly, she pulled his quivering erection inside her mouth. The right side of her forked tongue ran the length of his shaft, lapping at the head of his dick, while the left side lathed his balls.

Apparently curious to see Eris's serpentine tongue at work, Xavier ventured a peek. Eris caught him with his eyes open. She locked him with her gaze, mesmerizing the demon child with the brilliant blue shine from her eyes.

Abruptly, Eris stood. "You belong to me now, you little runt. I expect you to obey me. Is that clear?"

"Yes, goddess," he replied, his voice hushed. His opened eyes were unblinking.

Entranced, Xavier did not put up a fight. Eris lifted him up, digging her dagger-sharp fingernails into his side. The shock of pain broke Eris's spell and took his breath away. Before he could utter a sound, she yanked his shirt up.

Squirming and twisting at the waist, he gawked at her with loathing. Xavier tried to bash Eris with his huge head. Wild and desperate, he swung his head, aiming to knock the smirk off her face. Then, using his tiny fingers, he clawed at Eris's hands, trying to loosen her grip.

"Stop wiggling, you little bastard!" Eris pressed one palm against the boy's tummy and the other against the flat of his back, stilling his torso. Turning him sideways, she placed her hot lips against his skin.

Outraged, Xavier shrieked. "How dare you treat me like this? You ungrateful bitch!" He kicked his feet through the air, wheezing like crazy between shouted obscenities.

Unperturbed, Eris held him firmly. She drew his blood, feeding unhurriedly. Xavier's head lulled to the side; his heavy breathing quieted. The fierce kicking slowed down to foot flutters, and then came to a stop. Eris's former wise counselor went limp in her arms, completely drained. Lifeless.

It was time to rouse the governess and provide the dreary girl with nourishment to fortify her for the journey to Roanoke. Of course, there'd be pit stops along the way; Eris would need to replenish herself with human blood to keep up her dazzling appearance.

Xavier's useless form would join the rotting cook, she decided. Before making the trek down into the cellar, she gazed once more in the mirror. Her reflection thrilled her. She'd grown more beautiful since drinking Xavier's blood.

There was another reflection in the mirror. Eris frowned at Rome who lay collapsed on the sofa. She wasn't dragging him down into the cellar. He was too large and she might break a nail.

She glared at him for dying on her so soon, then closed her eyes in thought. Though he lay motionless, she could see that he was breathing. *Good!* Deciding to momentarily delay her journey, she glided over to the weakened male. There was still warm blood running through his veins and Eris didn't want to waste a drop of the beautifying elixir.

A sudden disturbance upstairs gave Rome a reprieve. Eris made a *tsking* sound. Boozer! She supposed he was trying to get in through the skylight. How dare that ogre try to gain admission after all the trouble he'd caused? It would serve him right if she left him here to fend for himself while she ran off to Roanoke. After witnessing all that depraved howling and shrieking, she realized that clothed or unclothed, he couldn't be passed off as a regular human.

Boozer was worthless to her now. And he was very lucky that he was not human. Otherwise, she'd devour his blood and just to be rid of him.

The clatter was persistent. With her eyes flaming, Eris stomped up the stairs, relishing the idea of scorching Boozer in several choice places.

Eris reached the landing at the top of the stairs and before she could determine the direction of the clatter, a burst of glittering light erupted at the far end of the long corridor. There stood an unwelcome sight…Tara with her winged lover standing behind her.

"It's time to go home," Tara said softly.

Eris laughed. Tara was so sentimental and pathetic. "I suppose the goddess council has finally come to their senses." She stared at her sister. "Either that or they've grown tired of having to listen to your lament. Whatever the case, I have to decline the offer. I've made my own way in life and I don't need charity from the goddesses."

"Had I not told you about the powers of the goddess ring, you would not speak so disrespectfully of our realm."

Eris took note of the ring on Tara's finger and it crossed her mind that she could save herself the burden of a long and hastily planned journey if she swindled her sister out of her goddess ring. She'd get to Roanoke eventually, but if she had Tara's ring, she wouldn't have to rush. Eris held back laughter.

"Go ahead and laugh. I can hear your thoughts, sister." Tara spat the words, shocking Eris into a brief silence.

"What I meant was…I'd like to borrow your ring. After all, your life is not in peril on the Goddess Realm. As I said, I can't return home. I'm staying here and it would mean a lot if I had something of yours to cherish…temporarily…until I retrieve my own ring."

"Do you really think I'm a fool?"

Eris's eyes lowered in feigned sorrow. "Why do you speak to me so harshly? Where is the compassion you once possessed?"

"I haven't changed. I am the embodiment of compassion. I know of your plan to harm Zeta."

"Oh, who cares about a winged servant? You're putting her on a pedestal, as if she's a goddess."

"She is a goddess to me. And the time will come when Zeta and I are viewed as equals by the entire Goddess Realm."

This time Eris didn't stifle her ridiculing laughter.

Tara stepped forward, arms behind her. Zeta lifted and spread her majestic wings.

"Oh my, should I be fearful?" Eris asked snidely. "Did you travel all the way to this Earthly Realm to challenge me, little sister?"

"I came to defend Zeta's honor, to ensure her safety and well-being." Tara brought her arms forward, revealing the two sparkling swords that she held in each hand.

Recognizing Kali's powerful swords, Eris took a step back.

"I'm also here on the goddess Kali's behalf to protect her goddaughter, the young Stovall child."

"Exactly how do you plan to do that?" Furious, Eris charged forward, eyes shooting flames aimed at Zeta's feathers. Tara's arms, moving swiftly, used Kali's mighty swords to block the bolts of fire.

"You are incorrigible and wicked." Grinding the two swords together, Tara advanced.

"NO!" Eris shouted when she saw the sparks from the swords erupt into flames and billowing white smoke.

"I wanted to cleanse you with purifying fire, I wanted you to rest in peace, but I'm ordered by the goddess council to send your wretched soul back to the Dark Realm, your eternal home."

"Tara, have mercy. I'm your sister." Eris used a voice that was tiny and meek, appealing to Tara's natural kindness.

But imbibed with the power of goddess Kali, Tara was a warrior with a mission to complete. "You will not harm another innocent being."

Fighting back, Eris sent beams of hot blue light Tara's way.

Protecting her lover, Zeta flapped her wings, extinguishing Eris's fire and fanning the flame that Tara created. Zeta flapped faster, sending the ball of white fire rolling and bouncing speedily in Eris's direction.

She rubbed the swords again and blue fire erupted and blazed a swift trail, merging with the purifying fire—popping, bouncing, and leaping onto the hem of Eris's blood-encrusted gown. Highly flammable, the masquerade costume crackled as it became consumed by fire. Eris stretched her mouth open to curse her sister, but managed only a lingering hiss.

Zeta and Tara stood in witness as Eris burned. In the form of a dark streak of smoke, Eris's furious spirit whooshed and whirled about. The smoky spirit began to lose its vigor, floating to the floor, and then began to dissipate.

Grudgingly, the goddess of destruction rejoined Boozer and the other wicked beings on the Dark Realm. All that was left of Eris's physical body was a mound of ash.

Zeta lifted Tara in her arms and floated down the stairs. With a fiery hot sword, Tara sliced through the lock on the basement door.

Jen had to be dreaming. Two magnificent women—one with a pair of blue wings rescued her from the belly of the dreadful basement. Their glorious presence created sparkling light in the dark, dreary basement. She gazed down into the pit where poor Carmen lay sprawled. Jen flinched, and looked away.

"She's at peace now," Tara said softly, referring to Carmen.

"Who are you?" Jen asked in whisper.

"My name is Tara. I'm the goddess of compassion."

"I'm Zeta," the winged woman offered. "I'm Tara's faithful attendant."

"I've changed her title. Zeta's my lover," Tara added boldly.

Jen didn't know what to say. She was overwhelmed by the presence of these two magnificent beings sent from above to save her. There weren't words to express her gratitude.

"Your wounds need to be treated." Tara shook her head. "Your husband is upstairs in the main room. He's going to need emergency medical attention as soon as possible or he will perish. You must hurry. Know that he loves you and would gladly give his life for you."

Jen squinted in bewilderment. "I'm not married."

Tara smiled. "You will be," she promised. "Kali, the goddess of fertility, wants you to know that she's blessed you and your husband with a fine and healthy son. Now hurry! Go upstairs. This dwelling will soon erupt into flames."

Before Jen could respond, the two women were surrounded in magnificent, glittering light and then they vanished, leaving behind a soft shimmer to help Jen find her way through the darkness.

Upstairs and out of the darkness, Jen was accosted by smothering smoke. Choking, gasping, coughing, she made her way into the living room and there he was...

43

According to authorities, it was all connected. The fire at the Provost home and the mysterious murder spree by an unknown assailant that took the lives of Carmen Diego, Doris Abramson, and young Ethan Provost. The public was not made aware that the DNA evidence in the rape kits of Carmen Diego and Doris Abramson was not human. And it was not animal. It was unknown. The DNA evidence taken from the puncture wounds of five-year-old Ethan Provost was also unidentifiable.

Romel Chavis was considered a hero. He didn't get the weird glances or gasps of disbelief when, from his hospital bed and in a weakened, barely audible voice, he recounted the Sasquatch story.

That bizarre DNA discovery and Rome's own injuries backed up his claim that the killer wasn't human. Still, top brass in the department asked him to keep the information to himself.

According to the record, the assailant was still on the loose. There was a huge reward for any information that would lead to his arrest.

There was an outpouring of public sympathy for Catherine Provost, the brave mother, who refused to sit home and mourn, but instead campaigned mightily, vowing to wage a war against sexual predators and child abusers if Americans cast their votes for her. Her party was expected to win by a landslide.

Rome had lain on the Provosts' lawn, shivering and bleeding. Jen had used practically all her strength dragging him out of the burning house. She wrapped her arms around him, keeping him warm with her body heat while they waited for the fire department.

During the first few hours of being in and out of consciousness, Rome repeatedly asked Jen to marry him, insisting that her engagement ring was in his coat pocket. Naturally, Jen thought he was talking out of his head. Even if his words were true, the ring, along with his coat, was gone—lost in the fire.

A week later, an infection set in. Jen didn't know if Rome was going to make it. The doctors were trying everything. He had a rare blood type and needed a transfusion with the same rare blood type.

Jen had an idea. It was a gamble, but she was willing to take that risk.

Twyla Tanning was on tour, staying at the Four Seasons Hotel.

Jen walked up to the front desk and requested Twyla be called. With all that had transpired in the past week, Jen had grown up a great deal and was no longer timid and afraid to stand up for herself.

"She's not staying here, ma'am," the desk clerk said, trying to look earnest.

"Okay, why don't you do this—"

"Ma'am," he interrupted. "Ms. Tanning is not here. I'm asking you nicely to please leave or I'll have to call security."

Jen inhaled. "As I was saying," she said, enunciating each word. "Call the room listed under the name that Twyla Tanning is using and inform her that Jennifer Darnell is in the lobby with a message from Romel. Tell her I think she should hear it." Jen stood firm, staring the man down.

The bandages on Jen's arms were concealed by the sleeves of her jacket. Both her arms were swollen and sore, but she refused to take her prescribed medication. She wanted to be alert for the showdown she was about to have. And there was another reason Jen was cautious about taking drugs—prescribed or otherwise. There was a chance that she was pregnant; Jen didn't want to risk taking anything that might harm her unborn baby.

She tapped her finger on the desk while she waited and found herself growing anxious and increasingly impatient.

The flustered young man picked up the phone. Repeating Jen's words, he spoke discreetly and then hung up. "Someone will be down in five minutes," he said, looking relieved that he didn't have to call security to have Jen removed from the lobby.

The elevator doors parted. Jen lifted her eyes, expecting to see beefy bodyguards, but instead, Twyla Tanning herself stepped out of the elevator.

Jen stood and watched as Twyla approached. As the international star grew closer, Jen could see that despite all the surgical procedures, Twyla still looked so much like Rome that it was startling.

"Jennifer?"

"Yes. I'm a friend of Romel's."

Twyla searched Jen's face, waiting for her say more.

"I think we should sit down," Jen said.

Twyla didn't budge. "Has something happened to Romel?" There was fear in Twyla's eyes.

Fighting back tears, Jen nodded. She really needed to sit down. Twyla ushered Jen to the nearest set of chairs.

Composing herself, Jen inhaled. "Rome's a police officer—"

"I know. He's been on the Philadelphia police force for two years," Twyla responded softly.

An image of Rome lying in the hospital bed came into Jen's mind. She couldn't keep her lips from quivering. "Something happened—"

Twyla shook her head, her jaw tensed. "Please don't tell me he's dead!"

"He's still alive…but he's been badly injured." Jen swallowed hard.

Twyla pressed a palm against her heart. "Oh, thank God." Her lashes fluttered closed. "He's going to be all right," she murmured, as though speaking to herself. "It's nothing life-threatening, is it?"

"I'm not sure."

"Was he shot?" The words came out in a frantic whisper.

"No. He was off-duty and he tried to help…uh…it's been all over the news," Jen said, frustrated. The unbelievable atrocity Jen and Rome had endured was hard to put into words. She didn't know where to begin. .

"I don't listen to the news when I'm on tour," Twyla explained.

"He was involved in a tragedy…trying to save lives," Jen stammered. "He lost a lot of blood. And right now…he's fighting for his life."

Twyla covered her mouth. An anguished sound was muffled by her palm.

"He has a rare blood type," Jen went on and noticed a flicker in Twyla's eyes. *God, please let her be a match*. "He needs a transfusion but it has to be his exact rare blood type. His father can't help him. So far, the hospital can't find a donor that matches. Even his birth mother on record…"

"She's not a match either. I have the same blood type as my son." Twyla nodded, punctuating the fact that she'd finally claimed Rome as her son.

"I can help him." Tears spilled down her cheeks. "I'm so ashamed of myself. Romel shouldn't have had to send me such a desperate message. I should have been there for him. It's this lie that I've been living—it's like a cancer. It's eating me alive. Of course, I'll give my son my blood."

"Rome didn't send me here with that message," Jen told her. "He's not aware that I'm here with you. I came on my own, hoping you would help. "

"The front desk called and said you had a message from Romel."

"I do."

Sniffling, Twyla waited.

"His message is that despite everything...even that day when he met you and treated him like one of your fans—"

Twyla gasped. "I'm so sorry. I was worried about my career. Look what being ambitious did to me..."

Jen squinted, not knowing how to respond. The woman seated next to her was gorgeous, successful, sexy, and rich.

"My life is a mess—a living hell," Twyla revealed.

A living hell? From the outside, Twyla's life looked good. Most recently, the entertainment icon had launched her own fragrance line...Insatiable Woman and Insatiable for Men. Twyla was getting paid, and after more than two decades, she was still at the top of her profession.

Jen wondered if the living hell Twyla mentioned was a reference to her five bad marriages or the constant scandals that plagued her family members. "Rome loves you," Jen repeated. "He's hoping that one day, when your career is over, you'll be a grandmother to his son."

"Romel has a child?"

"Not yet."

"You're more than a friend, aren't you?" she said knowingly.

"We're in a relationship; we were getting close before the... uh...accident."

A shimmer of hope lit Twyla's face. "Are you pregnant?"

Jen gave a wistful smile, thinking of Tara and Zeta, the two wondrous beings who had come from the heavens to rescue her and Rome. Those angelic women had promised that she and Rome would marry and have a son.

"No," Jen finally said. Locating a blood match for Rome had precedence over getting a pregnancy test. She wondered if Tara's and Zeta's prediction was true. Actually, she had started to doubt herself and wondered if she'd imagined the encounter. A winged woman and a beautiful goddess armed with two swords... crazy!

With all she'd been through, it was possible she'd hallucinated being rescued by otherworldly beings. Had she hallucinated Eris and Boozer, as well? Hell no! Her aching arm and Rome's critical condition was a testament to their biting and blood-sucking rampage.

As far as marrying Rome and having his child...well, time would tell. Right now, her only concern was saving her man's life.

"Excuse me. I have to call the hospital and let them know Rome has a match." Jen reached inside her purse, pulled out her cell, and looked at Twyla. "Don't worry; your identity will be kept confidential."

Twyla rose. "I'm sick of keeping secrets. I'm holding a press conference tomorrow. I'm telling the world that I've been blessed with a brave and forgiving son."

Jen felt brave, also. Brave enough to face her parents, and admit she'd been expelled from school.

She had no idea what the future held for her and Rome. If her role in his life was to reunite him with his mother, then she would accept that. But on a deeper level, she knew that they'd be sharing a future together. It would all unfold in time.

In the meantime, no more secrets. The cost to the soul is too high.

44

SPRING, ROANOKE, VIRGINIA

Ajali frowned. The asparagus fern displayed to liven up the parlor was tinged with brown. Had she given it too much water? No! She'd done her research, followed the care instructions to a tee but still, the showpiece fern was dying.

Huffing and puffing, Ajali lifted the potted plant and struggled to carry the gargantuan fern next to the piano where there was indirect light.

Kali skipped into the room. "Why are you moving that big plant again, Mommy?"

"I think it's getting too much sun. I've got to figure out a way to keep this plant alive, honey," Ajali answered, distracted as she lowered the enormous ceramic pot to the floor. She lifted a billowing stalk and sighed.

"What's wrong?" Kali skipped over to see what her mother was fretting about.

"This plant is in worse shape than I thought. It's not going to make it."

"I can save your plant." Kali said with confidence.

Ajali looked up to smile at her sweet child, but noticing an unusual ring on Kali's thumb, she made a tiny screech. "Where'd you get that ring?" she shouted, knowing that Bryce had donated every piece of that so-called buried treasure to charity.

"I found it." Kali said, leaving out Mr. Bear's involvement.

"Where?" Ajali was horrified. The ring looked ancient. It reminded Ajali of the Egyptian ankh, but with unique features of its own.

"This is a goddess ring. It was in the treasure box."

"Your father gave those jewels to charity."

Kali lowered her head. "He gave away the jewels and my musical jewelry box, but he didn't donate the wooden box."

"The wooden box was empty! I thought we threw it out a long time ago."

Shaking her head, Kali held her thumb up, showing off the ring and waiting for her mother's approval. "Don't be mad, Mommy. This ring is magical. It was hiding all this time in a secret slot at the bottom of the box."

"Oh, my God!" Ajali was beyond horrified. She couldn't believe her child was wearing something that the evil Eris wanted.

"Watch! Look at what I can do."

Kali touched Ajali's plant and miraculously, it sprang to life, turning a vibrant green all over."

"See. I can save things," she said proudly.

"Have you brought any other plants back to life?"

She shook her head. "No, but I made a baby bird come back to life and put it back in its nest with the other birds."

Ajali gasped, her eyes staring at the ring in horror. "Did you save anything else, honey?" she asked in a voice that trembled with fear.

"Uh-huh. A butterfly, a worm—"

"Just insects...birds...and uh, that worm?" Ajali asked her, brimming with hope.

"Can you keep a secret?" Kali whispered.

Her mother nodded, though her fingers were mentally crossed.

"Remember that day I had a play date with Marley? She was sad because her gerbil had died. And I brought it back to life."

"Oh, Kali. Take that ring off. It looks strange…and evil."

"It's not evil. My godmother told me to wear it for protection."

"Your godmother?"

"Her name is like mine, only she's a goddess. Guess what, Mommy?"

"What, sweetie?" Ajali asked, distracted by thoughts of the goddess who'd saved her life—whom she'd named her daughter after. How did her daughter know about the goddess? She'd never shared that information with her.

"I'm going to be a goddess, too."

Eyes roving fast from the ring to Kali's face, Ajali could feel herself going into a fit of panic. What was her daughter telling her? Was Kali going to leave her and join the others on the Goddess Realm? Ajali almost collapsed; her fear was so profound. She'd always considered Kali to be a gift that was too good to be true. She'd harbored a hidden fear that one day she'd lose her precious child.

"She teaches me the lessons of the goddess at night. While I'm asleep."

"Oh, God!" Fear gripped Ajali's heart.

"She meets me in my dreams. That's why I'm not afraid to sleep in my room. Kali says she will always protect me."

Ajali nodded. "Okay, but when—specifically—did she say you're going to become a goddess?" Motivated by fear and desperation, she clutched her daughter by her shoulders and shook her. "When?" Ajali screamed.

"Stop it, Mommy! You're hurting me."

Ajali looked at her own hands in shock and released her daughter. "I'm sorry."

"Being a goddess is not a bad thing, Mommy. Kali said I'm going to make you proud."

"I'm already proud." Ajali began to sob. "You don't have to leave me and become a goddess to make me proud."

"But I'm not leaving you. The transition will be complete when I'm twelve years old," Kali said proudly. "Kali is going to ascend to the heavens, but she's going to sleep until I turn twelve. She said the goddess Gaia looks after the planet earth, but I'll be the first goddess to actually live here. Our planet needs me."

Ajali wanted to cry. She didn't want her child burdened with the problems of the world. "It sounds like there might be a lot of responsibility. Is that what you want, honey?"

"I want to help all living things. The goddess Kali says it's my calling."

Brows drawn together, Ajali looked at her daughter. "Do you remember, Shanice…the little girl you met on last Halloween?"

"Shanice feels much better. Doesn't she, Mommy?"

"Yes," Ajali agreed softly. "I saw her last week. She was at the hospital for a routine visit. She's back in school and doing great. No symptoms of sickle cell anemia. Did you have something to do with her recovery?"

Kali nodded and Ajali knew the role that she and Bryce would play. Anonymously, they'd donate money—build a new wing at the children's hospital. She would continue to volunteer, bringing Kali along from time to time. The children Kali interacted with would heal.

Ajali and Bryce kept many of their various contributions, anonymous. They'd have to figure out a way to keep Kali's gift of healing a secret, too.

45

The sound of their harsh breathing filled the room. Recovering from an extremely passionate lovemaking session, Jen and Rome lay side by side, panting. They were always good in bed together, but this time seemed like the best sex ever. Intense yet tender.

Still trying to catch her breath, Jen stared at the animal art that decorated Rome's bedroom. As her heart rate returned to normal, a million thoughts whisked through her mind. She'd been so brave up to this point. But it was her last night with Rome until the end of summer. A sharp pang of regret knifed through her. Could she get through an entire summer without her man?

He had displayed such unabashed affection; there was no reason for her to doubt his love. But here she lay, taking in every aspect of his bedroom as if it might be the very last time she perused his personal space.

Suddenly she felt his finger touching her...tracing her stomach. His hand glided downward, fingers combing through the tangle of red hair that covered her mons. With the tip of his middle finger, he caressed her clit. Gently. Circularly. Determinedly. Until she released a tiny moan. That soft sound announced her arousal, and her temporary distraction from troubling thoughts.

"I can't get enough of you," Rome murmured.

Jen turned toward him, moving closer. She pressed her face against his chest, inhaling him. But a whiff of his fragrance, Twyla Tanning's signature, Insatiable for Men, was a harsh reminder of their pending summer separation.

Insatiable was a scrumptious scent, but it smelled like trouble.

Ever so slightly, Jen pulled away, using her palm to secretly dab tears before they trickled from her eyes.

Sensing a mood shift, Rome clipped Jen's chin, lifting her face. His worried eyes searched hers. "What's wrong, Pretty Red? Why you crying, baby?"

"You haven't left yet, but I miss you already."

"Aw, come on, baby. Don't cry. This summer is going to be rough on both of us, but you know I'm going to call you…text you…and send you flowers every day."

Sniffling, Jen nodded. "I know. I'm being silly. Allowing my insecurities to get to me."

Rome looked shocked. "Insecurities? About what? I'm not leaving you behind because I want to. I invited you to come with me."

"I know, Rome. I'll get it together." Jen said, her tone unconvincing and pitiful.

"Jen. Baby," he said patiently. "Didn't we both agree that I would spend the summer with Twyla while you went back to school?"

"Yeah, but—"

Motioning impatiently, Rome shushed her. "You promised your parents you were going to take summer classes to make up for that semester you lost."

"I know," Jen whined. "I just wish you didn't have to go."

Rome spoke softly, taking on the patient tone one would use

with someone who suffered from memory problems. "When you got accepted to Saint Joe's, you said you wanted to hit the books hard. You even said that trying to study with me underfoot would be a distraction." Rome chuckled.

"You're right. Back when we made those plans, I was feeling a lot more confident than I do now."

"What happened?" Soothingly, he smoothed wiry strands of her hair, and stroked her neck as he waited for her to answer.

"To be honest, I'm feeling really vulnerable. And jealous. I'm so scared I'm going to lose you."

Rome stared at her. "Who are you jealous of? Twyla?"

"No! It's just...well, you're like a celebrity now. I guess I'm feeling like I can't compete with all those fly chicks you'll be hanging out with while you're on the road with your mother."

Rome gave a hearty laugh, indicating he thought her comment was absurd. But Jen felt too vulnerable to even crack a smile. Her heart was aching and Rome didn't seem to be experiencing any pain over their separation.

As if reading her mind, he put a comforting arm around her. "Baby, the thought of getting on that plane without you is killing me. Look, the last thing you need to worry about is me getting involved with some aspiring actress. Do you really think I'd let somebody use me to get a photo op with Twyla Tanning's lovechild?" He laughed loudly at his self-description.

Again, Jen saw no humor. She kept a straight face.

Twyla's admission that she'd given birth to Rome during her teens had created hot tabloid fodder. Rome's uncanny resemblance to his glamorous mother had stirred public fascination.

With his face splashed alongside Twyla's on magazine covers throughout the world, Rome had become a celebrity by association. Twyla's sold-out European tour would be filmed as a documentary featuring concert performances as well as poignant moments between mother and son.

Jen frowned, dreading the additional female attention the documentary would cause.

"What's that frown about?"

Jen shrugged.

"Seriously, Jen. I'm going to be old news in a minute and everything will get back to normal. But right now, Twyla and I need to spend some time together. You know—get to know each other. That's the only reason I'm joining her on her Return to Love tour. It's why I agreed to let cameras follow us for that documentary."

"But you're gonna be in Europe…a whole continent away. And women are going to be camped out outside your hotel room. Not to mention the ones who'll be in your company every day. Background singers, makeup artists, Twyla's dancers…" Choked up, Jen looked away.

He shook his head. "Yeah, the media coverage is out of control. I mean…I want my mother in my life, but I'm not enjoying the fame."

"I don't want to get hurt, Rome. I can't help worrying that now that Twyla has acknowledged you…well…you might be out of my league."

He gawked at her like she was out of her mind. "Look, I had no idea that my going away was causing you this kind of pain."

"I was trying to keep it to myself." Jen's voice sounded squeaky and weak, making her sound totally irritated with herself.

"You want me to cancel?" he asked bluntly. "You know I will." His tone was dead serious.

Jen was quiet, her eyes downcast. She didn't know what to say.

"So what's it gonna be, Jen? You want me to cancel and stay

here with you? Will that make you feel secure?" He stared her down, demanding her final answer.

Weighing the gravity of his proposal, Jen's mind went into hyper-drive. If she fed into her insecurities and asked him to stay, he'd probably grow to resent her. Now was the time for Jen to have some faith. Faith in love. And faith in the unseen.

If the Goddess Realm truly exists, and if the goddess prophecy was true, then she and Rome were destined to be husband and wife. And parents of a son.

She'd never told him about Tara and Zeta. She wasn't sure if she ever would.

Taking a leap of faith, Jen smiled at him and said, "I...uh... I'm just being silly. Separation anxiety, I guess. Don't worry. I'll be all right."

"You sure?"

Changing her tone from meek to confident, she said, "I'm positive. I want you to bond with your mother." She leaned over and kissed him softly on the lips. "End of August, I'm going to be right here." She patted the bed. "Right now, I'm ready to pick up where we left off." Jen spread her legs invitingly.

Instantly ready for round two, Rome's lips traveled to her neck, nipping the spot that drove her wild.

But before Jen succumbed to passion, she pulled back. "Do me a favor?"

"Anything." He spoke with rasping breath.

"Don't wear that cologne while you're away."

Baffled, Rome frowned. "Why not?"

"You're only allowed to wear Insatiable when you're with me."

"Is that right?" Rome's lips spread into the boyish smile that made Jen's heart do flips.

She kissed his neck, and then inhaled his scent. "Um," she

uttered. Enjoying the blend of his natural scent mixed with the heady fragrance, she sniffed him from his neck down to his chest. "You smell delicious." Jen licked her lips. "Good enough to eat."

Proving her point, she slid off the bed and eased down to her knees.

Releasing a groan of pleasure, Rome inched to the edge of the bed. Jen moved inside the space between his legs. She held his dick in her hand admiringly, and then inhaled his pungent masculine aroma deeply.

She brought the smooth head of his dick close to her lips and kissed it gently. Flicking out her tongue, she administered love licks. Pausing, she looked up at him. "See what you do to me? I can't help myself."

"Don't try."Aroused, Rome kept his words to a minimum.

"I won't, then." She sucked his hard flesh between her lips, causing him to let out a growl that was rough and primal. Enraptured, his eyes were at half mast.

Drawing in the full length of his bulging shaft, Jen relaxed her throat, permitting his length to travel further than it ever had.

Rome's eyes opened. Awestruck, he watched as Jen deep-throated him for the very first time. Her mouth was moist and hot as she slowly...methodically...and deliberately gave him the ultimate blowjob—the best oral sexing she'd ever given him.

"So good," he moaned.

She was giving him the kind of tender tonguing he'd never get from a meaningless encounter on the road.

"Oh, baby," he shouted, his body beginning to convulse from the loving sucking she was putting on him.

Jen rose from the floor and straddled her man. She rode him hard and fast, meeting his desperate thrusts.

He tensed and groaned.

She collapsed upon him.

He held her tight, pressing her sweaty breasts against his chest.

Roaring a primal cry, he released his seed.

Suddenly, sparkling light spilled into the darkened bedroom; trumpets blared.

"Rome!"

"Yeah, baby?" he said dreamily.

"The bright light, don't you see it. Can't you hear the music?"

"Stop playing. I know it was good, but you don't have to try to blow up my ego like that."

The light began to dim; the sound of music faded. Jen heard soft wings fluttering in the distance.

Tara and Zeta had stopped by!

Filled with a sense of peace and well-being, Jen knew with certainty that Rome would return.

She touched her stomach and smiled.

The goddess prophecy was fulfilled.

AUTHOR'S NOTE

If you're ever in the Chestnut Hill section of Philadelphia, you don't have to worry about spotting an apparition running aimlessly across a bridge.

When writing the scene where Jen first encounters Eris, I envisioned Jen jogging along Kelly Drive, looking up, and seeing Eris pacing on Falls Bridge, which is located in East Falls.

On foot, there's quite a distance between Chestnut Hill and East Falls. Being that Jen didn't have access to a car, and was only out for a short run, I had to keep her in Chestnut Hill.

Taking creative license, I constructed a fictitious bridge, named it Piper's Bridge, and placed it in Chestnut Hill.

I hope you enjoyed *The Sorceress*, the continuation of my first paranormal novel, *The Enchantress*.

ABOUT THE AUTHOR

Allison Hobbs is the national bestselling author of eleven novels and novellas: *Pure Paradise, Disciplined, One Taste, Big Juicy Lips, The Climax, A Bona Fide Gold Digger, The Enchantress, Double Dippin', Dangerously in Love, Insatiable* and *Pandora's Box.* She is one of the contributing writers of Cinemax's *Zane's Sex Chronicles.*

Her novel *The Climax* was nominated for the 2008 African American Literary Awards Show.

Allison received a bachelor of science degree from Temple University. She resides in Philadelphia, PA where she's working on her next novel.

Visit the author at: www.allisonhobbs.com, www.blackplanet.com/allisonhobbs or www.myspace.com/allisonhobbs

The Enchantress

Chapter 1

ROANOKE, VIRGINIA
1806

The whispered grumblings in the slave quarters on the Stovall Plantation were usually about Eris.

"Now, a gal like dat—black as tar—ain't got no business workin' in de big house," the old man named Make-Do complained.

"You sho' 'nuff right, Make-Do. In all my years, ah ain't nevah seen nothin' like it. Dark-skinded gal wit dem big ol' clumsy feets tendin' to Missus and givin out orders to de cook and e'rebody else workin' in de big house," agreed Peahead. "She sho' got Massuh fooled."

"Hmph! Don't nobody seem to know where she come from, but wherevah dat was, ah bet she wasn't nothin' but a field hand jes' like us," groused Peahead's wife, Florette.

Make-Do scratched his head. "If ah 'members co'reckly, Eris

showed up here in de middle of de night. She told Massuh she been on de run from some evil slave owner way down in 'Bama somewhere."

"You mean to tell me dat gal ran all de way from 'Bama to Virginy?" Florette scrunched up her lips and shook her head. "Don't make no kinda sense dem slave catchers nevah got ahold'a her 'long de way."

"Massuh got such a good heart; took her in promisin' to hide her and all. She showed up buck naked—ain't had nothin but a box filled up with potions and such. Told Massuh she was good at nursin' folk. Dat why he keep her up in de big house," explained Peahead.

"Well, it don't look like her nursin's worth mucha nothin'. Missus be gittin' sicker by de day," said a young woman by the name of Willa. "And why somebody blacker den soot talkin' like de white folk? And why she got dem strange-lookin' blue eyes?" There was a collective confused shaking of heads.

"Bet y'all don't know…" Willa paused, waiting to get the group's undivided attention. "Eris done started wearin' all the Missus's clothes." Willa's bottom lip jutted out in disapproval.

"Wearin Missus's clothes!" Peahead and Florette chorused incredulously.

"Sho' 'nuff is." Make-Do confirmed with a nod. "Eris done give all her old frocks to Molly and Tookie." Make-Do had been on the Stovall Plantation long before the current master was born. Now, too old to work the fields, Make-Do kept an eye on the children and performed easy tasks that didn't require agility or a strong back .

"I done told dem girls they ain't gon' have nothin' but bad luck from wearin' dat evil woman's clothes," Make-Do continued.

"Uh-huh. I tried to warn 'em, too. Dey so happy to have spare frocks, dey won't even listen. But dey gon' see. Mark my words, dey sho' 'nuff gon' see," Willa said, staring off into space and shaking her head as if a future fraught with unparalleled horrors was being revealed.

"Lawd, look ovah dere." Peahead pointed toward the big house. All heads turned. In the distance, illuminated by moonlight, Eris was kneeling on the ground.

"What she up to now?" Florette inquired in a hushed tone.

Peahead stood up and squinted. "Look like she tendin' to dat garden a-hern."

"At night!" they all exclaimed loudly, then looked around anxiously, hoping Eris didn't catch them spying on her. But Eris was intently involved with gathering the herbs and roots she needed for the mistress's remedy.

"You know dat woman's stranger than a two-headed chicken," Peahead whispered nervously. "Wouldn't surprise me a bit if she diggin' a hole so's to holla down dere and talk to Satan hisself." Peahead gave a shudder. "Come on, Florette. We goin' inside. Ah don't wanna be nowhere near Eris after daylight. And 'specially not with dat full moon burnin' while she dealin' wit' de devil," he said ominously. Peahead and Florette gathered themselves to go inside their cabin, careful not to look in Eris's direction.

Willa latched onto Make-Do's arm and helped him to stand upright. After he was safely on his feet, Willa respectfully handed the old man his walking stick. She hurried to her cabin while old Make-Do shuffled on down the dusty path to his own shanty.

Edith Stovall, the mistress of the plantation, was so consumed with fever she had no idea that her fine garments had been relegated to adorning a lowly slave. Had she known, she would have diplomatically excused her husband's lack of judgment, but such impudence by a slave girl would have warranted a visit to the whipping post. Nine and thirty. That's how many lashes the ill-mannered, uppity heifer would have incurred if the mistress of the house had her strength and wits about her.

The mistress was stricken with a serious illness and according to her husband, Arthur, she was delirious. Talking out of her head—accusing him of unspeakable acts since she'd been banished from his bed. Having the fever and carrying what appeared to be a deadly and contagious disease, of course she had had to be exiled from the marital bedroom. She was being quarantined until she got better or—God forbid—she died.

Since none of the local physicians could figure out what was wrong with Edith and none wanted to risk catching her strange sickness, it was lucky for Edith that Eris seemed immune. Eris could go in and out of Edith's sickroom and administer to her without so much as a cough or a sneeze.

Arthur was more than grateful to Eris. As master of the plantation, he couldn't afford to come down with the strange illness that had gripped his pitiful wife. Why, he'd lose everything his daddy had left him if he caught whatever was ailing his wife.

It was for the good of the plantation and the future of the Stovall family if Edith stayed far, far away from him as well as any essential slaves whose labor he depended upon. Until her health improved, Edith would have to stay tucked away in that cramped and musty bedroom up in the attic.

But in the meantime, a man had his needs. Manly desires that a sickly wife could not fulfill.

Eris used a sharp-edged rock to grind the mixture that she'd concocted in the moonlight and then carried it up the stairs to the attic. With the wooden bowl and ladle in hand, Eris used her hip to bump open the door to the quarantined room.

"Missus," Eris said sharply. "Wake up, Missus. It's time to take your remedy."

Although Arthur Stovall never came into the room personally, he'd been known to send in slaves whom he considered dispensable to periodically check on his wife and give him a report on her condition.

Eris wasn't willing to risk having unexpected visits from loose lips reporting that she wasn't giving the mistress the best treatment possible, so she set the bowl on the bedside table and used the hem of her apron to blot the perspiration from Edith's forehead. Then, certain that no prying eyes could see her, she roughly wiped the sickly woman's face and mouth, using the lace-edged pocket of the apron. With a hateful grimace, Eris dug the crust out of the corners of her patient's rapidly blinking eyes. The friction of the stiff lace was painful and caused angry red blotches to pop up all over Edith's frail face.

As far as Eris was concerned, the red blotches further proved that the mistress was contagious and required an extended quarantine. And more doses of her special remedy.

Eris gave a low chortle as she recalled the last slave the master had sent to the attic infirmary. Scared to death, old Make-Do had limped into the room holding a rag over his face. The rag covered his mouth, nose, and eyes.

He wasn't going to be able to give the master a detailed report being that he had neither seen nor smelled anything, so out of pure spite, Eris instructed Make-Do to empty the mistress's almost overflowing chamberpot.

Having to walk with a cane made carrying the *contagious* waste material cumbersome. One would have thought Make-Do had seen a ghost the way he whooped and hollered when bits of loose excrement splattered on his hand.

Imagining he'd been infected by the mistress, Make-Do coughed up blood for a week, but he finally pulled through. Eris found Make-Do's near-death experience extremely humorous and made a mental note to take better advantage of his simple-mindedness in the future.

Eris was anxious to report that the Missus's ailment was not better, that she was even more emaciated and pale with a curious eruption of red welts, which were spreading all over her face. The Missus, Eris would sadly state, seemed to be getting worse. Excited, Eris hurriedly left the room, forgetting to administer the poisonous concoction.

Edith was weak and very thirsty. But her heart was filled with relief that the vile black slave had forgotten to force-feed her the twice-daily dosage of poison. Eris's lethal "remedy" was the instrument of the mistress's slow and agonizing demise.

Experiencing an unusually lucid period earlier that day, Edith had kept the poisonous mixture hidden beneath her tongue. She'd spat it out as soon as the slave woman left the room. And now, having skipped the evening dose as well, she was feeling strengthened and hopeful that she might survive this vexation dealt upon her by the hands of a slave. The gall!

Unwilling to risk exposure to his wife's malady, Arthur Stovall insisted that Eris shed the clothing she'd worn while attending to Edith and wash thoroughly before entering his chambers.

The mistress's nights on this earth were numbered. It was just a matter of time before Eris became the Mistress of the House.

Although her name would not be affixed to any official documents, she'd be the mistress no less, and she would inform the slaves to address her as such. She'd already begun training Molly, the cook's assistant, to refer to her as *Mistress*.

Hearing her addressed as such would be a problem with the white people, of course. Therefore, she'd have to prohibit visitations by business associates who'd come snooping around. She'd insist that Arthur—yes, she now called him *Arthur*—conduct his business away from the home. She would not kowtow to lawyers, bookkeepers or such. No, Arthur would have to arrange his life to suit her needs.

Feeling powerful, Eris did not cover herself with even a wisp of fabric. Boldly, she glided naked from her room to the master bedchamber. She did not care if curious eyes peered from corners or slightly cracked doors. *Let them behold my beauty—my full breasts and wide hips. Yes, let them admire me from a distance but cower in my presence.* Intoxicated with power, Eris, dark and statuesque, with refined facial features, strode through the corridors with the regal carriage of a queen. Heavy coils of dark hair fell past her shoulders. She did not carry a lantern; the full moon brightened the path to Arthur's chamber.

"My beloved," Arthur said when Eris opened the door and crept to his bed. "I've waited for what feels like ages. Hurry! Come!" He patted the bed.

She peered at him in the dark room. "Wait! I must part the curtains."

"Why, beloved?"

"The moon is full tonight. You've given me many things; but never have you given me the moon."

"Ah, you're a strange one. But I have no power in your presence. Part the curtains if you wish. Have your moon; have the stars as well." Arthur waved his hand extravagantly and laughed.

Eris parted the curtains and for a few moments, stood naked in the window. She threw back her head in ecstasy as she became energized by the light of the moon.

In the cramped slave huts below, candles were quickly snuffed when the slaves saw Eris's naked silhouette. Such a sight seemed unholy and they all wished to escape through sleep as quickly as possible. With prayers on their tongues, they hoped that by morning's light, the chilling image of Eris basking in the moonlight would seem like a bad dream.

Eris walked to the bed. Her breasts were full and tender; a red streak trailed down her inner thigh. Smiling, she pulled back the heavy covers and joined the master whose look of worship assured her that behind closed doors, he'd always be her slave.

Chapter 2

*E*ris awakened at dawn. There was great clattering in the kitchen as the cook and her help prepared the morning meal for Arthur and her.

Molly, an obedient young girl, rapped on the door twice as Eris had instructed her. "Good morning, Mistress," the young girl greeted Eris. Molly did a double-take and looked quizzically at her master, who still asleep, sucked loudly on the knuckle of Eris's middle finger.

"Will that be all, Mistress?" Molly asked, averting her gaze as she set down the breakfast tray.

"No. Go out to the slave quarters and tell that worthless Make-Do to go tend to the Missus. Tell him to empty her slop..." Suddenly remembering that she hadn't given Arthur's wife her evening dosage, she further instructed, "Tell him to add a little water to her remedy; it's in a bowl on the nightstand. He must give her two spoonfuls. Is that clear?"

"Yes, Mistress," Molly said. "Two spoonfuls," she repeated, and whirled around and hurried out of the room. Through the window Eris watched Molly race across the lawn to give Make-Do the distressful news.

Eris was famished and sore. The power she'd derived from the full moon had enhanced her femininity, bringing on her menses and causing her full breasts to lactate although she'd never given birth to a child.

The moon had allowed her to nurture Arthur—to claim him as her own. Last night, she'd encouraged him to suckle her breasts and her bleeding womanhood until he cried from sheer bliss.

Different from other women, Eris's menstrual cycle lasted for just one evening per month, and though Arthur cried and pleaded for more of her delicious dark red nectar, she had nothing left to give; he'd suckled her dry.

Like a fretful baby, he'd cried and whimpered throughout the night. Not wanting to awaken the slaves, Eris had given him her knuckle to suck. This soothed and kept him quiet, allowing him to sleep like a contented child for the remainder of the night.

Depleted and famished from her nocturnal activities, Eris, propped up by three plump pillows, enjoyed her own breakfast and Arthur's as well.

Praying he did not become afflicted again with the doomed Missus's illness, Make-Do hobbled up the flights of stairs, carrying a pitcher of fresh water. When he reached the attic, although it hadn't entered his mind before, the thought of just upping and running away seemed like a better idea than risking another chance with the sick Missus. All that choking and coughing up blood was bound to kill him this time. But trying to run with his bad leg…well, he wouldn't get very far. Nope! The hounds would have a hold on him before he even got close to the river.

Accepting his fate, Make-Do pushed open the door. The room smelled like a pigsty. The Missus looked all dried-up and half-dead, with her thick and cankered tongue hanging out the side of her mouth. Momentarily oblivious of his fear of contagion, Make-Do rushed over, lifted her head and tried to give her a drink of water, but the water rolled off her thick, blistered tongue.

In a quandary, he looked around the room. There was a spoon stuck in the dried-up remedy that Eris had instructed him to give to the mistress. Make-Do cleaned the gook off and began spoonfeeding drops of water to Edith. "Here you go, Missus," he said, carefully aiming the spoon toward her dry lips. His doctoring seemed to work. The Missus began to utter sounds. Incomprehensible noises, but the gibberish was progress nonetheless. Wanting her to get better, Make-Do poured a little water in the remedy and tried to soften it up enough to give to the mistress.

But the mistress started making an awful growling sound in her throat. It scared old Make-Do so bad, he thought she was drowning from taking in too much water. Not wanting to be blamed for killing her, Make-Do slipped out of the room and hobbled as fast as he could down the stairs.

He ran smack into Molly. "Ah give de Missus two spoonfuls of dat remedy jest like you said." He turned to hobble away.

"Did you empty the slop bucket?"

"No, Lawdy, Ah didn't," he said sadly. "Ah sho' is gittin' old and fo'getful. Lemme git back up dere and fetch it."

When Make-Do reentered the infirmed woman's room, she looked surprisingly brighter. Her complexion wasn't as pasty and her tongue didn't look as thick. Encouraged, he picked up the bowl of remedy and started stirring.

Edith Stovall began to moan and Make-Do put down the bowl.

"You don't like dat remedy, do you, Missus?"

She looked at him and grunted.

"Okey-dokey. Ah'm jest up here to fetch yo' slop bucket anyways. So you git yo'self some sleep now, Missus."

Grateful that he hadn't killed the Missus, Make-Do whistled a happy tune as he took care of emptying the slop bucket.

By nightfall, when Make-Do hadn't started choking and coughing up any blood, the slaves breathed a sigh of relief. They loved Make-Do too much to have to beg his pardon and ask him to kindly stay in his own cabin. Yes, they were mighty obliged that they didn't have to turn old Make-Do away.

"Ah's done beat dat ol' sickness," Make-Do told the awestruck slaves. "Maybe de Missus will, too."

The slaves all smiled hopefully. If the mistress recovered, Eris would be put in her place and things would be back to normal on the Stovall Plantation.

Chapter 3

*A*rthur Stovall believed his wife was under Eris's expert care, but Eris, disgusted by the awful stench in the sickroom, preferred the sweet smell of her own quarters, which Molly filled with fresh cut flowers daily.

Expecting Edith to expire at any moment, Eris had stopped providing personal care and now the sickly woman's pasty-colored skin and wildly tangled hair was a completely unappealing sight. In fact, everything about the sickroom and its occupant was unpleasant and not a suitable place for a woman such as Eris, who was living in the lap of luxury.

But with the mistress's unwillingness to just go ahead and give up the ghost, Eris had no choice but to make the remedy stronger—more toxic. She'd left the handling of the infirm woman to Make-Do, giving the old slave strict orders to now give the mistress three heaping spoons of the concoction every day.

Eris had custody of every article of clothing Edith Stovall owned. In order to prove his devotion and the sincerity of his love, Arthur had recently given Eris a cameo brooch, and upon his wife's imminent death, Eris fully expected to inherit the woman's entire collection of jewels, especially her beautiful wedding ring. Of course, she wouldn't *wear* the woman's wedding ring; she'd keep it along with the treasure of jewelry she'd acquired and hid in the box she kept buried near her vegetable patch.

Then, when it was time to move on, she'd leave the useless garments, hats and other finery—but the box of jewels would accompany her on the journey to the next plantation.

Eris's plan was to make her way up north. Once settled there as a free woman, she'd cash in her jewelry and live the good life without having to rely on the males that drained her powers with their greedy mouths, depleting her of her womanhood.

Ever so sweetly, Eris persuaded Arthur to take the buggy and meet his banker in town. She considered sending Make-Do along under the pretense of tending to the horse, but she'd instruct him to keep an ear out for any important financial information. However, needing the old man to empty the slop jar and take care of the mistress, she decided Arthur could make the two-day journey alone.

Having not stepped a foot inside the sickroom in weeks, Eris had no idea that Make-Do had stopped administering the lethal potion to the mistress and had been hand-feeding her mashed fruit, soft boiled vegetables, and several glasses of water per day. Thus, Edith Stovall was slowly but surely coming back to good health.

Eris stayed so far away from the attic, she hadn't heard all the laughter and sounds of merriment that emanated from the sickroom. Nor did she hear the Missus clunking around with Make-Do's cane as she taught herself how to walk again.

And so it was a tremendous shock when Eris awakened in her beautiful, sweet-smelling, flower-filled room to an oddly familiar odor. She thought she had to be dreaming when she opened her eyes and beheld the mistress, looking like an old crone propped up with Make-Do's cane, as she observed with increasing rage the splendid surroundings that Eris had become accustomed to.

The wedding ring on the frail hand that gripped the cane caught Eris's attention. She'd wanted that ring so badly; now it was too late...